"I was in love with you," Rossiter said, but his gaze told her that nothing had changed.

"But that was years ago," Clara murmured. She closed her eyes and remembered. "I was in love with you too. And we were good together, weren't we?" Did one ever forget the warmth, the sensation of merging, the smell of it, the wetness, the thumping excitement, and the climax, resounding as thunder, like the sky being torn like a sheet?

She remembered all that, couldn't deny the pleasure that had been hers, theirs. But then she'd married his father . . .

"Look at me, Clara, and tell me you don't want me now," Ross commanded. He pulled her against him and brushed his mouth over hers.

He tasted right on her lips, like a liquor that made her high, not drunk. A few minutes before, she'd been sure she could handle seeing him again. Now everything was turned upside down. She turned her face upward, and let her tongue glide along the line of his clean-shaven jaw. He dropped his head and they kissed again, gently first, then hungrily.

"You're just the same," Clara whispered. "Unbutton me. Then button me up."

He understood what she meant, what she wanted. Undo her, then do her. *He undid me, then did me, and I was undone.*

It was crazy, merely crazy. But nothing could stop them now . . .

Other Bantam Books by Barney Leason.

North Rodeo Drive

Rich and Reckless

Barney Leason

BANTAM BOOKS
TORONTO • NEW YORK • LONDON • SYDNEY • AUCKLAND

To Josephine

RICH AND RECKLESS
A Bantam Book / August 1988

Necklace of pearls, diamonds and amethysts from
FRED Joaillier, New York.

ISBN 0-553-27328-0

Published simultaneously in the United States and Canada

Bantam Books are published by Bantam Books, a division of
Bantam Doubleday Dell Publishing Group, Inc. Its trade-
mark, consisting of the words "Bantam Books" and the por-
trayal of a rooster, is Registered in U.S. Patent and Trademark
Office and in other countries. Marca Registrada. Bantam
Books, 666 Fifth Avenue, New York, New York 10103.

PRINTED IN THE UNITED STATES OF AMERICA

O   0 9 8 7 6 5 4 3 2 1

Chapter One

*T*om Addey was as close to sleep as a man could be without declining into actual unconsciousness. During this period of truce, with the events of the day swarming in his head, unfiled, unedited, he heard Martha come back—the whoosh of the elevator, click of the hall light, and then, in a few seconds, the scratch of her fingernail on their door. If Clara and Tom were awake, they'd hear; if asleep, be undisturbed.

"It's me." Her low, husky voice crept in, as substantial as a whisper in his ear.

Martha. It was startling how much Martha reminded Tom of her mother. She seemed more like Clara than Clara. One might have been the reflection of the other—both so blond and slim, vigorous, fast-moving, built to a rakish style, like the racing sloops that crowded San Francisco Bay on weekends.

Tom wondered: Would Martha have been the exciting stranger? Or familiar territory to him, well-mapped? Vile thought, but there, alone, on the edge of sleep, he permitted his mind to range in odd directions. And over women.

Right then, for example, he could have constructed Hildy Beckmann out of memory and imagination. Kissing her good-bye just a few hours earlier, Tom had already formed a mental picture of her neat body under the green loden coat; warm breasts, yes, with nipples the size of small money. The sensation had been like a knife twist to the heart; how it had hurt when she smiled. Good-bye. And he might never see her again, unless she happened to marry his son Seth.

1

Would Clara let him fly back east by himself to see Hildy—
and Seth—again before they returned to Germany? Hullo, Thelma,
old girl, ex-wife, isn't Hildy there with you? Please let me talk
to Hildy, for I am crazed by her moist beauty.

Thelma. She'd never been so forward or seemingly up-front
as the young goddess Hildy. There had always been such ritual
involved in his relationship with Thelma, a neurotic but dazzlingly
theatrical woman. Thelma was a woman of classical proportions,
kind of Wagnerian despite her New England heritage. She was
one of the last, it was to be hoped, of the inbred, purebred,
Dumb Drysdales, as he'd always called them.

Clara. A blond minx—his opulently furnished Etruscan,
Tom had always thought of her, created for comfort *and* speed.
She was at her best veiled in mystery, walking toward him
through a misty night, as she had the first time he'd ever seen
her outside the Music Center in Los Angeles. Clara, of the
unrelenting blondness, her high cheekboned face always turned
into the wind. She was so serene, so reserved, suggestive of
depths unplumbed.

He did love her, didn't he? Did he?

His mind slipped back to Martha, then Hildy again. Who
else? *Never Serena*, his oldest son Rossiter's wife. No, not her,
the silly anorexic bitch, a young woman so thin of body and
starved of spirit it was shameful. There was nothing to her
except a bosom; a creature to suckle, but her milk would be
poison. Rossiter had to be crazy.

Hildy. Tom tried to focus his thoughts on the succulent
German, but inevitably, as it always did, his mind jumped to
Ludmilla. There had never been any problem about summoning
up Ludmilla while sliding toward sleep, Ludmilla of the long
thrashing loins, a woman so much larger than life, a throwback
to far more romantic days. . . . A woman outrun by history but
determined to survive come what might, doing whatever she had
to do. She'd always rejected age as a kind of Darwinian termination notice.

How mysterious life was, Tom Addey might have thought
later, or how maddening, the way things happened when you
least—or most—expected. Why, he'd just been thinking about
Ludmilla when the bedside phone bleated softly.

"Hullo." Not his most vivacious voice by any means. But

the sound at the other end of the line was nearly garbled. Yet
. . . "Is that you, Alex?"

"Yes, yes, my dear Tom! I called before . . . so many
times!"

"Alex, we were all out to dinner. My sons are here and—"

Alex Spurzov had always been excitable. But he was so
distraught now, he could barely get words out. He stuttered, then
tried again.

"Ludmilla is dead, Tom!"

A horror came and went. "Christ! Alex!"

"It is terrible, Tom. We found her in the pool, early this
evening. She went for her usual swim . . ."

Clara was wide awake now. Never mind Tom's voice;
Alex's was loud enough. Tom put his hand over the mouthpiece.

"It's about . . . Ludmilla." Even transmitting this information, he felt awkward. Clara had never known Ludmilla, had
never even met her.

Clara sighed loudly. What would she say when she heard
his news about the mad princess?

"Alex . . . Alex . . . What the hell! Swimming? It's the
dead of winter!"

But who could stop her? As clearly as he had imagined
Hildy and Martha, Tom saw Ludmilla strutting naked, out of the
boudoir of her Bel Air palace called Richlands, striding like a
cavalry officer through the stone mausoleum . . . down the stairs
and into the night and the ice-cold pool. Or had they taken to
heating it since the death of her last husband, the wealthy but
parsimonious Rodney Richards? No, why heat it? Ludmilla would
have said. Ice water was good for the skin and bowels; it was
life-extending to swim with the polar bears.

"Ludl lived as she pleased, Tom!"

And died. Alex had choked on the words. He must look
terrible, red-rimmed eyes dripping with tears. His features had
always seemed half melted and in the process of running off his
facial bones. He would be blearier than ever now.

"Dear God! I cannot believe it. We were waiting dinner,
having a vodka, and she didn't appear!"

"We?"

"Cazimir is here," Alex whispered.

Cazimir? Tom felt his stomach heave, with something
closer to nausea than surprise. Cazimir Ben Gazi, that miserable

son of a bitch, was the latest and—as it had turned out—last of Ludmilla's lovers. Cazimir was miles younger than Ludmilla, but had age ever been known to deter her? She had once boasted to Tom that she'd never seduced a lad younger than twenty-one— but when they were old enough to vote, they were old enough for *bamboomski*!

Tom disliked Cazimir even more than was reasonable, because it'd been Tom Addey who had been tricked into introducing the vile Lebanese to Los Angeles, and to Ludmilla, some years before. This he had done, thinking nothing of it, at the behest of a Washington client, the same Sol Betancur whom Clara had discussed so hatefully during dinner, the man who was a power within the Republican Party, and now, during the George Washburn administration, a reigning star in Washington. Clara disliked Sol intensely because he treated his wife badly, and Alice Betancur had been a schoolmate and one of Clara's best, oldest friends.

Why Sol had decided Cazimir Ben Gazi should get to know Los Angeles society, at least its so-called ranks, or why Cazimir himself would want to, was beyond Tom Addey. But so it had turned out.

It had not been difficult to launch Cazimir. At the time, he'd been plus or minus thirty-five, good-looking in a dark and rather oily Levantine manner, and rich enough to impress even Beverly Hills.

"Cazimir is in from Paris, Tom. *Thanks to God*," Alex whispered hoarsely.

Yes, and how headline-grabbing that would be. Ludmilla Spurzova, lover *extraordinaire*, found floating in her Olympic-sized pool at palatial Richlands by ex-husband (several times removed) Prince Alexei Spurzov and current lover, the Lebanese arms dealer and international fixer, Cazimir Ben Gazi.

"The paramedics could not save her, Tom!"

Clara turned on the lamp at her side of the bed, punched up her pillows and raised herself to a sitting position.

"The *police* were here, Tom!"

Tom's legal mind turned on. "Did you make a statement?"

"Yes, but what could I say? Should a person worry that Ludmilla would go for a swim in the dark?"

"And nobody saw her?"

"No," Alex whispered, his voice fading. "The cook and

the maid were in the kitchen. The butler—this *corpse* called Peat—was with me making my vodka. I was reading Peat something out of *Pravda.*"

"*Pravda*? Since when are you reading *that*?"

"My dear!" Alex forgot Ludmilla for a split second. "I must keep up with what the filthy goddamn Bolsheviks are doing."

"Yes, yes . . . and *Cazimir* was there with you?"

"Cazimir?" Alex stopped to think. "No, he was not. I remember now. He went out. He took one of Ludl's cars and went to the Polo Lounge for a drink. Yes, that's right," Alex recalled bitterly, "the *Lebanese bastard* met some woman. He should have been there with Ludmilla. Then—"

"He was *out* with a broad! Did Ludmilla know he was playing around?"

Listlessly, Alex replied, "Would she care, Tom? Gooses and ganders, you know the game. . . ."

Yes. And Ludmilla had never stopped playing it. Even with Cazimir in town and Alex back living with her at Richlands, she'd still had something else on the side. Merely to use the term "playing around" in conjunction with Ludmilla was inappropriate; and, as far as Tom knew, Ben Gazi had married a Middle East oil heiress in the years since becoming one of Ludmilla's lovers and had a couple of children in Beirut or wherever it was that his wealth kept him immune from kidnapping, car bombing, or whatever.

Alex's voice rose again. "I know you loved her, Tom—as did we all."

All of us, that was right, and the numbers were legion. Tom didn't look at Clara; he hoped she hadn't heard that.

"And Cazimir? Did he talk to the police too?"

"Yes," Alex muttered. "He had his alibi. Now he is upstairs, doing what his people do—is it wailing? I can hear him, even with my bad ears."

Tom knew what was coming next. Despite everything that had happened—and there had been trying moments between them because of Ludmilla—Alex had always leaned on him.

"Tom . . . Tom, please come to Los Angeles. This old man needs you now!"

Yes, *especially now*, because Cazimir was there. As long as Ludmilla had been pleased with Cazimir Ben Gazi, Alex was too. Whatever was good for Ludmilla was, by definition, not just good but *wonderful* for Alex. But Ludmilla was dead now, and nobody had ever trusted Cazimir.

Tom would have to be harsh. "Don't let Ben Gazi get into her things, Alex!"

He remembered the heavy metal so many men had bought Ludmilla—her gold and silver. And the colored baubles, as Ludmilla contemptuously called them—the diamonds, rubies, sapphires, mounted and unmounted; the strings of pearls. None of it had ever meant much to Ludmilla. She'd been capable—if that was the word—of wearing cheap trinkets on one arm and priceless rocks on the other. Her attitude, though, did not detract from the fact the stuff would be worth a good deal, enough to warrant a good-sized chunk of a Sotheby's catalogue.

Tom had never given her anything. And it had never mattered.

"And the Egg, Alex—it's still put away, isn't it?"

"Oh, yes, my dear!"

The so-called Spurzov Egg, described as a "Fabergé Imperial" to distinguish it from a mere Fabergé egg, was the last of the family treasures, as Alex liked to tell close friends. But ironically it was by now the most valuable of anything the Spurzovs could have carried away from Moscow after the Russian Revolution. It had been especially commissioned by the czar for the Spurzovs, and was apparently one of the last produced by the great jeweler-craftsman who had worked by appointment at the court of the Romanovs.

Somehow, Alex's Egg had survived all the blood and bartering that had accompanied the Spurzovs' forced migration to the West. And Alex had pledged that so long as he lived, the Egg would not leave his possession. Selling it was out of the question.

"Tom, never fear for the Spurzov Egg!"

Once, only once, to prove to Tom the treasure existed, Alex had invited him to the vault in downtown Los Angeles where the Egg was kept and afforded Tom one quick glimpse of it, as if exposure to eyes alone would somehow tarnish the *objet's* value. This was when Alex had told Tom that when the time came, he would know what to do with the Spurzov Egg.

Tom shrugged helplessly at Clara. What else could he do?

"Sit tight, Alex. Get some sleep. Don't leave the house till I get there."

"Thanks be, dear friend."

After he hung up, the bedroom was silent until Clara asked, "Why did you tell him not to leave the house? You'd think the first thing he'd want is to get some fresh air."

"Uh-uh." Tom shook his head. "For all we know, the Richards family would change all the locks."

"Would they? Surely not."

"No? People are capable of some pretty surprising things, Clara. The house belongs to the family—*she* had the use of it." He wouldn't mention Ludmilla's name if he could help it. "Pretty generous when you think about it—she wasn't married to Rodney Richards more than eight or nine years."

Her irritation was showing. Clara had been edgy all evening, then openly angry after they'd said good night to Seth and Rossiter and the two women. Clara was upset about something, he wasn't quite sure what. Of course, he'd been nice to Hildegard Beckmann, and why not—wasn't she a guest from a faraway land? Tom refused to feel bad about that. Also, he was not a stone; she was an attractive girl. Did Clara want him to dry up like an old stump and decay? Surely he himself would remain interesting as long as he found *people* interesting. Why shouldn't a man be allowed to fantasize . . . hallucinate?

Now, vis-à-vis Alex, Clara *must* understand he had to help. What bothered her, he knew, was that people, including herself, would be reminded of his crazy love affair with Ludmilla.

It was as simple as that . . . and as ridiculous.

"If we fly down today, we'd be back in a week, plenty of time before Christmas," Tom said cautiously.

Clara turned over and flicked off her light.

Into the darkness, she asked, "Just what, specifically, can you do for him?"

"Show the flag, that's the main thing—"

"Why don't you get Rossiter to go see him—Rossiter and Serena are going back to L.A. early this morning."

"No," Tom said. "That wouldn't be any good. Ross doesn't know . . . What I've got to do is check into the various legal aspects. . . ."

Sardonically, she said, "Maybe Ludmilla left you something in her will."

He smiled privately. Unbelievably, Clara was jealous, even though Ludmilla was dead and Clara hadn't even known of Tom

7

Addey's existence when he'd written the wild Bulgarian chapter of his life.

"Anyway," Clara muttered, "I can't go with you. I told you why I can't go away right now."

Yes, they'd touched on that at Trader Vic's, where Tom had brought the reunited family for Sunday-night dinner. Seth and Hildy were here from Germany—Seth was posted to the U.S. Consulate in Munich—and Rossiter had come up from Los Angeles with Serena.

"Oh, c'mon, Clara," he protested. "I was just kidding about going to New York for a few days. *This* is serious."

"And I'm serious too. You're going to be busy down there—you won't miss me. And I'll be busy up here getting ready for our show."

"Just for a couple of days, Clara, that's all. *Seriously*. Biff Percy can get everything ready for the show. You know you're not going to hang the pictures till the night before it opens, and that's not for ten days."

"There's a lot more to it than that, Tom, and you know it. Besides, Biff gets nervous and uptight on his own. He hates the responsibility."

"Poor Biff . . ."

"And," she sniffed, "he's also got his own art to do, remember. He doesn't work full time."

"The Picasso of North Beach."

Highly put out, Clara yanked on the covers and curled up. "I'm sleepy."

So he gave up. He'd let her stew. He would try to come to terms with the concept of blank, cold nothingness. It was not easy. Even nothingness should have a shape; or was life, mind, thought nothing but a dream, merrily . . . merrily . . . merrily, like in the song? Could there be a dream, though, without a dreamer? An end without a beginning? An infinitely expanding universe, expanding where and whence . . . an end to life without death as an end?

Ludmilla would be out there now, conducting her own eager exploration of the unknown. It was not possible to think of her as dead. Ludmilla dead? That was, as she loved to say, *to laugh*! He could see her up there, in the flesh, laughing wildly at the irony of it all. Ludmilla had always held that nothing was as

8

it seemed to be or was said to be. Behind every truth was a lie. On the reverse of white, black. Back was front. Up was down.

No, she remained too real to be actually dead. How vividly he remembered them making love. Drinking and telling stories all day and night, weeping, laughing, yelling about her mother and the Black Sea marshes, her church, her town; and then, without warning, she would fall upon him, with a hunger for flesh that could never really be satisfied.

Poor Ludmilla, how she had behaved.

If he thought of Thelma as a screechy Wagnerian soprano . . . Clara as a slinky blond tart . . . then Ludmilla was something more Grecian than Bulgarian, a goddess of grand proportions, more mythical than human, a woman magnificent enough to drive the gods mad.

Clara rolled back toward him.

"Tom . . ."

Her voice was husky. For a second . . . but no. Not Ludmilla. "You're thinking about her, aren't you?"

He could not deny it. He wouldn't.

"I guess so."

She slid closer to him, her body warm. Was it his imagination or could he feel her blood pounding? Her scent brought him back—the very subtle perfume she wore, the faint sweet remnant of the rum drinks they'd had at the Trader's. Her breath heavy on his neck, Clara kissed him there with moist lips, then, as he turned his head, on the mouth. She pressed the length of her body against him. Clara on the prowl was like an opened treasure chest, glittering and gleaming with gold and jewels and magic surprises. In this, she was very like Ludmilla.

"Oh, Tom," she whispered, "Tom . . ."

"You're not mad at me now?" He teased because he didn't know what else to do. It was his failing. "Strike that," he muttered. "Forget it."

"You bastard."

On such winter nights as this, Clara always wore oversized white cotton pajamas. Cleverly, he pulled the drawstring on the bottoms to loosen them, caressing the smooth skin of her belly, the curly short hair at her crotch, pale blond, true blond.

Clara sighed steamily as he prepared her skin with his fingers. He ran his hand along her ribs, unbuttoned the pajama top and pressed his lips to her breasts, bringing the nipples to engorged points, kissed her throat where the veins throbbed, then moved his hand back down to pull off the bottoms.

She lay revealed before him, yes, familiar territory, yes, but ever mysterious. Clara kept her distance emotionally. He was never precisely sure how she'd react when they were in bed; in this way, she continued to intrigue him, probably longer than he would have been by most women.

Clara kissed him again, fervently. Maybe she did understand and was making the best of it; yes, she'd outperform anybody on the block, including the fabled Ludmilla Spurzova. Yes, he thought, did she understand this fascination he had, always had had, in spreading himself alongside the body of a stranger?

"Tom," she murmured, "now . . ."

The invitation was enough. Desire bolted within him, a precipitous, runaway need. Had this to do with the emotional fallout of the evening, first seeing his sons, then hearing about Ludmilla? Whatever it was, it had affected Clara too. She moved her legs and rocked him atop her, taking him slowly, easily, into her warmth.

This was good too, familiar, of course, but, as always, different.

She drew him forward, leading him into a deep place he'd never reached before, sighing, then locking him there, in extremis, with her strong legs, and against her breasts. No, he did not remember this, or this about her. Tom passed into a kind of euphoria. He was lucky . . . yes, damned lucky. And happy!

Her want was very powerful. Clara's fingers dug into his back, ravenous. Never before had she actually punctured skin; now, or was it again his imagination, he was sure she'd drawn blood. But he didn't care.

She must have felt before he did the powerful rush of his fulfillment, for she reached for him with all her body and held him with her knees as he crested; as she did too, with loud cries, then sighs as she came down.

Forget the fragrant stranger, Tom told himself.

"Oh, Tom," she whispered.

Had he made her forget about Ludmilla? At least for a little while? Better yet, had Clara helped him put aside his own memories, the yearning, the regret? This was most important, Tom told himself slyly. It had never stopped, his own thirst for adventure . . . *the adventure,* the only adventure worth talking about.

Hildy? He wanted to tell Clara that because he'd behaved in a slightly lecherous fashion, it didn't necessarily mean he aimed to sleep with Hildy, even if he had a chance, which was unlikely.

Of course, given the chance, then he might have to reconsider. Laughing. Was that Ludmilla he heard laughing?

"I'll bet you woke up Martha," Tom said.

"Tough. She should shut her ears. This is my house."

"You scratched me, madame."

"I didn't hear you cry out, sweetheart."

"I bit my knuckle," he joked.

Clara chuckled to herself, beginning to withdraw already toward her private self.

"I guess I'll go with you, Tom," she whispered. "For a few days. I'm afraid to let you loose by yourself."

"Ah, good. I'd worry about leaving you alone too." Yes, she was still remembering Ludmilla. "I don't trust Biff Percy. . . ."

She chuckled again, too readily, Tom judged, far too casually to suit him.

"Why would you say a thing like that?" Clara asked. "Poor Biff . . ."

Poor Biff? Hardly. The ugly little bastard had ingratiated himself with Clara. Clara adored artists of all types—watercolor, oil, pastiche . . . good, bad, indifferent. Tom wasn't exactly sure where Biff fell. Penniless, for sure, in the age-old tradition. But as to talent, perhaps somewhere between good and bad.

Sometimes, when Clara was in one of her dark furies, she would tell Tom that Biff was her single joy.

Not, he thought, turning again toward sleep, the most flattering remark she might make.

Chapter Two

*T*he morning dawned clear, a strong offshore wind having blown the mist out of San Francisco Bay. The day before, everybody had come to the apartment for brunch and they hadn't been able to see past the windowsill. But now a metallic December sun was shining through low clouds, and far down below, Clara could easily spot the incoming commuter boat beating the whitecaps near the island of Alcatraz.

The daily help, one Kharma Quinn, had fixed morning coffee, served with fresh croissants she'd picked up on her way from home. A crisp, buttery smell invaded every corner of the apartment.

Tom was looking at the *Chronicle*, his face impassive, the dark brows and eyes steady on the page. His powers of concentration were remarkable, the result, Clara supposed, of all those years studying and writing boring legal briefs. He hardly moved; you couldn't really be sure he was breathing. But he didn't fall out of his chair, so he must be alive.

Sometimes Clara wondered. She had heard so many people say, as a half-serious joke, that Tom Addey, the legal eagle, was so cold that ice wouldn't melt in his mouth.

But this wasn't exactly true. The night before, at the Trader's, he'd been far from cold with Seth's German girlfriend, the starchy but come-hither number called Hildy Beckmann. He had done his best to dazzle her. Seth might as well not have been there at all. Or Serena, Rossiter's wife, who was sitting on Tom's right.

Whereas, Tom would have said coyly, the defendant might *seem* cold and distant, actually he is a warm and affectionate person, yes, God knows, even passionate, wouldn't you say?

No, what Clara would say was that sometimes—not so very often, thank God, for nobody could take a steady diet of Tom at his most supercilious and conceited—he acted the pain in the ass. And he was extremely lucky to have Clara Morelli Gates Addey, Mrs. Patience Personified, to put up with him, to understand him. In her understanding, Clara did not doubt, she was better than his first wife, the ballbusting Thelma Drysdale, famed magazine editor and doyenne of *style* with a capital S.

And Tom should understand something too—that he could push his luck only so far.

He'd been far too blatant last night, for instance—though, she had to admit, he had made up for it later, and very nicely too. There had been only the six of them at the table, and for Tom to keep bringing Hildy's small, well-manicured hand to his lips and kissing it, that was too much. And there had been people in the room with very alert eyes. She and Tom were well-known; there could be no anonymity for them in San Francisco. *That* columnist from the *Chronicle* had been sitting nearby with two tired sophisticates, a couple of people close to Madame Mayor were across the room, and Clara's old friend Bette Toland cooed in the corner with her latest husband—Number Five? Clara had lost count.

Sunday night at the Trader's was like the village square; every gossip had her window open.

Naturally, Tom Addey did not give a damn. He never had. Never did. Probably never would. What you had to know about Tom was that he was greatly attracted to females such as Hildy, aged more or less thirty, women of ambition and career. She had been presented by Seth as a photojournalist of growing reputation among the awful German picture magazines.

But what about Tom's roving eye for wild women?

Like Bette Toland, the barracuda, aged approximately thirty-eight. Clara was better-looking overall than either Bette or Hildy, if it came to that. She was blond and free-flying—like a parachutist, she had often thought, rocketing through the sky. Clara was a striking blonde; she looked good with sunburn on her nose or in a negligee in front of the fire.

Still, sometimes she had to wonder how much such qualifications meant to Tom. After eight years of marriage he showed signs of returning to the exploration; he was fascinated by strange faces and exotic places.

How her luck had spun out, Clara thought wryly. Her first marriage, at a tender age, had been to a gay young man, Martha's father; the second, when she was supposedly older and wiser, to a cocksman. Or did she exaggerate?

Deliberately, Clara interrupted Tom's attention to the newspaper.

"You know, your sons are very nice," she said carefully.

He nodded, not looking up. "Not bad. They're quiet, I'll grant you that."

"Black-haired Addey men—all the same. You all look alike."

Tom studied her. "That's understandable."

Clara smiled at him distantly. "I'd like to see you in a triptych—father and sons. Clever black eyebrows, furrowed white brow, keenly intellectual Tom Addey, attorney-for-the-defense—"

"Or plaintiff," he muttered. "Doesn't matter. I'll take the case, if the money's right."

"You unprincipled dog!" Clara said lightly. "Then Rossiter, uncomplicated, absentminded Rossiter—*the good boy*."

"Right on that," Tom said.

"And sinister Seth."

Tom laughed easily, accepted what she said as not a personal putdown.

"Too true, dear. Seth likes to look sinister. He's made for his profession."

"Do you needle them too much?"

"Do I? Well . . . don't I needle everybody?"

"I think fathers and sons are apt to be a little uneasy with each other. I've watched my father and Fred."

Fred was Clara's younger brother. He was a partner in Morelli Vineyards, had been married ten years and had three young sons—but Alberto treated him like he was still sixteen.

Coolly, she observed, "I thought Seth got a little frosty when you kept calling him 'My son, the secret agent.' "

Again Tom chuckled. "Well, that's what he is—a spook. What do you think happened in Moscow? Why he's in Munich all of a sudden?"

"Well," Clara continued, even more carefully, "Rossiter? 'My son, the stockbroker.' I think you . . ." Clara chose the word cautiously. He was quick to take offense, and indeed, his eye sharpened. ". . . well, demean him. He wanted to talk to you about a business thing and you just brushed him off."

"Oh, for crissakes!" Tom rattled his newspaper. "Must you be Ross's PR flack? It was something about Chet Arthur Limited taking over that company that publishes Thelma's magazine. Should I give a good goddamn about that, *I ask you*?"

It was nine-thirty and they'd have to leave fairly soon. But Clara wondered if she wanted to work herself into such a lather that she could renege on her promise to go with him.

Poor Rossiter.

No! There was nothing poor about him, either materially or spiritually. He was tall, handsome, healthy, and he made a good living stockbrokering in southern California. Christ alone knew why he had apparently freely and presumably happily married this little pain in the ass Serena, née Slagger. Part of Ross's problem with his father, of course, was Serena. There was plenty of snob in Tom. He could not forgive Serena for her father, the ex-baseball player and now Las Vegas executive, or her mother, inaptly named Tiny, who had apparently once been a chorus girl at one of the Vegas casinos.

But no, *not* poor Rossiter. Rossiter's briefest touch still made Clara weak in the knees, ready to drop at the drop of a hat. Tom couldn't have any idea of that, could he? Even thinking about Rossiter so obliquely made her short of breath. But she couldn't let on.

"You hardly said a word to Serena."

"*What is this?* I treated everybody just fine! Even Serena!"

Then he smiled, and Clara saw why. Martha strolled into the breakfast room stretching and yawning like a five-year-old.

"Serena?" She took up the little conversation. "That woman has got knockers big enough to derail a train."

Clara glared at her. "That's a horrible thing to say!"

Martha shrugged. "Sorry." She sat down at the table. "Didn't I hear the phone last night late?"

"Tom had a call from L.A.," Clara told her tersely. "That's all."

She noticed how he put the paper aside for Martha.

"A friend died," he said, "that's what it was about."

"Oh. Sorry."

Death didn't have any big effect on kids of nineteen. They registered condolence, then went on to other things. Martha poured coffee and milk and cradled the big café au lait cup in her hands. Slowly but surely Kharma Quinn was getting the hang of making the coffee smell like morning in Paris.

Martha shoved her nose into the steam, elbows planted on the edge of the table. She made a throaty sound as she sipped, causing Tom to smile at her warmly. Oh, yes, that would alert him, wouldn't it?

"Did your kiddies have a good time last night?"

"I thought they did," Tom replied. He glanced at Clara. "Though now I'm told I behaved like a boor."

"So what's new?" Martha joked heavily.

"I didn't say you behaved like a boor, Tom," Clara disagreed crisply. "I said I thought you needled your sons more than is absolutely necessary."

Martha nodded enthusiastically.

"Does he ever! But none of us kids pay any attention. The man's bark is worse than his bite—or is it the other way around? Not that *I'd* know, of course," Martha hinted coyly. "Anyway, they're all leaving today, aren't they?"

Tom stared at her blackly. But he could never be angry at Martha, not even very irritated. As far as Tom was concerned, Martha could do no wrong, and she played this for all it was worth.

"Yes, they're leaving. Back to the real world."

Tom said this in a way that made Clara want to scream and kick him in the shins. He actually envied Seth, that was the truth of it. Tom envied Seth his job, envied Seth the fact he'd been expelled from Moscow after the run-in with the KGB—Clara wasn't sure of the dirty details. Tom was even a little jealous of Rossiter, although he always claimed loudly that he never could've done Ross's job—buying and selling stocks, creating arbitraging situations. But it had been Tom's own choice to leave L.A. and semi-retire from the world, declaring himself for all to hear alienated from the legal profession, at the age of fifty, at the peak. Clara had always presumed alienation was for the young; *she* had been alienated herself for two or three minutes. But at fifty, wasn't a man supposed to be slotted for good into society's machinery?

16

"Will you miss them?" Martha asked curiously.

Tom shrugged. "The world goes on."

"And *we're* going to L.A.," Clara said.

"Why? Oh! The phone call." Even Martha's sleep-drugged mind could put that together. "So who died anyway?"

"The woman who died," Tom said ponderously, "was called Ludmilla Spurzova. She was married to a good friend of mine—Prince Alex Spurzov."

Martha nodded. "Sure. She was your mistress, wasn't she?"

"How do you know that?"

Clara laughed to herself. "She's heard us mention Ludmilla."

"Of course," Martha said, "everybody knows."

"Well, *you* don't," he decreed, "and the point is, we're going down to Los Angeles this morning. I've got to see to Alex's affairs."

Martha didn't flinch. "It was Princess Spurzova who broke up your first marriage, wasn't it?"

Tom glanced grimly at Clara. Had *she* put Martha up to this? It couldn't have been planned better to provoke him.

"Well, I'm sorry," Martha went on, undeterred. "I hope you're not too sad."

"I haven't seen her in years."

Martha sighed. "She must have been a woman and a half—a model, wasn't she, and an actress, and a fashion designer?"

"She was a Bulgarian," Tom said, as if that explained her. "She was a great character too. She did *everything*."

"And *everybody*," Clara put in sardonically, not able to resist.

"Now, Mother!" Martha shook a finger at her. "That's not nice." Then, solemnly, she asked Tom, *"Are* you sorry?"

Tom looked uncomfortable. Whatever he said wouldn't satisfy Clara.

"Well, aren't you usually sorry when people die? Sorry that I knew her?" he growled. "No! That'd be a silly waste of time." He paused and then went on smoothly, "Look at it this way—if it hadn't been for Ludmilla, I'd never have come across Clara Morelli and her cute little daughter, Martha Gates."

"Cute?"

"As a bug."

"Jesus!"

"Some big bug," Clara noted critically, "flouncing around in her jammies in the middle of the day. . . ."

As well as, Clara might have added, showing her stuff for all to see. The way she was sitting, Martha's upper arms pushed her breasts against the pajama top, revealing large patches of sleep-pinkened skin. Clara wondered if Martha did it deliberately, to provoke Tom. Now, she leaned back in the roomy Windsor chair and crossed her legs, pulling the bottoms tight at the thighs. There wasn't much hope for Tom to miss seeing all of it.

Clara said tensely, "Now, listen, while we're gone, I want you to donate me some of your time. I want you at the Morelli Gallery to help Biff out. I'd be doing it myself—we have a show opening the middle of next week."

"Biff?" Martha wouldn't be happy about that. "Biff Percy is a dangerous man, you know that, don't you?"

"You can handle him, *my sweet.*"

"Biff Percy is the grossest artist on the West Coast, mother. And I hate his goddamn cigars!"

"I said—you can handle it," Clara said sharply. "I just want to make sure all the things for the show are ready, that's all. It doesn't involve very much . . . it's the least you can do. . . ."

"Oh, I see, sure, in return for my room and board."

Irritably, Tom cut in, "You know what your mother means, for God's sake! Check it out, that's all. Make sure Genius Biff doesn't get drunk and burn the place down with one of those stinking cigars of his."

"Exactly," Clara said testily, thinking to herself she could have cheerfully kicked Martha into the street and maybe Tom along with her. She pushed back from the table and stood up. "I've got to pack a couple more things. . . . If you want to go, Tom, then maybe you'd better think about calling the car."

He glanced up. "Aye, aye, sir!"

Naturally, Martha's look was also defiant. It wasn't that mother and daughter didn't like each other—there was simply this competition. The problem was, Clara wasn't old enough to be her mother; she'd had Martha at much too young an age, thanks to the beautiful Stanley Gates—and because Stanley had been so young at the time himself, he thought those funny feelings he got was because he liked girls.

Bitchily, Martha said, "Speaking of which, it sounded like somebody was getting killed around here last night. . . ."

Clara smiled at her sheepishly. "You just do what I tell you."

Tom got up from the table and so did Martha. As she was leaving the room, Clara saw Martha throw herself at Tom and hug him.

"Good-bye, sweet prince!"

"Now, listen, you—"

"I wish I could go with you."

"Well, you can't. You've got school and . . . Biff."

"I may just . . . give myself to Biff," Martha threatened.

From the hallway Clara called, "Stop talking like that! You know Biff Percy is socially below your station."

"Oh, Jesus, that is so funny!"

Around the corner Clara stopped to watch them in the mirror that covered the short wall of the breakfast room.

Martha wouldn't let Tom go. She plastered herself against him, hanging from his shoulders. Then she slid her body upward onto her tiptoes to kiss his cheek, then his lips. Tom did his best to look surprised, and confused. But he made no move to back away from the attack. Martha positively ground her pajama'ed bottom against him, laughing good-naturedly all the while, as if this were just a great big joke. Tricky time.

Yes, her husband. It wasn't enough she had to watch him with the flirty German, ignore his gallantry with titty Serena, and guard against leaving him alone with Bette Toland . . . and try to forgive Ludmilla retroactively.

But her own goddamn daughter couldn't keep her hands off him—what was Tom, some kind of satyr? Did he give off some kind of irresistible aura?

Yes, in a way, he did. Why else did she stick with him, as infuriating as he could be? Last night she had been angry, bitter, frustrated . . . And then? Then she had forgiven him. That was how she'd put it. Forgiven him, and very positively too. Vehemently, if Martha had heard something. There was that about him, that hateful thing, appeal, a kind of funny fatal attraction. Or a fatal funny attraction.

Once in a while Tom let himself out of his shell; now and then he showed his true colors. That was what made him bearable, and the fact, of course, that he was a very good lover. He must have known this last part of it.

Well, she thought, he practiced enough.

Sure enough. She could see it all. His right hand dropped so he could pat Martha paternally on the ass, then stroke the spot a few times, then pat again before he finally . . . finally . . . pulled away from her.

"Tom!" Clara yelled.

She heard Martha call out, "Bon voyage, handsome."

"Same to you, hot-buns."

Chapter Three

*A*lex hadn't bothered to sleep. At the best of times he got in only a couple of hours a night. As dawn slipped through the shutters at Richlands, he was still pacing his room, as if alone in a prison cell with his grief. He counted, then recounted the steps from door to window, back to door, now and then stopping to light a cigarette. He would take a few puffs, then stub it out. Once, Alex had been a heavy smoker; nowadays the doctors said smoking would shorten your life.

He laughed to himself about that—he was already seventy-three years old. The fact was that Alex was not much good anymore at smoking, as he was not so good at certain other things. He didn't drink heavily, nothing like he had during his days in the caviar importing business. He found it unwise to take more than two or three good shots of cold vodka a day.

And Alex never stopped eating heartily of good red meat. People could talk all they wanted to about fish and fiber. Alex needed his meat. Somewhere in his background lurked his Cossack ancestors, men on horseback with the digestive tracts of a meat grinder.

And Alex wished he had an ancestor with him now, a crazy Cossack with his saber.

With one sweeping cut, he'd slice off the balls of that son of a bitch Cazimir Ben Gazi.

How he hated Ben Gazi now—for, injustice of injustices, had it not been Cazimir who had last spent himself between Ludmilla's dear thighs? Admittedly, Alex had been in her bed a mere few hours before Cazimir's arrival, but then she had booted him out. Yes, all right, Ludmilla was *always* kicking somebody out of her bed to make way for somebody new. And he *was* too old for her now. What did you expect of a man?

He was not sure of his precise age; all that had gotten confused in the drama of the century. His family had fled Russia a few months after the Revolution, first to Helsinki and then Berlin and finally to Paris in the 1930s. Yes, the Spurzovs had survived the slaughter, but there had been little left, only a few jewels and other portable treasures, such as the Spurzov Egg. After a spotty education Alex had been sent into commerce—perish the thought! A family connection secured him an apprentice position with Tarnowski et Frères, a commodities firm owned by descendants of Polish nobility who had retreated across Europe with Napoleon after the defeat in Moscow.

Eventually Tarnowski had sent Alex to the Balkans in search of a superior slivowitz, the numbing plum brandy never, never to be partaken with beer in the form of boilermakers. There, along the Black Sea coast of Bulgaria, as he pursued his mission, Alex discovered the perfect woman, the chubby and extremely high-spirited daughter of a prosperous Bulgarian kulak.

And so it was that Luba, quickly Ludmilla, had run away with him to Paris—what Bulgarian peasant girl could resist the invitation?—and then on to New York just before the outbreak of war in Europe.

There, in America, with nothing to recommend her but sheer Gypsy beauty, a naturally aristocratic bearing, and bubbling vivacity, the newly minted and slimmed down Princess Spurzova had become an overnight sensation . . . not only as a fashion model.

People said she walked like Garbo. In truth, like Garbo, she was a woman of the Earth—and earthy with it.

Alex did not begrudge her that. For Ludmilla anything and everything was permitted. Ludmilla loved love, to be loved, and to love. She did it often and well. It amazed Alex to watch her progression, her career. Never was there anything ill-spirited about her behavior. Ludmilla was generosity itself; and generosity began with herself, her body.

This did not mean Alex did not live in the First Circle of Hell.

Before his very eyes she became the mistress of Edward

Stringham, a ranking vice-president of the World Commerce Corporation—and Ludmilla, with her contempt for money!

And then the war. Heroic service for Alex in the OSS . . . Stringham's death in France.

And on to Hollywood. But it was already very late for Ludmilla. People said she was pre-war merchandise. Was that fair? Or polite?

During the long night at Richlands Alex remembered all these things. The betrayals, mainly . . . *Betrayal,* the favorite pastime of the twentieth century. Yes, he had betrayed Ludmilla too, finally, in a lonely farmhouse in Occupied France—he hadn't even known the girl's real name, and she was dead soon afterward.

And Stringham betrayed as well by an informer and destroyed as his parachute came to ground in the farmlands of Normandy.

How sad and exciting and catastrophic it had been, this century.

Alex stopped at the window again, staring through the slats of the shutters. Richlands was soggy with heavy morning dew. The pool, on the other side of a barricade of hedgerow, was calm, its surface unchanged by the recent presence of death. *Goddamn water!*

His watch said it was eight-thirty. Ludmilla had given him this beautiful gold watch; she had passed it to him carelessly one lunchtime, Here; beloved one, a little gift for you. They still spoke a mad mixture of Russian and English when they were alone.

Finally, of course, Alex had divorced her, but they had never stopped being lovers when the opportunity arose. Alex traveled back and forth to France from California and he'd forced himself to take several mistresses—one in Paris, one in New York who worked as a curator at the Met, and a Hollywood writer who'd killed herself one day, not because of Alex but in despair over the cancellation of her TV series.

However, no one but Ludmilla had ever touched his mainspring. She married a singing cowboy and later divorced him. Alex had always come back to her, to be enfolded once more in the supple limbs, then to be ejected again to make room for yet another somebody, or nobody. . . .

Alex adjusted the shutters and sunlight flooded the room.

The birds had begun to make a serious racket down in the garden where, among other greenery, Rodney Richards had developed his prize-winning collection of cymbidia.

Ah, yes, Richlands was a paradise on Earth. Or a hell. It all depended where you were standing.

Time to get a move on. There were things to be done before Tom Addey arrived, if only Alex could bring himself to concentrate. Looking in the mirror, he saw a haggard man with a mass of wavy white hair and a long, hound-dog face. He felt his cheek, which she had so recently kissed good morning, or good night. Alex had not undressed; shaving could be put off until later.

The house was very quiet as Alex stepped into the hallway. Yes, Alex remembered, the butler Peat had begged for the day off, to get away from the house; he usually visited his mother in Pomona when he was distraught, which was not infrequent. And the other servants wouldn't be coming in; Peat had seen to that before he left.

The hallway ran the length of the house, past a tightly curved, no-nonsense staircase. Richards had wasted neither money nor space. Ludmilla had caused the master suite to be riotously redecorated when she became the second Mrs. Rodney Richards . . . as Rod's Harem, she boasted preposterously, to offset Rod's boring personality, in colors and fabrics and furniture foreign to Rod's nature. The decor, Alex had always thought, without saying so, reminded him of Berlin, circa 1935.

He might have locked the boudoir door the night before, after the police and Peat had finally departed, but he hadn't thought to do so.

He should have.

Cazimir was there before him, crouched on the fluffy white carpet and holding in twitching fingers a white-framed picture Alex recognized as Ludmilla in full regalia of her own inimitable design, a theatrical white negligee and flowing robe edged with ermine. Pure Ludmilla. Pure bliss!

"Good morning, Cazimir."

How he hated the presumptuous Arab for handling the picture. Gently, he took it from him.

Cazimir waited suspiciously.

"You have not slept, dear boy? All night, you have been sitting here?"

Perhaps, it occurred to Alex, he should not be so skeptical of Cazimir. Perhaps Cazimir was *truly* broken-hearted. After all, these people were different; they could be honestly emotional in ways Westerners would not understand.

"Father Alex . . . I am so sad."

Was the loathesome sigh genuine or merely a variation of Cazimir's usual petulant whine? Alex hated it when the lad called him father. That was something Ludmilla had thought amusing. Cazimir might have been her son; thus, Alex the father.

Nauseating.

Even more so when Cazimir moved his hands. There, where he had been holding the picture, he revealed an erection straining against his skintight black pajamas.

Alex snarled, "Not the most stunning expression of grief, dear boy."

Cazimir, as Alex might have expected, laughed hoarsely, without shame.

"I have been thinking of Lud-mullah, Father Alex. *She* would understand . . . and appreciate. Always, she appreciated . . ." Registering Alex's shock, he went on lasciviously, "Only last night, Father Alex—"

"You went out!"

"*Before* I left, Alex, I was here, with her. . . ."

But then, fortunately, he stopped. Alex especially hated the way the little bastard pronounced her name, barbarized it: *Ludmull-ah*, the sounds of a man eating a handful of dates. And now that she was dead, he was permitted to hate Cazimir too. Alive, Ludmilla had glossed over Cazimir's ugliness, his grossness—what was it about the man that fascinated so many women so completely? Perhaps the mere fact of his association with Ludmilla. Until the very end Ludmilla had reflected her own sheen on to another lover, transformed yet another toad into a prince.

Alex might well wonder how his own image would rot now that she was no longer there to dress it like a théatre set.

"Gallop! *Gallop*," Cazimir cried wetly, derisively. "She and I were playing bedouin in the desert."

The fool!

Alex said, "My friend Tom Addey is arriving today."

Cazimir didn't seem interested. He continued to sit on the

carpet like an ungainly lump. Surely he would remember it had been Tom who had brought him to Ludmilla.

"So . . . all Lud-mullah's lovers are gathering, then?"

Alex drew himself up. "*I* was her husband."

"*And lover* . . . after being her husband. But not too often, no, Father Alex? The ancient tool, no?" Cazimir giggled. "Lud-mullah told me all!"

"It would be best for you to be silent."

Cazimir defied him, though. He pointed at his crotch.

"Well, old man," he taunted, "then you know it was *this* Lud-mullah loved to roll in her mouth . . . *like a Cuban cigar*." Cazimir giggled again, on the edge of hysteria. Poor lad, Alex told himself quietly, he was obviously very tired. Cazimir mistook Alex's expression for acceptance and went on, making it all the worse. "But she was very useful to me, Alex. There were so many people she helped me with—"

"What the hell are you going on about?"

"Nothing, *Père Alex*," Cazimir teased, "nothing which would concern such an old *fart* as you." A clever smile, a smile of such immense superiority formed on his lips that Alex had to restrain himself from delivering a karate kick to the pouty red lips. "I will tell you something, Alex—*I was Lud-mullah's last husband!* You were first . . . I was last!"

"Last lover . . ."

Cazimir mocked gleefully. "No, *last husband*. You were the last lover, *Père*. . . ."

A strain of fear, like poison, began to leak into Alex's bloodstream.

"Liar!"

But sharply, words slashing, Cazimir assured him. "I tell you no lies. Lud-mullah and I were married in Paris . . . last year. Do you not remember when she met me in Paris?"

Uncertainly, Alex shook his head, then vaguely nodded, wondering if his heart had stopped beating. No, it revived and began to pound in his chest like a drum.

Could Ludmilla have married this swine?

"Never," he exclaimed angrily. "Ludl would have told me." Another truth dawned on him. "And you . . . you're married already. You have a wife in Lebanon."

"But of course," Cazimir replied nonchalantly. "And little ones . . . You forget I'm allowed more than one wife."

"But you are a Christian! Christians have one wife . . . not two or three!"

"Of no consequence, *Père Alex*," Caximir said carelessly. "Moslem first, Christian second."

"Liar first!"

"No." Cazimir shook his head. "Lud-mullah was my wife. I have the paper."

"Where? Where is it? Let me see!"

"When the time comes, I will produce it."

Alex trembled with rage. But Tom Addey had once warned him against talking instead of thinking. He regained control and stared down at Cazimir; there must have been something in his eyes, for finally Cazimir began to rise, like a snake uncurling. His pajama top crept up to reveal his ludicrously hairy belly.

"I leave you here for a few moments," he announced. "But I do not leave the house."

"Leave or stay," Alex said mildly. "This house has nothing more to do with you."

"I will stay to protect my interests, Father Alex."

"Your interests?" Alex echoed scornfully. "You? The wealthy Sheik of Araby? What could interest you here?"

Eyeing Alex in an infuriating way, a pitying way that was most infuriating of all, Cazimir murmured, "Do you expect me to surrender what belongs to me now, *Père Alex*? *The Egg* . . . among other riches?"

Alex stepped back. He could not help showing shock.

"You cannot be speaking of the Spurzov Egg!"

"The same."

Alex was aware that his body temperature dropped. It did so, he had learned during the war, at times of extreme stress.

"The Egg has nothing to do with you. It has belonged to the Spurzovs through the ages. It is a heritage. Would you understand that?"

A malicious glint appeared in Cazimir's eyes.

"But there are no more Spurzovs, Father Alex. You are the last. Make me your son," he teased spitefully. "Besides, study the law a little—in California exists what they know as community property. Lud-mullah owned half your Egg and I inherit that fifty percent—you should nicely give me the rest. *Please*?"

Now Alex's blood was congealing, bringing it closer to near absolute zero in temperature.

"Not possible."

"Then there will be no shortage of buyers for it in auction."

Silently, Alex watched Cazimir slither from the room, then crossed to lock the door after him.

There was a point to what Cazimir had said: Alex was the last of the Spurzovs. What, then, after Alex? Did the Egg return to the goddamn Bolsheviks? Admittedly it was a treasure that belonged to all the Russians, a breed that had nothing to do with the present usurpers. They would be swept from the land in due course. The People—they were like the sand and the tide. Sand castles were always swept away.

But there was a way of ascertaining how closely Ludmilla had gathered Cazimir to her dear bosom.

Ludmilla's vast closet was a repository of international fashion, a museum of gowns and robes and caftans, evening dresses, day dresses, sports clothes, negligees, naughty lingerie, which she liked to wear in the evening.

But the secret place inside the closet was all Ludmilla, typically Ludmilla—at heart she had never stopped being a peasant. It was a wonder she hadn't kept her valuables in the mattress. The hiding place was so obvious no one would have thought to look there. Merely slide back a piece of paneling and within was a metal safe with a combination lock.

The question was whether Ludmilla had confided in Cazimir. If so, the safe would've been emptied of everything already . . . and all was lost.

But no, nothing had been touched. Inside the box, Ludmilla kept only a modest selection of her jewelry—the walking-around stuff or daytime jewelry, people called it, too valuable to be left laying around the house, not valuable enough to be stored in the bank vault.

Mainly this assortment was of the gold pieces Alex had bought for her over the years—still, for sentimental reasons, the things Ludmilla liked most. Thank God, yes, she had never really stopped loving him.

More to the point, the box contained a key to a deposit box at a Westwood bank, as Alex had always known, where he would find the main force of Ludmilla's wealth. Even more significantly, within a soft Italian-made leather holster, was Ludmilla's lady-sized automatic. It waited there like a Mafia hit man to be called into action.

Alex pocketed the key, then removed the deadly black automatic from its leather pouch. He checked the clip—it was full of ugly little snub-nosed slugs—and snapped it back into the grip, then jacked a round into the chamber and set the safety. Unceremoniously, not really aware of what he was doing or why he was doing so, he tucked the automatic into the back pocket of his gray flannels.

Next, still carrying out a ritual for which a script had yet to be written, Alex gathered handfuls of the gold jewelry and returned to the bedroom. Stiffly, he stooped and knelt down to spread the gold pieces on the fluffy carpet, arranging them neatly, as in a showcase, as the young Peruvian woman had always done.

She had come up to Los Angeles once or twice a year to sell the work of the mountain craftsmen. For a time she had been another of Alex's on-again, off-again mistresses; each of his purchases had evidently, by some Indian custom, entitled him to an allotment of pleasure.

The centerpiece was a heavy golden chestplate, as substantial as a piece of armor and, indeed, with a lurid scene of sacrifice etched into its surface and a fringe of gold fish dangling from the bottom.

Everything meant something.

The gold shone. There was a specific color to gold, as well as weight. Its color was Greed, if that was possible, something at the far end of the rainbow's visible range. When men thought of gold, their heads filled with a color frequency quite different from that which produced red or green or yellow. Greed was its own thing.

And so, also, had Ludmilla kept the little automatic. When the world dropped over the brink, gold would still buy goods and shelter, but one needed a weapon to protect the gold.

It had been years since Alex had thought seriously of defending himself. How swiftly the memories of war came back, then slipped away.

The habits of war too.

Alex replaced the sliding panel inside the closet and wiped the wood clean of fingerprints with his handkerchief. There was no reason to point the way to the secret compartment.

Then he unlocked the bedroom door and waited for Cazimir. There was no question Cazimir would come back. By now his

29

subconscious would have picked up the pulsing frequency of the gold.

If he had been blind, Alex could have identified Cazimir from his scent. The Lebanese gave off waves of pungent aftershave; he smelled as high as a squadron of harlots.

Behind him Alex heard Cazimir's sharp intake of breath. As he turned, Cazimir's eyes widened and his hands fell out of the pockets of the shawl-collared cardigan.

"From where is this?" he gasped.

Alex laughed gently. "Ludmilla."

Forgetting Alex was there, Cazimir dropped to his knees and fell on the gold like a plunderer. As rich as he was . . . He looped long, seemingly boneless fingers around the pieces, lifting them toward his nose and letting them slide away, weighing and caressing. He even began to purr; ululating sobs throbbed in his throat like love sounds.

How touching.

There was a certain inevitability about things, Alex had always believed. In a quiet moment he would accept, for instance, that Ludmilla's time had come. And that it was also inevitable that Alex Spurzov, on this particular day in December, had been tethered to the planet Earth in this crazy place called Los Angeles . . . and that squatting below him, moaning with greed, was Cazimir Ben Gazi, this awful man who never wore underwear.

Alex drew the little automatic out of his back pocket and silently slid the safety catch to *Off*. So far, brilliant.

With his left hand, almost lovingly, Alex touched the top of Cazimir's head, the hair bunched up in a conceited sort of pompadour, resilient enough to cushion a fall.

Then, decisively, as he had once been taught, Alex took a big handful of the hair and yanked Cazimir's head backward and to the side.

Before Cazimir could do more than squeak in alarm, never mind fear, Alex put the muzzle of the automatic to his temple and fired.

Pop!

The sound was surprisingly neutral, and hardly louder than the opening of a celebratory bottle of champagne. And Alex knew about champagne.

So simple. But killing, Alex had been taught, should be

simple. It didn't do to doll up an assassination. Do it quickly and get it done. Efficiently, without great emotion.

Am I right, Eddie? he heard himself asking silently.

The noise was not a consideration, since there was nobody else in the house. And a wound like this wouldn't bleed much. Such a small caliber slug got tangled in the gray matter and didn't exit—or hadn't, as far as Alex could make out.

Cazimir was kneeling already, so when Alex let go of the hair, there was nothing for. the body to do but sag. Cazimir didn't fall headlong but, rather, folded at the waist, slipped into a posture suggesting an obeisance, his forehead coming to rest on the golden breastplate he had been so noisily coveting.

Alex again took the handkerchief out of his blazer breast pocket and wiped down the automatic, then carefully pressed it into Cazimir's right hand.

Still brilliant.

Cazimir was right-handed, so there could not be any foul-up that way. Alex was pretty sure he had thought it through; suicide was suicide and the poor lad had been distraught, no question of it.

But Alex was older now, there was no question of that either.

Things could go wrong. Suppose, for example, Cazimir was merely very badly wounded? But no, unquestionably, the poor lad was dead; final, involuntary muscular spasms, his expiring life, made the body quiver, like the last drops running out of a bottle.

People, if it did come out, would say Alex Spurzov was a beast, a heartless murderer, and this would be partially true. A murderer, yes; but not heartless. He had killed Cazimir because he did have a heart, a very large heart.

Cazimir *was* dead. The body spasms declined, fading to nil. Alex had plenty of time to watch. Yes, Cazimir was just as dead—*kaput!*—as Ludmilla, even though a person might have thought he was praying—to Mecca? Or toward St. Peter's in Rome? Both were to the east and on adjacent latitudes.

Well, Eddie, did this make it any better?

Other than that, what did Alex feel?

Young! Yes, and alive!

This was not the first time he had killed a man—and he had killed better men than Cazimir Ben Gazi.

Finally, though, staring down at the fallen enemy, Alex felt his hands shake, his fingers begin to tremble.

He shouldn't be a fool about it. You didn't get away with it without paying some kind of a price. Not because God wouldn't approve. He would settle that part of it with God later.

Alex tucked the handkerchief back into the breast pocket of his blazer and turned away. Leaving the former Cazimir Ben Gazi there in the middle of the carpet, he crossed to the door.

Somebody would have to discover Cazimir—in due course.

Right now it was time for a drink. Alex hoped he could find the vodka bottle in the butler's pantry.

Chapter Four

*R*oss Addey wished to hell they'd driven to San Francisco, though there were pros and cons about that too.

The flight into Burbank was normally less than an hour—he'd done it often enough, into San Fran for a breakfast meeting, back to L.A. for lunch—but in Serena's company any airplane trip was interminable.

She began her initial nausea attack even before the door was closed, and by the time Flight So-and-so was in the air, Rossiter had already had to ask the stewardess for another airsickness bag. Was it his imagination or were people around them hustling for different seats, in an already crowded plane?

But . . .

Rossiter was long-suffering, you couldn't take that away from him. With Serena, for sure; his mother too. He had always allowed himself to be pushed around by women. He'd buy that. They took him for granted, used him for exorcizing their bad moods. He talked to his mother on the phone all the time and exchanged long letters with her, composed largely, it seemed, of Thelma's paranoid outbursts and Rossiter's efforts to reassure her.

When you thought about it, Seth must have inherited Thelma's fearful and suspicious disposition. And *they* communicated very seldom.

But Rossiter was first-born. He was responsible. Thelma hadn't ever put it so bluntly, but it must have been in her mind.

And now he was going to be in a big jam with her, for he

had utterly failed to get his father's input on the matter of Thelma's latest anxiety—the very strong possibility that media giant Morris Communications Inc., publisher of Thelma's hugely successful magazine *Classics*, was soon to be taken over by a corporate raider named Chester Arthur Ltd.

Big trouble lay in the fact that Thelma, once upon a time, had published a story that came close to accusing the maverick Chet Arthur of corporate behavior as piratical as his personal life was adventuresome.

To keep to the metaphor, Thelma had been having nightmares of herself walking the plank.

In his mind's eye Rossiter, too, could see the battle-scarred ship, the Jolly Chester, the plank . . . Serena. Serena?

She was kicking at his knee.

"Move your goddamn legs. I've gotta get out—quick!"

He jumped up. God, no, don't delay her. Serena pushed past him furiously, heading up the aisle for the johns. Pray God one of them was vacant. Better yet, maybe the can would yawn open underneath her and Serena would decorate the great outdoors.

Christ, yes, he thought worriedly, there it came again, his delicately homicidal feelings toward Serena. This could be dangerous.

She disappeared behind a partition long enough for him to know she had found an empty spot. Thankfully, he sat down again and tried to re-form his previous thoughts.

Tom Addey. His father didn't make his feelings very secret, even confidential. Serena gave him a pain in the neck; this could not be more obvious. Just once, over the weekend, very circumspectly, he had inquired whether Serena might be pregnant— why else was she behaving like a pregnant woman—and seemed very relieved when Rossiter replied that no, he didn't think no.

Rossiter did not think she was; but strangely, Serena had been making pregnant noises now for a couple of weeks. He could not imagine why. Pregnancy was not in the cards, one would have thought. It was not something Serena would have deliberately sought; the fact it *might* have happened would have been accident compounded.

For, as Rossiter had learned to his regret, Serena was much less highly sexed over the long haul than she had been in the short run. This, plus the protestation she really didn't want a child, made for good odds she wouldn't have one.

Of course, life was full of surprises.

What was incredible was that Serena had anything left inside her with which to be sick. She'd eaten almost nothing the night before, nothing for breakfast except a cup of coffee . . . oh, yes, and the last of the fortune cookies she'd carried away from Trader Vic's.

VAST WEALTH.

Rossiter's eyes flew open, in dull shock. Serena had returned. "Let me in!"

Rossiter nearly gagged over the burst of sweet-sour *après-vomit* breath Serena shot at him as she trampled across his feet. "Jesus!"

She flopped down, barking, "You don't care!"

Her eyes were remarkably bloodshot behind green-tinted contact lenses, like she'd been made up to play the living corpse from the black lagoon. Serena had an idea green eyes coordinated with her artificially blond hair.

It would surprise no one to learn that Serena was *not* a natural blonde. Down at Ice Station Zero the hair was dark as night.

People often wondered why Rossiter had married Serena. They were not much alike—he tall and beefy, she so small, almost emaciated; he stolid and unemotional, Serena excitable, loud, insecure, even neurotic; he more interested in the simple things of life and Serena bound hand and foot by the worst of southern California flash—if you've got it, flaunt it!

Well, what *had* possessed him? What had been so special about Serena that he'd fallen for her? Good questions, and Rossiter did have some answers—if anybody had ever asked outright.

Basically, details of Serena's earlier, traumatic marriage, he admitted, had fascinated him. The pure decadence of her relationship with her first husband had tickled his shock-horror nerve. Hearing her stories gave him a kind of delightfully sick feeling in the pit of the stomach. Rossiter didn't think he had ever actually heard of two people doing such things to each other. Good God! Deliciously awful!

Oh, Ross, how disgusting it was! I thought I'd go stark-raving mad before it was over, until I could escape from him!

Poor doll! Yes, and here was Rossiter, was . . . *would she?* Not all, but just a few selected dirty tricks?

Of course not. Rossiter was much too proper. Yes, it must always be a challenge for a man to turn an unhappy and misused woman into a happy and sheltered one. There was more to being a missionary than the position. Rossiter would help save Serena. Oh, yes. Poor Serena, poor doll, she had always put on a front, so brave it was positively heartbreaking. And on her good days she did bubble with energy and high spirits. *And* her outlook, it could have been said, was sportsman . . . sportswomanlike. She had jumped into Rossiter's bed without a second thought, oh God, yes, seemingly head over heels in love with the tall, dark, and handsome investment tycoon. He hadn't dared ask her for a demonstration of purely sordid practices. Like a good girl she'd then merrily gotten pregnant.

The wedding had been nice enough.

Then it turned out she wasn't pregnant after all.

Now Serena shot another bitter round at him.

"Your father was not nice to me."

"Daddy-Addey?" he tried to joke, lamely.

"Daddy-Addey is a shit."

So she'd noticed it too. Well, at least Daddy-Addey took her mind off being sick. Maybe they could fight the rest of the way into Burbank.

"He was making fun of me in front of Seth's girlfriend—that German *bitch!*"

"No, no. Surely not, surely not. Serena," he said patiently, "when we get home you should go straight to bed."

"I am! I'm sleeping all afternoon. Then, *up!* We're going out tonight!"

She knew what he'd say, that he'd object. Serena smiled at him childishly, trying to assuage his misery.

"I'll be fine. Look," she said eagerly, "we'll be landing soon."

Sure, better already. Serena's basic problem was she couldn't bear to leave Beverly Hills. She didn't much like even driving out to Santa Monica for dinner. If you brought her with you to New York, she was only good for a day or two.

"We could skip a party for once."

Especially during the week, when he had to be at the office by seven, or seven-thirty at the latest.

"Gloomy old beanpole." Wheedling, forgetting once more the death-shock of her fetid breath, Serena leaned to nuzzle his cheek with her clipped-off nose. "It's Kit Morosco's party of the year—'Christmas Tra-La.' Last year you had a ball. And you looked just like Tom whatshisname."

"I *did not* have a ball."

Then, trying to be tricky, she said, "Maybe it's the other kind of ball you're after, Rossiter, my love." He didn't answer yea or nay or baloney, so she went on smugly, "Look, I have to go to this party. My friends from the Society will all be there."

Oh, yes, of course, Serena's big benevolent activity for which he laid out a sizable tithing: The Society of the Madeleine, a second-ranking collection of Los Angeles/Beverly Hills young marrieds who'd dedicated themselves with much fanfare and, naturally, quite a bit of publicity, to the preservation of historical bridges in France. Every summer a group went over to the Loire or Seine to help with the sandblasting.

Thus, Serena seemed to have what she wanted out of their marriage—security and some social standing. After all, Rossiter's father had been well-known around town before moving back up to the northern California of his birth. Clara was well-placed and popular too, the daughter of the rich, old, Sonoma County winemaker Morelli; during her few years in Los Angeles, Clara had gotten around as a hard worker at the Music Center, and she'd become quite friendly with many of the Mighty in the process.

So there was that . . . *and* the money. Rossiter had made a comfortable living since beginning in the business—and in the last couple of years had been pulling down, on the average, one hundred fifty thousand a year as a hard-working West Coast representative of New York–based Sandor Veruckt & Associates, of that breed of money company called arbitrageurs.

Veruckt & Associates dealt in commodities, precious metals, and the securities of companies looking to be on the brink of either dissolution or merger.

Serena liked her life, though she might never admit it; and it was beyond her, as he was learning, to be nice to the man who provided it.

He had made a big mistake. Serena had taken him for a ride. But at the time . . . well, no sense thinking about that now.

Divorce? Murder? One or the other—but Rossiter feared he
didn't have the moral strength to commit murder, even if she
deserved it.

Soon after their marriage six or so years ago, Rossiter and
Serena had acquired a small house a block or so north of Santa
Monica Boulevard in Beverly Hills, barely on the right side of
the tracks but not so bad for a young couple without great
financial resources. In a few years, Rossiter had promised, if all
went well, there wasn't any reason they couldn't get close to
Sunset; and, if luck held, before it was all over, maybe they'd
have located *north of Sunset* and would have well and truly
arrived. And, if things really went their way, a house in Bel Air
was not out of the question.

A baby-blue Seville with a Nevada plate was already parked
in the driveway of their mock-hacienda.

"Daddy!"

Serena high-tailed it toward the house. More leisurely,
Rossiter got his overnight bag and Serena's suitcase out of the
back of the modest Ford. From the house he could hear Serena's
overpowering noises of greeting.

The pint-sized maid they'd imported from south of the
border came to the door, a curious expression on her face. Yes,
she had seen him before, he wanted to yell. He lived there.

"Good morning, Lourdes."

It was true—she was named for the shrine. And Serena
dressed Lourdes like a lay nun, in tight white uniforms she
bought at a price-slashing dump in East Los Angeles.

Lourdes muttered at him direly and tried to grab the bags
away.

But Rossiter wouldn't let her. It embarrassed him to let a
woman, especially one as little as Lourdes was, carry heavy
things. He followed her back toward the house.

Reluctantly he looked into the drawing room—what Serena
called the drawing room, a room too rectangular for its square
footage. But never mind—they weren't here forever.

Serena clung to her father like a shroud on a corpse. Indeed,
despite his rough, suntanned good looks, you knew Bud Slagger
was a man flirting with high blood pressure. He was a man of
about sixty, a former nationally known baseball player. Slagger
had swung a mean baseball bat once, but he had gone to pot.

Even as Serena clung to him, Slagger managed to shake a cigarette out of a pack he extricated from his shirt pocket, put it in his mouth, and light it.

"What say, Ross!"

Slagger pulled loose of Serena and dragged on the cigarette.

"Daddy! To what do we owe this special treat?"

Serena planted her fists on her slim hips and stuck out her chest, interrogating him lavishly.

"Drove in last night." This did not answer her question. "Your mother's over at the condo . . . sleeping."

Read *passed out*, Rossiter advised himself. Bud and Tiny Slagger owned a one-room flat over in Century City.

"Sit down, Daddy. Sit down!"

Slagger walked backward to an easy chair by the fireplace and dumped himself into it.

"Coffee? A drink?" Rossiter asked.

For an instant Bud looked worried, preoccupied.

"Daddy! What's wrong? What's the matter?"

Serena hurried across the room and dropped beside his chair. She seized his hand and stroked it, pulled it to her lips, kissing his knuckles passionately.

"Baby," Slagger confessed guiltily, "Daddy's got to go in the hospital."

Enough said. Serena burst into tears. She pushed her whole face into the palm of "Slugger" Slagger's hand, muscles and bones all kneaded into something as broad and soft as pounded fur by a thousand summers of catching baseballs.

Slagger looked ready to cry himself. "Nothing so serious as all that, baby."

"*Tell*, Daddy!"

"I'm going into Cedars for a couple of bypasses, that's all."

"*All!*" She shrieked the word. "Oh, my God!"

"Now, baby, it's done all the time, am I right, Ross?"

"Of course."

Serena whirled around. "You! A lot you care!"

Bud Slagger shook his head at Rossiter. Understand, he was saying wordlessly, that was an unfair thing for her to say, but pay no attention. It's just that she loves her daddy so much.

"The cigarette! At least put out that goddamn cigarette, Daddy!"

Slagger nodded philosophically. "Right. I've got to knock off the cigarettes . . . and the booze." He touched a fond finger to Serena's teary cheek. "They tell me I've got my good health to see me through this. The years as an athlete are a plus." He tapped his chest. "Except for this, I'm in damn good shape."

Exhibit One, Rossiter thought, Ailing Heart. Sure, the man was in wonderful shape, until he died unexpectedly of a heart attack.

Slagger continued boastfully, "If I knew I was going to live so long, I'd'a taken better care of myself. That's what my pal Shorty Estoril used to say."

Serena reared back on her haunches. "Put out the goddamn cigarette!"

"Baby, it's one of the last, I promise. After I check in this afternoon, that's it!"

"This afternoon?" Serena screamed. "Then put it out!"

"Now, look, baby, I'm not supposed to get excited," Slagger bawled. "This happens to be one of the last goddamn cigarettes of my goddamn life so let me enjoy it . . . without yelling at me. . . ." Sternness failed him. *"Please?"*

Serena staggered to her feet, betrayed, ruined.

"I feel absolutely nauseous, I'm so sick to my stomach from what you've told me. . . . *My God!* How can you do this to me?"

"I don't mean to make you unhappy, baby."

Serena pulled at her belly with both hands, as if her guts were spilling out. Stiffly, she exited to the hallway, grabbed the banister, and hauled herself painfully up the staircase.

"Holy shit," Slagger grunted, "who's sick, me or her?"

The answer was so obvious.

"She gets like that."

Rossiter felt a million years old compared to Bud and daughter—both were such children, in infinite terms born within a second of each other.

"You think I'm nuts," Slagger apologized, as he puffed.

Rossiter was surprised Bud hadn't stopped. The way he understood it, the scare was enough to make a man sick just walking past a dirty ashtray. Bud had to be a brave man.

"How's your dad?"

"Ulcer," Rossiter lied, "kicking up again."

The last thing Bud Slagger wanted to hear was that Tom Addey was fit as a fiddle, tip-top, walking the hills of San Francisco and keeping a beautiful and passionate young wife happy.

Yes, beautiful. Yes, passionate. Rossiter tried never to dwell too long on Clara, though.

Suddenly as forlorn as Bud, Rossiter watched cigarette smoke curl toward the ceiling. But Bud was not one for lengthy contemplation. He tossed a different question at Rossiter.

"How's our little investment doing?"

Little? On Rossiter's say-so, Bud and some Las Vegas associates had put up ten million dollars to take a very minor position in Morris Communications, to bet on the Chet Arthur takeover Rossiter had mentioned to his father.

There was a short answer. "Just got to wait it out, Bud."

"Yeah, but what's happening?"

Rossiter considered his reply.

Bud and his boss, Lorenzo Diamond, had been around the gambling scene long enough to know there was no sure thing unless it had been fixed. Yet they seemed to believe Chet Arthur's takeover of Morris Communications was one hundred percent guaranteed—maybe the simple fact was that Diamond wanted it so much, the wish by itself would get the deal done.

Chet Arthur's empire stretched far and wide—into the media, oil, high tech, and real estate—but most usefully into the hotel-motel business. King Arthur Hotels were known to be among the best in the Far East. Small European family hotels carried the name Chester—thus the Chester Arms in London, Hotel Chester Premier in Paris, and so on.

Chet Arthur's Las Vegas place went by the fancy name Le Roi Arthur Desert Resort Hotel.

Significantly, it was located across the street from Lorenzo Diamond's Las Vegas Alhambra Hotel and Convention Center and, compared to Lorenzo's place, was a very classy operation. In fact, Le Roi Arthur cast a shadow over the Alhambra, and for some time Lorenzo had been trying to get Chet to sell out to him.

No such thing. Chet Arthur, a very straight-arrow sort of man, despite Thelma's slightly libelous article, wouldn't give Diamond the time of day.

41

The Diamond boys responded with a mix of hate and envy.

Diamond wanted to be liked and respected. To be scorned by a man like Arthur, particularly with all the latter's political connections, was completely unsupportable. Thus, or so it seemed to Rossiter, the reason behind the investment in MorrisCom was to force Chet Arthur to acknowledge Diamond's existence.

Out of this might come several beneficial things: Arthur might agree to sell Le Roi Arthur just to get Diamond off his back; or pay a nice premium over and above the share price to oust Diamond and his group out of the MorrisCom situation. There could be a three- or four-million-dollar profit there on the ten-million-dollar investment.

Or maybe Chet would just say Hello some day.

Everything revolved around that beautiful two-letter word, *If*.

He repeated Bud's question. "What's happening? Right now there's no movement. The wheels are grinding."

Bud kept his eye on the staircase in the foyer as he sucked smoke out of the cigarette.

"I hope so. We're in at forty, right?"

"An average of forty, that's right."

This was what Rossiter had hoped would catch his father's interest. According to Rossiter's belief, and bits and pieces of information he'd dragged out of his unwitting mother and well-placed contacts, Arthur would begin buying on the open market, then take the remaining stock he needed for control at sixty a share—therein lay the twenty per share profit on which Rossiter was betting his own future.

But Tom Addey wanted nothing to do with it. He didn't think about the stock market if he could avoid it. Moreover, if Thelma believed he was a close friend of Chet Arthur's and would somehow intercede in her behalf, she was wrong. At a certain point, when he had been considering suing Thelma and *Classics* for libel, Chet had figured it'd be "droll" for Tom Addey to represent him. But Tom said no, refused the offer. Chet never sued.

"If she's worried," Tom had said cruelly, "tell her to get the Morrises to build her a golden parachute. Besides," he went on, eyeing Rossiter amusedly, "you're more interested in the money part of it. I always said you'd sell your mother down the river for a quick buck."

"That's not fair," Rossiter had protested hotly. "She *is* my mother, for crissakes, Dad. She, well . . . she just thought you might know something about this."

Tom had looked at Rossiter sharply. "*Are* you buying into this thing?"

"A little."

"Be careful. Chet's a shark—God knows what he'll get up to."

Remembering Tom Addey's warning, Rossiter shivered. What made him even more nervous was that he'd done the Diamond investment outside the bounds of Veruckt & Associates. Thus, his boss, Sandor Veruckt, knew nothing about the investment, or the potential for a killing. If Rossiter had ever considered praying, he should pray Sandor never found out.

He'd done it strictly for the money—Diamond, via Slagger, promised Rossiter ten percent of the profit, if any. And that was a lot more than he'd make if the transaction went through the Veruckt books.

So, he'd pray.

"Chet is going to offer sixty?"

"So we believe, Bud."

God forbid, however, that Rossiter was one hundred percent sure. Never let it be said he was operating on insider information, like some others who'd got their hands caught in the SEC wringer.

"So *who* believes?"

They'd been over that before too. Ben knew Rossiter had several reliable sources. Rossiter had never told him that one was Thelma Drysdale. His mother had had the information from her boss, the highly strung and more than a little wicked publisher of Morris Magazines, Wilkey Morris, Jr., son of the company chairman, Wilkey Morris.

Wilkey Junior had never liked Thelma; she had been taken into the company under the wing of Junior's father. And so the context of his tip to Thelma was that Chet Arthur was going to buy the company and when he did Thelma could just kiss her ass good-bye, ha-ha-ha, because Chet would throw her out.

Naturally, therefore, Thelma had looked to Rossiter for help, and Rossiter, lamely, to his father.

Rossiter had also been apprised of the takeover situation by a good friend at Arnold, Callay, and Crux, an investment banking firm that'd most likely be selling the "junk bonds," if any were needed, to power the deal.

Bud smashed his cigarette into the ashtray. A second later his hand jumped to his shirt pocket. He resisted the impulse for a moment, then quickly gave in.

"Lot of money tied up there, Ross. People getting impatient."

"Everybody gets impatient when it comes to money." There was no point in being subtle about it. "You guys want to take a bite out of Chet Arthur, Bud, this is what you've got to put up with."

Perspiration sparkled in Bud's thin hair. Clumsily, he lit up again.

"Can't help it, can't help it. Last one, Ross." Bud puffed until he calmed a little. "Remember, I'm low man on the totem pole. Personally, I couldn't give less of a shit about Lorenzo and his vendetta with Chet Arthur."

"Vendetta?"

Bud grimaced, almost comically. "If you remember a skimming investigation a few years back. . . ."

But there was always a skimming investigation in progress in Las Vegas.

Bud shrugged dismally. "Somebody wrote a letter, packed with accusations. One of our guys got indicted. Chet's *never* had any problem at the *Roy Arthur*." Looking suddenly boyish, he murmured, "Like my deathbed revelation, what do you think, Ross?"

"Bad joke."

Rossiter couldn't actively dislike Bud, even though the man was at least partially responsible for the ruination, if you wanted to call it that, of his daughter. Hadn't Bud gotten her involved with that first husband in order, somehow, to promote himself among the people he thought mattered? Slagger was a weak man with bad judgment, and after they'd relieved him of his baseball bat, he'd also lost self-confidence.

Bud had sort of fallen in with the Diamond group for lack of anything better to do. He was one of the oldest friends and eventually bosom pal-bodyguard of Diamond's favorite bandleader, the Shorty Estoril whom Bud so often mentioned. Shorty Estoril and his Royal Vibes had been in and out of the Alhambra for years. Then, sadly, Shorty had died the sudden death of a failed and owing gambler. To make a long story *shorty,* as Bud would say, he found himself in due course nominally in charge of the Alhambra's public-relations effort, a heavily budgeted activity.

Fortunately, Serena had not heard Bud's bad joke. Nonetheless, her voice ripped into their tête-à-tête.

"Daddy! Put out that *fucking* cigarette!"

Serena had washed her face but still looked wasted.

"I can smell the goddamn cigarette all the way upstairs and into the john!"

Bud groaned and surrendered.

"One would think," she said acidly, "if one was warned by his doctors and was about to undergo heart transplant at Cedars-Sinai Hospital, that one would have the good sense to quit with the goddamn cigarettes already!"

Bud tried to smile. "Not transplant, baby. Simple old bypasses."

"I just talked to Mama, your wife, *Daddy*, and she says she's given up on you, that you smoked two packs yesterday just in the car and that's the reason she's sleeping so long today, because she was knocked out by the *fucking* fumes, Daddy, and you're trying to kill her too, and me, and if you are, this is the one sure way of going about it."

Buffeted by the language, Slagger never ceased smiling.

"Besides," Serena screamed, as if in triumph, "you big *dumbo*, you don't know but I may be having a baby one of these days and I want him or her to have a grandfather around for baby-sitting!"

Serena finally tried a smile. Bud's face tensed and a cry burst from his throat. He grabbed melodramatically at his chest.

"Baby! You could knock me right out of this chair! *True?*" For once speechless, Serena nodded. "Baby, come to me!"

He held out his arms and Serena collapsed on top of him. Good thing she wasn't any bigger or heavier.

"Ross! Congratulations," Bud whooped.

A smile backed against Rossiter's lips. Congratulations?

"I said *maybe*, Daddy."

Rossiter had to say something.

"Bud, persuade her it's not fashionable to be skinny if you're pregnant."

"Hear what your husband says, baby!"

Serena snuggled in Bud's arms.

"Oh, fuck my husband!"

Bud winked at Rossiter. She didn't mean it, big guy. She was just being cute.

"Look," Rossiter said, glancing at his watch, "I've got to get to the office. I'll try to be back early."

Serena didn't bother to turn. "Don't hurry. The party is off. I'll be going to the hospital with Daddy."

"Now, now," Bud began to protest, "go to your party, baby. . . . They just pop you in bed and you're half out of it already."

"No way! When you get back, I'll be at the hospital with Daddy."

"I'll come over," Rossiter offered.

"No way!" She barked again. "I don't want you sitting around moping and long-faced."

Bud looked worried—and suddenly sicker. He knew what he was in for—Serena couldn't wait to make him comfortable, pat his pillows and stroke his hand, coo at him like an idiot, and yell at the nurses. By the time she was through, Bud would be wishing for the anesthetic.

Chapter
Five

*T*om Addey finally decided to answer Alex Spurzov's question, for him evidently the crucial question.

"Yes, I can imagine Ludmilla falling for Cazimir. I'm sorry to say so—but I can. Yes."

Alex's cynical Mongolian eyes flashed fiercely. He hit the arm of his overstuffed easy chair with his fist.

"Yes, Tom, goddamn! Ludl gave her love so easily. But, thank God, took it away easily too—as she would have from that swine Cazimir even before she died."

"That wouldn't surprise me either."

Alex swallowed noisily. His prominent Adam's apple jumped out of the silk of his foulard, then settled back. Tom couldn't remember the prince dressing in any other way: the gray flannels sharply pressed, the double-breasted blue blazer, gray silk shirt unbuttoned, and the scarf knotted to hide his gobbly neck.

"We will cremate the dear body," Alex suddenly announced.

He had veered. They hadn't exactly gotten to that yet. And dump the ashes where? Tom wondered.

"Is that what she wanted?"

Alex nodded blackly. "God would be kind if I could go with her, Tom. There is nothing left for me now. My dear," he half sobbed, "I ache when I think of her—her dear legs, her beloved breasts, like planets, orbs of delight . . . those loins, like a mare's. Ludl was an artistry, Tom, born of the gods. She carried a man to Heaven . . . *Nirvana!*"

This was not merely overwrought sorrow speaking. It had

been so—maybe not to the extreme Alex mentioned, but there was no doubt Ludmilla had been something special—child-woman, earthbound goddess.

"So, therefore," Alex added, "it destroys me, Tom, to think of the swine Cazimir enjoying her."

"Alex—forget that. Cazimir is nothing. A pig. Not worth talking about now that she's dead."

"True! *A nothing!* Ludmilla's last lay!"

Alex reached for his vodka again—already a little bit plastered, Tom would have said. The butler Peat had brought a bottle of Stolichnaya to set between them on one of the art nouveau steel-and-glass coffee tables in the long, cold, two-story gallery that ran the length of the house, overlooking Rodney Richards's prized garden.

The stoop-shouldered Peat scooted across their line of sight in the marble-floored entry foyer. He wore noisemaking clickers on his heels.

"Look," Alex said, "he moves like a rodent. He has a rat face, does he not? And has Fascist tendencies; he wanted to enlist in the Bel Air patrol. Ludl dissuaded him. Poor man—he was sobbing his eyes out. I would not have thought it possible. The Ludl Effect, it was felt in the most unlikely places. I gave the poor fool the day off; I didn't want him around. Why he is here, I do not know."

Tom grinned. "Good thing he did come back, Alex. You wouldn't have known how to buzz me through the gate—or find the vodka."

"Ha!" For a moment Alex forgot his sadness, long enough to snap his fingers and cry, "Never fear about the vodka, my dear! I had already found it before Peat came back."

Glumly, Tom tasted the vodka. Looking around, he shivered.

"This is a goddamn depressing place, Alex. I should think you'd be happy to get the hell out of here."

"Yes." Alex sneered, following Tom's eyes from patches of peeling paint to spots of moldy plaster. "I hate everything about it."

The basic problem, Tom supposed, was that Richlands was in crying need of renovation. Richards had built it in the 1930s as a sort of instant ancestral home. Patina had come on much too fast; or, as the theory went, you hired fifty good men to stand on the roof and piss over the walls. That would age the stone and

48

brick work in short order. At the time of its construction, Richlands had been state-of-the-art estate. Now it was rundown, seedy, threadbare. Richards had been a miser and his two sons were certainly not prepared to spend anything on the house after he died and Ludmilla was in lifetime possession. This very salon, the long gallery, had been fitted with furniture which, to this day, had not been changed or even much refurbished—long, uncomfortable couches, square-shaped easy chairs, and an abundance of glass-topped tables and light fixtures.

Pots of half-dead ivy and wilted palms only contributed to the dulling ambience of decay and death, or perhaps merely death, en route.

"I don't know, Tom," Alex murmured, sweeping his hand back over his white hair. "What should I do? Where should I go? Back to Paris?"

"Well . . . you've got a lot of friends in Paris."

Alex smiled a little, then winked. "Several. And beautiful friends too. More than here, Tom. Except for you—you are my one true friend. Am I yours? Will you visit me there?"

"Sure I will." But the question reminded him of his purpose in Los Angeles. "Now, Alex, I don't like to mention this. What about money? Financially, are you okay?"

Alex ignored the question. He winked again, grinning almost idiotically. Then he leaned forward and nonchalantly touched his glass to Tom's once more.

"All I need, my dear, is a little time to collect my breath. Life goes on and I suppose Ludmilla would want me to enjoy the few moments that are left."

"Okay, then . . ."

Tom wasn't sure of the answer, but there was little more he could say. Alex was too proud to discuss it; had he been on the verge of starvation, he'd never have admitted it. Alex was one of the last of the great Russian emigré playboys—he'd run with Obolensky and Toumanoff and Troubetskoy, with any number of fake Romanovs and in the company of people like Rubirosa and the old Aly Khan, visited Gulbenkian and sailed with Onassis and Niarchos. In the days when he'd still traveled on business, Alex had been entertained in Paris during the winter and Monte Carlo in August. Alex had become a regular on the society pages, finally as well-known as Ludmilla.

He'd never lost it either. Alex couldn't be a sex object any longer but he would never lose his distinguished and dashing look. He retained that elegance which derived from family. Breeding did matter, Tom realized once again, not in the manner that made Alex some sort of superior being, but in providing self-assurance. And the latter in turn granted grace, a ready smile, and an apparently sunny disposition. A man might have nothing, but if he possessed Alex's intangible, then he could pretend to anything.

Over the years, one might have figured, Alex should have put aside a considerable amount. On the other hand, he might not have a bean to his name. Except for the Spurzov Egg, of course; but it was worthless if Alex was sworn never to sell it.

Alex waved a hand at the mirrored walls and the chipped fresco ceiling of the long gallery.

"What do you suppose the Richardses will do with it, Tom?"

"If it was me," he replied, "I'd tear the goddamn place down and start over. . . ."

Gloomy, gloomy, now, especially at this time of day. The December light was nearly finished in the late afternoon sky; the chill of evening had set in and the heating system did nothing to dispel it.

"The gardens are still very good," Alex said. "You did not care for Rodney, did you?"

"Did you?"

Alex smiled. "I could, shall we say, tolerate him. His sons didn't like him at all, you know. Ludl said they fought about everything. They never forgave him for putting so much of his money into the Richards Foundation."

"They won't starve."

Actually, Tom had never expected to see the insides of Richlands. His last sight of Rodney Richards had been that awful but redemptive night at the Music Center when he'd first caught sight of the lovely divorcée Mrs. Clara Gates. She'd happened to have been escorted to the opera or ballet or whatever it was by none other than her astute financial advisor—Rossiter Addey.

Tom always laughed to himself about that particular irony. Did they still remember this was how he and Clara had met?

Naturally Rossiter had been with her in the course of duty. She was a client of his firm—the one before Sandor Veruckt & Associates—and had been assigned to escort her. It happened all the time. Rossiter had been single then, so why not? Tom's old law firm had used Alex the same way, he remembered, and Alex had loved it. Alex the Arm, they'd called him. Call the prince if you've got a footloose lady.

Anyway, if Clara hadn't known Tom, she'd never have come to his rescue at the moment of confrontation with Rodney Richards. Tom had had a bit to drink and there were nasty words exchanged—though not quite fists, he remembered with lingering shame—when he'd had something rude to say about Ludmilla's pedigree and the circumstances of her meeting Alex Spurzov in the depths of a Bulgarian haystack.

And so it had been. How things did come around!

"By the way," Tom asked, "where is the little son of a bitch?"

"Son of a bitch?"

"Cazimir."

"Oh." Alex glanced toward the entry again and sipped a finger or two of vodka. "Well, I wonder too. Perhaps he has gone out . . . to the Polo Lounge again, of course. He would not let sorrow interfere with the hunt," he said briefly, bitterly. "I have never known such a man for pussy, my dear. Not even you . . ." He laughed jocularly. "Nor I."

"I'm sorry I ever introduced him to you," Tom said. "I don't know why I did. It was stupid—"

"No," Alex corrected him wisely. "You did it because you were asked by this important man in Washington."

"Yes."

"Sol Betancur," Alex added. "The man who sits at the foot of the throne."

"Betancur has an involvement in the intelligence community. He's on one of those oversight committees. I don't know exactly." Tom shrugged. "I always thought Cazimir was one of their . . . You know what they call such guys," Tom went on in a low voice. "An asset. Maybe he helps them out in the Middle East. . . ."

Alex laughed sardonically. "How? By screwing everybody into submission?"

"Like wise old King Solomon, Alex, remember—Solomon married the daughters of all his enemies and got them with child and nobody had the the bad taste to attack him."

"Well, then," Alex said reluctantly, "Cazimir may be your man."

Soulfully Alex lifted his vodka glass above his head, then touched it to Tom's in salute. Without warning he cried out, his voice high and unsteady.

"Oh, God, Tom, she made love like an angel. Tom, we must never forget Ludmilla loved life and all living things. . . . Yes, she tried to love every last living thing!"

Yes, it had to be said. The essence of Ludmilla, like the core of the Earth, was located between her flying legs.

It was, therefore, safe for him to interject, "Only the men, Alex."

"To Ludmilla!" Eyes bleary, Alex drained his glass again. Tom realized the man must by now be very weary. He hadn't slept and it was now late in the afternoon. But Alex went on, undiminished, "I know Ludmilla enjoyed you, Tom, because she told me so. Ludl vowed to me that of all the American boys she had known, you were the best, Tom, absolutely the best . . . *tops*!"

"Really?" But why not believe it?

"Tom," Alex said curiously, "did Ludl not tell you about her first American boy, Eddie Stringham?"

"No, I don't think so."

Had she? He could not remember. Ludmilla had talked at great length about other men . . . but at a certain point he had always tuned out.

"Eddie was a great man, my dear," Alex said wistfully. "A banker. Ludl met him not long after we arrived in New York—before the war." He laughed modestly. "Ludl, one who despised money so much. She transformed Eddie's life. He became a man of daring. General Donovan, called 'Wild Bill,' was a friend of his, and when Wild Bill organized the OSS during the war, Eddie joined. He brought me to Donovan too. Me, *the cuckold*! Would you believe, my dear, Eddie and I were such great friends. We both became heroes. And Ludl? Well, we left her in New York."

Tom shook his head. "She never told me about . . . Eddie."

"I think," Alex said sadly, "she loved him too. She was completely wild, you know, crazy in those days—she and Eddie made love once in the back of a carriage in Central Park. Did she not tell you about that?"

"No, no."

"It was a terrible scandal, Tom," Alex recalled fondly. "And then at parties—in the bedroom where all the coats were piled. It gave them pleasure to be discovered."

"She never told me anything like that."

No, and just as well. Even though he'd known her only in the years after this Eddie was gone, Tom would've been devoured by the monster.

"I am surprised," Alex murmured. "You see—half the joy in it for Ludl, I came to understand, was to know I was an observer. Not so much observer as that I knew what was happening."

"Sort of cruel, wasn't it?"

Alex shrugged again, wanly. "Ludl didn't do well with promiscuity during the war—largely, I think, because we were not there to act as sounding boards, to react to her infidelity. She had begun to torture Eddie in this way."

Quelle bitch, Tom might have said, but didn't. Had it been this way when he knew her? Yes, he supposed it had. Ludmilla had thrown him over—Jesus! For Rodney Richards?

"Eddie and I, you see, went to the OSS's best finishing schools. In Georgia and then in a little town in Scotland called Jedburgh we were trained to parachute into occupied France." Alex paused, then abruptly completed the story. "And we did—except Eddie was killed. He had been betrayed—a German patrol killed his unit when they were still in the air. . . ."

Tom watched soberly as Alex filled his vodka glass again and downed it.

"I'm sorry."

Alex smiled mournfully, but otherwise did not respond.

Tom had always figured he had been slightly more exciting than Rodney Richards—but perhaps not. Was this a good time to ask Alex about another of Ludmilla's affairs—that short-lived one with the Italo-American musicologist Amos Virgilio who, people said, had died in Ludmilla's arms, which when you came to think about it was a surprisingly rare way for one of her liaisons to end. The Reaper, it had been joked, had caught Virgilio *in coitus*.

But there was something more important Tom wanted to say.

"You know, I've always regretted . . ."

The bony chin snapped up as if the elderly man could sense what was coming.

"Regretted what?"

Tom shook his head. "That I offended you. I'm sorry, you know. I never wanted that."

"My dear, *of no consequence*!" Alex averted his eyes. "I know what you are saying. But do not regret. You must remember you were able to make love to one of the most wonderful women ever born. *Please!*"

"I know, I know. But still . . ."

Alex shook his long forefinger in caution. He smiled at Tom in a secretive way.

"You do not regret, Tom. I do not regret either."

"What? You regret *nothing*?"

"Well," Alex shrugged, "I've done things too. Would *you* pardon me?"

"I have nothing to pardon you for, Alex."

"But *if* . . . *if* . . . would you?"

Tom nodded. It was the least he could do. "All the way. Sure."

All very mysterious, but it didn't really matter. If it had not been Tom Addey, it would've been somebody else—and was anyway, despite Tom Addey; Tom Addey and many others had been swept into Ludmilla's insatiable embrace.

The cadaverous Peat appeared at the top of the steps at the far end of the gallery. Slowly, moving with stately resolution, he paraded toward them.

One might think of Peat as old. Seen from a distance he would surely appear old—the way he moved, the stiffness of his arms, his stoop. One would have given him seventy years, when in fact he was probably not more than forty-five or fifty.

As Peat approached, Alex seemed to stop breathing.

"Yes? Yes, yes?" he barked fraily. "What is it, Peat?"

Peat drew up a couple of yards from the table. His eyes were small and quick, placed too close in his feral face.

Peat's voice was deep. It must bounce around in the ribcage a certain time before finally emerging, Tom thought.

"I wish to announce a body, Prince."

Alex snapped forward, as if on a spring. His eyes bulged.

"My God! Where! Peat, *where*? Upstairs?"

Peat shook his head.

"No. The body is in the garden, down by the pool. It is our visitor. I think he's killed himself. There's a gun in his right hand and a hole in his right temple."

"By the pool?"

"Yes, by the pool, near where the Princess died, Prince."

Carefully, Alex put his vodka down. Then he slumped backward in the chair. It was in the cards that he might faint. This was a shock, of course, even for one in the best of health.

Cazimir dead, a suicide? It was difficult to give Cazimir so much credit. Was Peat suggesting Cazimir had shot himself out of grief for Ludmilla?

Not bloody likely, Tom told himself.

Chapter Six

*T*here was no way Hildy could have known why Sol Betancur had called that morning at the Plaza Hotel, an hour or so before they were due to meet Thelma Drysdale at the *Classics* offices on Madison Avenue.

Betancur's exchange with Seth had been all clipped and cryptic, the sum and substance being that (a) Tom Addey had apprised him of Seth's existence, (b) had advised Sol where to find Seth in New York, and (c) that Sol—he insisted Seth call him Sol; after all, wasn't he an old friend of Seth's father—wanted badly to see him in Washington.

Therefore, Seth was hereby invited to come to the Betancur house in Georgetown the following night. There was going to be a Christmas party of some kind or other, Sol wasn't sure, but they'd have a chance anyway to talk. Sol's wife Alice—didn't Seth know this, for God's sake?—was an old, old friend of Tom's wife Clara.

No, Seth was not particularly aware of that, he admitted carefully. Best never to confirm, concur, or agree. Of course, he was aware of Betancur, as he would be since Betancur was a long-standing member of the president's intelligence oversight board, a panel of retired businessmen, military heroes, and ex-statesmen who "watchdogged" the nation's intelligence activities. As was abundantly clear in Sol Betancur's case, personal connections also played a vital role in the selection process.

There was definitely no reason Seth should tell Hildy about the conversation or invitation. Something, evidently, had happened, but Sol was not prepared to discuss it over the phone. And, even more important, Seth did not want Hildy, by sheer accident or misunderstanding, to mention to Thelma that he'd been invited by Betancur, whose wife, by the way, was a great friend of . . . guess who? Clara, the second Mrs. Addey.

Hell-fire, no!

As ordered, then, innocent and uninformed, Hildy went with Seth to meet Thelma Drysdale.

It was always said that the editorial offices of a major publication were exciting, nerve-tingling, disorganized places. Seth supposed this was true. Not that bedlam suited him; he preferred the quiet atmosphere of analysis to the noisy one of creation. Whatever, Thelma Drysdale had put her highly strung mark on her offices, no question of it. *Classics was* noisy. Electronic machinery whirred, writers blabbered vehemently on telephones, doors slammed, things fell, and people rushed around wildly.

Thelma was crouched over her desk in a large corner office, glowering at what seemed to be blownup page proofs and ranting at two young female assistants about typos and color register.

When she finally finished and shooed the others out of the office, Seth performed a rather formal and strained introduction— Hildy and Thelma, of course, had never met. They shook hands like fighters and seemed to circle each other mentally, taking measure. Both were professionals; that's what had to be remembered. But Thelma had the upper hand—she was the editor, the woman of power, the source of possible work.

Thelma wanted to introduce Seth to the two Morrises, father and son, but only Wilkey Senior was available. Seth shook hands with the tall old gentleman and they exchanged words about Germany. Mr. Morris Senior, it seemed, had studied there once; could it have been before the Second World War?

Thelma had them in the elevator by twelve-fifteen. A couple of minutes later they were standing on Madison Avenue in front of the Morris Communications building.

"We'll walk," she announced, pausing to tighten the belt of her heavy tweed coat, so substantial and English, and to set her sable fur hat firmly on her iron-gray curls. "We're almost at Fifty-seventh, and then it's only blocks across town to the Russian Tea Room—have you been there yet? No—then it'll be an experience for you."

She set out, making the pace demonically. But, Seth could appreciate with some satisfaction, Hildy was more than a match for her. Hildy Beckmann was athletic, to say the least. On any given day, never mind the weather, she was prepared to drag him across the street from their flat in Munich to march through the Englischer Garten. When there was snow, she used the park for cross-country skiing.

Hildy was a good modern German, single-minded and disciplined.

Seth lagged behind, sluggishly, feeling like a fifth wheel. He wouldn't have much part in this outing: Thelma would do the talking, and Hildy the listening. Seth would moderate, if that became necessary.

Thelma was already talking volubly. Seth picked up speed so he could listen in, moving up behind Hildy's churning hips. She did have that about her, he had to admit: great hips, strong, muscled legs, a beautiful round bottom which, on occasion, she wasn't bashful about using. Just being with her was good exercise.

Was Hildy receiving the magazine? Thelma had asked sharply.

"I *directed* that you be sent *Classics* in Munich in the first mailing every week, Hildegard, and I trust you have been getting it and studying it carefully."

"Yes, it comes every week," Hildy said crisply, "and I read every word."

"Good!" Seth's mother spit the word into the wind. "And now tell me—how *was* California?" She glanced over her shoulder at Seth. "We are aware, are we not, that *the Princess* is dead?"

"It was in the paper, Mother."

"Yes, yes!" Thelma tilted her generously featured face toward the cloudy sky. "Darlings, I don't mind admitting I'm thinking *vermilion* today, the absolute color of revenge devoutly prayed for."

Now, now, Seth wanted to tell her.

"But, of course," Thelma continued, glancing at him again, "I would not want to show that I care. It was all so long ago. And my life has moved on—to an astonishing degree, I think everyone would say." She paused. "But, nonetheless, I wonder what your father's reaction is? You had already left by then . . . But I do wonder."

Thelma pulled up smartly at the corner of Madison and

Fifty-seventh and tapped her heels impatiently as they waited for the light to change. She smiled at Hildy, frankly and curiously. Thelma was a few inches taller, the difference accentuated by her boots, soft leather which reached up under the bottom of the tweed coat.

Seth wondered for a mad moment if Thelma ever considered suing the City of New York for wasting her time. Then they were under way again.

"My reaction was," Seth heard her say, "no sooner than did I hear that Seth had become a . . . friend of a German fraulein named Hildegard Beckmann . . ."

Seth marveled at how difficult it was for Thelma to admit to herself that he was simply living with Hildy. In this modern age, Thelma remained prissy, even though she edited a sometimes-racy magazine. But that was all right—Seth also found it difficult sometimes to get at the heart of their relationship. He and Hildy did live together, true, but it seemed so often merely a matter of convenience or logistics or maybe even simply a clinically safe and secure way of feeding their sexual appetites. He was, at the very least, fond of Hildy; but she often acted as though they would do well together until something better came along . . . as if they'd been mated by some cockeyed lottery.

"My point," Thelma pressed on, "is whether this beautiful *Heidiesque* girl is related to the German painter Max Beckmann?"

Thelma locked her eyes on Hildy's.

"No, there is no relationship, I think."

She looked so petite beside Thelma, so defenseless. Defenseless? Odd thought.

"But of course you cannot be sure."

Thelma would never accept No for an answer, not if she had her mind set on Of Course or Maybe. She radiated skepticism. Amazing, how he'd forgotten, or misplaced, this memory of his mother.

Yes, this *was* Thelma Drysdale. She came of an old New English family; the Drysdales had been down to the sea in ships for many generations. Imagine, *now* one of them was a magazine editor. Another a daredevil stockbroker—perhaps Rossiter, though, was closest to the original businesslike Drysdales who had hunted whales and swapped rum for slaves during a certain period of family history. And the other, himself, a loyal servant of the government, *a believer* like the Drysdale offshoots who'd been in the theological line. Thelma had always said that Seth had, like Nathaniel Drysdale, his ancestor from way back, the deadly look of a religious fanatic.

A warrior of freedom . . . of Democracy Militant?

Silently walking, listening, then not listening, Seth shoved his hands in the pockets of his trench coat. It was barely warmer than the usual damp, chill-factored weather of December in New York City.

Seth didn't like the fact of the Betancur telephone call; he surely did not thank Tom Addey for letting Betancur know he was to be in Washington. Fiercely, Seth hoped this did not signal some new and upsetting departure; he was just now getting over the Moscow business. Twelve hours in the hands of the "opposition," no, not easy to forget; but, still, think of—

No, he refused to think about that.

He wanted to go back to his well-organized life in Munich.

Were they getting set to move him again? Where? Specialization gave Seth a certain advantage—did you send a supposed expert on the USSR and Eastern Europe to Australia or Brazil or some spot in darkest Africa?

With this government, that was always possible.

Washington? Seth was due for a tour of duty there. Home, of course, might mean promotion. And he was ambitious; he'd like that. He'd done a good job in Moscow, barring the foul-up with the KGB. And that hadn't been his fault. There had been a betrayal somewhere along the line.

Christ, he remembered it like it was ten minutes ago.

Warsaw or Prague wouldn't be bad, he thought to himself. Lovely, intriguing cities, wide open for his kind of work. And he did love it—*he must*! Otherwise, he would've quit after the unpleasantness two years before.

But then? What about Hildy?

Does your mistress have a clearance, Addey?

No, but she had other things. This lush, green body to start with, green in the sense of birth and fertility, of being popped out of the oven of Creation only a second ago.

Like Thelma, and her *vermilion,* he would think *green* in terms of Hildy Beckmann.

"The reason I ask you this," Thelma was saying, "is that it occurred to me, in relation to the Beckmann exhibition we've just had in New York, that when Herr Beckmann served as a medical corpsman during the first war—the Great War, as they called it—he might have ministered to Herr Hitler, whom, you recall, was wounded on the Western Front.''

Hildy hated talk of the war, of Hitler, atrocities, and all that. There had been something in her family, he didn't know what, whether the Beckmanns had been sinners or sinned against.

He interrupted Thelma harshly. ''That's an imagination-stretcher, if I ever heard one!''

Thelma stopped in the middle of the sidewalk and drew him into the group.

''A conceit, I admit. I happen to find such historical happenstance fascinating. I firmly believe in the power of coincidence, and especially the ironies of coincidence.''

''I, too,'' Hildy said hesitantly. ''It happens—you will take a picture of a given something, and when the film is developed, there will be something else there you did not expect, something even more important than your intention when you snapped.''

''My God! We'll get along famously, Hildegard!''

Extravagantly, emotionally, Thelma clapped her hands on Hildy's shoulders and kissed each of her rosy cheeks. Then, seemingly all choked up, Thelma whirled and continued up the street, thumping her heels all the more violently. The rest of the walk, Seth thought, passed in a blur. Hildy was embarrassed that Thelma would not stop her prattle about Max Beckmann.

''Sick in his soul . . . suffering more than the men in the trenches, Beckmann served menially in the *sanitaire,* or the aid station . . . and on one horrible, shell-shocked night, on *one* such night of horror . . .'' She halted again and grabbed Hildy's arm. ''See this as a photographer, Hildegard! The horror. The men writhing in their litters, this scene of hell itself. Hitler is carried in—Schicklgruber, he was still called then, an Austrian misfit. Did he have that moustache at the time? It fell to Herr Beckmann to help *this man* who later became the anti-Christ, the beast of beasts, created by a shell burst on the Western Front like Frankenstein's by a bolt of lightning, out of the Hell of the Hell of the Hell, as beloved Miss Stein would have put it . . . I see Black, the color Black, Black, Black, Hildegard!''

Hildy nodded reluctantly, doubtfully, skeptically. What could she say?

''Suppose,'' Seth suggested sardonically, ''General de Gaulle was the one who shot him from across no-man's land.''

"Exactly!"

"You're getting carried away, Mother."

"Never!" Thelma spoke in high, good humor. "Until I am disproved, I am allowed to reconstruct the scene just as I like—and I will ask you, *Fraulein Beckmann*," she said aggressively, "how else to explain why Herr Beckmann was never molested by the Gestapo during the war?"

"But he had to flee to Holland," Hildy protested.

"And he was never bothered there either!"

"But he was incognito. He painted in secret all through the war," Hildy muttered.

Her face was flushed, not just from the cold. She was not used to losing arguments. It would be good for her, this experience, Seth told himself amusedly.

"No, not possible," Thelma disagreed. "A man of his stature, so hated by the Nazi art critics. He did not paint *Aryan art*, Hildegard."

They reached the other side of Sixth Avenue in physical safety. But Hildy was not happy. Sullenly, she pulled her green loden coat around her, tucking her chin down in the collar against a freezing wind which whipped down the hill from the direction of Carnegie Hall.

"My belief," Thelma declared, "is that Herr Beckmann was preserved from harm by Hitler himself. Herr Hitler had never forgotten that horror of a night on the Western Front when Max Beckmann breathed life back into him. . . ."

Hildy glanced at Seth. "It is possible," she murmured. "Possible."

Thelma laughed merrily. "Hildegard, you're much too literal. If Germans have a fault, it's that they're too literal. Remember, darlings, if one studies the Beckmann paintings of the thirties, in every one there is a face that resembles that of Herr Hitler."

Hildy realized that she had no hope. Whatever she said, Thelma would not hear.

"I suppose you are right," she conceded.

"Of course I am." But Thelma didn't like to win too easily either. "It all went back to that night in 1915 or '16 . . . *whenever*. You have a distinguished cousin, Hildegard."

Thank God, the history lesson carried them into the Russian Tea Room. There was no question that Seth's mother was known here. Just as she passed her heavy coat to Seth, Thelma was spotted by the hostess, who charged past the bar to greet her.

"Your table is ready and waiting, Mrs. Drysdale."

They were led around a jumble of people waiting at the reservations desk to a booth on the west wall, Thelma's usual spot. How could Seth know this was so? Thelma pointed at a heavy crystal vase full of red roses.

"My usual flowers . . ."

From this vantage point Thelma could see everything and everybody. Nobody made an entrance or exit without being reviewed by Thelma's eagle eye. Before sitting down, moreover, Thelma stood for a moment, towering over the proceedings, inspecting each table and performing small flutters of her bejeweled right hand whenever she saw anybody worth registering. For all the world, like royalty, Seth noted. Finished with this ritual, Thelma finally sat down.

"An aperitif? A person could definitely use a schnapps in weather like this, Hildegard."

"Will you?" Hildy asked politely.

Obviously, Seth decided, she wanted one. Hildy never stinted herself with the drinks.

Thelma hesitated only a second. "At the Russian Tea Room we will have vodka! Does that suit you? And a bit of caviar, an ounce or two or three of Beluga."

"That would be wonderful," Hildy said.

For his part, Seth was sick of the stuff. It also jogged his memory of very unpleasant times.

"We know *you* are the caviar specialist," Thelma said to him.

"Beluga's the top of the line, Mother, what could be more Russian?" Thelma looked peeved, as if she'd been caught in a truism. Seth continued blackly, "Do I get the feeling you've brought us here in my honor?"

"Perish the thought!" Thelma colored in annoyance. She hated to be nagged. "This is a *chic* place, and my favorite. I'd forgotten you were in Russia. Quite!"

"I'm not crazy about being reminded of Moscow."

Thelma seemed properly reprimanded. "It's almost two years ago, though, isn't it, darling?"

Seth shrugged. How could he tell her it didn't go away so easily? The memory was acute of that day in Moscow when the opposition had picked up him and Nick, his Russian "contact"; it was over in seconds, Seth dragged in one direction, Nick the other, white-faced, his fur hat knocked off, kicked and thrown in the back of the car.

The waitress arrived and Thelma ordered vodka. "Bring us the Polish stuff," with a look at Seth, adding, "I'm having the Stroganoff, no matter what you say!"

Seth laughed, trying to sound lovable. Thelma was not a total dragon when she remembered not to take herself too seriously.

"I'll have the same. Thanks, Mother."

"And for me too," Hildy murmured.

Clearly Hildy was still trying to decipher Thelma. She'd imagined that Thelma could not be so very different from her son. How wrong she was!

Thelma settled back complacently, and when the vodka arrived, toyed with the little carafe nestled in ice.

"I'm told the main pleasure in life is to outlive your enemies. I guess I'm reaching an age where I can start raking in such pleasures."

"Now, Mother."

"But I don't know whether to be happy or sad," Thelma went on, undeterred. "For years Ludmilla was my *scarlet* sustenance, and now that's gone."

"You'll find somebody else to hate," Seth said.

"True. I have Wilkey Morris *Junior*. A terrible man . . . nothing like his father, whom you've just met. A *true* gentleman." Fastidiously, Thelma tasted the Wyborowa. "Of course, Princess Spurzova, so-called, has to be given her due—she was one of the century's *leading courtesans*, you're aware of that? Had she lived in an earlier age, no telling what cataclysmic events she might have set off—the equivalent of Helen starting the Trojan War, something of the kind."

Thelma looked significantly at Hildy and Seth. No response was necessary, of course. Thelma was speaking rhetorically, hypothetically, philosophically.

"It occurs to me that *Classics* should do a retrospective investigation of the matter, using the Princess, so-called, as leit-motif . . . if you follow."

Seth began listening more closely. He could see she was up to no good.

"The place of the *courtesan* in modern society? Has television usurped the role of the *courtesan*—lady of the court? How does such a courtesan survive in the era of ERA?''

"It doesn't sound earth-shaking to me," Seth commented quietly.

"Well . . . you are not a woman, Seth," Thelma said reasonably. "I happen to think our *women readers* will be fascinated. . . . There are so many of this sort in Washington. And, of course, everybody would think of the Duchess of Windsor. . . .'' Thelma shrugged disdainfully. "But she's always used in pieces like this.''

Seth realized he had to respect her editorial intuition. Hildy had explained that Thelma *knew*; she felt in her fingertips and her bones what the public wanted, more vitally what *women* wanted.

"We'll need pictures of all her husbands and lovers, of course," Thelma said softly. This was for Hildy's benefit. "All of them that we can find, that is. There were so many of each.''

"Oh, yes, you would need many, many pictures," Hildy agreed.

Yes, she would grind her own axe, to be sure. Hildy never stopped doing that; Seth couldn't blame her. Hildy was a good photographer, but in a world of automatic cameras, even a good photographer had to be much more.

Slowly, Seth said, "I get it. Now I understand.''

"What is it you understand?''

"Tom gets a full-page picture . . . right?''

Thelma's face looked like thunder. "Not at all! You don't approve? Don't be ridiculous and unpleasant. Do you think revenge is on my mind? How insulting you are, my own son. I'm seeing a terrible, *terrible* yellow . . . I should leave! Waitress!''

"All right, all right, forget I said it.''

Deliberately, Thelma made herself deflate.

"As a matter of fact," she said, "I happen to be far more interested in *Prince Alexei Spurzov*.'' She glared at Seth, her eyes steely, eyebrows like hackles. "We know about her last husband, the boring Rodney Richards. We know about her lover, the financier, I forget his name. We know about a couple of husbands back, that one with the curious name, Jasper 'Heartburn' Brady, the singing cowboy.''

"You've already been studying the file, I see.''

"But more to the point, *Prince Alexei*," Thelma said bitingly. "You may not be aware that I am well acquainted with the prince—"

"No, I'm not aware of that," Seth said. "I didn't know that at all. . . . When—"

Thelma cut in, "*Post-partum*, dear boy, that is to say after the *entire* world found out about Ludmilla and your *dear* father, I met Alex."

Seth was almost afraid to ask. *"And?"*

Thelma smiled at him archly. "And what? He's a lovely man. I say no more. . . ."

Eyeing her keenly, suspiciously, Seth said, "Mother!"

Thelma chuckled and patted the back of Hildy's hand. The poor girl looked totally confused, as well she might. Just what the hell was his mother trying to say? Whatever it was, he didn't believe it, didn't want to believe it. Didn't want to? Why not? Of what importance to him was it if Thelma, as she was trying to hint, had carried on with Alex Spurzov?

"You see, Hildy," Thelma said, "perfectly wonderful for the men to have flaming affairs, but if the goose does the same, oh my! *Quelle scandale!* Scarlet! Lavender! Puce!"

Heavily, he asked, "You're trying to tell us you had an affair with Alex Spurzov?"

"Gooses and ganders," Thelma defied him jovially. "You know that game, to be sure. Do you not?"

She glanced at Hildy. What was she suggesting? That he and Hildy had an arrangement—that they were free agents? As a matter of fact, the veiled insinuation made him nervous. Seth never asked what Hildy got up to when she was on the road; she did travel considerably in her job, to the various European capitals. He had never checked; she had never checked on him either, so far as he knew.

"Well . . ." Seth thought about it. What was there to say? Only one thing she'd appreciate. "I guess if you like the irony of coincidence, that could serve you well."

"The irony of irony," Thelma agreed complacently. Changing the subject, she said, "The weather will not be nice in Washington, not at all. Freezing and humid . . . what a place!"

"Strictly business. I don't care for Washington even when the weather is good."

"You know," Thelma pointed out crossly, "some day they're going to transfer you there. You can't stay abroad forever."

"Worse luck . . ."

"And Hildegard's moving in with me," Thelma went on comfortably. "What a joy." Again she tapped the Beckmann knuckles.

Of course, Seth and Hildy had had to stay in a hotel because Thelma was such a Victorian throwback. What did she think they got up to when they were by themselves? Walks in the park? Skiing? Drinking Munich beer? Going to museums? Well, she couldn't know Hildy, could she?

Chapter
Seven

*S*o her time in L.A. wouldn't be a total waste, Clara spent all day Tuesday roaming the art galleries and visiting friends up and down Melrose Avenue, up on Sunset, and finally in Beverly Hills, before going back to the hotel about five.

Clara was tired, but she was pleased with what she'd heard and seen—the Morelli Gallery in San Francisco was holding its own and more. Tom always said she was a clever girl, and in this she did give herself credit. She had thought the thing through. Anybody could open an art gallery if they had the money to blow. To be successful, Clara had decided, one had to be very specific about what sort of stuff you were going to assemble and sell. Quite deliberately, therefore, she had chosen a theme: the Pacific. The Morelli Gallery became a specialist in art produced around the Pacific Basin.

Smart people said that over the next fifty years or so it would be the lands around this ocean that would develop the hypertech civilization of the future.

Would she live so long?

Clara's plan was to search out, catalogue, and sell or trade in the best of Pacific art —whether painting, sculpture, or native craft.

Great for travel, Tom would say flippantly, as usual—all their trips were a write-off. Not that he much liked Japan, though, and he was *comme-ci, comme-ca* about Hong Kong and mainland China.

Paris was more his place, actually, anything French appealed to him.

The show opening the following week was to be devoted to young California artists, and there were many, many of these, young and old, some not as young as they'd used to be. They worked in every school, or style; what they had in common, maybe, was a joyous outlook and sense of very far off horizons.

They were what you'd call very California. Laid back, mellow? Something like that.

Even Biff with his own, startlingly savage signature was Californian. But how different he was in person from his paintings—private, seemingly at peace with himself, quietly watchful, so unlike any other man Clara had ever admired, so different from Tom and Rossiter, certainly the opposite of smooth and svelte Stanley Gates.

Clara was giving Biff pride of position at the show—that would be a surprise for him. For Tom too, when he saw it. But Clara knew what she was doing by now.

People didn't refer these days patronizingly to Clara's "folly," her expensive hobby. The Morelli Gallery didn't make real money but it did better than break even and pay its rent, and that was saying something.

Even Alberto, her father, admitted now there might be something to her after all. Maybe in due course, he ventured, he'd be able to interest her in the vineyard. Her brother Fred would inherit the place for himself and his own sons. But in the meantime, Alberto hoped, Clara would take a small hand in management. Why not? After all, she did draw a certain income from the place.

This possibility was more appealing to Tom than an art gallery. Why? Easy answer—Tom liked wine. He liked the *idea* of wine; and he liked drinking wine. He was interested in art, yes—well, he'd collected a little California art himself; from time to time he'd had artist-clients, and some of them had even paid him in kind. Not a great arrangement, Tom admitted, but better than not getting paid at all.

Rossiter, tall, dark, and taciturn, dressed in a baggy tweed suit and knit tie, was waiting for her in the lobby of the Westwood Marquis.

"Well . . . hello," she said. She heard her own voice, small and shy. "Are we expecting you?"

Rossiter stared at her dismally. "Tom called me at the office . . . I didn't even know you were in Los Angeles."

Was he accusing her? Of what? Not informing him soon enough?

"We only got here yesterday. C'mon, I'm pooped, let's go sit in the bar."

Clara led the way. She could feel him behind her, his bulk, his strength. Rossiter was that much bigger than Tom—if you measured them together, Rossiter would have been a quarter or third bigger than Tom.

Next to the doorway a woman was strumming a harp, very restful music after a long day—a brilliant idea for a hotel bar, Clara thought. But this was a special place, the Westwood Marquis; whenever they came down to Los Angeles now, they usually stayed here, if they planned long enough in advance, in the same small suite of rooms.

"A glass of white wine, Chardonnay—you should have a bottle of *my* particular wine there, the Morelli Cabinet."

But, of course, the waitress knew by now. Clara seldom drank anything else. She was a good Italian, so stuck pretty much to wine, and a good Morelli, so she tried always to drink her father's wine.

"The same," Rossiter said.

"*You'd better!*" Clara laid down the law, then patted his hand. "So what did Tom say?"

"Well . . . to join you for dinner. I told him Serena would be at the hospital."

"At the hospital? My God! What's wrong. *And* . . . why are you not with her?" Even if she didn't care for Serena, well . . . all the same.

"No, no," he said. "It's Bud. Her father. He's at Cedars for a couple of bypasses. Serena won't leave him. And she kicked me out. When Tom heard that, he invited me for dinner . . . I mean, when he heard Serena couldn't be with us."

He grinned wildly. Jesus, Clara thought, he really was nuts about Serena, wasn't he? Again the question, why had he chosen her? Rossiter could've done so much better.

"Okay," Clara said succinctly. "When is he going to get here?"

"He said he'd be here by six. He's at Alex Spurzov's. I didn't know Ludmilla had died."

"It was in the paper."

"I never got past the business section this morning."

"He went over there yesterday," Clara said, "and now again, all day? I mean, there's just so much you can do. . . ."

"He said this thing has become unimaginably complicated."

To hell with Tom, she thought. She had known it was going to happen just this way. She'd come down to L.A. with him out of the goodness of her heart . . . and wouldn't see him again until they left. She had a good mind to leave right now, catch a plane, and beat it back to San Francisco, *her* world.

She tasted the wine. It was fine, and why shouldn't it be? Alberto Morelli was known coast to coast as a Chardonnay specialist.

Rossiter gazed at her, perplexed. His smooth, tanned face was unblemished by the slightest wrinkle. He was serenity itself. Rossiter might be disturbed, tense, worried, a ball of nerves, but no one would ever know it.

Clara remembered that about him from their very first meeting. Rossiter had been suggested to her by a friend of a friend, the usual way doctors or stockbrokers were recommended. She had had a bit to invest, not a lot, after the parting with Stanley Gates, and she'd called Rossiter out of the blue.

Now she was reminded. "Did I ever tell you that I made about four hundred percent on those stocks you bought for me? Do you remember that?"

"Of course I remember that." He sounded hurt. "Do you suppose I'd forget?"

"Well, anyway . . ." Clara hesitated. She didn't want to make him unhappy; or any unhappier than he was already. "I put all of it into my gallery. So . . . thank you. Your choice was splendid."

"I'm happy for you."

"Now look—"

Rossiter frowned into his wineglass. Behind them the harpist finished in a crescendo of notes.

"I remember," Rossiter muttered. "*Do you?* I think you've forgotten a lot. It's like you're a stranger . . . up in San Francisco you didn't even speak to me."

"Ross, what do you expect me to do?" This was not so

71

easy to get out. "It's a while ago now, you'd have to agree. But . . . of course, I remember. I was merely asking if *you* remembered buying those stocks."

"And I said I did."

"Oh . . ." She stared at him. His eyes came up, sad, woebegone. "Well, for crissakes, Ross!"

She did remember. Calling him afterward, her words replete with "good news-bad news" implications. Good news, she supposed, that she'd met Tom; bad news that she had complicated Rossiter's life. But nothing had been forced. She had never expected or wanted him to fall in love with her—if that was what he was going to say had happened.

The simple fact was that she had seduced him. She should never have done that. It had proved to be a disaster over the long run. But Clara wasn't making any apologies. She was not sorry about it, personally or professionally or publicly. At the time, of course, she had been suffering. She'd tried valiantly to turn herself into a rapacious female, to take her pleasures without regard to others. Including Rossiter Addey: young Ross, tall, dark, and handsome, a young stud. All the divorced ladies said that was the first thing they wanted to do after they got the papers—get a young stud.

So, she had chosen Rossiter.

It had not gone on very long, perhaps five or six weeks from start to finish.

Finish came that night at the Music Center when Tom Addey had barged into her life.

"We didn't have a bad time, did we?"

He shook his head, afraid to speak.

"Then let's be happy to remember that—a good time. We didn't hurt anybody, Ross. It was very good for me, you know. I was in terrible shape. . . ."

Though not as bad a shape, she might have added, as Tom Addey, who had suffered through his divorce from Thelma and, directly afterward, the shattering dissolution of his affair with that vamp of international renown, Ludmilla Spurzova. He, too, had been a walking disaster.

"Yes, yes," Rossiter agreed hastily. "Maybe it's better—"

"Not to talk about it? Why did you come here, then?"

"I was hoping I'd get here before . . . Tom," he confessed.

"To what end, for God's sake?" Cruelty might be the

greater of the kindnesses. "Do you want to run upstairs for a quickie before Tom comes?"

His eyes flashed at her angrily. "Don't be crazy. Christ!"

Rossiter was so much more vulnerable than Tom. Or perhaps he hadn't had time to build Tom's wall. Poor Rossiter.

Hell, there she'd gone and said that again.

Why poor? He would never suffer, no matter what happened. He wasn't like his brother Seth. Even sitting quietly at Trader Vic's, Seth had made her think of somebody in pain—as if under the table someone was pinching his balls. His very facial features bespoke pain and tension.

"I *was* in love with you, you know."

"Oh, c'mon, Ross. That was years ago. . . . It's *today*." Clara shrugged, then freely said, "I was sort of in love with you too, you know."

A smile lit his face. Maybe this would help, she thought.

"I don't believe I can hop in bed with a man without being somewhat in love with him," she said frankly. "And we were good, were we not?"

His chin loosened. Yes, he would remember that. And she too. Did one ever forget the warmth, the sensation of merging— he'd appreciate the term, being a stockbroker. The smell of it, the wetness, the thumping excitement and the climax, as re sounding as thunder, the sky being torn like a sheet.

Clara could remember all that, admit to the pleasure that had been hers, theirs. But she wouldn't make any big deal of it. Were women more realistic . . . or just *callous*? she wondered.

"Well, that's enough of that," Clara declared. "I'm too old for you now anyway."

Yes, by five or six years, what was that? Was thirty-eight so much older than thirty-two; or thirty that much closer to twenty-five? Clara's problem, basically, was that she'd married the first time too young; at eighteen, running away like that, her chronology had been distorted for good and all. It would've been fine if Stan Gates hadn't uncovered his true needs; then it would have been *just fine* that Clara had a daughter almost as old as she was. But, as it turned out, time had screwed her up. And there wasn't any way of correcting it now.

Rossiter agreed. They shouldn't talk about it, he knew.

"Anyway," he said, "you're happy. That's the main thing."

"Yes." She nodded. "I think so. But I'll tell you something—it's a damn good thing I've got something of my own to do, you know, my gallery. Tom can . . . well . . ."

"Bug you, right?"

"He needs a lot," she explained faint-heartedly, not covering all her list of complaints. "Demanding, I guess, is the word."

"He's hell on wheels, I know. He doesn't have much patience."

"No, he does not gladly suffer idiots or conceited people—"

"Being very conceited himself," Rossiter said sorely. "Conceited enough for any ten people."

"Now, Ross. You know that's not how you feel."

"Oh, no?" he challenged. "After he stole my girl?"

Fortunately, now, he was able to chuckle about it. Very fortunately. It saved Clara reminding him that she'd never really been *his* girl. What she had been was *Clara libre*.

She finished her wine. "Come on, let's go upstairs. We can wait for him up there." She signaled for the waitress and signed the check. "And, *no*, I'm not afraid to go upstairs with you."

"I'm not afraid to go upstairs with you either," Rossiter murmured, "for you are my stepmother and will do me no harm."

"That is so, young man."

In the elevator, thinking it best to change the subject, Clara asked, "So what's the prognosis on Slugger Slagger?"

"He claims to be in great shape except for his heart."

"And Serena?"

Mention of the name was enough to make his expression slip. Rossiter moved his shoulders as if adjusting a load—and everybody knew what the load represented.

"She's not pregnant, you know. Even though she's been doing her best to convince everybody she is."

"*Why?*" Bluntly, she wondered why would the stupid woman do such a thing?

"Beats me. Maybe so she can suffer another miscarriage," Rossiter mused. "I get the impression that for Serena it's more fun to have a miscarriage than a baby. Then you don't have to bother yourself about raising it."

"She makes her life so complicated?" Clara doubted it. "Maybe you're going to be surprised."

They stepped out of the elevator on the seventh floor and turned down the quiet hallway.

No, Rossiter said, he wasn't going to be surprised. Serena was that kind of a woman. She couldn't handle the idea of a baby; she wouldn't have time for a baby.

Pity, Clara thought. She herself wouldn't have minded another. But it had to be soon. She was reaching the extremity of possibility. A few more years and everything would shut down that way.

"You didn't know her very well when you married her—I guess that's stating the obvious," Clara said kindly.

"It'd be sort of amazing to me, I have to admit, if she did get pregnant, if you see what I mean?"

What should she do, bite her lip? Laugh? Clutch him sympathetically? Rossiter Addey had married Serena, and nobody had forced him to. But then Clara wondered—what would have happened, how would it have been, if she'd stayed with Ross those few years ago and not married his father? Maybe she would've had another baby or two by now. She wouldn't with Tom—he had never said so in so many words, but it was clear he believed he'd already done his duty as far as restocking the world with children.

But it had not happened that way. It had happened this way.

"Silly little slut," Clara muttered. She was speaking of Serena. "Her loss, isn't it?"

"Who knows?" He shook his head despondently. "Maybe it's me."

Clara gripped his arm, dug fingers deep into his muscles, his tendons, directly into his inferiority complex. "That's a lot of nonsense. I know you better than that, Ross."

He wanted stroking, though, didn't he?

"Not the greatest ego builder when she starts talking nausea as soon as you kiss her good night."

"No!"

"Fact!" he exclaimed. "Nausea is a way of life. Do you know how many times she threw up on the plane yesterday?"

"And so? *And so?*"

"I've had it," he said, just as Clara shoved the key in the door and clicked and swung it open.

The phone was ringing. Clara crossed the room and picked it up.

"Hello," she said.

The voice was hollow, reticent, even sepulchral.

"It's me."

"Me . . . who?" But she recognized the voice. It was Seth. Clara put her hand over the mouthpiece. "Washington calling."

"Your youngest . . . stepson," Seth said. "I was just told you and Tom are in L.A."

"Oh, yes, who told you that? As a matter of fact, we are, as you may have noted when you dialed. You know *why* we're here?"

"Yes," Seth muttered. "I . . . I need to talk to Tom."

"You can't. He's not here. But your brother is."

"Wait! Wait, I have a question to ask you—do we know the Betancurs?"

"Well, yes." She was more puzzled than before. "Why?"

"Tom was talking to Sol Betancur. Tom told him I'd be in Washington this afternoon. He told me you were—"

"In Los Angeles," Clara finished, laughing. "Neat! Well, of course. Alice Betancur is one of my oldest friends—didn't you hear me say that? So you'll be able to meet her."

"I'm . . ." He hesitated. How he hated to share his information. "I'm going there tonight. I'm invited to a Christmas party. Christ!"

"Well . . . do go, Seth! Alice is a sweetheart! Say hello to her and give her a big kiss for me. Will you?"

"Well, I . . . I don't know about that. I've never met her."

"Seth," she said impatiently. "Here's Ross—good-bye."

Saying no more, she passed the phone. Awkwardly, Rossiter reported what he'd already told Clara—that Bud Slagger was in the hospital and Serena was with him, which accounted for the fact, if you were very suspicious, that he was here with Clara in the hotel room, unchaperoned.

Dunce, she thought darkly. Clara went to the tiny wet bar near the door and poured a big shot of vodka out of the bottle Tom kept there. Gin and vodka. Gin *or* vodka.

Rossiter was laughing jovially by now, going on about Bud being built like a brick you-know-what, promising Seth he'd advise Tom to give him a call . . . and so on. Rossiter finally said good-bye and hung up.

The phone rang again, almost instantly.

This time it was Tom. He wasn't going to make it by six,

76

maybe not even by eight. Was Rossiter there, he'd arrived? Well, then, they shouldn't wait, they should go ahead and eat dinner without him. No, it wasn't particularly Alex screwing things up.

Something else. He'd explain later.

And good-bye.

"Well . . ." Clara turned to Rossiter. She handed him the glass of vodka and busily he began tapping ice cubes out of a tray. "Seems like we're on our own, guy."

She flopped down on the couch under the long window. Behind her the lights of Westwood winked and blinked. In the distance a police siren blared. Down below, the parking boys were screaming at each other.

Rossiter came back with the vodka on the rocks. He handed it to her and Clara pointed to the cushion beside her. Obediently, Rossiter sat down, clasping his hands between his legs. That was maybe what made Clara remember the other time, so long ago now, how awkward he was. Rossiter was as socially graceful as a snake.

Clara sipped on the drink and handed him the glass. "Have a little?"

He tasted too, right where her mouth had been. She remembered the other time; she had been a little drunk then, and she felt a little drunk now. A few minutes before, she'd been so sure she had the drop on Rossiter. Suddenly everything was turned upside down.

There was a reassurance about his body. She wouldn't say he gave off overpowering electricity, as people sometimes described sexual attraction. There was a warmth about him, rather, an enveloping, protective aura which made her think of intimacy, closeness, the liberating effect of passion, not so much of the passion itself but the commitment to it.

She dropped her head on his shoulder.

Rossiter did not move, though his long bones and muscles did stiffen. That she could feel. God, what Tom and Thelma had wrought with the help of Wheaties! she marveled.

What a striking couple they made, what with her near-albino blondness and his dark beauty.

Funny how all these Addeys looked more Italian than Clara, and she was the most Italian of them all.

Clara turned her face upward, gazing along the line of

Ross's clean-shaven jaw. He dropped his head and they kissed. First gently, then hungrily.

Horrors! was her first conscious thought.

Horrors, hell! her second. Then Clara laughed.

"You're just the same," she whispered.

"And you . . ."

"Unbutton me," Clara told him. "Then button me up."

He understood what she was saying. She could have said anything, any gibberish, and he'd have understood. Undo her, then do her. *He undid me, then did me, and I'm undone.*

It was merely, purely crazy. But it seemed right.

"I still love you, you know," Rossiter stammered.

Clara laughed a little, as best she could. She had begun to tremble. Well, what the hell, she thought.

Substantial. Real. In the flesh. Rossiter made strange noises but did as he was told, unbuttoning sweater, blouse, loosening her bra. Then his mouth took possession of her breasts, tonguing them to attention. She was appreciated, and it felt damn good. And she did her own appreciating in return.

There on the couch, quickly—she hadn't been far off, joking about a quickie—as if they'd been waiting and abstinent, like Ulysses' wife. Clara forgot the last eight years or whatever the hell it was. Like there had been nobody in between, even Tom was so far away. How she had forgotten; it was incredible and shocking that she could have. Needing her, Rossiter ran riot. It was like Clara wasn't even in the room. But she was, because she could hear the other voice imploring, passionate: hers.

He kept coming at her, forcing life within her and taking it from her. Until finally . . .

Overhead, behind her, on the other side of the window, she scarcely heard a helicopter come to land on the roof of the nearby UCLA Medical Center, lights flashing and whirling blades hammering the night. Emergency!

Chapter Eight

At this time of the year Washington was at its quietest, its dullest. Congress was either recessed or about to shut down, and the *weather*, well, it was terrible, as Tom Addey had predicted to Seth it would be. Wintry without being really winter as the season was celebrated in healthier climes. Particularly along the Potomac, which flowed beneath the windows of the Watergate Hotel, the bone-chilling character of December was set.

Seth was not on his way to Sol and Alice Betancur's because he expected to enjoy himself or even because he might realistically expect to gain somehow from the evening. He was going because he hadn't known how to refuse the invitation, and powerful Betancur being who he was, it seemed best simply to surrender and go along.

Of course, it was not impossible that Betancur, even inadvertently, could help Seth's career. A word in the right ear and at the right moment was more weighty than a dozen citations.

Seth paid off the cab driver outside the Betancur's Georgetown treasure and, holding the brim of his new brown trilby against the raw wind, mounted the steep steps to a white, brass-fitted front door which opened to a scene that might have been dressed by the editors of *House & Garden*. Dead ahead, a Christmas tree blazing with lights was tucked into a tight curve of highly polished staircase.

The maid was collecting his trench coat and hat when a voice from behind him called for his attention.

"Could you tell me your name, please, sir?"

A tall woman was taking names and checking them against a list on her clipboard. She had a telltale little button in the lapel of her blazer top and to Seth looked suspiciously like a Secret Service agent. The general public wouldn't have known.

"Seth Addey."

She found him near the top. "Fine. You're alone, Mr. Addey?" She paused, as if it hurt to have to ask. "Would you mind showing me an I.D.?"

Not resisting, Seth took his wallet from an inside pocket and flashed the State Department identity. Why all this, he wanted to ask, for a goddamn Christmas party?

He paused for a moment to collect himself. To the left of the small foyer he saw a piece of what he took to be the library: two leather wing chairs visible through a half-open door, a coffee table, a fireplace whose fire reflected off a small window with leaded panes, and pictures—hunting scenes and old family portraits.

To the right was where the security person pointed him: a drawing room overcrowded with people, and beyond that a dining room with sideboards jammed with silver trays, braziers, punch bowls, and big serving plates of hot and cold food, heaps of French bread, cheeses, and iced half-kilos of the inevitable caviar.

Sol Betancur—for the man could be no other—was approaching. He looked exactly as his voice suggested—careless of dress and physically sloppy. He was of middle height but heavy, shoulders wide and sloping. Betancur's head seemed too small for his frame; it hung in a loose, disconnected manner. He was bald save for a fringe of white hair, but his eyes were a sharp, bright blue.

The Betancur paw when it came at Seth was warm and soft.

Yes, with a fake beard and slightly more pillowed belly, Sol Betancur could have played Santa Claus—if that had been part of the entertainment.

"I'm Seth Addey, Mr. Betancur."

"Hey! I'm glad to see you! Hoped you wouldn't stand us up. Alice is over there . . . someplace. . . ." Betancur swung his head amiably. "Remember, Alice is a great friend of Tom's wife Clara. But now, *your* mother is—"

"Thelma Drysdale, Mr. Betancur."

One of the women Sol had indicated looked in their direction. If this was Alice, she was years younger than Sol; yes, indeed, about the same age as Clara. Tall, pencil-slim, she was one of those elegant women for whom expensive clothes were conceived. She could have been a model herself, and for all Seth knew, maybe she had been. Tonight she was dressed in a long black skirt and a silvery blouse that hinted at small, perfect breasts.

But most striking was her perfect complexion, pale ivory, almost too pale. Curly brown hair was brushed in an upsweep away from her face. Her eyes were calm and direct, unblinking but warm.

"Sorry about the security," Betancur mumbled. Maybe he was not quite as jovial as he had first seemed. Way in the back of his eyes glittered little nagging points of skepticism and doubt. "There's a good chance the President will drop in a little later, and we've got to be extra careful. You understand."

"Sure."

Well, Seth thought, maybe it was a good thing he had accepted the invitation. He was pretty cool about most things—but, after all, Sol was talking about the Big Boss.

Sol put his mouth closer to Seth's ear.

"There's something else," he said. "Have you spoken to your father?" No, Tom had been at Alex's. "You know about the old lady—Ludmilla Spurzova—dying out there. Well, There's somebody else dead—a guy named Cazimir Ben Gazi. You familiar with that name?"

Betancur hissed the question. Seth would not forget it right away. But he had to say no: He had never heard the name Cazimir Ben Gazi.

"Ticklish business, bub. I want to talk to you later. Right now, come along. I want you to meet a few friends."

Jesus Christ! Seth felt his stomach yipping. He should have suspected there was something more involved than a mere invitation to a party.

It would have been difficult for Seth to report how many people were at the Betancurs that night. Both front rooms were crowded and people kept arriving—four or five more couples right after Seth. Obvious, though, why they'd all be here—Sol and Alice were as close to the First Family as any friends could be. Just being in the vicinity of the Betancurs did wonders for social standing in this most self-conscious of capital cities.

Moving along behind Sol, Seth spotted two pairs of French doors open at the end of the dining room. A long narrow garden had been completely covered with a jolly candy-striped tent, and several dozen tables were set up, lavishly decorated with red tablecloths, silver, crystal, and batteries of votive candles, all atop a portable parquet dance floor. Electric heaters on stanchions gleamed amid more Christmas decorations—chains of braided evergreen, tinsel, and blinking opera lights—and additional blinking Christmas trees flanked a three-man combo playing seasonal music.

A waiter hustled them with a napkin-wrapped bottle of champagne and glasses.

"Whatjalike?" Sol demanded. "Champagne? Wine? A real drink?"

"I'll have champagne, thanks."

"You heard him, Roscoe," Sol said. "I'm staying dry myself—for the moment anyway."

Sol led him on, muttering Excuse-mes, Hiyas, and How Are Yas as he pushed and shoved and sidled through the crowd. He stopped, finally, next to a young woman with blond hair and a strong jaw.

"Corky! Finally," Sol puffed. "I want you to met Seth Addey. This is Corky Corcoran here . . . and Mac Kindling. Mac, meet Addey."

"Hi," Corky Corcoran said huskily.

Seth shook hands with Kindling. Jesus, didn't they ever say anything except *Hi* in this country?

Sol laughed wheezily. "In case you wondered, Mac is our next ambassador to Portugal."

"In the event our present ambassador dies or quits," Kindling said dryly.

"Take care of him, Corky," Betancur ordered. "There's General Matthews and his wife . . . 'Scuse me . . ."

Corky Corcoran stared across the room. "The last time I saw Matthews he was wearing his uniform and ribbons up to his earlobes." Briefly, she explained to Seth, "I'm a reporter. He was testifying at some committee. . . ."

"Are you working tonight?" Kindling inquired. "If you are . . ."

"You haven't said anything yet worth quoting, Mac."

Corky Corcoran laughed in Kindling's face, not unkindly, but in a tolerant way, as a mother might at the antics of a child.

Kindling was a State Department undersecretary involved in African affairs, so far as Seth remembered. The more reason to be careful, very careful. But he couldn't remain anonymous for long. Kindling very quickly had it out of Seth that he worked at the Consulate in Munich. And Kindling's memory had been piqued. It would come to him in a minute.

"How do you come to be a friend of Sol's?"

"It's my father, actually. This is the first time I've ever met Mr. Betancur," Seth said.

Kindling's eyes gleamed suddenly. He had it. "Don't I remember your name? Weren't you in Moscow?"

Seth nodded. "Yes."

"*Right,*" Kindling said with such great pleasure Seth knew he must remember *everything*. "Well! Ummm . . . I think I saw Jim Madison a few minutes ago—if that interests you."

"Uh-oh!" Seth tried to keep it light.

Corky Corcoran looked annoyed. "What are you talking about?"

Her long chin cocked pugnaciously. Yes, she looked ready for a fight. Corky gazed at Seth critically, as if he smelled of something sour. Her eyes were deep green, Seth noticed, heavily lidded. She used green eye shadow. Corky was good-looking, he decided, without being beautiful; solidly built, or seemed so in a dark-red suit, the jacket top open over a pink oxford shirt. There was not a piece of jewelry upon her, except for a businesslike digital watch on her wrist.

Mac Kindling straightened his glasses, looking professorial and clever. "Madison is a sort of mutual . . . friend," he said teasingly.

Seth studied Kindling calmly; he believed his look was calm. Inside, he was a mess. Was there any way Corky Corcoran couldn't know who Madison was or where he worked? But he shouldn't have concerned himself. Kindling's eyes quickly began to wander. Seth understood—Mac Kindling would want to circulate. They chatted a little about Munich. Kindling did not mention Moscow again. Finally, he spoke brusquely.

"Excuse me, I see the Secretary has arrived. Addey, drop in

sometime. I'd like to talk. Nice meeting you—and seeing you, Corky . . .''

After he'd gone, Corky Corcoran said, "Now you're stuck with me. I'm not official. The only reason I'm here at all is because Alice and I are chums. Sol-baby hates the press.'' Sardonically, she watched Mac Kindling's progress. "He can't wait to get over there and kiss his boss's . . . ring.''

"Dan Whitten . . .''

"Secretary of State, ducky,'' Corky muttered. "Look, there he goes.'' Kindling was shaking hands with the Secretary. So what? A man shaking hands with another man, *so what?* "If Mac had a brain in that egghead of his, he'd know Dan hates ass kissers. Dan's a good old boy, from my part of the country.''

"Which is?''

"Texas, where'd you think?'' How was he to know? She hadn't any accent. She turned to him, smiling slyly. "By the way, saying you work on visas is a bunch of crap—I know better than that. You were in Moscow? What happened? Kindling remembered quick enough.''

Seth shook his head. "Why do you need to know?''

"I can find out easy enough . . . was it in the papers?''

Unwillingly, Seth admitted, "A couple of items. *So?* I got picked up by the KGB and tossed out of the country. That's all. Nothing much.''

She eyed him sourly. "I'm not writing a book, you know, and I can't say that you're exactly a big news item. . . .'' Corky Corcoran paused to reflect. "Still, everybody who's anybody is here tonight—secretaries of whatever, people from the Kennedy Center, Smithsonian, leading social lights—and that includes you. What's the story?''

"Friend of my father, I said before.'' Seth shrugged. "I guess the Betancurs are a very big draw.''

"Sol thinks of himself as a kingmaker,'' she said. "And actually, I suppose he is—''

"Why doesn't he kingmake something for himself?''

Seth thought he might as well get as much out of her as he could. She'd gotten his story easily enough.

Corky shrugged almost scornfully. "There was talk once that he'd get an ambassadorship. But it couldn't happen. First of all, the *occupants* would never let Sol and Alice out of their

sight, and second, his enemies say Sol is crude of mind as well
as body. A slob, in short. Sorry—don't quote me.''

"As long as *you* don't quote me.''

Corky Corcoran continued to watch the door. "Here comes
Health, Education, and Welfare. . . .''

A tall man with a straggly moustache posed in the archway
between the drawing and dining rooms. He looked things over
with an amused smile.

"They say Whittaker's not going to last much longer,''
Corky continued informatively. "He's too left-wing for Washburn.
Whittaker wants to give *all* the money to the huddled masses. He
hates the defense budget and them that wrote it. And there's Al
Carter, he works at the White House, appointments secretary or
something.''

"The man with the meaty red face?''

"Carter happens to be Sol's second cousin or nephew or
something.'' Corky shook her head disgustedly. "We *could* have
something to eat—you want to get plates and go outside? Or *are*
you afraid of seeing this Madison character? I do know who he
is,'' she said sourly.

"A guy I . . . work for.''

"I say no more. There goes Sol.''

Betancur brushed past them, barking over his shoulder,
"Okay? Don't leave without seeing me, Addey.''

"Washburn must be on his way,'' Corky surmised. "Now's
our chance to get some food.''

Corky helped herself to caviar and a moderate portion of
sliced smoked salmon and brown bread.

"Is that all you're having?''

Seth was suddenly hungry. Having seen Madison across the
room, Madison evidently having not seen him, he felt like he'd
been reprieved.

"I eat too much,'' she said. "You've got to be very careful
at parties. You gorge.''

Seth took a plateful of the stew—beef and oyster, Corky
told him, the favorite of the social season—and allowed himself
to be led to the first table down in the garden. With the heaters
blazing, it was balmy there, even too hot.

"We can sit here,'' Corky said laconically, "then leap up
when the Prez appears. You'll hear the clapping—for some

reason everybody claps when he comes into the room. And I can't think why Sol hasn't got the Marine Band outside in the street playing 'Hail to the Chief.' "

Seth grunted. "By now I've sort of lost interest."

"Poor baby," she mocked. She winked one green eye solemnly, taking a liberty with him, acting as though she'd known him since childhood. What the hell was going on? Seth wondered. They were *strangers*.

"I guess I'll not get to meet Mrs. Betancur after all."

"Not right now, anyway. She'll be at the front door . . . curtsying."

"She's an old friend of my father's wife," Seth said. "Clara. Has she ever mentioned Clara Addey . . . or Gates . . . or Morelli?"

"Maybe . . . Clara is your—"

"Stepmother—oddly enough." Seth spoke more easily. He'd lost his tenseness, some of it. "She doesn't seem old enough to be a stepmother . . . or a mother, for that matter."

Corky chewed vigorously. She had strong white teeth, he noticed, and a generous mouth.

"My name is actually Katie," she said. "They call me Corky for obvious reasons."

"Katie is nicer."

"Tell that to the yokels." Corky finished her plate and sat back to cross her legs, exposing smooth knees. "We can go up now, if you're done. Anyway, we need more wine."

She had described Sol Betancur as a kingmaker. Now, back up in the dining room, on the fringe of people pressing toward the front of the house, Corky expanded on the matter of the Famous and Powerful, in Washington Power being more important than Riches.

"You know, all these people organize their December schedules around the Betancur Christmas party. You better not plan one for the same night—you won't draw anybody outside the C group."

"I can understand that."

"You understand Power and Influence. Of course. You must, if you've worked in *those* places. That's why Sol would never leave Washington. He feeds on Power, needs it like oxygen. And the women," she added knowingly. "Women gravitate to it. Groupies . . ."

"Not all women," Seth observed nicely.

"Not me, you mean," Corky drawled amusedly. "Don't you think I know what I'm talking about?"

"You?" Seth couldn't make it plainer: she wasn't that type.

Laughing disdainfully, Corky pointed surreptitiously. "See that woman there, in the black dress with the cut-out back? You see a bit of her bra strap?"

Yes, tight black dress, cut-out back, bra strap . . . smooth skin, the back of a short-cropped auburn hairdo, a neat figure.

"Her name is Mabel Harrey and she's a very mysterious woman about town. A political hanger-on . . ."

"If you say mysterious," he flattered her, "then she must be *very* mysterious. . . ."

"I don't know absolutely everything about everybody, you know."

Could this Mabel Harrey have heard? No, it was too noisy. But she must have sensed Corky had mentioned her name. Coolly, a painted face swung around and deadly dark eyes stared. Seth would have found it difficult to fault Mrs. Harrey's appearance. Her dark hair lay in perfect place, eyebrows plucked to matching swirls in a smooth forehead notched by a distinct widow's peak. Her lips were colored glossily, in what was very nearly an archaic cupid bow. She might have been made up by an expert, for all Seth could say. A gently rounded chin spliced into a curved throat. Pulsing throat? The smallest of smiles, curious yet challenging, turned one corner of her smooth lips. After a second or two she turned away.

They had been looking at her, talking about her—and she knew it.

"Mabel does whatever is necessary," Corky whispered. "She is said to be *very* decadent—if such is required. Her parties are extravagant. I've never been invited, thank God. But she doesn't draw Alice's caliber of people."

"But she's a friend of Alice's?"

"Yes," Corky said grimly, "I'm afraid she is."

Meaning what? It was too late to ask. Things began to happen. Like an approaching tornado, Washburn was preceded by a rush of noise, people clapping, a few "Bravos" and shrieks of "Mr. President, Mr. President," then more sustained applause as Washburn apparently reached the front door of the Betancur house and came inside.

"Well," Corky growled, "he's here."

Washburn was a tall and weary-seeming man. He was in the company of friends now—there would be few in the room outside of government who were not political allies. Sol kept him moving, but there were so many people to greet, Seth thought, they'd never make it as far as Seth and Corky Corcoran. Ignoring Corky's muttered critique, Seth kept his eye on the Great Washburn, and sure enough, by force of sheer will, he brought the presidential attention to him. For a second they eyeballed. He would never be any closer to his commander-in-chief.

But Seth had underestimated Betancur. Sol must have worked such crowded rooms very often; he knew where to steer the presidential elbow.

"Mr. President, let me introduce Seth Addey," Sol said. "Son of a good friend of ours, a good, good friend. And Corky Corcoran, you know, the lady journalist."

How a woman must hate to be introduced like that, Seth thought.

"Hello there, Corky," said Washburn cordially. He had a smile for her and even squeezed her arm. "And . . ."

"Seth Addey," Sol supplied.

"Seth . . . Good to see you . . . Merry Christmas."

And he moved on. Sol *was* a master. Now you see him. Now you don't.

Suddenly he realized Alice Betancur was standing in front of him. Surprised, shaken, he felt himself flush. Unlike her husband, Alice Betancur was much better looking at close range. Her pale face was luminous with beguiling friendliness, even an eager sort of innocence—as though Alice Betancur had never been disappointed by life, had never seen the dark side. Was this possible? Could a person be so good?

The next question swiftly followed the first—what was an Alice Betancur doing with a man like Sol?

"At last. If you wouldn't come to me, Seth Addey, then I come to you." He could have fallen over. *"I know about you!"* she cried.

He didn't believe it. "From Clara? I'm supposed to say hello."

"Is *this girl* keeping you amused, Seth?"

"Yes," he stuttered, like a little boy, then rashly blurted, "Clara said I was to give you a kiss for her."

Alice came closer and turned her cheek into the position. "Let's have it, then. . . ."

Embarrassed, awkwardly, feeling the fool more than ever, like a child Seth touched her cheek with his lips. Smooth, cool but hot. Maybe they'd be joined by Superglue, frozen like this, sent to the hospital . . . No, no, the kiss was instantaneous; but it was as though he had put his lips to a hot wire. The bolt carried down to his toes, farther . . .

Corky Corcoran snapped the spell. "Madame Washburn didn't come?"

Eyes still on Seth, Alice shook her head. "The wheelchair doesn't negotiate in such crowded rooms. . . ."

Ah, yes, dunce. He had forgotten Matilda Washburn was something of an invalid.

"This is just a drop-in," Alice said. "He's got something else tonight. You'll see the cabinet leaving with him. Well . . ." Her eyes returned, wiltingly, to Seth, "so happy to meet you."

"Thank you," he said.

As Alice moved along, Corky muttered, "Well, what do you think? Mrs. Ice Palace . . . or what?"

Meaning she was cold, or unfriendly? Certainly not. Even now Alice Betancur had turned her head and looked back. Her eyes seemed to swarm, to flood with an intimacy aimed specifically at him, excluding her friend Corky Corcoran.

It was only a few moments later when the Betancur butler came for Seth.

"Mr. Betancur would like you to join him in the library, sir."

Corky shrugged impatiently. "Well, go on. Duty calls . . ."

"You'll wait?"

She nodded, smiled thoughtfully, nodded again more positively. "Yes, I think I will wait for you."

Seth was in for a surprise. The man who turned from the fireplace in the snug library was none other than presidential advisor General Homer Kraszewski.

"Krash," Sol announced, as Seth was closing the door, "I want to introduce Seth Addey."

"Hello, Addey," Kraszewski mumbled.

Seth *was* impressed. Whatever had gone before, now he was shaken. Homer "Krash" Kraszewski was one of the legendary figures of American intelligence. He was aging now but his dates went back to the days even before America's entry into the Second World War. In character, Kraszewski's eyes, behind slightly dusty rimless glasses, were opaque. People didn't call him the Polish Fox for nothing.

Aside from the fact that Sol didn't wear glasses, the two men resembled each other physically, both heavy-shouldered and slightly stooped and shambling in appearance. Obviously they'd have been acquainted even if Sol had not been a member of the oversight board. Both were personal friends of the President—Kraszewski an ex-officio advisor way back when Washburn had been a new senator from Tennessee. Krash clearly had the upper hand in the relationship—Betancur treated him with exaggerated respect.

"I guess I know your father, Addey," the general said.

If sounds had been photographs, Kraszewski's enunciation would have produced double exposures. Seth thought he heard right, but he was not totally sure.

Now Kraszewski coughed violently, swallowed, muttered something about cigarettes of the past, then stared keenly at Sol.

"Now . . . where were we? Remind me, Sol."

"The trouble in California, Krash."

Kraszewski sighed. "Yeah, Ludmilla . . . and our friend Ben Gazi."

"Right." Sol spoke rapidly, as if trying to hold Kraszewski's attention. "It was Seth's dad, Tom Addey, who alerted me about Cazimir . . . Tom's in L.A. right now, sitting with Alex Spurzov."

The general nodded, then lifted his chin with a dogged grin. "Hell of a guy, Alex. *One of us,* you know." For a second one might have imagined the Fox going mushy. "Ludmilla drowning in her own goddamn pool." He shook his head dolefully. "Gorgeous woman—and a red-hot vulgar Bulgar to boot. God, Sol, our friends are dropping like goddamn flies!"

"Ludmilla has been in the papers. But *not* the other."

"And won't be!" Kraszewski fixed his vacuous eyes on Seth. "Young man, you know the whole story, do you?"

Seth faltered.

"He doesn't know anything about the suicide, Krash."

Kraszewski's voice broke cheerfully. *"Suicide?"* Spittle flew. "Bloody nonsense, Sol. Ben Gazi *did not* kill himself.

Why would he? He had everything to live for—family, country
. . . *us*."

"Something to do with Ludmilla? Grief?"

"More *bloody nonsense*!" Kraszewski coughed violently
before continuing. "Do you suppose a world-seeded scoundrel
like Ben Gazi would kill himself over a woman?" Merriment
crowded Kraszewski's gullet. "*We know, don't we, Sol,* that
Ben Gazi had broads in every port. Maybe they weren't all
princesses. But they weren't peasants either."

Watching them together, listening, Seth reminded himself
yet again that there were other things a man could do with his
life. Banking, for instance; a convenient career sidestep for
people of his profession when they tired of solving riddles.

As he droned on about the unsettled Middle East, Kraszewski's
eyes settled behind the glare of his glasses. People would be
wrong to doubt his mental capacity; he could have gone on like
this until morning.

"Ben Gazi was *our boy*, Addey. Being a Christian but of
deep Moslem roots, he was doubly anti-Soviet. He'd have fought
those bastards to the bitter end . . . *Those bastards!* And he
did!"

Seth did not need to be reminded that, according to every
account, after the Second World War had been wrapped up, the
general had turned his full attention to the Soviet menace. Of
Polish extraction, Kraszewski had been a Cold Warrior from the
word go.

"Addey, we are *not* about to announce Ben Gazi's murder—
and we *do know* it was murder. We *will not* admit such a murder
on *our own turf*. We send no bouquets, understand? *Nothing
happened in California.*"

"I see." Seth nodded. "Or do I?"

Kraszewski looked pained, then patient.

"For all the opposition knows, Ben Gazi has simply gone to
earth. The only guys who know he's dead are us . . . *and
whoever did it*. What I'm getting at is that those bastards are
trying to make us look stupid—like we can't defend one of our
own. So—we keep mum, they can't prove anything to their
clients. Understand?"

Seth did understand. There was a certain logic in the reasoning. Kraszewski went on about the various factions who
might have had a hand in Ben Gazi's assassination, and of other

groups not even identified who could, possibly, have pulled off such a thing just to exacerbate Soviet-American relations, already bad enough.

Kraszewski smiled.

"But not bad enough to suit me." Slyly, he added, "And don't exclude some jealous husband having him hit. That's possible—*right*, Sol? But probably not likely. Too simple."

Was it Seth's imagination, or did Sol Betancur change color and shudder ever so slightly? After all, it occurred to Seth, was there some connection between Betancur and Ben Gazi? Why else would Tom Addey have called Sol?

"Enough," Kraszewski said grumpily. "We could speculate until doomsday. Long and short of it, young man, is we want you to go to California and do us some *damage control*."

Finally, there it was. "But I just came from California. I'm due back in Munich next week."

Kraszewski chuckled moistly. "Pity we didn't know sooner—save us a trip." Then he waved his hand, brushing away a fly. "Jim Madison agrees, young man . . ."

No, no, the general had it wrong. Jim Madison might seem to agree but actually he'd be hating it. Taking guidance from Krash Kraszewski, that old has-been? Losing one of his men, even temporarily, for some purpose outside his own grand design? No, no, Madison was not the sort to nourish special respect for the elderly.

Anyway, Seth wondered, why the great to-do? Why should the death—suicide or otherwise—of a man with the concocted-sounding name of Cazimir Ben Gazi be so important? Even if the opposition had killed him, so what? They could always go to the fall-back position—suicide, and so what, again?

"I don't understand the problem, sir."

"I told you! Damage control! We don't want any leakage on this thing."

"You don't have to worry about my father."

"I'm not talking about him," Kraszewski said. "I'm talking about everybody else. Ben Gazi was big-time. He had money and connections all over the world. . . . Friends, but *beaucoup* enemies, right, Sol? A host of enemies. And naturally, we want you to find out who did this thing, if you can. . . ." Kraszewski's voice trailed away, then returned with a new thought. "Sol, does the boss need to know?"

Sol shook his head. "I don't think so, Krash, but that's up to you. I'm out of it, *as of now*. All I know is what Tom told me—Ben Gazi is slabbed at the L.A. County morgue as a John Doe. Tom's agreed to handle shipping."

Kraszewski held up his hand. "Now, wait, Sol! I know he's a friend of yours, and he's Addey's father, but is this *wise*?"

Seth could have told him. Sol did.

"Tom's an attorney, Krash. He's got a client relationship with me."

"With Ben Gazi too?"

"What I'm saying, Krash, is Tom is dependable and discreet. He knew exactly how to handle it."

Kraszewski's double chin wobbled as he pondered what Sol said. He finally nodded, though reluctantly.

"I guess it's just basically a logistical thing." He turned his head enough to fix his eyes on Seth. "You'll do okay. Sol reminded me about that business in Moscow."

There was no need to respond. Sure, Seth told himself dismally, put off the return to Munich. What about Hildy? Sure, it was a piece of cake, whatever was *really* involved. *Sure.* In situations like this, if something went wrong, you were on your own.

Kraszewski struggled against the smooth leather of the chair, pulling himself forward and up. "I gotta get going, Sol."

"Sure, Krash, sure."

Kraszewski offered a limp hand to Seth. And how had the living legend fared? Seth wasn't sure he revered Kraszewski as much now as he had when the general had been no more than a name.

In a moment, from outside, there was the slam of a heavy armored car door. Sol motioned for Seth to sit down. Only then did he speak again.

"The rest of this is between us and one hundred percent nonofficial. I'm telling you this," Sol said, "and asking your help as a friend of the family . . . a good friend of the President's . . . and of the country."

Seth was waiting. He didn't need this, he kept telling himself.

Slowly, Sol continued, "Ben Gazi was everything Krash said he was—one of ours and all that. But he also used us *to the hilt*." Sol's jolly little eyes turned stormy. "Ben Gazi was a grafter and a blackmailer. What Krash said is true—he had a stableful of women. All over the place. Ludmilla was only one . . . and she was sort of a sideshow anyway, as far as Ben Gazi was concerned. You see what I'm saying?''

Seth nodded. He did, and he didn't.

"He had as many girls on his string as the busiest pimp,'' Sol muttered crudely. "Not like they were hookers, nothing like that. They were high class, women of high position. . . .'' Sol groaned dismally; it was tough for him to get it out. "He used them on *friends* of ours. He sucked 'em in, the son of a bitch. Goddamn slick rug merchant bastard!'' Sol flipped his pudgy hands disarmingly. '' 'Course the women just fell on their asses at his tiniest smile. I never understood that. . . . The rest of us have to work so hard.''

"Can I ask?'' Seth hesitated. "Does the general know this? I mean . . . if the man was such scum, what good was he to us?''

Betancur stared at him bitterly. "You tell me, bub! Ben Gazi was stamped Extremely Valuable. I took it from there—he was approved for human consumption, all that.''

"The general doesn't seem to know all this,'' Seth observed.

"Not the seamy bits,'' Betancur admitted.

"But what are you suggesting, Mr. Betancur—blackmail, or what?''

"Sol, bub. Sol's the name . . . I'm not sure,'' he said unwillingly. "All I hear is he was using women, like *swallows,* the Russkies call 'em. I've been connected with this business long enough to know how they operate. These bimbos—swallows—are turned loose on our guys by the KGB. They ever try it on you?''

"Sure.''

"No shit!'' Betancur looked at him with respect. "But you didn't fall for it.'' No, Seth had been careful. "Anyway, I was fooled, I admit it. I sent him to your dad, ten years ago, so the *dear man* could meet some West Coast people. But I'm worried *here,* bub, in D.C. I'm worried . . .'' He pointed upward. "High level.''

"But you're not sure.''

"Sure enough, though.''

"But what, *exactly,* are you talking about?'' Seth asked desperately. "Sex for secrets?'' He sounded like a lurid headline. "Blackmail? What?''

"I don't know yet."

Well, it sounded stupid, according to Seth's thinking. Betancur didn't know what he was talking about. He might have had suspicions but he wouldn't be honest about them.

"Maybe Madison has a better idea," Betancur allowed sullenly, "or Scudder of the FBI. Or they're holding out on what they do know." He scowled even more blackly. "You heard Krash . . . hinting. *Hinting*. What, though?"

"Well, I sure as hell don't know," Seth muttered.

"The way I figure it," Betancur said, "is they weighed it up, the pros and cons. Ben Gazi weighed enough on the pro side, they didn't bother him in his *other endeavors*."

Harshly, Seth demanded, "Why didn't you blow the whistle . . . *Sol*? That's serious stuff—you could have had him hit at a better time and place—at least find out what he's got in his black book—"

"Jesus, kid! *We* didn't do it. I didn't arrange it!" Betancur yelped.

"You're sure?"

Betancur looked at him, some fear in his expression. "Did we? Could we? What do you think?"

"No. I couldn't say that," Seth muttered quickly.

But he could. He would always be suspicious, no matter who swore to what.

"I'm not happy you'd say that, bub," Betancur complained. "Look, we always knew the son of a bitch liked women. But something like this? I always thought women were just his amusement—"

"But now?"

Betancur's head swung loosely. "Yeah, yeah, I hear what you're saying. I'll tell you something nobody else knows. A close friend of mine who shall go nameless, a woman friend . . ." For an instant he looked puckish. "She sort of tipped me off. She kidded me about how close *Alice* had come to Ben Gazi. Alice!"

So! Finally! That was it. Spy plot . . . This man running a string of women . . . blackmail . . . compromising men of authority. It all reduced to Alice. Betancur was jealous, and Seth was ready to yawn.

"I cannot believe," Betancur declared angrily, "that Alice

would be mixed up in any kind of nefarious tricks with a *scumbag* like Cazimir Ben Gazi.''

"Nor can I!" Seth made his statement as emphatically as he could. "It's inconceivable, Sol . . . nonsensical!"

"Right! But I can still be concerned about other people. Political friends, Christ knows who all.''

"Does Alice know he's dead?"

Betancur shook his head. "No, no, I wouldn't tell her. I have to admit she always liked him. And *no more than that,* bub.'' He drew a long breath. "You'll be talking to Madison. I sure would like to know what he's got—he's supposed to have a dossier. Madison claims he always had his eye on *Caz,*'' Sol said disgustedly. "And that's why he assigned you, that and the theory being it's better to have somebody on it from out of town. Keep it from leaking all over the goddamn city.''

Seth removed his glasses and carefully polished them with his handkerchief, one of the world's great stalling tactics. In silence Betancur watched. Damage control? Hell, this was sewer work. Seth didn't like it.

"I can tell you I'm not crazy about the assignment,'' he said.

"So?" Betancur shrugged. "Anyway, I don't see why Krash says go to California. I'd forget that. The trail is right *here*. Who knows what's going to come tumbling out of the safe-deposit boxes? Who knows what instructions *Caz* left in case of his sudden death? Who knows about all the other stuff that's got nothing to do with broads and . . . maybe blackmail?''

"More yet?" Seth's heart tripped.

Betancur laughed hoarsely. "Cazimir worked on a lot of projects, and even I don't know the half of them. Remember all the times certain people have tried to kill Castro? That's been one of Caz's offshore projects.''

Seth noticed: *Caz*, was it? Were they back to the old days when Ben Gazi had been such a dear friend of the family?

"And there was the time Caz nailed a banker down in the Caribbean. Guy was tied into drugs and running guns to the commies in Central America.'' Sol clucked pleasurably. "Caz got somebody to put mustard gas in his snorkeling tank.''

"Very pretty . . .''

"Another job was in Spain. Shot this fat German out of a speedboat while he was sipping his sundowner.''

"Sounds like Ben Gazi was something of a hero once."

Betancur shrugged. "Times change. People change. Demands change. Caz used to be our man. . . . The things you learn when it's too late."

"And now he's dead."

"Yep. And I'm done talking." Sol Betancur smiled engagingly. "Would you believe such a man killed himself?"

"Not really."

Alice—her farewell smile was so tremulous, as though he and Corky were her dearest friends and she couldn't count on ever seeing them again. She had that gift—when Alice looked at you, you were alone in the world.

The impression stayed with him for several minutes after they'd left and were walking to find a cab. Corky didn't live far from his hotel, in a modern, small apartment building, brick-fronted and with a glass stairwell on the street side.

Seth got out to escort her to the door but she stopped him, saying, "Pay him off. I'd like for you to come up for a while. It's not too late, is it?"

It was not. Nevertheless, Seth couldn't bring himself to agree right away, without thinking it over.

"Please," she said.

In the elevator Seth's senses reported to him eagerly that Corky Corcoran smelled of the outdoors; moist and fresh from the rawness of the night. On the third floor they walked down a short hallway to a cluster of three doors. Hers was in the middle.

"My modest digs."

A studio apartment, the place was simply but effectively furnished—books across one wall and a desk with word-processor and printer, another wall decorated with bright and bold circus posters—a form of modern art in itself, from Czechoslovakia—and a few pieces of comfortable modern furniture.

"My den," she added, a bit shyly. "Sit down. What would you like? A drink? Coffee . . . tea . . . or milk? What about a little brandy?"

Seth took off his trench coat and threw it on top of hers on a chair in the entry. He glanced around quickly—for the telltale sign of Man.

"Brandy would be nice," he said. "Good for the weather . . . Nice place."

But why did she want him here? Was she going to pump him, try to find out why Sol had called him into a private consultation? Would Corky Corcoran try to get secrets out of him? She could forget it; he was very close-mouthed.

No, so far as he could make out, there was no clue of a male in residence. Corky lived alone.

She delivered the brandy and dropped down on the couch beside him, close enough so he could smell her again, that same heady femaleness. Maybe the cold brought it out, a protective, warming scent.

"What did you think of Alice?"

So, she wanted to talk about Alice.

"She's a nice woman. She seems very nice."

"She's beautiful, isn't she?"

Seth felt bound to play her beauty down. You had to, discussing one woman with another. "Good-looking, that's for sure."

"Too sweet. She never should've married a man like Sol."

"How do you know her?" he asked curiously.

"Hell . . ." Corky shrugged, as if this were the most obvious thing ever. "I met her when I first started as a reporter. Sol nabbed her out of a White House office and married her . . . about six years ago." Corky smiled. "And, naturally, I've interviewed her since then—subjects like Entertaining the Mighty in Washington, D.C. Deep-think pieces like that."

"My mother runs *Classics* magazine."

Corky's eyebrows did rise, just a little. "Indeed? Well!" She laughed loudly.

"I thought it might interest you," he said stiffly.

He moved his brandy glass to his lips but Corky intercepted. A wayward gesture, touching her glass to his.

"Cheers, Seth. I am interested. Sure."

"Cheers."

Laughing again, she showed her teeth, then abruptly turned serious again.

"I'm worried about her."

"Alice?"

"Yes, and nothing to do with journalism. As a friend."

It struck Seth that anything he could learn about Alice Betancur could only help him in his search for the identity of Cazimir Ben Gazi . . . and his killers.

"I don't rightly know *why* I'm worried, I must confess." Absently, she touched a finger to his knee, poked, then noticing her action, pulled her hand back. "She's not as approachable. Like she's harboring a worry, or secret." She glanced at him. "You'd know about secrets."

Seth shrugged. "Yes . . . and no."

Her laughter pealed once again and green eyes flared. She did have that, the ability to laugh joyously.

"The woman I pointed out to you—Mabel Harrey? She's Sol's mistress. The woman with the peekaboo bra strap, remember?"

"The predator? Sure, I remember."

"Unforgettable?"

"Sol's mistress." He nodded. "Very interesting . . ."

"One of many over the years, I might add," Corky said. "Of course, Alice was bound to find out."

"And did?"

"Yes, I'm pretty sure. Though she'd never say so. Madame Mabel came originally from Canada. She went to England and was married for a while to an earl. Then, either divorced or widowed—I've never checked it out—she gravitated to Washington. Toward the Power I mentioned before. And, naturally, latched onto Sol."

Seth remembered what his mother had been blathering about in New York, doing a *Classics* piece on such women: courtesans.

"Sol mentioned something tonight about a *woman friend*," Seth said rashly, as he instantly realized, but too late. "He didn't say who."

"She's who." Corky turned toward him more intimately, throwing her knee up on the couch. "You give interesting info, Mr. Stranger. And you? Unmarried man? In Washington, D.C., the City of Women?"

"Including you . . . unmarried?" He was surprised to hear himself asking such a question. The next was more forward. "And no man friend?"

"Yes, including me. And no, no man friend, nothing steady anyway. I'm not much interested," Corky said. "I've lived here almost all my life and I know the score. I'm not particularly crazy about men."

What was she saying? Did she prefer another species of

humanity, then? Seth's insides churned. What a pity; he always thought about it that way. A good-looking woman and—

Corky evidently caught his interpretation. Had his face fallen so far?

"What I mean is that watching Washington men in action might give you qualms—they're power-hungry monsters. It's always better to get your hooks into guys from out of town—like you," she said frankly.

"Me?"

Then he remembered what Sol Betancur had said, why Madison would assign an out-of-town guy to the Ben Gazi thing: No leaks. No gossip.

"Sure, *you*." She was straightforward, he'd give her that. Corky looked him straight in the eye, then tried the brandy on him again, clicking glasses the third time; Seth counted. Three times and out, or in? "You're an innocent. You're not after anything, are you?"

"Only to get the hell out of town and away from Jim Madison," Seth said wryly. There! He was being indiscreet. "Are you attempting to get me drunk?"

"If possible," Corky said. "See, you don't want publicity, do you? There's no way I can help you get your name in lights, is there?"

"Not that I can think of."

"And you're in town for *just a week*?"

"According to the schedule."

Corky laughed, loudly at first, then more restrainedly. She was very companionable, he had to admit it, easygoing, comforting even. He was aware of slipping further into the mold of the soft cushion. His high tension loosened. And she did surprise him, didn't she?

Her lips were strong. Determined. They curled against his mouth, as if she were still laughing.

"Then we'd better get started," she said quietly.

Chapter Nine

*R*ichard Richards folded small, skin-cancer-speckled hands under his chin, pursed his prissy lips, then swung his high-backed swivel chair to stare for a moment, maybe philosophically, out of the broad windows of a tenth-story suite in the Richards Corporation building.

"I never thought of Ludmilla being old enough to die." His voice was weak; he probably didn't speak more than fifty words a day. "She always behaved with great flair. I did admire Ludmilla very much, Mr. Addey."

If Richards was babbling for Tom Addey's benefit, he was wasting his breath. Ludmilla hadn't been Richards's mother; she would have dismissed Richards as a nonperson, if recognizable at all, only because he was Rodney's son.

Richards's eyes, behind small steel-framed glasses, were bloodshot, his hair grayish-red and stiff.

"Ludmilla made my father very happy. Lucky man, wasn't he?"

Yes, Tom thought, the old coot. He wanted to tell Dick Richards that if his own mother had possessed half the wattage of Ludmilla, he wouldn't be such a dull clod himself.

Softly, Richards said, "You knew her pretty well yourself, didn't you?"

Tom put a hand to his silk tie, then the top button of his vest. He'd dressed lawyer-style for the day.

"Ludmilla and Alex have been my friends for years."

"Yes, yes. My father got to be Alex's good friend too, you

know, and for that reason *we* weren't displeased when Ludmilla invited Alex to stay at Richlands upon R.R.'s death. We knew she'd be lonely.''

Tom wondered what it was Dick Richards wanted him to say. Did he want reassurance his father could really have been happy married to such an international slut as Ludmilla?

"But of course," Richards probed, "she had her young friend to amuse her. . . .''

"Young man?"

"The Lebanese. He is Ludmilla's lover, is he not?" Richards continued to stare at the globe, at the area of Europe and the Middle East from which all the players hailed . . . or had.

"Are you speaking of Cazimir?"

Cazimir. Tom would be permitted a curse or two. How indelicately, how inconveniently Cazimir had interfered in the course of Tom Addey's existence. Of course, if Tom hadn't responded to Alex's plea for help, he wouldn't have been bothered at all. It had been a bit complicated but, if Tom did say so himself, he had handled everything with ease, skill, aplomb. Few people would've known how to proceed with the police. But there were ways of keeping such things quiet. That very morning he'd arranged the final stage—for the shipment of John Doe's remains to that place in Maryland that dealt with confidential terminations.

"I've been waiting to hear from Mr. Ben Gazi," Richards murmured. "We met and became rather friendly while my father was still with us.''

"Cazimir's left town," Tom informed him.

"Has he?" Richards swung his chair around. "Then I'm very surprised he didn't call.''

"Well . . .'' He didn't have a good answer for that. "You know he always had . . . a lot of irons in the fire.'' Tom hoped Richards hadn't caught that; he must be very careful not to place Cazimir in the past tense. "He's probably back in Beirut *right now*.'' Liking the irony, Tom added, "He'll be missing the services for Ludmilla. Alex thought a short memorial in that little chapel—''

"I won't be there. I don't care for funerals.''

"It's not a funeral.''

"I understand.'' Richards began speaking in nervous spurts, as if mention of a funeral, or memorial, had thrown him for a loop. "We haven't decided yet what we'll do with Richlands, Mr. Addey. There's no argument that the estate belongs to us. Ludmilla was allowed its use—"

"No, no, no argument about that."

Richards smiled with some relief. "We intend to maintain the house as-is until a decision has been made on disposition." His voice faded, then surged. "Prince Alexei is welcome to stay as long as he likes . . . or until we make a decision."

Tom felt warmer toward him. "Alex is very appreciative."

"Is he?"

"Well, he will be when I tell him."

Richards frowned. "As you know, Mr. Addey, it's better to have a house lived in than not. One of the first rules of real estate. Empty houses are like empty glasses."

"Do I know that saying?"

"Ghosts breed in empty houses like germs in an empty glass." Muttering irritably, Richards returned to business. "As to personal property, we're not concerned. I understand Ludmilla owned one or two cars. They go to Alex, if he wants them."

"Again, he'll be grateful."

Absently, Richards twirled the globe.

"I think it's fair. Ludmilla was always *true* to Alex. So . . ." He looked at Tom meaningfully. "I think it's right Alex should have her personal things, don't you?"

"Yes," Tom said, "and I'm happy you do too."

"We'll keep a small staff at Richlands in the meantime," Richards continued, "a maid and gardener—and Peat, as sort of coordinator. He's been with the family for twenty or more years, Mr. Addey."

Ah, yes, Peat. *There* was a problem, the one fly in the ointment.

Tom had had a very unsatisfactory conversation with Seth that morning. Seth called from Washington, and to Tom's great surprise was very well briefed on the matter of Cazimir Ben Gazi. How had that happened, and why? Seth did not sound greatly thrilled with the assignment—what, evidently, had *become* an assignment. But Tom asked no questions; nor did he say anything leading over the telephone, beyond confirming that it had been arranged for "John Doe" to fly eastwards and that the situation on the coast was well in hand.

He had not told Seth about the loose link, Peat; that it had been Peat who'd discovered the body, and that Peat knew Cazimir Ben Gazi was not John Doe. What to do about Peat? Tom had not warned the gaunt butler to keep his mouth shut, reasoning that to do so would merely sound an alarm. This way, Peat would soon forget the whole thing. Body? What body?

It was a simple enough situation. No, there was no reason for Seth to come to California to make sure everything was okay . . . what the hell did they think Tom Addey was? Some kind of a neophyte? As it happened, Tom Addey had been in very touchy situations before this one—*and* more often than Seth, even with his son's experience in Moscow. Tom did envy him that. It seemed a man could not consider he'd ever lived unless he'd been grabbed for a few hours by the KGB.

But this was no justification for Seth to put on his little spook act or to play stuffy bureaucrat with his own father. No, Tom was not having any of that. He was not crippled or infirm or senile. Not yet.

Moreover, he'd enjoyed it.

Getting a dead man shipped across country like a load of fish on ice was just a little bit of a challenge to enliven his declining years, Tom thought sardonically. Amazing, wasn't it, how the old man had pulled it off!

And, as for Peat, if he did open his yap, Tom would have him committed to the booby hatch.

What he had not expected was that Dick Richards would claim acquaintance with the discredited Lebanese.

But he supposed he could deal with that too—if necessary.

"Well, then," Richards said, impatient to get it over with, "the cars. Personal jewelry? I'm not sure R.R. ever gave her anything in the way of valuable jewelry. Knowing him, probably not. And the clothes—I'm not sure what you do with such a collection, are you?"

"Easiest to give them to a costume museum, most likely— and try to get the write-off, if there is one."

"Yes, yes, let's leave that up to Alex too." Then something else occurred to Richards. "I almost forgot—this may sound like a strange request. But if Alex is agreeable, I'd appreciate it very, very much. You know, my wife and Ralph's both sort of worshipped Ludmilla from a distance. They were always in such awe of her. My wife Rose would really like to have a couple of Ludmilla's caftans . . . or something. Does that sound ghoulish?''

For a change Richards seemed a little embarrassed that he might have to ask for something.

"On the contrary. Alex will be flattered to know that the ladies thought of Ludmilla as a glamorous figure.''

"Good, good. I do appreciate that very much," Richards continued in his gracious mood. ''What do you think Alex will actually do? Will he stay in the house?''

Not giving anything away, Tom said, ''For a while. Then, he's talking about going back to France. For good.''

Richards looked out the window, nodding sadly. A few moments earlier, he had seemed so anxious to get rid of him. Now, nervously, he said, ''It's going on five, Mr. Addey. We're agreed—I'll have the necessary papers drawn up. Right now, I suggest you and I have a quiet drink to seal the bargain.''

Before Tom could say yea or nay, Richards jumped up and opened a built-in bar behind his desk. Inside there were glasses, ice bucket, decanters, a small refrigerator, and an array of bottles.

"Whiskey?''

"Yes, all right, with a little soda, no ice." Especially no ice, since Dick Richards was reaching for a malt whiskey.

Standing, Richards exhibited the figure of an active man—a yachtsman, Tom remembered. He handed Tom a glass, not generously supplied with whiskey but long on water. Richards drank, without saying anything in the way of a ''cheers'' or ''down the hatch'', then sat down again and stared across the table.

"There is something else, Mr. Addey.'' Uh-oh. ''Do I understand that you've retired from the law?''

Had he? Seth evidently thought he'd retired from everything. Tom had never felt right admitting he was fully retired. Who said God owed a man empty days?

"No,'' he declared. ''Not at all. I'm very busy.''

Richards had definitely lost his self-assurance. ''So you do still represent people?''

Hadn't he just said so? Actually, though, it'd lately been mostly old clients entangled in tricky tax situations. Such cases were not as fascinating as they'd once been—lawyers had come to spend more effort on the technicalities than the letter of the law, more on loopholes to the law.

Tom had been wondering about teaching a legal ethics course—he'd recently been approached to do so. He might not be the right person to transmit great faith in the law to a roomful of students. Once, true, he'd loved it, the law in its pure and perfect form, as one might fervently love a gorgeous woman. The law he knew now was a pockmarked old crone.

He answered Richards, "Represent, yes, and advise."

Abruptly, Richards said, "I want you to represent *me*."

"You'll have to explain."

Richards lifted his eyes bravely. "Look, can I call you Tom?" He chuckled embarrassedly. "I've behaved like a god-damn fool."

Tom recrossed his legs, waiting, drinking the whiskey. It bit his tongue and trickled nobly into his gut, like God's blood, a saving draught.

"I've never had to confess anything like this before," Richards muttered. "Maybe I should've been a Catholic, it might be easier." He clasped his hands, unclasped them. "Will you agree to represent me?"

Now was the time to say no. But Tom didn't.

"Listen . . . *Dick*. Whatever you have to tell me will be strictly confidential—you've got my word—but I can't commit myself."

Richards nodded nervously. Now was also his chance to retreat.

"I'm being blackmailed!" Richards yanked off his glasses and began vigorously to rub his eyes. "It's that Lebanese . . . Cazimir!"

"Ben Gazi is blackmailing you? That doesn't make sense. Weren't you saying he's a friend?"

Richards blurted it out. "He's got pictures of me . . . bad pictures. What you'd call compromising pictures."

Rich men should have better sense. Tom must have frowned critically, and Richards was annoyed.

"Look, if you think it's too disgusting—"

"It's not that. I just don't know what I can do." But he had the upper hand, didn't he? Tom knew Ben Gazi was dead and Richards didn't.

"I've already paid him . . . about fifty thousand. I want to negotiate with the bastard," Richards cried. "I need some kind of agreement drawn up and I *want* the negatives and his promise there'll be no more!''

Tom hesitated. "But he's left town, Dick . . . I wouldn't know where to look for him.''

That happened to be the unvarnished truth.

"Well,'' Richards said doggedly, "I want to end it.''

"Maybe he won't deal.''

Again, the truth. More than that—Ben Gazi would definitely *not* be dealing.

"I'll have him killed!''

"Don't be ridiculous.''

Tom could have laughed. *Too late, Dicky-boy.*

"You might say differently if you saw the pictures.''

Tom shrugged. "Pictures of what? You and some hooker? You can just say you were drugged. People believe that and then they forget right away. What's he going to do with them—print them in the *L.A. Times*?''

Richards snarled, "It's not a hooker in the pictures. It's *him! Ben Gazi!*''

Boom! The whole truth might have made such an explosive noise landing like a fat dossier in the middle of the desk.

"I don't know how it happened, Tom, believe me.'' Richards blinked tearfully. "I give you my word—never before! Sure, all right, I've been attracted to guys . . . maybe I was bisexual, but I never really thought about it.''

Richards jumped up nervously. "Another.'' He poured himself a large shot of the beautiful malt whiskey. Sad when a man was so upset he couldn't appreciate drinking the real thing, Tom thought fleetingly.

"The son of a bitch. He makes a career of it! Women . . . look at Ludmilla. *And men.*''

"You fell in a trap, Dick. Guys like him . . .'' He didn't have to go on.

"The thing is, Tom,'' Richards confessed, "I'm waiting to hear from him. I *want* to see him again—''

"And pay.''

"If necessary,'' Richards whispered brokenly.

"So,'' Tom asked him bluntly, "do you want to negotiate or not? Have him killed, or not? You can't have it both ways.''

"I know.'' Richards drank. "But I do want it both ways.''

Tom Addey was sorely tempted to level with Richards, to

tell him there wouldn't be any negotiating because Ben Gazi was dead. But he couldn't.

"Tell me, Dick," he asked, "is there anybody else involved?" Richards shook his head dully. "Outside of the Alex-Ludmilla circle? Doesn't he have other connections in L.A.?"

They would need to know. This could be vital information.

"If he does, I don't know about them."

The best advice was the only advice Tom could give in the circumstances. "Sit on it, Dick, for the time being—at least until Ben Gazi surfaces again."

Richards agreed. "If I'm lucky, I'll never hear from him again. Or unlucky."

"Maybe you'll get lucky."

Richards pulled open the center drawer of his desk. "You'll want a retainer."

"No. We'll see what happens."

It would have been compounding a fiction to take money from Richards.

Chapter Ten

Within two days of Bud's operation Lorenzo Diamond called from Las Vegas to inquire after the health of his dear friend and "associate" and Rossiter was able to tell him, as he later reported to his father-in-law, that the Slugger was doing very well indeed.

But Bud didn't like it at all.

"He could've called me himself. Why didn't he place a call to me here in the hospital?"

Rossiter explained that Mr. Diamond just didn't want to disturb Bud, or so he'd said, at least.

"I'm here days, or what is it, I'm out of intensive care and getting ready to leave, let us hope, and the guy doesn't want to disturb me. A man waits for a call. He gets lonely."

Serena huffed irritably.

"Daddy, I am here with you *all* the time, to the neglect of my home."

But Bud wouldn't listen.

"And did he send me flowers? Think about that—more than that he didn't call, he didn't even send any flowers. What does that say to you?"

"That men don't think about sending flowers to other men in the hospital," Serena said acidly.

"And Tiny—does Tiny even stick her head in for five minutes?"

Rossiter thought he could stop being puzzled how Bud

Slagger could have helped create a Serena—the two were hatched from the same egg.

"Anyway, you look good today, Bud," he murmured. "Like the Slugger of old."

In more recent years, as the days of baseball glory faded further and further into the past, Bud Slagger liked more than ever to be hailed by his old nickname: Slugger Slagger, Now that he was ill, this was even more true. Go get 'em, Slugger! Ross would say to him.

"Feeling like a new man, Ross." Bud did his best to bounce his voice off all the walls. He looked like he wanted to beat himself on the chest, but Serena was sitting so close to him on the bed he couldn't move. "Rarin' to go, Ross! Up and at 'em!"

Serena sighed dramatically.

"Fine for you, Daddy. But this has been Hell, pure Hell for me."

Bud patted her hand, her thigh, her knee, slid his hand down her leg.

"Don't worry, baby. When it's all over, I'm going to buy you a great present."

His look and touch should have been enough to melt her down.

"Rossiter," she said comfortably, "Daddy has been very good. Not once has he asked for a cigarette."

"Cigarette?" Bud howled. "Ugh! Ugh! Make me nauseous!"

They were alike, this father and daughter. Serena chortled with hysterical laughter. Daddy was *so* funny! Bud hugged her, his fingers spread across that substantial bosom. Okay, okay, he was the daddy. Serena giggled and dropped backward, turning and twisting her head around to kiss Bud stickily on the mouth.

It was embarrassing to watch, even though they were all more or less related.

Serena stroked Daddy's chest, above the place where the surgeons had reconstructed a heart. "*Uum,*" Serena sang, "*uum, I can feel it humming, Daddy.*"

As he liked to do in order to reassure Rossiter this was all in innocent fun, Bud winked broadly. Daddy's little girl could do no wrong.

Rossiter tried to smile but was conscious only of a sick feeling inside himself, of an internal unrest that threatened to tear him apart. Serena was awful; this thing had come to a head. Clara had made him see, with a stark and shattering clarity, what a mistake he had made. He'd probably known it always—but being with Clara again, he felt so wonderful he didn't care. There was nothing about Serena that could even faintly please him now.

"Sit down, Ross, sit down."

"I've been sitting all day, Slugger."

Hearing his voice, Christ, he sounded so weak and wan and ineffectual. He'd like to kick her off the bed—Serena cuddled in Bud's arms, giggling and baby-talking in Bud's ear, much to Ross's discomfort. She caressed his damaged chest, his belly. What next? Hadn't she said something disgusting about renewed sex drive, having a new heart on him, or in him?

A reasonable stranger might have been justified in thinking the worst, that Serena was prepared to defy a fundamental no-no right there, careless of nurses or visitors roaming the corridors.

Who is this mad woman? I'm sorry, I don't know her.

"Yeah, yeah," Serena jeered, "sit down, Ross. Take a load off your feet. Say something interesting for a change."

"Jesus, baby. Jesus, take it easy. . . ."

Bud was a schmuck. He'd never known how to handle her, or Tiny for that matter.

For lack of anything better to do, just to shut them up, Rossiter took a chair on the other side of the bed, as far from Serena's evil eye as he could get.

Above them all, Bud's TV showed a silent picture of a game show in progress. The set was anchored in the wall, so that a man stretched flat, even half dead, was nonetheless as one with his TV. Rossiter smiled to himself, thinking evil in his own way. How would it be to check out in the middle of a soap—maybe along with a patient on the operating table in one of those hospital series?

Bong. Pull the plug. Farewell.

How had this happened? How had he managed to dig himself into such a hole? He was better than Serena. His father was better than Bud; and Thelma, his mother, was certainly superior to Tiny. Not to be snobbish about it, but Jesus! What could there have been about Serena? Her spirit? Kindness? Ability with the language?

"What else did Legs have to say?" Bud asked. Serena

111

stirred but Bud stroked her back, the nape of her neck, took little detours over her shoulders. "I mean Lorenzo . . . We call him Legs sometimes, not to his face."

"Nothing."

Actually, Diamond had referred to the big investment, asked how it was going.

"He just wanted to know how you were getting along, Slugger. He said he hoped he'd be seeing you soon."

Serena said sharply, "Daddy is not going back to Vegas until after Christmas!"

"I'd like to be with you, honey," Bud muttered. "It kinda depends—"

"You just tell them you're not coming back until January and that's that. We want you at our home for Christmas, don't we . . . darling?"

Darling? Was she speaking to Rossiter Addey?

Bud, however, wasn't thinking about the holidays.

"Lorenzo's got a very good telephone voice, doesn't he?"

"Very dignified. Melodious. He sounds like a newscaster."

"He used to sing," Bud said. "Then he did telephone sales. You know, calling people out of the blue and selling them shit they don't need or really want . . . And now he's boss of the Alhambra. A very big man."

Rossiter hoped he'd never have the honor and pleasure of making the personal acquaintance of the talented Lorenzo Diamond.

Fortunately, he had been able to pass on to Diamond encouraging news on the Chet Arthur-MorrisCom merger. Word that something was cooking must have leaked out in New York, for Morris shares had hopped a whole dollar that very morning, not so bad when you figured the pre-holiday market had been so slow. The formal bid was scheduled for early in the new year, Rossiter had been led to believe. So, Lorenzo had purred, they were looking at collecting their winnings in the first quarter.

As Rossiter's mind wandered, Serena sprang the surprise question on him.

Had he bought *the tree*? She'd been yelling about it the night before, when she'd finally come home from the hospital— luckily for Bud, unluckily for Rossiter, Serena wasn't allowed to sleep there. "Make sure and buy the tree, a good healthy, full one," she'd ordered. She wanted to put it up just inside the "salon" door.

Rossiter hadn't bought it yet; his intention had been to do so on his way home from the hospital.

Serena began to mutter viciously. "Daddy, Ross is such a fuck-up. I tell him. He forgets. What am I going to do with him?"

"Take it easy, honey, take it easy. You know Ross just came from the office."

"Office or not, I want him to buy that tree and I mean NOW!"

Slowly and deliberately Rossiter got up, smiling at Bud, feeling like a horse's ass. Bud stared back at him, a troubled look in his eyes. There was nothing either of them could do. They were *both* horse's asses.

"I'd better get going," he said. "I'll see you at home, Serena."

"Don't forget the goddamn tree!"

He said neither yes nor no. Maybe he would. Maybe he wouldn't.

"Take it easy, Bud."

"Keep your eye on the ball, Ross!"

Dumbly, Rossiter negotiated the maze of corridors, walkways, escalators, and elevators, got lost once, but eventually found the parking structure and his Ford. He didn't drive a modest car just because he was a modest man. It was a matter of money. A family with the resources of his was pretty well limited to one Mercedes, and that was Serena's.

But that was all right. Cars were the least of it. There were things far more important than cars.

Once clear of the hospital environs, Rossiter drove carefully on up Third Street and eventually into the heart of Beverly Hills. Skirting City Hall, he crossed Santa Monica Boulevard and headed toward Chez Addey.

Chez Addey? Who the hell was he kidding? Chez bullshit! And he'd forgotten the tree again.

Despite his best effort to focus on the rush-hour traffic, Rossiter's mind wandered. Where was Clara right then and what was she doing? And Tom Addey, his father, what of him? It was terrible, Rossiter supposed, very bad luck, that it had started up again. He had figured that, whatever else happened, Clara had bypassed him. It had been an embarrassing time for Rossiter when his father and Clara had married—she'd counted on him to keep his mouth shut, of course, without ever asking him in so many words to do so. Communication between them had just, bluntly, stopped.

But time did heal, Rossiter reminded himself, not that there had been so much healing to do, at least on his side. Yes, it was true what people said—he was probably too easygoing; nothing ever really devastated him. He didn't worry very much about things like love; in fact, Rossiter was ready to admit, he was far more concerned about the stock market.

Though he *was* kind, solicitous, friendly, helpful . . . what else did the Boy Scouts swear by? Brave, clean, and reverent—yes, put it all together and it spelled Rossiter Baker Addey.

Besides, there had not been anything much between them. The whole episode, over the years, became a nonevent, a nonrelationship. He'd forgotten all the intimate details and hadn't really thought too much about it in ages. Until the weekend in San Francisco. Sitting across from her . . . feeling his own desire for her echoed.

Goddamn, he felt good. And wasn't it true that men often fell in love with the same woman? Unusual, maybe, for a son to fall in love with a stepmother. But there was no good reason, beyond social morality, why he shouldn't—nothing in the way of blood bonds to frighten them off, as might have been a factor in the case of Serena and Bud Slagger.

Rossiter thought perhaps he'd never be able to look Tom in the eye again. Not that Tom would notice . . . and maybe that was the problem.

Clara would never leave Tom—even if she *was* discontented, even unhappy. She'd as much as said so. And why should she, really? Her life was pleasant and busy enough, with her gallery. And she didn't really love Rossiter, at least according to his judgment. It was more like a raw and selfish passion that had reignited. Amazing, wild, reckless, yes; but, no, she didn't, couldn't love him. If she did—or had—would she have gone off with Tom Addey without a second thought, with hardly a good-bye to Rossiter, that night outside the Music Center?

How vividly he remembered that. Clara had simply walked away, leaving him, Rossiter, gaping.

But was the future hopeless? No, he wouldn't believe it was.

About Serena, did he have a choice? Yes. About Clara, though, and Tom, and everything else? Little choice. Driving home, Rossiter suffered fleeting visions of escape—of running away with Clara, perhaps retreating to the vineyard and placing themselves under Alberto's protection, indenturing themselves; giving Alberto his pound of flesh? He probably had never fully forgiven Clara for her original transgression—eloping with Stanley Gates, against all Alberto's wishes and commands.

Rossiter and Clara . . . what? *For what?*

Nothing made very much sense. Rossiter's mind was a jumble. Along with euphoria, there were black moments too, and it was then Rossiter considered the ultimate descent down the spiral of depression: suicide. People did it all the time. But did he consider his own bad luck sufficient to kill for it? Kill *himself* for it, that is?

No, no, his delicious misery was not ripe enough. Life would have to turn much worse.

Professionally, though, there was a bright side. Envious people said Rossiter was rapidly becoming one of Sandor Veruckt's favorites. And Rossiter wasn't even a Hungarian.

Lately, even more to the point, Sandor had begun inquiring very often after the health and well-being of Thelma Drysdale. It seemed she and the Hungarian wizard had met at one or another dinner party in New York.

"How is your dearest mama?" Sandor had asked about her again that morning. Odd, because normally Sandor didn't waste time on the telephone. He stated his business, got it over with, and hung up, often without saying good-bye. "A remarkable woman," he purred. Then he got to the business point, asking how she was getting along at *Classics*.

"Morris Communications, my boy," Sandor said knowledgeably, "surely a *classic* case of corporate chaos."

Veruckt knows all. Sandor made the claim up and down Wall Street.

Rossiter had experienced a more than vague sensation of a dagger point trailing across his throat. Sandor had heard about the Chet Arthur bid? And had noticed that upward blip in price!

Rossiter's intuition, which often operated at lightning speed in high-risk situations, told him the moment had arrived to *divulge*.

"Speaking of my mother," he said warmly, "has she whispered anything to you about Chester Arthur making a bid for Morris?''

Sandor produced a thin, sucking sound. He switched his telephone from loudspeaker to the more confidential mode.

"You have heard something?" His nasal burr thickened. Sometimes Sandor Veruckt's voice seemed to slip and fall over that accent.

"She mentioned it in passing," Rossiter admitted casually. "But you know her understanding of money is *zilch*."

"No, no, Rossiterre," Sandor drawled mellowly, sounding somehow relieved, perhaps of the embarrassment of skinning Rossiter Addey alive. "On such clues, my boy . . ." He didn't finish what sounded like a weighty aphorism.

Rossiter had dared to play a deceptive game with such a man? Yes, he had. It was true. He had not previously reported Chet Arthur's rumored bid; and he had still not informed Sandor about the Las Vegas money. Or that he, Rossiter, was to be paid ten percent of Lorenzo Diamond's profits.

And it was too late to tell Sandor now. Rossiter was out of bounds, and Sandor did not react lightly to disloyalty. Rossiter had heard of him letting colleagues go merely for forgetting an insignificant bit of market gossip. *Nothing* was too insignificant for Sandor's astute ear—at least that was what Sandor said.

Great success supported Sandor's claim to brilliance. He'd escaped from Budapest in 1956, on the run after the uprising against the Soviets. Arriving in New York with nothing, in hardly more than a generation Sandor had made his name and fortune in the cutthroat world of capitalism, that system against which the communists had always been thought to have so effectively brainwashed.

So much for brainwashing, somebody said.

Sandor had already commenced to reel off, from memory, a complete financial summary of Chester Arthur Ltd. assets—media, property, the hotel empire.

"Consistently have I considered MorrisCom to be underpriced, Rossiterre." Sandor's tongue enwrapped Rossiter's name like a smooth, snug sheath. "This is a very possible thing for a man like Chet Arthur. Did you know his grandfather came from Pécs, a Hungarian provincial city?"

Yes, that too. Sandor never stopped hammering on the central Hungarian role in history. Think of any human endeavor and you will find involved a Hungarian. The atomic bomb, look, and a Hungarian! Money—Hungarians are the assault troops of investment financing. Writing and philosophy. Religion. Inventions—Hungarians had a hand in the invention of almost everything worth inventing. Art? The theatre? My boy, the theatre is a Hungarian art form.

Only once had Rossiter heard Sandor challenged—at an investment seminar in Chicago. Somebody had said, Phonies? Eighty percent of the phonies in captivity are Hungarians.

"We will check it out, Rossiterre," Sandor said cheerfully, rattling his tongue on the roof of his mouth.

"I should tell you, Sandor," Rossiter cautioned, "the reason Mother mentioned this at all, I think, is that she's very worried about Chet Arthur. She ran a story one time in *Classics* which he didn't like. He tried to get her fired—but the Morrises stuck up for her."

Sandor laughed ominously. "Revenge is the motor of much human endeavor, Rossiterre, sweet balm on the wounds of the *wronged*." Good will oozed, but Ross made no mistake, the Veruckt mind was ticking along. "I think *brilliant* Sandor Veruckt will telephone your mother and ask her for the pleasure of her company at luncheon or dinner. Do you think Mrs. Drysdale would consent to have dinner with me, Rossiterre?"

"I'm sure she would."

What did Sandor want? That Rossiter call Thelma and tell her she was going to hear from a Mr. Veruckt and to be nice to him?

"And perhaps, then, Sandor Veruckt Associates will take a *very small* position in this matter of Chester Arthur vis-à-vis MorrisCom."

So there, Rossiter had covered himself as best he could. He patted himself on the back. Yes, he had come across in the nick of time—and if Sandor did throw money at MorrisCom, it could only help push the price up. Rossiter Addey might yet acquire hero status in Las Vegas.

He pulled his Ford into the driveway and disentangled his legs.

The Maid of Lourdes met him at the door of the house, bursting with a Message.

117

There had been a phone call. *Señor Mr. Addey to telephone Clara*.

Rossiter was not surprised. He was pleased Clara had called. It would not have been easy for her, waiting for a moment alone, against her better judgment, calling, hoping to get him. She hadn't been able to stop herself. She couldn't help it, could she?

Poor Clara . . .

Chapter Eleven

*I*t was tragic, Thelma Drysdale always said, that Wilkey Morris Senior had spawned such an ugly and malicious twit as Wilkey Morris Junior, that such an overfed precosity should be scion to the family business, which they called Morris Communications but was MorrisCom on the stock exchange.

Wilkey Senior had always given Thelma full credit for making *Classics* the brilliant success that it was—a style setter and publishing pacemaker. But Wilkey Junior would never, ever do the same. To speak of generosity or magnanimity in the same breath as Wilkey Junior was out of place.

Well, Wilkey Junior had come to work after college not knowing a hem from a hamstring. He'd practically needed toilet training, and to be told where to sit . . . all the while blinking those big blue eyes so disingenuously; he made Thelma quite ill.

What a God-awful monster he had become. He preened, his manners were disgraceful. He was coy, sly, and right now he was giving Thelma's features editor, Esther Murat, the very hell of a time about her fondness for "boring" stories about women's rights, abortion, care of unwed mothers, and the like. Wilkey Junior was specifically bothered by a long feature on Paula Keats, brain surgeon and divorced mother of six, currently running for the U.S. Senate from one of the mid-western grassroots states.

"Boring, Esther, boring, boring, *boring*," Wilkey Junior raved. "The woman has nothing *to say*! Her children *hate her*!

She doesn't know how *to dress* . . . *and* her ex-husband tells us she's lousy *in bed*. I mean, Esther, what year are we in?''

Thelma didn't flinch. Esther was tough enough to take it; she was always on the edge of violence, always ready to quit, to shove Wilkey Junior's tonsils right up his . . . Thelma wouldn't repeat it, not even to herself, privately.

"We got good mail on that!" Esther growled.

"So, you disagree, Esther? You disagree with me?" Wilkey Junior's voice rose; he passed into his familiar ecstasy of intimidation. This was *his* conference room—he could say what he wished.

"Wilkey," Thelma stated, very deliberately, "we are a serious publication." She stared down her nose at him; she'd been told she had the nose for doing precisely that. "A serious magazine . . ."

Wilkey Junior laughed shrilly. He tried on his most supercilious smirk. "Thelma, you know very well that women are interested in three things, and *three things only*." He was in Heaven. His puffy cheeks quivered. Was he not the most conceited man in the world? "Women are interested in *clothes* and fashion and how they look *and smell*. Number two, they're interested in where to go for *vacation*. And number three, *romance*. Tell me I'm wrong."

"You're wrong," Esther exclaimed heatedly. She shook her small head defiantly. "As you know, Wilkey," Esther added, "I disagree with you most vehemently on that point."

"I do know that, Murat!"

Thelma said coolly, "Wilkey, *Classics* cannot be one hundred percent frivolous.''

His frown turned to a scowl. She was taunting him and knew it. But, Thelma considered, things were reaching a crossroads, particularly if the Chet Arthur rumor was true. Wilkey Junior might not be their master much longer.

She felt Esther tensing beside her, getting ready to attack.

"Wilkey, women are interested in life too, not merely Trivia. . . .''

Wilkey Junior's body jerked furiously. He was aware that his detractors, more than a few of them right in these offices, referred to him behind his back as the Prince of Trivia; and he was very sensitive to any such allusions. Somebody had filled his office with all of the editions of the game by the same name, and he'd hit the ceiling.

"Never mind!" His spare chin shook petulantly. Lips pursed, he ran his hand back through his salt-and-pepper hair. "Jesus! I think we've discussed everything, wouldn't you say? You may go, Esther!"

Esther jumped up gratefully. She'd had it.

"And Thelma?"

"I've covered everything I had."

Her main item for the meeting had been to propose the series on Twentieth Century American Courtesans. Wilkey Junior hadn't any negative thoughts about the idea—the subject was much closer to his heart than abortion. Thelma suggested they hire an outside woman writer for the job, somebody of the caliber of Shana Alexander.

"Oh, *her*," Wilkey had snorted angrily.

Thelma was getting up to follow Esther out of the conference room when Wilkey Junior stopped her.

"A word, Thelma . . . ." He waited until Esther had shut the door. Whatever was coming, Thelma was ready, clipboard held protectively across her chest. Fortuitously, she had worn one of her prized rings that morning—young Hildy Beckmann had admired it excessively over the breakfast table. The ring was a huge, uncut emerald shaped like the Rock of Gibraltar, in a heavy gold setting. If it came to that, she could always slug Wilkey Junior with it.

It caught his eye. But he forced himself to look away. "That woman has *got to go*!"

"Esther?"

"Of course, Esther! The woman hates me. And I hate her. Besides which, I have the feeling she doesn't have the *vaguest* idea what she's doing."

"But she does, Wilkey. She is my right hand."

"She's ugly, Thelma, and a *pain in the ass*. She doesn't know how to dress and all she's interested in are those *boring* women's causes. . . ." He paused, waiting to come to the boil, then hissed, "Thelma, I'm telling you, I think the woman is a dyke or something!"

"A dyke? *Dyke?*" Thelma repeated the awful word as if she didn't know what it meant, or didn't want to know. She struck her ring forcefully against the edge of the conference table. "That is an awful thing for you to say!"

"Thelma, Jesus! Where do you live? Up in the clouds someplace?"

Coldly Thelma said, "If I do, Wilkey, I certainly don't choose to dirty my silvery wings with such filthy black thoughts as you've just expressed."

"Jesus!" Wilkey Junior's mouth dropped open for rebuttal but nothing came out. He grunted to himself a few times, squealed like a piglet, then finally was able to say, "Chet Arthur's offer is becoming very real, Thelma—and you may be out on *your ass.*"

Thelma prided herself on putting a brave face to any adversity. And she did so now.

"Whatever happens, Wilkey, I *will* survive."

"Congratulations," he sneered. "You are aware, I take it, that Chet Arthur hates you."

"I'm aware of that."

"We saved your bacon once."

She knew all these arguments. "Your father did, not you. Also, may I remind you, Wilkey, if you had gone ahead and fired me, as Chet Arthur demanded, your organization would've lost all claim to journalistic independence."

"We *could* save you again," he said, surprisingly. "If we wanted we could probably write you into the merger agreement."

"I would not expect your father to go to bat for me again," Thelma said, shrugging. "If Chester Arthur wants my head, he can have it. *I will survive,* Wilkey."

"I'm sure you will," he said. "I should just tell you, the way it's stacking up now, I'll be staying with the company as president of Morris Media, a new division of the combined companies." He paused, to make sure Thelma got the point. "So I'd be in charge of the magazines . . . including *Classics.* And I wonder how you'd respond to a little idea of mine, Thelma? I've been thinking it'd be interesting to have a *man* as editor."

She didn't react, not at all, not a blink or cry. He would be very disappointed if he expected Thelma Drysdale to cave in.

"It seems to me," he continued, "that a magazine aimed at women might better be run by a man—is that not a *delicious* thought, Thelma?"

"Not merely delicious, *Wilkey Junior,* but totally *yummy!*"

Grasping her clipboard in her arms, Thelma stood up next to the end of the conference table, staring him down, the uncut emerald only inches from his nose. The temptation . . .

Without another word, she left the room. Wilkey would be livid—but so be it. Forcing herself not to scream in anger, Thelma headed into the big editorial office, marched between filing cabinets and reached her corner office.

Her secretary Terry was waiting impatiently. It was nearly time for her lunch break.

"A guy called . . ." Terry read carefully off her *While You Were Away* note. "His name was Sandor Veruckt. Says you two met at a party and your son Ross works for him. Is that right?"

Thelma rapped an affirmative.

She went into her office with the piece of paper on which Veruckt's number had been jotted. How many years of hard labor had she given Morris Communications? In the end, what had she gotten for her brilliance—a poke in the eye with a sharp stick at the hands of a low-grade moron like Wilkey Morris Junior. Thelma knew there was nothing Wilkey Senior could do for her this time.

She sat at her desk, staring at Sandor Veruckt's name. What could *he* want, this Hungarian whom she remembered looking like a magician or Gypsy violinist, not a banker—not her sort of banker, anyway.

But maybe . . . maybe there was something in it for Rossiter. God knew, Rossiter needed all the help he could get.

In the old days, before the era of her glass cubicle, whenever Thelma had had a very private call to make, her practice had been to crouch behind her desk so that nobody could possibly read her lips or overhear.

She had never lost this habit. She punched Sandor Veruckt's number, then doubled over so she was in effect speaking to her knees.

"Hallo?"

"Mr. Sandor Veruckt, please."

"This is Sandor!"

Surely the man could afford a secretary.

"Ah, Mr. Veruckt. You *are* Mr. Veruckt?"

"It is not *Santy Claus* speaking. You have reached Sandor on his private line. And who is this speaking?"

"I am Thelma Drysdale."

Chapter
Twelve

*P*rince Spurzov, his blood as old and gnarled as the most terrible of the Ivans, this same Alexei stared for some time at his reflection in the heavily gilded mirror hanging over the Louis Something chest of drawers with legs as pretty as any ballerina's in the dressing room of his apartment at Richlands.

He looked wonderful, better than he had any right to look, given his mourning for Ludmilla—which *was* receding. Alex had dressed with care in his usual costume—sharply pressed gray flannels, a gray silk shirt open at the collar, loosely-knotted silk foulard to cover his neck—foulard brought to him, he hated to remember, from Paris or Rome, he couldn't recall, by the poor lad.

With his silver-backed brushes, Alex persuaded his wiry hair into straight-back retreat from his high forehead. He'd had Peat drive him down to the Beverly Hills Hotel barbershop for a trim. Nothing like having the works to boost your spirits, the Americans always said—and he wanted to look just-so for Ludmilla's memorial, called for early Friday afternoon.

Finally Alex slapped a bit of astringent after-shave on his face. The fumes made his eyes water, but only for a second. Spurzov eyes had always been clear; his sparkled like sixty.

Alex was taking special care this morning because the Richards wives were calling. According to Tom Addey, the two Mrs. Richards had always harbored a secret admiration for the way Ludmilla adorned herself and they asked for the privilege of rooting through her closets and *the honor,* if Alex didn't mind, of choosing for themselves one or two of Ludmilla's caftans.

Wasn't it, after all, a very flattering request? Ludmilla, of course, would laugh. In life she had never treated the two Richards women with any great kindness.

But she was gone now, and Alex was still alive. Dick Richards was, according to Tom, prepared to be very generous about Alex's use of Richland. Alex was to have the cars and most of Ludmilla's jewelry.

So, he could afford to behave like a Prince among princes.

His blazer hung ready on the butler's helper in the sitting room of his suite. It was not quite the appointed time of eleven A.M.

Alex glanced again at the front pages of the *Los Angeles Times* and sighed. Nothing ever changed, did it? Plane crashes, ecological disasters, nuclear arms negotiations, politics, lottery winners, assassinations . . . a good many of the latter. History was constantly re-upping itself that way.

Did history repeat, double back upon itself . . . or *backfire*? So unexpectedly too. Alex could muse for a while about that: Ludmilla was suddenly dead, and for the first time in decades Alexei was alone. *Alone!* Ludmilla was gone. This one beloved woman, this woman who made sense of existence, of life . . . even justified the creation of the Universe, *she was gone*, forever. And Alex, he told himself again, *he was alone*.

It was a shattering thought. And its effect on his life might be devastating.

He picked up a cigarette and lit it thoughtfully, sorrowfully, mournfully, and carried it to the window. The garden was damp from a light rain during the night, but now the sun was out. He could feel the warmth of it, watch the steam rise from the walkways through the garden, next to the pool.

How had Cazimir gotten down there from Ludmilla's bedroom? The walking dead? Pistol in hand? Staggering rigor mortis?

No, this was impossible. There had been no sign of life in the poor lad when Alex had left him. The only possibility was that somebody had moved the body. It had not been Alex Spurzov. It could not have been Tom Addey.

That left Peat.

Just then the house phone rang. It was the same Peat, announcing the arrival at Richlands of Mrs. Rose Richards.

Alex shook himself free of the puzzle, of his thoughts about Ludmilla, Creation, and Eternity. Slipping into his blazer, he brushed imaginary lint from his shoulders, checked the mirror one more time, then stepped into the corridor, trod the thin carpet to the staircase, and descended to the circular marble foyer.

Peat was waiting, his ferret face haunted but secretive, uncommunicative—uncooperative, if it came to that.

"Mrs. Richards is in the gallery, Prince."

Peat adored calling him Prince. Alex nodded his thanks in princely fashion.

Alex didn't see too well at long distances. Perhaps it was that he sensed her presence first, her scent, could that be? The electrical emanations from her person? The vibes, as such sensations were called.

Alex began to tremble. His step became insecure. He gripped the wrought-iron railing which guarded the three steps down into the gallery.

Carefully, he walked toward her.

No. Yes. He was stunned. His mind began to overflow with Russian words. The words for amazement, horror, shock, adoration . . .

No, he did not remember ever having seen *this* Mrs. Richards before, this very dark-haired Mrs. Richards with the Gypsyish face, lighted from a hundred different angles, its planes faceted like a precious stone. In such a way did her features react to the light. She stared at him sullenly; at the same time eagerly, curiously; with hostility, but at the same time with a fondness or amusement in her eyes. Her skin was dark, not of tone but of resonance, of depth, as if she was turned partially inside out, showing her innermost being outside herself, like a heart on the sleeve. Her lips were full, lipsticked carelessly, her eyes gray and round, and they were fixed on him alone as he came closer.

"Prince Spurzov, I'm Rose Richards."

Her voice was low, contralto, tremolo, husky, like a stringed instrument.

For the love of God—*was this Ludmilla back from the dead*?

Alex hardly dared touch her hand, for fear there would be nothing there, that she would fade and turn to smoke and drift away. He tried to smile.

Realistically, he knew Mrs. Rose Richards was there! His smile became bolder.

126

Alex dared to speak. "But there were to be two Missus Richards."

"At the last minute Marcia couldn't come, Prince Spurzov."

"Please . . . I'm Alex."

Her hand was plump and warm like a child's, and childlike too. It seemed sticky, as if she'd recently eaten a Danish pastry and hadn't wiped her fingers quite clean.

"And I'm Rose. We've never met, Alex." Alexei was always sensitive to accents. Rose's was a bit coarse, tuned by a background he didn't at once recognize. "We didn't come here that much when the old man was alive," Rose went on, "and so I never met Princess Spurzov more than three or four times."

"And, unluckily," Alex gushed, "I would not have been here often in those days. Though I sometimes was. Rodney and I became friends, despite our love for the same woman."

Rose nodded. "The old man didn't have many friends."

Calling Rodney "the old man" didn't sound to Alex very respectful, but it would be like her to despise Rodney.

"So now, Rose, you are Richard's wife, or Ralph's?"

"Oh, sorry . . . Dick's."

"And a mother?"

Rose didn't have to answer. Yes, there would be the difference. Ludmilla had never had children—God knows, she *should* have. She'd been built for it, expansive of loin and deep of pubic cavity, lush like a sweet swamp. If she had had children, she might have looked more like Rose, whose figure had not gone untouched by the experience.

But Rose wore her clothes exactly like Ludmilla. Black slacks were tight over her buttocks, and a loose, woolly, bright red sweater covered her top, sleeves pushed back carelessly from blessedly slim forearms. Alex concluded immediately that Rose wouldn't be wearing any undergarments, not in the morning, not if she was as much like Ludmilla in spirit as he had concluded she was.

"I've got a couple of daughters," she acknowledged, but not with any great pride or enthusiasm. She was obviously not greatly pleased either that he had asked.

"Please," Alex blurted. Please, what? He was confused by the moody face she showed then. "Could I get you coffee, or a drink?"

"Thanks, Alex," Rose muttered. "What I'd really like is a

diet drink." She patted her behind disgustedly. "I'm trying to take some inches off this. . . ."

No, no, Alex wanted to scream, *don't touch it*! Leave it exactly as is!

He went back across the gallery, pressed the button for Peat and quickly returned to her.

"You are . . . a most striking woman," he cried happily. "I congratulate you." So saying, Alex touched his hair, then puffed up his foulard. "You are perfect!"

"Fat," she said perversely, enjoying that too—as she would.

When Peat appeared at the steps, Alex ordered her the soda, and for himself, daringly, a very cold vodka. Then he closed on Rose again, hardly able to keep his hands off her, urging her to sit down in one of the more comfortable overstuffed chairs at the far end of the gallery, which was warmed by the sunshine.

Then, only then, he took her fingers and carried them to his lips.

"It is so wonderful to have a beautiful woman in the house again. I beg you to believe me!"

Rose's eyes jumped, leapt, cavorted with joy and gratitude and the beginning of invitation. She wet her pouty lips, exposing sharp white teeth.

"You call *me* beautiful?" she challenged.

"I surely do!" He stared, unable to pull his eyes away from her face. When Peat appeared carrying a silver serving tray with crystal glass, the can of diet soda, iced vodka cup, and the Stolichnaya bottle, Alex hardly looked at him. Her gray eyes were destroying him. Alex felt his age, so old, but at the same time, simultaneously, very young—as young as he had been when he'd found Ludmilla in a Bulgarian sheep pasture.

Stumbling, not finding sensible words, Alex asked her about the children again. Rose frowned.

"The oldest is fourteen and the other is twelve. And they're both brats. Don't laugh. I mean it!" She did mean it. Her lips dipped into displeasure. "Thank God I don't have to see them in the daytime. At night when they get home from school, I can duck upstairs while they're making up to their father and watching TV."

Alex could not contain himself. "Beautiful Rose . . . excuse me, but how fortunate you are to have children. I regret so much that Ludmilla and I never—"

She stopped him derisively.

"Oh, yes, of course, I'm only kidding. Actually, we get along wonderfully, they're beautiful children, and I love them madly!"

"Ah, better," Alex sighed. "And then too, you have Dick."

"Oh, yes, Alex!" she said. "Open the door, Richard. But don't close it on me, Dick!" She laughed boisterously.

The awful play on words didn't register immediately. Then he cried, "Naughty! Naughty!" and shook his finger at her.

Abruptly, Rose stopped chuckling and surprisingly announced, "There's Russian blood in my family, you know."

"As I suspected!" Well, he'd known she wasn't Mexican. Now his smile *must* dazzle her. "I knew it!"

"My great-grandfather came from Odessá. He was a Jew."

Once again! How else to explain Rose's cheekbones, the flashing eyes?

"So, we have something else in common."

"What else? Besides that we're both Russian?" Rose demanded coyly.

Alex shrugged. He didn't want to tell her about Ludmilla, how closely she resembled Ludmilla, in mind and body. No, it would be far too complex a thing to explain—it was not something that would occur to everybody. One would have to be very old, or very young, to appreciate what he was feeling. Rose stared at him probingly, her lips parted in a way that might jar him loose of his bones.

"Well," he muttered, "that you're a woman . . . and I'm a man."

"Aha!" she said. Impulsively, Rose seized his arm, grabbed his hand and squeezed it. Her eyes gleamed. Then she changed the subject. "I know all about your Fabergé egg, Alex."

"But there is no secret about it."

He kept his eye on those lips, devouring them in his mind, as if taking small bites of a delicious piece of fruit.

"Could I see it?"

Alex shook his head. "I am so sorry, *darling,* but the Egg is not kept here. Oh no, it is deep and darkly guarded in a bank vault."

Rose looked disappointed. "If I owned a thing like that, I'd want to see it every day—"

"But for the insurance!"

"I'd hold it in my hands," she exclaimed, eyes shining, "and against my cheek. I'd kiss it and I think I'd rub it all over my body."

Oh, God, he thought, yes, Ludmilla had said the same thing—exactly—the same words.

"Would you?"

One could never take Rose for a married woman living in the lap of luxury in opulent, dullest Bel Air, the priciest suburb of Los Angeles. She sounded faintly . . . what? Like the voluptuous Narcissa created by Emile Zola, Nana. That quality had been present in Ludmilla too, the hint of narcissism. About both of them was this slightly sluttish thing.

A charming sluttishness, perhaps like Madame Bovary. Forget Nana. Yes, rather in a driven, single-minded devotion to love and passion.

Charming, charming.

Rose glanced at him inquiringly over her glass. She had downed half of the soda thirstily, reminding Alex of his untouched vodka. He reached for it and hoisted a toast.

"To beauty!"

Rose beamed again as Alex gave himself the vodka in one fiery shot.

"I think you're trying very hard to flatter me, Alex," she teased.

"Am I?" he responded quickly. "Yes, I suppose I am. I beg your pardon, dear young lady, but you see I cannot help myself."

"Really?" Her eyes dared him to go on.

"As I said, darling, such beauty starts the words flying, like game birds flushed in the forest."

"My," Rose said quietly, her hot eyes never moving, "that's some way of saying it . . . really beautiful, I think, Alex. I *am* flattered."

"You should not be. I speak the truth," he whispered hoarsely.

Alex took more vodka, gazing at her devotedly, then pushed himself forward to take Rose's hand again. The stickiness had run a little from her cold glass but Alex ignored it, pressing fervently and making to kiss her fingers again.

Distinctly he heard a small gasp of pleasure. No, Rose was not merely a settled California matron. The heat was in her blood, as it was in his. But remember, he warned himself, she was the wife of Dick Richards, his benefactor, upon whose good will Alex depended—at least until he was prepared to pack his Vuitton luggage and be on his way. The way he felt, departure could be at any moment.

Alex chuckled softly. This soothing, massaging laugh was one of his most powerful weapons. Rose sighed deeply.

"But," he said softly, watching how her lips twitched with lust, "you've come here to have a look at Ludmilla's closet. Shall we go upstairs?"

Upstairs? Rose seemed to gasp again and faintly blush. This was a surprise, but he must remember something else—she was *not* Ludmilla. To him, she might seem like Ludmilla Reincarnated. But Rose was not Ludmilla. Mention upstairs and the most liberated woman blushed. But not Ludmilla. To her, upstairs meant bedroom, bedroom meant bed and bed meant passion. The associations were all there, all logical and improper.

Still holding Rose's hand, Alex rose and helped her up too, much as he might have a Royal Princess, escorting her to the dance floor . . . or boudoir. Back across the gloomy galleria he walked her, to the steps, to the circular, circular entry, then up the curved staircase.

What went around, came around.

A happy thought tugged at his sleeve. How would it be if Alex cuckolded Richard Richards? And had the pleasure of young Ludmilla all over again, at one and the same moment in time?

How that would make Ludl roar!

Chapter Thirteen

*I*t was a fifteen or twenty minute walk back to the hotel, on the longer side perhaps, because of the Friday-afternoon traffic on Wilshire Boulevard and Westwood Village side streets. In early afternoon people were already heading out of town for the weekend, producing more smog and congestion just in order to escape the same thing.

But Clara supposed you couldn't blame them for trying.

She and Rossiter were stuck on the corner of Wilshire and Westwood Boulevard for what seemed like an hour waiting for the light to change. Then, the street was so wide you practically had to run across to make it before the light changed again.

After the service Tom had gone off with Alex in Martha's cramped sports car—returning to a gathering of the bereaved, mainly men, it seemed, at Richlands.

"Why they had to jam into her car, I can't tell you," Clara muttered.

"Togetherness?"

"Well," she said, staring straight ahead, "it's like they plot to leave us alone, dear boy."

Then why did he look so indifferent?

There was no use trying to ignore how she felt. Her whole body was flushed; pins and needles seemed to pick at her legs, her thighs. She was warm and uncomfortable. Anticipatory, was that it? Trying to shake it off, she said, "There couldn't be much more of a finality to a life. . . . If I'd been close to Ludmilla, I might have come apart too."

For Alex Spurzov had wept uninhibitedly into his handkerchief at the service.

"Tom said that's what Ludmilla wanted. No eulogies, just the music. One hour of it and good-bye. Farewell with Chopin."

Say what you wanted about her, Ludmilla was dead. Clara had to admit she'd begun to wish she'd known the lady, though Tom had told her that Ludmilla had never particularly liked women or made an effort to get along with them—maybe because she never knew when she'd be taking a husband or two away from them.

"I did not expect there'd be so many people," Clara said. "Did you know who any of them were?"

"I recognized a couple of bankers," Rossiter said disinterestedly. "Tom says Ludmilla always had a thing about bankers. Two or three dress designers. A couple of guys there from the studios, I believe . . . and just a crazy collection of her friends. She knew a lot of people."

And now a bunch of them were on their way to Richlands for a farewell drink to the old crone. It was mainly the men, obviously—except for Martha, her daughter, who'd go anywhere for a party, invited or not. But of course it would pep Alex up to have a pretty girl around, Tom had said.

Tom, Tom, did it always have to be Tom saying things, telling them things, pointing out *things?* Why was she so sick of Tom saying things?

"It's very depressing, if you ask me," she murmured, half to herself.

Naturally, she was speaking of Tom.

"Chopin *was* her choice," Rossiter said.

"Oh, shit on Chopin! I'm sorry I ever mentioned it."

"I'm sorry too," Rossiter said calmly.

"Oh, never mind."

She wished it was dark, at least then she wouldn't have to look at him anymore, and everything else she didn't like about this place.

Poor Rossiter, why did she treat him badly? It was not his fault she had these bad feelings of self-disgust mixed with desire. Self-hate butted against yearning.

"How's your father-in-law?" she asked neutrally.

Rossiter glanced at her. "He's okay . . . seems okay."

"So you're not coming up to the city for my opening?"

Rossiter shrugged. "Tell me how I can get away."

"Just come!"

"I don't see how I can. And even if I did . . . . I mean, Clara, where is this getting us?"

More angrily than before, she snapped, "You weren't thinking about that the other night."

"You're married to Tom."

"Your father," she reminded him cruelly. "Bastard! Look what you've done to him—no." She backed down instantly. "Forget I said it. Sorry. Sorry."

By now the Westwood Marquis had come into view, like a ship afloat on walls of ivy. It was a cheerful presence.

Clara took his arm, trying to match Rossiter's long strides. At least he was here. Tom seemed so far away from her now. Clara couldn't explain why; had he been so knocked out by Ludmilla's death? But there was a new restlessness between them, a strange, silent clamoring of *Man the Lifeboats,* though she couldn't pinpoint anything that had changed.

Maybe it was Clara who was changing. Was it *that*? Wasn't she too young for that?

"It also occurred to me," she mentioned matter-of-factly, "that you might like to come up to the vineyard for Christmas. We're all going to be there, as usual. There's always room. . . ."

"At Morelli Vineyards?" Rossiter sounded shocked. *"To drive myself crazy?"*

"It doesn't always have to be *that*," Clara retorted grimly. "You'd think that's all there was to a relationship. You know I'm fond of you, besides *that*."

"That?" he repeated, grinning.

"I mean making love, you bastard! I said I'm fond of you. I can look at you without wanting to tumble, you know."

"I can't!"

He put it innocently enough, this truth that fond looks were not enough. Clara pushed herself ahead in time, imagining they were upstairs. She was wet with desire—and even now didn't understand why. What was there in Rossiter that she couldn't find in Tom? You couldn't tell them apart in the dark, and certainly not lying in bed. Wasn't it all too stupid?

"You know I can't get away," Rossiter said. "Serena . . . Bud is supposed to stay in town, after he comes out of the hospital. It's such a goddamn mess, Clara."

Fiercely, she clutched his arm. "Come by yourself! You'll have to run away eventually—it might as well be now."

"Run away?" Again he seemed shocked.

"Of course," Clara exclaimed softly. "You don't think I can keep this up, do you? 'This lie,' as they say in the movies?"

"Well, Clara . . . I—"

"You don't know what to say, do you? Well? What *do* you think? That I shouldn't have married Tom. That I should've known better . . . and you should have too."

"How could I have stopped you?" He looked at her in disbelief. "You walked away with him."

"He was thrilling. A big lawyer, well-known, invited everywhere. Remember, Stan Gates was a nothing, less than a nothing. . . ."

"Like me," Rossiter said miserably.

Poor Rossiter. Poor Rossiter, but *not nothing*.

"No, for God's sake!" she said. Clara could have kicked herself. What was she suggesting—that she run away with Rossiter, a repeat performance of her elopement?

"I'm not sure you know what you're saying. Do you mean that we—you and I—are going to get together? After all these years, you're going to—" He couldn't say it.

Clara did. "Leave Tom? I don't know. What else can I do? I can't go on deceiving him."

"We could end it!"

"No," she cried. "Not today . . . anyway. Next week. We end it when I leave. That's it. Tomorrow, finished! Yes."

"Okay."

She glared at him. "But whatever happens to us, you've got to get away from Serena. Promise! She's destroying you, Ross."

Slowly, he said, "I am going to get away from her. I'm picking my time—"

"Are you?"

Was he? She'd bet he couldn't name any time that he had picked. Rossiter would never do anything by snap decision. The decision most likely would be made *for* him . . . probably by Serena herself.

He'd want to flee but he didn't know how.

Nor did she. Sometimes Clara dreamt of waking up in cities like Venice or Nice or Paris in big beds covered in heavy cotton sheets, awaking with a mysterious stranger beside her, a body warm with sex, the bed smelling of crisp laundering, the smell of fresh coffee and bread, the smell, just the plain smell of *life*.

It was as simple as that. She was that way, that was all there was to it. Never satisfied, always searching for more and better. Perhaps she had to admit it—she was no good at living a secret life of disrepute. But this was the only time. She was faithful . . . to the family, at least.

The lobby of the hotel was warm, and brilliantly friendly.

Rossiter stopped. "Shall we say good-bye?" he asked uncomfortably.

"No. I'll get the key."

They didn't say anything in the elevator. Awkwardly, in the hallway, Rossiter spoke.

"I was surprised to see Martha."

Stiffly, hardly able to answer, Clara said, "She's on her way to Palm Springs to see Stan."

She stuck the key in the lock and opened the door. It swung back and she stepped inside. He followed and shut it.

"Put the chain on," Clara ordered. "Do you want a drink? Take off your coat."

He was wearing a raincoat and carrying an umbrella, the ever-cautious Rossiter.

"What would you like?" he asked politely. "Should I make it?"

She nodded at him, still not understanding what was happening to her. Now and again, she believed, people did come to spots in the road, not precisely crossroads, but places where they stopped and asked themselves where they were bound, what on earth they were up to.

"Where are we going?"

He paid no attention, of course, not literal-minded Rossiter. In a moment he was beside her with a glass.

"Here."

That's where they were going? Here? Well, it did look that way.

It was vodka on ice. Clara sipped gratefully; maybe this would straighten her out.

"I want to speak very frankly," she said, her gaze direct. He didn't falter, didn't try to look away. "I'm married to your father and he's a fabulous man. He really is. So why do I want something . . . else? Is it Ludmilla come to haunt me?"

Rossiter looked uncomfortable. "You're upset, that's all," he said. "The Chopin . . . oh, sorry."

She shook her head. "Don't you understand what I'm saying? Would you kiss me, right now?"

There was great concern in his eyes. He did not understand her. But he wanted her.

Impatiently Clara turned her head and their lips met.

He reacted as violently as he always did. A tremor shook him. But he should not be frightened, Clara thought; her kiss was warm, and very beautiful. And as it continued, his shoulders untensed. Clara did not move; she did it all with her mouth, arms hanging limply at her sides. His big hands were on her shoulders, holding her there . . . yet *not holding her there* if she should choose to run. Even in this he was polite.

Clara touched his lips with the tip of her tongue. He uttered a sharp cry.

It was up to Clara now. They were hanging in midair, like trapeze artists—they would catch the rope, or fall. Rather, *she* would catch it or they would fall.

This would be the worst sin. Not absolutely the worst; there were others, more unholy things than this. Nothing could be so bad if you desired it so much. And why not do it, why not make love to him, *why not* seduce him, for it came to that. He would never make the first move.

Clara dropped her head but didn't move from those hands. She didn't dare look at him for fear of what he'd see. They stood like that for seconds, and seconds more, touching lightly. Clara heard her heart pumping.

It was not as though she didn't have opportunities to cheat on her husband. Nor did she hesitate because she was so sure of him. Tom was capable of adventure too—remember Ludmilla! They had never discussed the matter of faithfulness. She had been in love with Tom then; was she in love with Tom now?

"Sit down," she whispered. "I'm so tired.'

She pushed him to the couch and knelt beside him, her arms around his neck. She kissed him again, firmly, decisively.

"I'm undone," she said.

She pulled at his tie and unbuttoned his shirt, then slid her hands to his pants, pulled the buckle loose and unzipped him, never losing her momentum, then put her mouth to flesh, hardening beneath her lips.

"Jesus, Clara!"

She stopped long enough to say, "Me thinks he doth protest too much."

His hands were around her, then, swiftly, clumsily unbuttoning and unzipping and again, within the count of ten, on the couch, then sliding off the couch to the carpet. She turned him around and he put his lips to her, as she to him, at once focusing the flush she'd felt through her body, focusing it there at the core of her trouble. And then, lastly, the *grand finale*, she had taken him inside her, holding him tightly, he making love to her for the last time. Yes, it would be, she promised, ready to scream it out, this very last, definitely last, time. Ever. He must have felt it too. He was so gigantic, his force, his flesh, his fire.

And then it was not possible for him to hold back. It was all much too exciting making love to Clara Morelli Gates Addey. With a last plunging dive, as if from a cliff into the blue Caribbean, he crested and grunted, and grunted and crested, continuing until Clara uttered a muffled scream, then bleats of fulfillment, satisfaction, pleasure.

She realized he had begun to cry. She didn't acknowledge it, merely lay beneath him, stroking his back. Then he shyly pulled away.

For a second Clara feared he would say Sorry or Thank You. She didn't wait for that.

"Positively," she muttered, "positively, assuredly the final performance, ever. . . . Help me up, please?"

On her feet, Clara gathered her things, scattered by now here and there, and went into the bathroom. There wasn't time for a shower. No, she'd better not leave him alone—his despair was so fierce it moved her.

Tom had been a very good lover, Clara admitted it. But Rossiter was different—more than just forbidden fruit. Rossiter's quality of quiet desperation made him attractive, special; she knew it. He made love as if the world was at the moment of ending—and maybe it was.

So what, then? Drop all caution and make love? *Poor Rossiter.* Had he enjoyed it?

Clara was dressed again. Now, she ordered herself, wash away the tears of sweat, of desire, and fulfillment. Then fresh lipstick. She was ready. Instant self-rejuvenation. Now what about Rossiter?

But he was all back together when she emerged. In itself this was a little surprising. Rossiter had even put fresh ice in their vodkas.

"Here . . . Clara," he said, handing her the same glass the second time.

He was smiling.

Clara took the glass, then held it up. "Farewell . . ."

"Farewell, Clara." He continued to smile. She realized, though, he was not happy. The happy expression was false. "It was nice while it lasted. . . . I'm sorry."

"Sorry?" Now, she was put out. "Why sorry? Don't get the idea you forced me—".

"No, no," he said, too complacently. "I'm just sorry I couldn't go longer—you know what I mean."

"Yes, I know," she hissed. "That's all right, Ross. Older women get a little tired . . . faster."

His face fell. He wasn't as clever as he figured.

Glumly, from his chair, he pointed out the window. It was already getting dark.

"Look," he said. "See the initials? R . . R . . . C? That's the Richards building. The Rodney Richards Corporation. Rodney's son didn't come to the memorial, Tom said."

"Forget Tom," she demanded. "Tell me something."

"Sure."

"Do you feel you got your money's worth? Not that you paid . . . I mean, I bet Serena's never given you a . . . what do we say? Piece? A piece like that? Tell me the truth."

He stared at his crotch. "Never."

"Just remember that, then, Ross. . . ." *Poor Rossiter.* "There's plenty of it out there. You're not dependent on that little nothing. You promised me you'd dump her! Don't forget, I'll hold you to it. Come to San Francisco. I'll fix you up with somebody good."

"You."

"No. Last performance. I don't need this momentary madness, a passing madness in my decreasing years."

"Please, Clara—"

"You know what they say," she went on defiantly, "there's winter in her bones, but spring in her ass."

"Stop it, Clara."

139

"Sorry," she muttered. "I'm glad we're leaving tomorrow."

"I'm sorry you're leaving." He meant it too. When had Tom made her feel so *necessary*?

Clara sighed. "C'mere."

Chapter Fourteen

"**B**y the way," Jim Madison said coldly but with surprising sympathy, "our Russian friend has been executed. We just had word. It happened three months ago, in a military prison in Kazakhstan."

"You mean Nick?"

Madison nodded. "I'm sorry to tell you this. But, of course, you have to know."

Seth went numb. He stared at Madison's bleached-white face.

"It was inevitable in the circumstances," Madison said. "If it means anything posthumously, he was a terrific asset, for us a gold mine of information."

Seth nodded slowly, then bitterly said, "You know we were betrayed. Somebody here—"

"No! This has not been proven. It is not known," Madison said severely, "and it does you no credit to say so. You can't be sure Nick didn't stumble."

This was possible, but Seth's intuition told him otherwise.

"*So*, it's because of *that* you don't want me back in Munich. I don't see the logic. . . ." Ordinarily Seth wouldn't have dreamt of speaking to Madison in such a way. "I see this is why you've put me on this nutty Ben Gazi thing."

Fortunately, Madison was in rather a good humor.

"Keep your head down, Addey. There's *somebody* out there. I would not like to lose you."

Seth didn't even try to reply. The intrigue had definitely

begun to sicken him. Now, to hear this news of Nick . . . Fortunately, Madison interrupted, saying there were other matters to be considered.

Madison delicately flexed his long fingers on the keyboard of a computer console to the left of his desk and called up on one blank wall of his monkish cell a picture of a swarthy-looking individual.

"The *very late* Cazimir Ben Gazi," Madison said pleasantly. "We would describe the features of his ugly face as bulbous, pouting, and decidedly not gorgeous." He chuckled a little. "The body has been shipped . . . thanks to your very helpful father. I would not personally have involved him. In any case, through a screw up of the airlines, the corpse was misdirected to Detroit," Madison growled disgustedly.

He hit another combination of his magic keys and now a blownup map of the Eastern Mediterranean appeared on the wall.

"I confess, Addey," Madison said, "that the most relaxing thing I know of is playing this machine. It is astonishing." He stood up and walked to the map. "Now then, Addey, we have Cazimir Ben Gazi on ice. What say we move him . . . where? Rhodes, Cyprus, Alexandria . . . Sicily?"

Pointing at the various significant locations, Madison's smug smile was like something painted on porcelain. In fact, he looked like a Dresden doll—albino eyebrows, long supercilious face, pointed chin; Madison exuded bleakness, as if he'd decided there was little hope for the future and had even jettisoned despair.

"I think Cyprus, sir."

"Why Cyprus?"

"There's a good deal of movement in and out of there these days."

"Correct!" Something new flashed in Madison's eye: malice. "We'll wash the deceitful Ben Gazi ashore in Cyprus. Yes, and thus will his murder, though presumably well-deserved, be transferred to another theater of operations."

It appeared, despite the flippant tone, that Madison and his boys were deeply disturbed by the Ben Gazi business. Nobody was buying the suicide angle. What a reversal of judgment about Ben Gazi there seemed to have been.

By the simple device of taking ten seconds of the time of a high-speed computer tucked away in the hills of Virginia and using only one phone number as a reference point—that of the

Richlands estate in Los Angeles—Madison's boys had unearthed Ben Gazi's Washington hideaway.

"Leased in the name of Smith." Madison laughed. "But this Smith turned out to be a wog of the Ben Gazi description, with an Arabic accent."

Madison would have known. During his years in covert he had specialized in Albanian affairs and had thus been exposed to Moslem terrorists.

"We would like to know, Addey, what information Cazimir Ben Gazi was carrying around in that oddly shaped head." Madison stared at him frostily, finally getting around to answering Seth's original question. "And *this* is the reason we've assigned you—not particularly to keep you away from Europe. You see, if somebody were *after you*, it wouldn't much matter where you were . . . *would it*?"

So, at the present time, Seth Addey was sitting in back of a functional designer desk in what would be termed a second bedroom-study of the Ben Gazi hideaway, not more than a few blocks from the power base of the Western world. Someone had been here before him, snooping; papers had been assembled by category on the desktop—receipts and bills addressed to J. Smith, stacks of neatly cut newspaper clippings. But not a letter or postcard. Not a diary. Certainly not the black book Sol Betancur had been concerned might surface.

Once again, having heard his boss's untiring exposition of the Devil's Theory—that there was a black purpose behind every political happening in the world, and that therefore not only Ben Gazi but Ludmilla Spurzova had been murdered, the wonder being that Alex Spurzov hadn't been *done* as well—Seth was definitely thinking about alternative professions. What about an advanced course at Princeton, for instance, at the feet of the master, George Kennan?

It was tricky, but a man *could* escape this line of work.

The study in which Seth was sitting was furnished anonymously—desk, two dull prints on the walls, a couch—in contrast to the living room, which was like a desert chieftain's tent: masses of pillows, low-slung couches, brass-topped coffee tables, and even a camel saddle or two.

The somewhat disgusting and dismal ambience made Seth think of Munich, and with regret, of the simple gemütlichkeit it looked like he'd be missing at Christmas time. Hildy had remained in New York. Just as well. He was in Washington. And yes, Katie Corcoran was also in Washington. Seth had dropped the Corky bit; Katie was her name. And he was half in love already.

But she complicated matters so enormously.

As the day moved toward darkness, the cold winter dusk stealing down the streets like a bandit, Seth allowed his thoughts to travel back to Moscow.

Poor Nick! Obviously Seth would have to settle it in his own mind. It would not be easy to put Nick's death into perspective. But as Madison had said, execution was in the cards. A highly placed bureaucrat within a sensitive ministry could not pass documents of any kind without knowing the ultimate price. Nick had never had any illusions about that. Why, then, had he risked it?

Or had Nick merely been used to set Seth up? That was also possible. No one would ever know the truth of it.

Seth stared morosely at a heap of cheap paperbacks and tatty news magazines his predecessor had made on the couch. He would have to go through them page by page, searching for a carelessly written note, phone number, whatever. . . .

And to what end? Ben Gazi was dead. If he had been blackmailing people, there'd be no more of that. So he had been involved in assassinations and the shipment of weapons to good and noble Freedom Fighters, the moral equivalent of the Founding Fathers? Well, he'd also been a swine.

They were not talking about any Nick.

As night fell, Seth considered ringing Katie-Corky Corcoran; no, better not use this phone, a hundred ears would be tuned in. He was going to see her later at her place. Should he call Hildy before he went over there?

Did the Madison-Kraszewski theory make sense at all? That Ben Gazi had been *done* by one of the Mideast terrorist gangs? Why would killers travel all the way to California to bump off Cazimir Ben Gazi? Why the big rush? It was fortunate, Madison said, that they had entrée to Alex Spurzov. And that General Kraszewski thought so highly of him, remembered him from the old days.

Obviously Madison had not been told the worst about Ben Gazi.

Three Italian-made suits hung in a closet in the bedroom; in drawers by the bed there were freshly laundered and cellophane-packaged shirts, a half-dozen new ties conservative enough to be worn to one of Jim Madison's morning conferences. The bed was made up; when he pulled the covers back, Seth saw the sheets had been in place long enough to smell musty.

Ben Gazi was a shadow . . . a foul shadow, if there could be such a thing. Seth remembered what Sol had said about Ben Gazi, that he deserved to be dead.

Seth was about to turn on the lights when he heard the sound of a key being thrust into the front-door lock. His nerves leapt, screaming; flashing regret struck that he hadn't taken Madison's speculation more seriously. He was defenseless, terrified in the gloom, remembering Madison's scurrilous remarks about the November Sixth Brigade and Rommel Lipschitz, others who might want Ben Gazi.

Quickly Seth stepped back into the study and pressed himself against the wall. There was, unfortunately, nowhere to hide; he hadn't time to duck under the desk. He stood, quaking, thinking he might just have time to leap out of the darkness.

Then, astonishingly, he heard a woman's soft voice.

"*Caz* . . . ?"

Unless he was very mistaken, it was Alice Betancur.

Seth was shattered. But actually not surprised. Sol Betancur's behavior, the way he had spoken, his bitterness, made better sense now. Made sense, also, of Alice's arrival at Ben Gazi's apartment.

"Where are you, Caz? Are you here at last?"

She was in the living room. He heard a light click on. Then she came back to the short hallway. Her head appeared at the door of the study.

She saw him as he stepped forward. "My God! Who are you? Where's . . . Mr. Ben Gazi?"

"Mrs. Betancur, it's Seth Addey," he said quietly, so as not to alarm her. "You remember me?"

Her eyes glinted white terror. "Well . . . well, yes . . . of course . . ." She laughed softly, nervously. She must realize she had been nailed, caught dead to rights—what was *she* doing with a key to this terrible man's apartment? Bravely she went on, "Are you here waiting for Cazimir? He's a very good friend of

145

ours, did you know? I guess you did not. Did he go out
somewhere?''

Alice edged forward and reached for him. Her hands were
shaking. What was Seth to say? Without telling her the whole
truth, how could he answer the question? Should he give it to her
straight? *Your lover is dead, Alice.* No, he couldn't tell her. He
was not allowed to. He didn't say anything. His silence urged
her on.

''I did not know *you* were a friend of Cazimir's—but that
isn't surprising. He knows so many people.'' Alice hesitated but
kept hold of his hand. Not aware of what she was doing, she
rubbed and caressed it. ''Well . . . let's go sit in the other room,
if we're both *waiting*,'' she suggested softly. ''Caz always has
so many interesting friends. You would interest him, of course,
because of your background, Seth. It is Seth, isn't it? Yes, of
course, Clara's stepson—*how funny*! She called today, you know,
from Los Angeles, to remind me. She *said*,'' Alice said girl-
ishly, ''you were in this country with your girlfriend . . . *fiancée*.
True?''

''Yes.''

She pulled him into the living room.

''Where should we sit? Were would *you* like to sit, Seth?
On the sheik's couch?'' She giggled. ''Once down, you can't get
up again.''

Alice shrugged out of her fur coat; it dropped on pillows by
the door. She had already turned on a dim table lamp; its shade
produced filigreed patterns on the walls. Seth lowered himself
into the couch; it was low-slung, suspending him just a few
inches above the floor.

''Have you known Cazimir a long time?'' Alice asked
softly. She held out her hand for support as she crouched down
beside him. Again she did not let go.

''Not long.''

What she wanted to find out, he realized, but hadn't the
guts to ask, was whether Seth knew of her relationship with Ben
Gazi. Seth might have a few questions too: Why? What was this
willowy innocent doing with Ben Gazi?

''I guess,'' she whispered, ''you've gathered that Cazimir
and I are rather good friends . . . or perhaps he's already told
you about that?''

"No," Seth said, not lying, "he's never mentioned you to me. I'm very surprised to see you here."

"*Are you?*" She gasped in disbelief. "Well . . . *the key*. I can explain . . . Cazimir is a true friend. He helps me. He's a very wise man, you know . . a philosopher."

Alice extended her long, slim legs in front of her and crossed them at the ankles. Her skirt was above her knee, a beautiful knee.

"Cazimir," she continued shyly, "has acted almost as my therapist, Seth. . . ."

All his hope for her began to disintegrate. Seth understood now the fear in Sol Betancur's eyes.

"I wouldn't have thought a woman like you needed a therapist."

Alice clung to his hand, held it between them on the cushion, wringing his fingers feverishly. Seth was aware of her breathing—measured, deep, as if she were consciously willing herself to relax, keep calm, stay in control.

"No," she murmured, "no, no. I have deep troubles, you see. I understand nothing! Nothing! My lifestyle is so self-centered. We live such selfish lives . . . Cazimir makes me understand. We have it too easy, Seth. *We must atone*. Do you see?"

He nodded reluctantly. He didn't quite get it, however. Was this part of Cazimir's game? Psychological warfare?

"Cazimir," Alice cried, "instills a healthy humility . . ." Her words came more urgently; she moved closer to him, close enough that he could feel her body, haunch against haunch, the warmth of her long legs. She gripped his hand more tightly, dug her fingers into his arm. "There is no guarantee, Seth, that no matter who you are or where you live or what you have, that something terrible can't happen to you. . . . Caz gave me guidance. I'm far more serene now . . . after my trouble."

What trouble? Seth did not dare ask.

She laughed, a bit breathlessly. "You know . . ." She looked around. "It's sort of scary, isn't it? So quiet and dark. But Caz always likes it that way. Ambience is everything, he says, for studying the soul. Don't you think so?"

"Could be."

"You know, he's done this to me before," she continued. "I'll come here and find a perfect stranger, sitting . . . *waiting*.

147

Cazimir says it's good for me to face up to unfamiliar situations. . . ." She smiled brightly. "Of course, in your case, it's not that you're a stranger. Not at all. But Caz would've known that too, wouldn't he?"

"I—" He didn't have to dissemble, for she went right on.

"It's good for people to suffer—do you agree?"

Seth had begun to perspire a little. He felt wet at his armpits and the back of his shirt. Was it her body heat, or fire of belief in the rotten Ben Gazi? Seth feared he might be learning things about Alice Betancur that would turn out very ugly.

Awkwardly, he said, "I'm afraid I don't understand the purpose of all this."

"Well, didn't he tell you?" she demanded in a low voice. "Or weren't you supposed to be here? Or didn't you know I was coming?"

"I don't know," Seth said worriedly. "I can't say what . . . he had in mind."

"Sometimes," she confided after a moment, "the strangers don't seem to know themselves, that's true." She laughed confusedly. "Why am I telling you all this?"

Seth shrugged. "*Cazimir* must have a plan."

Alice nodded thoughtfully. "Yes, I suppose he must. Should I light a candle? A single candle flickering in the night? And turn off the lamp?"

"I don't mind," he murmured.

"We don't know, do we, how long we'll have to wait."

"It's going on five, Alice."

She paid no attention, rummaging around in a corner. She'd found a candle and matches. She placed the candle in a holder on one of the brass tables, then, as she'd said, turned off the light.

"Now then . . ." Alice kicked off her shoes with studied carelessness, crawled back across the room to the couch and slid up beside him, closer than she'd been before, squeezing against him. The heat of her was accentuated. Together with the strong scent of the perfumed candle, the effect was staggering.

"Sol took mistresses, you know," Alice whispered, "even though I worshipped the man. You think that funny, probably, he's so much older than I. But I was his slave. I would do anything for him. Anything. But then," she boasted, "it was the same when I met Cazimir . . . and had my trouble."

"Alice," Seth had to say, "that's the second time you mentioned trouble."

"The operation, my sweet," she murmured coyly. "Due to Sol, I can no longer have children. I have transferred my feelings. I became *Caz's slave*. I *am* his slave! I submit to his will. I do what he tells me, Seth, whatever that might be!"

He watched her face in the flickering candlelight. Her confession was all the more moving, dramatic . . . depressing for it.

"I tell you this because you're here. This place, on a night like this, like a cave, a prehistoric meeting place . . . a sacrificial shrine."

He should have said it right out then, frankly, to her face: she sounded nuts.

"There's a plan," she cried. "You're here. Cazimir made me undress after my operation, with the horrible scar down my front, and I had to stand there in front of him and he stared at my body, it seemed like for hours at a time . . . until all the scars disappeared. . . ."

"Disappeared?"

"Yes, they're gone. Caz did it by the great force of his will. Do you see now?"

Seth nodded carefully. Did he? He was not quite sure what she was suggesting—that Ben Gazi had willed the scars off her body? That was a very neat trick—the man could have had a great future in plastic surgery, if he'd lived.

Alice pressed insistently against him, her head next to his, her mouth at his ear. Her voice was a shadow of sound.

"I have been very successful at being unfaithful, my dear. No man ever reached the hard truth of me, no matter how deeply he penetrated, as I grasped him with deadly persuasion. No man ever hurt me. No man ever interfered with *my* soul. The sin of pride grows within one like a poisonous mushroom."

"Alice . . ." What was he to say? She was operating under entirely false assumptions. He was not here for *this*; but how was he to tell her?

"Do you believe Cazimir erased my scars?"

"Yes." He nodded briskly. Her mouth was on his chin; he felt her lips working toward the corner of his mouth, his lips. Her breath was very sweet against his face.

"Do you think he'll be back soon?"

"I . . . don't know. No, I don't think he'll be back right away."

"Should we wait for him . . . before . . ."

"Before what?"

Plaintively, she moaned, "I need to see him. He's my lover, you know."

"So I gathered."

"Throwing us together like this," she gasped. "I don't know what he intended for me. . . ." She seemed to hold her breath for a moment, then let it go. "For God's sake, Seth, what is it you want me to do? Just say it!"

"I don't understand, Alice." He was confused, out of it. This was beyond him.

"I do whatever you want, Seth, those are the rules of the house!" She laughed huskily. "I'm never but never surprised by anything. I can be a very naughty little girl, Seth! I may need to be punished . . . after."

"Listen now . . . Alice—"

"Now do you see?"

Her hand, yes, her right hand, long fingered, the nails filed to creamy ovals, was on his chest, fingers under his shirt, against his bare skin, scraping at his resistance.

Seth couldn't put in into words. He was too clumsy, not worldly enough. But he could not avoid accepting that this son of a bitch Ben Gazi used Alice as some kind of a whore to do his bidding with men who came and went after speaking of high politics.

"You're saying . . . you're . . . available to perfect strangers, is that it?"

"Not all of them, dear."

Sol had had it exactly right—but he hadn't the balls to admit it. Alice was one of Ben Gazi's string. This elegant, sweet-tempered . . . confused woman. She was Ben Gazi's slave—*had been*; the bastard was dead. And yes, he *did* deserve to be dead.

There were scientific definitions for all this, Seth told himself, these puzzling hang-ups that mixed power and sex, dominance and submission.

Her hand was on his thigh, unmoving, dormant, but he could feel the pulse beat of blood in her fingertips. She was ready . . . *waiting.*

Quietly Alice said, "Everybody fantasizes . . . I guess I'm just a garden variety masochist. I'm sorry if it puts you off your feed."

"But," he protested vehemently, "you're so *beautiful*. Why? Why do you need this?"

"You forget—Cazimir cured me. I invite you to see for yourself."

Alice pulled her wool sweater up over her bra, then yanked down the top of her plaid skirt, exposing an expanse of unmarked white flesh, dotted only by a curvy bellybutton and rosy-tipped, perfect breasts.

"Look!"

He looked, feeling hot and bothered. After all, a man could stand just so much. Seth, as wary as he was, did have a breaking point.

"Do you see anything? A shadow of a scar?" Alice demanded of him. "The scar ran from my breastbone down, almost to my knees, it seemed like. All gone. All gone!"

"I don't see anything, that's right." He gulped nervously.

"Well, then . . ."

She made no move to adjust her clothes. Her hand lay flat across her smooth belly, her skin so rich in the candlelight.

"I never liked being beaten, you understand, but I accepted it when he did," Alice said softly. "I would not like to allow you to do that to me, Seth."

"Alice, I wouldn't!"

"Dear boy . . ." She chuckled huskily. "Sometimes Cazimir tied me with golden chains—I wonder what's happened to those? Then . . . ravished me, made me surrender. Do you see what I mean?"

It was fairly explicit, he would have thought.

"I'm defenseless before you and all you do is ask me silly questions," she accused him tearfully, already into yet another mood change.

"I haven't asked you any questions, Alice."

She found his mouth and kissed him so wantonly he was concussed. And rock hard. Her hand leapt back to his legs, seeking proof. She caressed him greedily and he moaned.

"I want this!" she exclaimed. "You have to help me now, dear, please. I don't know when Cazimir will get back. Please!"

"Alice . . ." He wanted to tell her to stop, slow down, not to put herself through the ritual of giving herself to him.

"What is it?"

She was at him relentlessly. It was not that he wasn't willing; how could a man right in body and mind resist such an onslaught? He feared *for* her; she seemed so unbalanced. And a part of him simply feared her.

"I'm taking off my clothes, Seth!" she warned, pulling at them with abandon.

"Yes."

"Pull off my sweater." He did, over her head as she protected her hair-do. She unzipped the side of her skirt and dropped it to the floor. Then her bra and panty hose. "Now, tell me, Seth, tell me what you want me to do!"

She knelt in front of him, hands clasped together under her breasts in a gesture of submission and respect. Seth put his hands on her bare shoulders, drew her closer. She lifted her lips to his again, kissed him with open mouth and seeking tongue. Her breathing changed tempo.

"You can tie me with my panty hose if you wish!"

"No, no."

"Shall I—"

She fondled him with both hands, then dipped her head to engulf him.

"No, no!"

She smiled at his protest. Then she dropped backward onto a mass of cushions and spread her legs.

"Come, come, dear . . ." She held out her arms. "Take me. Do whatever you want."

Softly, like an animal, a big cat, Seth crept to her, extended himself over her long lithe body. Alice welcomed him wetly, warmly, taking him silently, almost secretly, arching with a cry of something—was it joy?—and wrapping him in those smooth legs.

"Seth . . . dear . . ." Eyes closed, she found his rhythm, adapted, molded her body to his. "Seth Addey, Seth Addey," she crooned, rocking. "Seth Addey, Seth Addey . . ."

He would have preferred her to keep quiet. But what could he say? He was the guest.

"Seth, Seth," she moaned, "go on, go on . . . I know Caz will be back and he'll discover us. Seth, Seth . . ." She paused, drawing a sharp breath as he dug. "Do you mind, dear? You won't mind, will you?"

He shook his head against her shoulder. He didn't have the strength to speak.

"If he watches? Seth? A picture, Seth, a picture or two?"

No, Ben Gazi wouldn't be getting Seth Addey's face in a picture. Maybe his ass, but not his face. But anyway, she shouldn't hold her breath for Cazimir Ben Gazi.

"Seth, dear, Seth, dear, Seth . . . dear. It's all right. Now . . . Seth . . . Now!"

Chapter Fifteen

*F*ortunately, as it was said, time did pass. The most dramatic of events dimmed; memories faded. For Clara, her time with Rossiter did become a thing of the past.

When Clara returned to San Francisco, she turned her attention to the gallery. But Biff had managed all the preliminaries with a sort of stubborn, relentless skill, and then there was nothing left to do but the hanging.

The hanging . . .

Biff, surprising them all, pleasing Clara, curbed his cigars and put a stop to the gin.

The Morelli Gallery Winter Show had gone amazingly well. The newspapers paid attention, criticism was favorable, sales had been brisk, and people even came back to look again.

Speaking of which . . . Biff. He had been the star of the show, just as Clara had planned it. His lithographs had sold out, and in a reversal of his usual, unruffled coolness, he was effusive in his gratitude, so adoring of Clara that she was shocked.

This unusual and unlikely Biff Percy then introduced Clara to his newest bimbo. Yes, he admitted, he was into another mistress, yes, it was true, he was playing Pygmalion for the umpteenth time. Biff Percy's hobby was to transform sexy waifs into man-killers, then to turn them loose to prey on happy marriages. Certainly there had to be something about Biff to compensate for his short, brash, and portly persona. Never mind that he was the Picasso of North Beach—that alone was not enough.

The *hanging*. Clara smiled at the way they used the term.

In one wild moment toward the end of the opening night party, Biff had found her in the back among the glasses and bottles and kissed her, kissed her Thank You, for an instant holding Clara against his body and hugging, for all the world just then like Alberto Morelli.

But Biff Percy was too far out on the limb for Clara to risk him. Take care, she told herself. People fell out of trees; it happened all the time.

No, Clara Addey was too far gone to be remade by the likes of Biff's Pygmalion.

Fortunately, there was the little matter of Christmas to divert her. Tom always left the holiday details to Clara, and that helped get her mind off all sorts of other things. This was what she was good at, the details. In truth, maybe that was all she was really good at.

As always, at Christmas, they'd be going to Morelli Vines, a command performance really. Clara and her father, the old winemaker, had had their problems, but that was the past; and this was a visitation Tom never minded. It got them away from San Francisco, saved them making up excuses to dodge the more tiresome of the Christmas parties.

Between Tom and Alberto there was an emotional empathy often found in men of very different professions. Tom was effusive about the Morelli product, of course, and that didn't exactly hurt.

The land would be beautiful this time of the year, brown and sere before the heaviest rainfalls of the winter, vines cut back and ready for rebirth in the spring. Clara's brother lived at the other end of the four hundred acres. Before she'd died, Clara's mother had had Alberto build a roomy cottage next to the main house, a big old frame Victorian, in which Clara and Fred had been raised. This was to be for Clara and her children; there, the Addeys always stayed when they visited from the city.

The usual schedule was to drive to the vineyard on the twenty-first or twenty-second, the morning following their annual Christmas party for old friends, close friends, and useful professional acquaintances—women Clara had known in high school and her one and only year of college, before she'd taken off with Stanley Gates; Tom's legal cronies, those who still talked to him, and a few of the men he'd grown up with in Sonoma.

They didn't seem to make *new* friends. At a certain age, Tom said . . . Well, he definitely was not a clubby sort, not a joiner. He kept away from the old-line San Francisco groups—the "drones," he called them. Solitude, he claimed, that was the stuff of ripe old age.

Old age!

In time, Clara mused, Rossiter would turn into another Tom unless a smart woman took him in hand. Out of bitterness and disillusion, he would retreat.

But she hadn't meant to think about Rossiter.

One of the big Christmas affairs that Tom would acknowledge was the Bohemian Club cocktail party—they'd asked him to join. No thanks. But they didn't begrudge him a one-time-a-year invitation. And then the dinner party Bette Toland always threw at Trader Vic's. Clara's friend Bette belonged to one of the pioneer California families, which Tom had once maliciously described to Seth's German girlfriend—though it was farfetched to link Bette and her mother and her mother's mother to Donner Pass cannibalism, unless latter-day social cannibalism qualified.

Bette, of course, was responsible for Clara's misadventure with Stanley Gates—Bette had dared Clara to elope. They didn't mention that anymore. Bette had to be forgiven much, for her mother was one of the city's social arbiters, a darling of the artistic clique and well-established in San Francisco's minor-league diplomatic corps. And, fondly, old-timers remembered Bette's father, the infamous Gerald, who'd left town for a skiing holiday in Switzerland and never returned.

Yes, people were sometimes a little weird in San Francisco.

Not Clara. In the first place she didn't really come from San Francisco. Secondly, Albert Morelli had never spoiled his children. Clara was nothing more, she liked to think, than a good solid peasant. She was by no means a vamp of Bette's dimension.

In fact, Clara had observed Bette with Tom from time to time. They were so alike. If Bette hadn't found husband number four—or was it five, or six?—Clara wouldn't have been surprised if she'd made a play for Tom Addey. Of course, it wouldn't have worked as a long-term thing . . . a hushed, rushed affair, yes, but Bette and Tom couldn't have made it over the long haul.

So, Clara didn't mind, did she, that the two had dallied in the daisies? Dilly-dallied . . . what did people call it between best friends?

Actually, Clara and Tom were quite happy together these days. The marriage was steady, or as steady as it could be, Clara knowing what she did, Clara suspicious . . . Clara having her own little fling.

Only the once. This was, she swore, the one and only time. And it was not going to happen again.

No. They were happy. They traveled well, like good old wine. They had fun together . . . *Talk yourself into it, Clara.* She had learned to ride out his dark moods, like taming gravity— though gravity, in comparison, was a simple sort of physical phenomenon. Tom was not simple. He was critical and demanding; but he was more vulnerable than people guessed.

Clara couldn't help but feel melancholic, sitting at her desk in the study. Tom had gone off as usual to see the bank regarding the family's redwood land and she had business letters to write. It seemed more like April than December, sunny out and warm, something to do with the jetstream high above the Pacific—a winter storm had just been blown away from San Francisco to the south, Los Angeles. Another good reason not to be *there!* It was like spring, not early winter. The waves down on the bay were choppy but friendly.

The world did not have to be gray and hostile; nor was it. The trouble was, Clara didn't know what she wanted. She was so restless, dissatisfied; there was a vague hollowness within her. Sometimes she felt lighter than air, other times heavier than the Earth. But no, she did not love Rossiter; she didn't even miss him, not at all. He was a nice man, adoring, comfortable, solicitous—the very word for him, but he didn't fascinate like Tom. He was a kind of plaything, poor Rossiter, yes, a stud, as awful and cruel as it was to think so. An abstraction, an expression of Lust II, Advanced Lust for Graduate Vamps, not to be taken at all seriously beyond the established fact that men and women attracted.

She would not think about it anymore; but she could not stop thinking about it. She *must* shake herself loose of this dismal preoccupation.

Clara jumped up. Well, she could deceive the *old coot*, meaning Tom, just as well and trickily as he deceived her, and handle it with the same aplomb. Rossiter was something else—she'd crack him up, drive him out of his little mind. She was too much for him, yes; Clara was built for passion, raging, thumping, screaming, humping passion. She was not one of those stolid New Englanders from whose dusty loins Rossiter Addey had sprung.

Clara passed through the large, high-ceilinged living room. She remembered Seth's girlfriend—Hildy—that rainy, foggy day they'd all been here for brunch.

"I *could* leave my heart in San Francisco," Hildy had gushed, almost weepily, clutching at Tom's arm, Tom the Lecher's arm.

And Clara thinking if Hildy kept on, she'd be leaving a little piece of something else behind for sure.

It would be a shame, a crying pity, Clara told herself, to have to leave this place. She had decorated the living room beautifully, everybody said so, all in greens, starting with dark slubbed green silk upholstered to the walls, lighter green satin covers on the furniture, and a red- and pink-rose embroidered Chinese Celadon-green carpet. Above the center of the carpet hung an antique Tiffany chandelier; the mantlepiece was a white marble treasure they'd found in Paris.

In the hallway Clara remembered she had to pick up Tom's present from Wilkes-Bashford before they left; she'd had a brocaded smoking jacket made for him, except Tom didn't smoke anymore. Well, then, it could be a reading jacket, a lying-around-in jacket, a drinking jacket, perfect for Morelli Vines on Christmas Eve. Being richly patterned, it would never show a wine spill.

And Martha? That pushy girl, her daughter, was due back from the south sometime today or tomorrow, in time to drive with them to the vineyard. At least, she had better be back. Clara still hadn't bought Martha's present; maybe it was better if she didn't show up. Martha had everything—and if she didn't, then what did you buy a girl her age? Half the time you'd get it thrown back in your face.

Daydreams carried Clara into Martha's room. A book? The last thing the child needed was another book. Jewelry? Martha didn't wear it. Cosmetics, cologne, perfume? She would have been insulted. Boots? Warm boots, shoes?

What about a round-trip ticket to Paris? Or Kashmir? Or the moon?

Idly, Clara gazed down at Martha's messy desk. The rest of the room had been tidied, but nobody dared touch this desk. Martha was such a character. Clara felt envious of her daughter's riotous youth. To be that young again, to have it all to do over again! Some people thought that'd be horrible; but not Clara. She'd have lived and loved it all over again, mistakes and all.

Tom said . . . yes, Tom said Alex Spurzov had pronounced Martha a charming and beautiful and delightful girl. And intelligent. Tom said Alex brought out the best in Martha, her razzle-dazzle. According to Tom, Alex could've tutored Martha into a devastating femme fatale . . . as he had Ludmilla? Alex, said Tom, would've made a great teacher at one of those Swiss finishing schools for young women with very visible means of support, i.e., Daddy.

A diary of sorts lay atop the heap of notes and scraps of paper.

December . . whatever the date. Clara didn't notice the date.

What she saw was written in big, bold, red letters.

TOM LOVES MARTHA.

And directly below that,

MARTHA LOVES TOM.

Clara slammed her hand down on the diary. She flushed . . . choked.

The little bitch! And Clara had been cautioning herself to beware of Bette Toland!

Then she heard the elevator, rising, coming to rest at their floor. That would be Tom.

But there were loud voices, and as the door opened, Clara heard Martha's laughter, loud, and brassy, yes, brassy and loud.

"You just wait, Tom Addey, you just wait!"

"Stay where you are, girl! Come no closer!"

Clara stepped back into the hallway. Tom saw her first; his eyebrows leapt. Yes, he could justly be startled. Not caught in the act, maybe, but surprised. Martha saw her too, but was unperturbed.

"Hi, Ma, I'm back."

"So I see."

Clara did her very best not to give herself away. Nothing

she'd seen or heard of course meant a goddamn thing. The words? Adolescent doodlings and, actually, for all she knew, Martha might have been referring to Tom the Gooney Bird. And what? *You just wait, Tom Addey!* What did that mean? Nothing . . . on the surface.

Tom spoke very gravely. "Everything okay?"

"Yes. Of course. What wouldn't be okay?" she demanded coldly.

"C'mon, Ma!"

"How come you're feeling so good?"

Martha frowned. "Actually, I'm not . . ."

"What's wrong?"

"Nothing . . . I'll tell you later."

Martha's mood turned, and without another word she walked past Clara and into her room and closed the door.

Tom pursed his lips, then shrugged. *Who* understood Martha?

"Now that you're back," Clara said, "I'm going out. I've got an errand to run."

"Bought your present," he drawled, grinning at her, shaking off his coat and hanging it up in the closet. Clara didn't respond. "Aren't you going to guess what it is?"

"I don't see anything."

"It'll be delivered later. It's that kind of present."

Clara nodded, staring at him, *the bastard*. What *had* they been up to in the elevator?"

"I know," she said, "an elf . . . a little Christmas elf."

"Nope."

"A little elf with a big dick . . ."

His very expressive eyebrows lofted again; a little whistle formed on his lips.

"That kind of a Christmas, is it?"

It had not been easy for Clara to keep her mouth shut the previous evening, and now, in the car, she sat up front with Tom as they drove out of San Francisco. As he had promised, her Christmas gift had come by delivery boy—in fact, a delivery boy with a guard: A string of perfectly matched pearls, the real thing; the people at the store had only just finished polishing them up, tightening the clasp. Receiving them, emotionally, Clara had burst into tears. It *was* that kind of a Christmas. Her brocade jacket for Tom seemed so insignificant afterward that she'd almost started crying again.

True to the way she'd been feeling, Clara had bought Martha an open ticket to Paris; then, thinking it was a bit impersonal for a gift, went to Saks and picked out two nightgowns. Did that make any sense, in the circumstances? She handed Martha the envelope after the pearls arrived and she'd given Tom his brocade jacket.

Martha scowled. "I'm going by myself?"

Clara had wanted to snarl at her, And what do you want, to take *him* with you?

Instead she muttered, "You're lucky I bought round-trip."

It began to rain as they drove down the hill toward the bridge. Morbidly, Clara stared out the side window, determined to ignore them, and her own demons. The streets were slick; light rain persisted, became steadier in the middle of the bridge. Tom had set the wiper on slow; he had to speed it up. It *flumped* and *whooshed*, flumped and whooshed, in tempo with her mood.

Clara wanted badly to be home, at the farm. Once there, she promised herself, she'd dig out her old yellow rain slicker and matching hat and the boots and tramp away, leaving them to their own devices—which were probably infernal.

Martha still hadn't said anything about Palm Springs. Clara's impression was that she was depressed about . . . whatever it was, something to do with Stanley, her father, and his chum, Will Sorge—they were lovers, she could say it. Stanley Gates and Sorge had been partners in business and otherwise since the day Stan had fled. It was to be expected Martha was worried about her father. It occurred to Clara that Stan had been married to Sorge now longer than he had been to her. Anyway, maybe it was good that Martha had something substantive on her mind . . . something other than Tom Addey.

Martha was hunkered down in the back seat of the Volvo, eyes half closed, the familiar mopey and sullen expression on her face. She'd caught a little cold in the desert; although alert and lively enough at the party the night before, Martha was in a down mood now, very much so.

She sniffled miserably, deliberately loud enough for them to hear.

Tom ordered, "Put the blanket around you, for God's sake. Otherwise you're going to be sick all day tomorrow."

"I don't give a damn if I am."

Oh, charming, Clara thought. Tom's little *protégé* was in a foul temper, and what was he going to do about it? And Alex Spurzov had declared Martha *wonderful*?

And Tom frowned at Clara. *Her* daughter.

The bitch! Wasn't Tom aware how obvious was Martha's continual, continuing, and open flirtation with him? Clara had watched it with tolerant amusement over the years—fool, that she was, had never taken it seriously. A few years ago, not that long ago, Martha had been quick to kiss and hug—but the girl was a grown woman now. There would be an end to such nonsense!

And what if she'd never had Martha? Without a child, without Stanley, dopey Stan, Clara could have done what she wanted—played the piano, become an opera star, painted, done architecture. Even, at the minimum, become a vinicologist, as Alberto had wanted.

The trouble between Martha and herself was that they were too much alike. Clara resented Martha for her youth, yes, especially today. But more—Martha was headstrong, and just as stubborn as Clara, always ready to take the plunge, to risk all. Emotionally they were sisters; and sisters often fought. But Clara was older, presumably wiser . . . and *maybe not*, all things considered.

Clara had always been too easy on her men, that was it. She'd even taken Stanley at face value—and why not? At the time, Stanley hadn't known about himself. She supposed it had been Will Sorge who led him to self-discovery.

And Tom? Clara had always catered to him, hadn't she? Been subservient, yes, goddamn it! Always tuned herself to his fork. There would be no more of that! Tom Addey, big lawyer, internationally known, Mr. Clever Dick, yes, he'd pulled lots of fat out of the fire. Including Mr. Sol Betancur's, who'd shown his gratitude by foisting upon them the *late* Cazimir Ben Gazi, God rest his soul. *Don't mention it, Tom had said*. Ben Gazi, certainly one of the reasons they'd had to be in L.A.—with such disastrous effects!

Ah, but she was being so stupid, to sit there going on like this, pumping up her discontent and fury, taking out her frustrations on phantoms. Contritely, Clara put her hand on Tom's on the steering wheel—right there, where Martha could see it, see what she was doing, and maybe understand the signal—then squeezed his knee. He glanced at her quickly. Something was troubling her, he could see that.

"Martha will be fine as soon as she sees her grandfather," Clara said.

"*Sure,*" Martha sniped, "here comes the spaghetti and meatballs—"

Clara whirled around, more than furious. "Don't you mock him!" Martha flushed, bit her lip. "If you say one smart-aleck thing, just one, I'll take you out behind the barn and beat the hell out of you, *Miss!*"

"Okay, okay!" Martha tittered behind her hand. The threat was not realistic, anybody could see that.

"You'd better be careful, kiddo," Tom cautioned lightly.

Again Clara felt weepy. They were mocking her! But why should she give a damn? Normally, when Martha and Tom got on her case, she merely laughed them off, called them names and went on to something else.

Not today. A green creature with very sharp teeth was eating at her. Rossiter! Clara was sorrier than ever he wouldn't come for Christmas; he would have given her a sort of relief, a weapon to use against them. But what a price to pay if Rossiter were to bring Serena with him! Maybe she should pair Martha with Rossiter. What a thought! But why not? If Martha could fall in love with Tom, then Martha could just as well fall in love with Rossiter, who was as much like Tom as Martha was like Clara.

Good God! And people would say, if this was so, was Clara in love with Rossiter? And Tom with Martha? Did the diary lie?

Clara glared at him, wanting to slap his face. He was so sure of everything, so amused by the world, whistling to himself as he drove.

Never deterred for long, Martha boldly declared, "I'm going to get me some of that old Morelli rotgut tonight and get stinkin'—that'll fix this cold."

"*You will not!*" Tom hoisted those supercilious eyebrows. "It's very un-Italian to get drunk."

"I'm only half Italian."

"Yes," Clara murmured, seizing the opening, "and the rest is half-assed."

"Ma! *Tra-la!*" Martha trilled sarcastically. "I wouldn't dare anyway—Alberto would thrash me very soundly."

"And if he didn't, I would," Tom said.

"Oh, would you? I'd like that!"

Tom groaned, perplexed, finally a little embarrassed. "Madame, would you please curb your daughter?"

Clara didn't bother to turn. "Martha, shut up!"

"I'd do anything to get people to pay a little attention to me."

Clara twisted around. *"Are you serious?"*

Martha grinned, a clownish expression on her face. "Of course I am! You know I'm made for him!"

Tom scowled at her in the mirror. "God preserve me!"

"Martha, you are always the center of attention—"

"Am not!"

The child, child-woman. Now tell the truth, didn't Tom see what was going on? He must. And, of course, he was too astute, too nimble of wit, too self-protective, to allow himself to be caught in anything so silly as Martha's trap.

Clara stared out at the storm clouds rolling over the Marin hills, billowing down at them from the top of Mount Tamalpais. After they cleared the bridge and drilled through the tunnel over Sausalito, rain began falling more intensely and northbound traffic slowed on Route 101.

Please God, Clara prayed, for once let it be sunny at Morelli, let it be clear and sunny and beautiful . . . and without a care.

Absently she muttered, "Martha was absolutely the center of attention last night. . . . All the *old coots* were courting you."

"Old coots is right!" Martha laughed obnoxiously.

Tom looked in the mirror again. "You're speaking of my peers, *ducky*, my generation."

Martha cried self-righteously, "I didn't say it first—*your wife did*, didn't you hear her?"

Tom glanced at Clara. *"Old coots, eh?"*

Yes, they *were* in league against her, goading, scheming to drive her mad so they could have her committed and then run away to debauchery in Paris.

Coldly Clara said, "Merely an expression . . . affectionate, at that."

"Yeah, sure," he grunted.

Too bad . . . she'd hurt his feelings. After a moment, thinking to shake up his apple cart of smugness just a little bit

164

more, Clara murmured, "I didn't tell you. I sort of invited Rossiter for Christmas."

Truly alarmed, he cried, "God, I hope they can't."

"Maybe Ross could come by himself . . . Serena's all involved with her father. *Poor Ross* . . . he sounds sort of dismal."

"Wouldn't you be, married to that dame?"

Clara shrugged. "Maybe she's so awful because she knows you don't like her."

"Good! I wish we *could* break up that God-awful marriage."

"Yes," Clara said quietly, "he'd be . . happier."

"You're sure?"

"We spent time together in L.A., Tom . . ." She didn't go on.

Let him wonder what she meant; let him begin to wonder.

Martha, naturally, had to pipe up with her opinion, which nobody wanted.

"He should get rid of the little *klutz*."

"Not for you to say."

But, of course, there'd be no stopping her now. "What a pain! Wonder woman—she must be carrying twenty pounds of silicone."

Clara's jaw caught peevishly. "Don't be coarse!"

Tom, as usual, laughed. Martha delighted him so. The nastier she was, the better he liked it. Maliciously, he drawled, "She's a simple case: Beverly Hills psychotic, garden variety."

"You two are very cruel."

"Just the facts, ma'am," Tom said, switching his eyes to the mirror—for Martha's approval, to be sure. "I just can't think why the boy married her in the first place."

"You know why—she convinced him she was pregnant," Clara said.

"He should sue her for entrapment, am I right?" Martha asked.

That was another thing, if Clara was putting together all those instances of ostentatious flirtation. Martha had begun talking about shifting to a pre-legal course at the university, and lately she'd begun drawing Tom out about his cases. Maybe she *was* fascinated—at any rate, Tom, as one would expect, was flattered. The law was his life. Despite all his bitter complaining about it having become debased—adulterated by modern interpretation, with lawyers, like fallen doctors, turning into legalistic abortionists—despite all that, Tom still loved the law, his law. He was like that, attached to *things*, immaterial things. Maybe he would finally say yes to teaching the legal ethics course at Berkeley. Clara hoped so—for both their sakes. How *convenient* it would be.

"That'd be a job," Tom opened. "You'd have to prove Serena had deliberately misrepresented. Just impossible . . . No, she got old Ross to do the honorable thing. And that's that."

"*Old* Ross?"

"*Old coots?*" he echoed her sardonically. "Ross acts sometimes like he's two hundred years old."

And Tom Addey, she asked herself wearily, how old did he act? How old and sour and introverted and nasty?

"We will try to think kindly of Serena," Clara said, "although it will not be easy. You know, at one time, according to Rossiter, she was nothing more life-threatening than a chubby little California beach girl. . . ."

"Ross told you that?"

"Sure. Then Bud Slagger threw her to this horrible show-biz personality—he thought it'd help him somehow in Las Vegas. Nobody ever discovered what happened, except one fine day Serena ran screaming and naked into a Beverly Hills street, you know, all palm trees and pale beauty. So ended her first marriage . . ."

"Ross told you about that, did he?"

Martha threw off her blanket and scooted forward to put her chin on the back of Clara's seat, already recovered or recovering, on that edge of boisterousness that always made Clara so nervous.

"I say," she hooted, "send that boy to me! I'll make him see the light!"

Chapter Sixteen

*C*azimir, the poor lad, had been well-beloved by very influential people in Washington, Tom Addey had told Alex, and that had to account for all the trouble that had been taken in the rather insignificant (as far as Alex was concerned) matter of his death.

The police had been and gone several times and then the whole affair, for some reason, hushed up. Totally. There must be no leaks, Tom advised; if anybody asked, which they would not, Alex was merely to say that Cazimir had left town, headed home, hours before Ludmilla's death.

They had talked to Peat too. After all, he had found the body.

Why not simply say it? The lad had killed himself out of grief. Was that so odd? He had been overcome by grief, consumed by it, even more than Alex who, after all, had loved Ludmilla better than had any other man on Earth.

No, no, Tom said, it was not as simple as it seemed. Cazimir Ben Gazi had been a true-blue friend of America. He had acted as diplomatic bridge to the warring and paranoid countries of the Middle East, as a booster of American interests and a doer of deeds never discussed.

Talking to himself, Alex muttered aloud, "If the lad was such an important individual, he should've taken better care of himself. . . ."

Peat removed his eye from the curly back road of Bel Air Heights to stare at Alex in alarm.

"*You say*, Prince?"

Alex shrugged. There was not much point, he thought, in pretending Peat didn't know about it.

"They seem to believe, Peat, that our guest was murdered."

The car swerved. If Alex hadn't known better, he might have leapt to the conclusion that Peat had not only found the body but done the deed. Good thing there weren't any policemen around.

"Prince," Peat muttered laboriously, his tone as acrid as his breath, "the little gun was tight in his hand. . . ."

"I know, Peat, I know."

And, of course, he did. Life was often repetitous. Peat was bringing him clear across the Bel Air estates to the home of Rose and Dick Richards. Alex had been invited for a festive Christmas Day luncheon. At first he wasn't going to accept—better, Alex thought, to keep Dick Richards and Rose at arm's length. But then he couldn't make himself refuse. He was feeling Ludmilla's absence so acutely, and Rose . . . well, Rose! She was as extravagant as Ludmilla, her moods, he knew already, cruel and thoughtless. She would be at times just as coarse as Ludmilla. But that was all right . . .perfectly all right. In the end, Alex had said, yes, please, he would come.

He and Peat were in her small Mercedes, the one with about ten miles on the odometer; Ludmilla had been such a horrible, erratic driver, they'd feared to let her on the road. Peat drove well, his hands wrapped lovingly around the handmade wooden steering wheel. The car was a treasure, an *objet*; it would bring a collector's price at auction time. And, true to form, Peat was wearing a high-peaked, black officer's hat, though it was bare of insignia.

"I thank you for driving me, Peat."

"Call when you want me to pick you up, Prince."

"I'll mooch a ride home, my friend."

My friend. Could they be closer now? Ludmilla had always created division, as if Peat were jealous of her attentions to Alex . . and Alex jealous himself of Peat's service to Ludmilla. Now there was every reason for them to be friends.

"Well, Peat, you know we are not supposed to say anything about our . . . guest. You were told so too, were you not?"

Peat nodded, his sallow face impassive. "I was, Prince."

That seemed to be the end of it. Alex could not imagine

Peat would shoot his mouth off. His expression said he'd be unwilling to share even the time of day.

It was Rose who had insisted Alex join her family for Christmas Day. Did she mean it? Or merely feel some revolting pity? Alex would hate that. Perhaps, even this was possible, Rose found Alex . . . well, a good friend. Was it too much to hope that he might become as precious to her as he had been to her sister-of-spirit, Ludmilla?

Many of his stuffy friends would have laughed over his infatuation with such a pretentious nothing. But Alex didn't care. Citizen Alex, after all, had adopted as his own the democratic spirit of the Republic.

He was proud to be American, to be boiling away in the melting pot with Rose and all the Mexicans and Koreans and Chinese and Irish and Germans and Africans. Wasn't it ironic, too, that Rose seemed to be descended from the very people whom Alex's forebears had raped and pillaged? Yes, Rose was a survivor of all those centuries of killing and looting. Alex tried to make her see how miraculous it was that she, her blood and family genes, had survived, while other families had been wiped out to the last man, woman, and child, simply ceasing to exist . . . so tragically to be obliterated in one afternoon of pogrom for which his part of the world had become infamous. Alex was not proud of his ancestors. And he thought Rose might be the instrument by which he would pay retribution for the things his people had done to hers.

But Rose refused to listen to such talk. She was American! But she was something else too, whether she knew it or not. Her face, the way she moved, her body was a reminder of the little feudal villages Alexei had known years before in Poland . . and Bulgaria. The blood had come a long way, yes, but there persisted in Rose the shadow of the peasant.

After that first morning, Rose had come back to Richlands several times—she couldn't make up her mind, she insisted, what she wanted of Ludmilla's.

All of Ludmilla's finery suited her—they had the same complexion; only the body was not as wonderful. Of course, Ludmilla had never had children; she had not lost tautness, the power of her thighs, the firm clasp of her sexual bud vase, as Alex often thought of it. In the end Rose had stubbornly refused to choose anything. But the purpose of her visits, Alex argued, was precisely that she *should* pick something out. Ludmilla would be offended, he told her. Rose would have to think about it, to come back another day. Did Alex mind? Far from it. Alex sat and admired the slightly bowed legs, the chunky behind full of promise.

Alex had become fond of Rose. She might have been Ludmilla's daughter. But she was more. They sat for hours in the boudoir where the poor lad had died—either died or by superhuman effort picked himself up off the fluffy carpet, torn himself away from the gold pieces, and dragged himself downstairs and outside.

The carpet—it must show something, some trace of blood. But not even a blur of bloodred remained.

And the gold? It was gone too. Alex checked the box in the closet wall, to assure himself that he had not dreamt the whole thing. No, the gold had not walked away by itself either.

There was more to Peat than met the eye. Peat had some explaining to do. But how to ask? Hard to frame a question if you were not supposed to know anything. Peat drove on impassively; did he have any idea what Alex was thinking, how thin and frayed the tightrope was upon which he balanced?

Dick Richards presented Alex a flute of fairly flat champagne, muttering about how pleased he was to have the prince in his house and how sorry he was, of course, about Ludmilla's passing so close to the happy holiday.

Alex thanked him and looked around the dull, dark Richards living room. Leaded, smoked-glass windows of the mock Tudor house allowed little of the fabled California sunshine inside.

Was Dick Richards a man who hated truth and daylight? There were people like that. Count Dracula came to mind. But Alex remembered what Tom had said: Richards was a yachtsman of sorts.

Rose finally descended the choppy little staircase, dressed in a green velvet hostess gown. Dick Richards handed her a glass of the same champagne. She tasted cautiously, then spit it violently on the floor. *"Flat as horse piss!"*

Dick was unimpressed by the critique. He laughed dryly, explaining to an embarrassed Alex that they didn't do much drinking in this household and that he couldn't actually tell the difference between flat champagne and proper bubbly.

"He does his drinking at his office," Rose charged brashly, "just like his father before him—*that old sot*! Alex, Ludmilla must have been bored out of her skull. . . ."

Alex winced. Was it so? The mystery, of course, could never be settled. Why *had* Ludmilla given up, married Rodney Richards and surrendered herself to such boredom? Was it the money? Certainly not—Ludmilla had always scorned money. Half the time she hadn't bothered to pick up the change from a dollar bill. What was it, then, that had brought her to Richlands?

"Oh, for God's sakes," Rose cried good-naturedly, "give me a vodka . . . and one for Alex too. He can't drink that stuff."

Richards sighed. "All right, Rose."

The Richards daughters were pretty red-haired girls, Sindy and Sue, dressed in matching green-red plaid dresses, white ankle socks, and black patent-leather shoes. Unhappily, they sat by the big, unfired fireplace like two mummies and stared. Alex prayed to the good God to see him through the afternoon.

"A beautiful tree," he murmured.

At least there was a tree; nicely decorated too, it stood to one side of the dead fireplace.

Dick Richards smiled cagily. "We get it down out of the attic every year."

"It's plastic?"

Alex must have sounded surprised. Richards calmly nodded.

"Jesus, Dick, give him another vodka, can't you? He *is* a Russian!"

"Yes, *please*."

"My brother and his wife are dropping in for coffee after lunch," Richards said. "Did Tom Addey tell you about our talk?"

"Oh, yes . . he did, Dick. I was very glad to hear—"

Rose interrupted raucously, thrusting out her glass. "Another, please!" She touched Alex's arm conspiratorially. "Yeah, Ralph and his wife are coming, darling! And that's going to do you in, I promise. Every succeeding Richards is more boring than the last. . . . *Am I right, Richard*?"

"Not . . . exactly, Rose."

Grim-faced at last, Richards put another dollop of vodka in her glass.

"More!"

"Remember your quota, Rose."

One of the daughters had the bad sense to chime in, "Please, Mommy—"

Furiously, Rose whirled around. "Shut up, you little pieface!"

Oh, my God. Alex felt himself declining, his physical powers failing him. It was going to be one of those days. Strange that Rose could change so. With him, she was by comparison a perfect lady.

Worriedly, Alex asked himself a rather crucial question. Being so much like Ludmilla, Rose . . no, if Ludmilla had borne children, would *she* have treated them as Rose treated hers?

Was it possible?

"Have another, Alex," Rose exclaimed, "take the frost off the lily—what is it they say?"

She had mentioned Rodney Richards's drinking habits—had Rodney been a closet alcoholic? And what about Rose? At Richlands she'd always asked for diet sodas.

Although he did desperately need another drink, Alex said, "I'm fine."

"We're ready to eat anyway." From somewhere, Richards had received the signal. He seemed so relieved, poor man, Alex thought.

Grandly Rose said, "You may bring me to the table, Alex."

Her fingernails were sharp, desperately sharp. Alex tried not to cry out, did his best to smile.

"So happy to be here, helping you at Christmas—"

"Not half as happy as I am that you're here!"

Perhaps he'd been a little off base about Rose. It was very naughty of her to be so scornful of Dick Richards and her daughters. But she calmed slightly over dinner; actually it was a very tasty and traditional feast. Dick Richards even served a passable white wine, chilled, with a first course of carrot soup, a culinary thrill discovered that year in Beverly Hills, and with the turkey, a red wine—unfortunately, slightly off. By this time, Alex told himself stoically, Rose would not have noticed.

It was not Alex's assigned role in life, after all, to worry about Rose Richards, or to make small talk with Dick. Once he had reminded Alex of Tom Addey's visit, Richards ran out of things to say. He registered Rose's recourse to the wineglass, but said nothing more about quotas either. He had written her off. He was that sort of businessman, too hard-boiled to throw good anxiety after bad. Cut your losses and run for it!

The two daughters, unfortunately, were not so toughened. They didn't know where to look, where to hide. Alex tried to speak to them; he was, after all, a cosmopolitan man and subtle enough to get through such a bad patch as this. But, no, the frightened little things were scared to death. Finally Alex gave up, turning his attention to the noble bird and in praise thereof.

He lifted his glass of sour red wine. "To the chef!"

Rose laughed uproariously. "The chef? Jesus, Alex, we had it catered!"

"Catered?" Why should Alex be surprised, though, after discovering that they kept a plastic Christmas tree? He blustered it out. "Well . . . to *that* chef, then! Somebody has cooked the bloody bird."

"Alex," Rose said sloppily, "this goddamn family doesn't know how to eat. The old man and Ludmilla dined off trays watching TV—Peat brought them TV dinners. It didn't matter, though—the old fart was pissed the whole time!"

Alex stared at her. This was true?

Dick Richards hurled his first thunderbolt of a look, like a silenced shot from a Colt automatic.

"Tell me why," he demanded angrily, "why we should keep a full staff here for *four* people?" Alex would have, even for two people. "Figure it out, Alex," Richards went on insistently. "We've got a maid for cleaning and we're not even as big as Richlands. Besides, Rose enjoys cooking!"

"The hell I do!" Rose exclaimed, her face flushed.

"And the *handyman*," Dick Richards added solemnly.

Rose chuckled. "Lance, the Hammer," she elaborated. "He's Welsh, his last name starts like they do with a double-F. Lance F-F-Fart."

"Now, Rose . . ." Dick Richards frowned reprovingly. "Lance *Ffarthing* is his name." His voice dropped to a squeaky whisper. "Anyway, everytime you hire somebody, you're stuck with Social Security, just for starters. And what you have to pay a cook nowadays—it's highway robbery!"

Rose just smiled. Alex had seen Ludmilla like this—

unforgiving. A staccato laugh emerged from Rose's red-lipsticked mouth. Her face was deathly white with too much powder, and the mascara, perfectly applied to highlight those unearthly gray eyes, had run a little, he was sad to note.

"I love it! Alex isn't a man who concerns himself about the *mundane* things, Dick. Not like you, worried about every toothpick." Rose turned to her daughters. *"Do you hear what I'm saying?"*

The eldest, whom Alex believed was Sindy, nodded dejectedly. She didn't want to hurt her father, but she was afraid to disagree with Rose. What a mess!

"Why should Alex worry about who cooks his meals? And why should *I* have to worry about it either?"

Mouth set, Richards hunched over, listening, not listening, twisting the bottom of his untouched wineglass into the tablecloth.

"Oh, shit!"

Rose jerked back, jamming her chair legs against the rug. She jumped up and stalked out of the dining room.

Richards didn't even turn his head to watch her go.

"Will you please excuse us, Daddy?" the oldest girl asked.

"Yes, all right." His voice was dead.

The eldest spoke, surprisingly, to Alex.

"Good-bye, sir."

Alex was speechless, touched. God Almighty, he felt for these two. They wrenched his heart. And they were gone, their feet making a racket on the stairs. Now, what *did* he say to a man who had been so humiliated? But Richards was completely unaffected. As if he'd been waiting for the ladies to leave the room, he blandly broached the subject of Cazimir Ben Gazi, the poor, dead lad.

"An interesting man," Richards murmured. "I'm taken by his prognosis of business opportunities in the Middle East."

Alex remembered the formula. "Cazimir has returned to the bosom of his family. . . ."

He might have said to God's bosom, but it wouldn't be nice to tease poor Dick Richards.

"Peat told me he was here," Richards blinked, as if remembering something crucial. "Coffee, Alex, would you care for some coffee?"

"No. No thank you. I never drink coffee after breakfast, Dick."

"Very wise. More wine? Should I open another bottle, Alex?"

Richards sounded so eager to please, the more so certainly since Rose had gone. Alex turned down the wine too; what he wanted, obviously, was another vodka. But he wouldn't disappoint Richards by asking.

"I expected Cazimir to call before he left," Richards said guardedly.

Had Dick Richards *really* conceived of doing business with the poor, larcenous lad? Did he really have so many pennies to lose that he'd dare a business venture with Cazimir?

"He was here only very briefly. I'm surprised Peat even noticed." Alex studied the dregs of his red wine.

"Oh. So he'd already left . . . when . . ."

"Yes, *before Ludmilla's accident*, Dick."

If Peat had the audacity to report anything different to Richards, then, of course, he was dead wrong and in big trouble. *This was the formula.*

"Well," Richards said testily, "the next time he's here, I hope he will call. But . . ." Doubt struck. "Maybe he won't come back now, Alex."

Alex laughed gently. He understood—what Richards meant to say was that there wouldn't be any reason now for the lad to return to California. No use denying it—Cazimir had been Ludmilla's lover. He wasn't interested in Alex. *Too true!* And certainly the feeling was . . . had been . . . mutual.

"You could supply me with his address?" Richards asked.

Alex shrugged. "Ludmilla kept the records. . . . It's sure to be there."

Richards could understand that. He nodded perfunctorily, then began to get up. Alex was already planning how he could escape before brother Ralph and wife appeared.

"I . . . um . . ." Richards hesitated. "Rose is high-strung, isn't she?" he asked innocently. "She gets touchy whey you mention Lance. *I wonder why.*" He smiled fleetingly. "I'm prepared to offer you a brandy, Alex."

"I mustn't—"

He didn't have a chance to finish the ritual statement. Richards gripped his arm and stopped him at the livingroom doorway.

"Rose! What the *hell* are you doing?"

Shock exploded out of Richards, his first genuine outburst of feeling.

What Rose had done, rather innocent fun, really, was push a coffee table over close to their man-made Christmas tree. More thought provoking, Alex supposed he would have to agree, was that she had removed her hostess gown and was standing stark naked upon the table, holding a big enameled Christmas ornament over her head.

"I am the Spirit of Christmas Disastrous . . ."

"Rose! Get down!"

Dick Richards was huffing disapproval. His sunburned face flamed the more as Rose swayed to some private beat, ogling them benignly.

Alex had been right about her body. In shape it had been rather sabotaged by the two children—but evident instead was something more precious, a depth of fertility, a lushness Ludmilla had possibly never possessed.

"I am the Ghost of Christmas Pissed . . ."

Dick Richards began to yell angrily, but Alex stood quite still, feasting on something better than turkey: the unveiled female form.

"Rose! Cover yourself, for God's sake!"

One did not expect wholesome, pneumatic Miss America, did one? Rose's was the fulfilled body of motherhood.

At the midriff, he noticed appreciatively, she was as hairy as a bear, a Russian bear. Alex chortled to himself, not yet deprived, he realized with relief, of yearning. Very acutely he felt the pressure of desire in his loins. It came in a rush, perhaps reflected off Rose, a surge of desire that swept up from his feet, like charging horsemen. Of course he hadn't forgotten! And he never would! Ludmilla had never faulted him, even in the later years—he had always been the best of her boys. And Rose wouldn't either, he pledged to her smorgasbord of flesh, which he felt was signaling to him in a semaphore.

Alex snickered like a schoolboy while Richards danced around in a total dither. What a telling defeat for a man! All very well for a man's wife to get smashed on vodka and wine but . . . to strip in front of a stranger, in front of a man like Prince Spurzov, what a horrible loss of face!

Richards grabbed up her discarded hostess gown and leapt across the room. But Rose pushed his hands away.

"I am the Ghost of Christmas Future . . ."

Rose crowed with laughter, waving Richards away, her breasts jogging violently, the nipples like pug noses. Riveted, Alex watched, thinking, yes, yes, yes, thinking Ludmilla . . . Ludmilla.

Dick Richards grabbed for an arm. Rose screamed at him to leave her alone, kicking viciously. He ducked out of the way. Then, without warning, Rose toppled forward, howling.

Her weight was too much for him. Richards staggered sideways and, with frightened screams—particularly from Rose, whose bare skin was exposed—they crashed into the fake tree. How did you help people who had lost their dignity?

Rose shrieked with anger, then the pure joy of violence. Cursing Richards brilliantly, she tried to crawl free of him, and the tree ornaments scattered, and shattered.

Alex watched, his mind fuzzy, then confused. He could not decide—should he stay, or go? Go. Alex moved in slow retreat. Rose was *delightful*. She lay on the floor now, roaring, her head thrown back, laughing herself crazy. It was the sort of thing Ludmilla would *adore*, total madness. Everything was out of order, the world out of joint. Dick Richards began to cry, and this reminded Alex of something very apropos—once upon a time he had spent a short holiday with Ludmilla and her husband of some time back, the singing cowboy. Alex couldn't even remember his name.

And it had come to this sort of breakdown of logic and order and good sense, and Ludmilla had begun to smash the cowboy's guitar, his prized "singing guitar," over his head. She had busted the fragile instrument into kindling wood.

Alex found his coat in the hallway, opened the front door . . . and fled. He would have to walk back to Richlands. But the way was mostly downhill.

Out of sight of the house, he began to laugh too.

Yes, Rose! Yes, indeed! Ludmilla would have laughed too.

Chapter Seventeen

*V*AST WEALTH.

Remember Serena's fortune cookie?

Not vast. Maybe moderate. Sandor Veruckt was talking bonus, and if Sandor was talking that way, then Rossiter might reasonably expect to get his rake-off from Las Vegas too.

Sandor had made the investment in MorrisCom, and now, he told Rossiter cautiously on New Year's Eve day, "it appears *our friend* will make his *démarche* in the next week or so for the family-owned media mammoth we have discussed."

Sandor liked to be clever. But the message was clear.

"Good news, Sandor."

Rossiter had heard from the financial genius personally that day and also as part of the audience for Veruckt's usual bombastic year-end message to the troops.

"On a scale of one to ten," Sandor had proclaimed, "I give this expiring year a seven-plus. *For next year*, your leader, Sandor, forecasts continued prosperity, great progress for the nation, significant growth in GNP, healthy investment climate, falling interest rates, and a market sure to rise to five thousand on the Dow. In addition, Sandor sees relative quiet on the international political front, reduction of nuclear tension, and a beginning of solution to all the world's outstanding problems. . . . *I salute you!*"

After the bell sounded, signaling the end of the financial year in New York, Rossiter as usual made his way downstairs to the Bull Market, the bar he and his chums frequented. He was in

178

no great mood for celebration—but not anxious to go home either.

Betwixt and between, that was about it. Happy New Year? He was not at all sure of that. Vast wealth? How vast after taxes? How vast after splitting everything with Serena? There was the fly in the ointment of his sunny world view; there was an unseemly wart on the beautiful ass of forward-progress . . . and her name was Serena.

Dump her. Clara was right about that, as she was about most everything. Don't delay, don't piss your life away down the drainpipe of unrequited love. Clara, Clara was the ticket.

There must be another Clara, somewhere, that he knew. You had to poke around a little, do a bit of exploratory drilling, but she would be there!

"Hey, Ross! Buddy! Another?"

No, he did have to get going. Happy New Year and all that.

Anticipation did heighten just a little, thank God, as Rossiter neared the house in Beverly Hills. After all, they'd be going out to a couple of pretty good parties. He didn't have to work the next day and . . . who knew, maybe he'd get lucky. Whole lives could change in a matter of seconds. People could be alive, then dead, in the blink of a eye.

But it never went the other way—dead, then in the blink of an eye . . . alive. Too bad.

Sandor had been on about Thelma again. Somewhat to Rossiter's surprise, Sandor said Thelma and he would be spending New Year's Eve together. Yes, they had become such great, good friends. Thelma Drysdale was a wonderful, intuitive woman, though her intuition was on an entirely different plane than Sandor's—his pragmatic, hers ethereal.

"But a very good harmony, my dear boy!"

Rossiter thought about warning his employer that Thelma was perhaps not quite as harmonious as she seemed on the surface. But why? Sandor was a grown man and surely experienced—after all, Hungarian women were not noted for being saintlike.

The timbre of Sandor's voice definitely darkened as he spoke of Thelma, his nasal accent seemingly too much for the fragility of mere tissue. Hungarians had stringed instruments built into their throats, along with drama in their hearts.

"Thelma and I are like marching armies of the night,

Rossiterre,'' Sandor bubbled. "We seek no trouble, but if attacked, our retaliation is total. Understand me—that is our way!''

What was this? Rossiter shivered. Was Sandor warning him again not to play fast and loose with private financial transactions? But then, immediately, Sandor was congratulating him for his alertness in spotting the MorrisCom opportunity.

"We have taken a strong position, my boy,'' he hissed.

"'But the market was down today, Sandor . . .''

"No, no, not down, dear boy! *Unawares* is the word!'' Sandor pounced, like a tiger in the jungle. . . .''

Well, it was done, then.

Sandor had almost forgotten to tell him that his brother Seth would be coming to New York from Washington to join Hildy, Thelma, and himself for the festive celebration.

It would, Rossiter thought glumly, have been thrilling to be away somewhere . . . anywhere—especially when he spotted the big white truck parked in front of his house. A sign on its side read:

FURNITURE RENTALS
HOME AND OFFICE

What the hell was Serena up to now? They weren't having a party at Chez Addey as far as he knew. Or was Serena surprising him? She loved causing unpleasant surprises.

Rossiter parked and walked across his springy lawn. This was the "winter lawn,'' green and thick, planted by their Japanese gardener, probably richer than most of the people he serviced and one of the last of the breed. For the Japanese gardener was being rapidly replaced by the Mexican gardener. The Japanese gardener's children were up to something new, like banking and brain surgery.

Two men in white coats were just emerging from Rossiter's house. Appropriate, he thought. Had they come to take Serena away?

"Happy New Year,'' one of them snarled.

Which probably meant, simply, that Serena hadn't tipped.

Warily, Rossiter went inside, half expecting to come upon balloons and streamers, dozens of tables laid in white with sparkling glasses and silver.

But no—parked in the middle of the living room was a

crisply made-up hospital bed, and propped up in it was Bud Slagger.

Feebly he lifted his hand. "Hi, Ross! Surprise!"

Rossiter nodded casually. Of course, Bud was always lying there like this in the afternoon, waiting for him. Nothing could surprise Rossiter Addey, could it, in this world of high finance and low-down shenanigans?

Rossiter dropped casually into a chair by the study door just as Serena slipped into the room. She crossed to drape her hand on Bud's shoulder. Her look, and Rossiter hadn't yet said a word, would have scorched wallpaper.

"Where *the hell* have you been?" She was too hot to handle.

"Downtown."

"Drinking with the boys!"

Bud squirmed, glancing at Rossiter apologetically. Now, had Rossiter crudely asked what the hell Bud Slagger was doing here in the middle of the Rossiter Addey & Family living room?

"Serena," he pointed out patiently, "it's three in the afternoon, not three in the morning."

"So . . . *fucking* . . . what?"

Bud opened his mouth; a squeak emerged. *"Tiny wouldn't take me."*

Rossiter looked blank. He was not, after all, extrasensory.

"Dummy!" Serena snarled. "When the ambulance got him to Century City and the guys rang her bell, she wouldn't let them bring Daddy upstairs. What do you think of *that*?"

Tiny would not take delivery on her own husband? Not too shabby a gesture.

"I had to call and rent a bed—because you weren't here to take care of it!"

"Sorry, I was at the office."

"Having drinks with your friends, that's where you were."

Freely, he confessed. "We had a couple."

This was all so much easier than it might once have been.

"That was very *insignificant* of you, Ross!"

He was never quite sure what she meant by insignificant. Inconsiderate? Insufferable? Or that he was some kind of worm?

"We usually have a couple at the end of the year, nothing new about that."

"You bastard!"

"Baby . . . baby . . ." Bud's lip shook. "How was Ross supposed to know? Please, baby, take it easy. I don't feel good."

"And a lot *he* cares," Serena yelled, "a hell of a lot that son-in-law of yours cares!"

"I do care," Rossiter objected. "I'm sorry. So what are you going to do, Bud?"

Serena's eyes lit again, like a double-barreled flame thrower. "Do? What the hell do you think he's gonna do? Daddy is going to stay here until *his wife* . . ." She formed the words viciously, evidently forgetting that Tiny was also her mother. ". . . wakes up to her senses. You have got to go over there, Ross!"

"Me? Why?"

"To speak to her, for crissakes."

Bud slipped down, trying to duck. "Baby, baby, what's Ross going to say to her? She wouldn't let him in either."

Rossiter stared at him, at Serena, then got up. "I'm going to make myself a drink. You want something, Bud?"

Bud sighed rapturously. "Give me a touch of scotch, just a finger, on the bottom of the glass."

"Daddy! Jesus!"

"Babydoll . . . please. Listen, the doctor said a little bit, just a little, is supposed to relax you. They tell me it dilates the blood vessels."

"Who says that? *Who?* I'm going to call the hospital right away. Give me the name!" Serena blamed Rossiter, glaring at him. He didn't care. "I might have known. You would ask him to have a drink, wouldn't you? You're trying to kill him."

Rossiter didn't bother to answer. Bud knew she was crazy; yes, she had suffered something of a breakdown at the time of the breakup of her first marriage. Maybe the nerve ends were fraying again.

"You'd kill him just to get him out of the living room!"

"Baby, baby, that's enough."

Finally Bud had remembered *he* was the father, that he had a certain authority. Serena faltered; from one second to the next she sagged physically.

"I feel sick, nauseous."

"Go lie down," Bud said hopefully.

Serena's eyes fluttered groggily. So obstreperous a moment before, now she was hardly able to drag herself out of the room.

When she was gone, Rossiter asked quietly, "With water?"
Bud laughed weakly. "Yes, lots of water, Ross."

Rossiter sauntered into the kitchen. After all, why should *he* feel embarrassed merely because his wife was insane? Lourdes was standing at the sink as if she'd been put to sleep on her feet. Absently rubbing a sponge back and forth, back and forth, she stared out the window into the yard, at the trees, at their abbreviated swimming pool. Hadn't she heard Serena yelling?

For a second Rossiter considered goosing her back into the present tense.

Instead he barked jovially, *"Hello, Lourdes!"*

Lourdes whirled around, grinning like an idiot, as if she couldn't recall where she was. Finally she recognized him, and her face flared bashfully. Rossiter didn't speak to her often; when he did, it was a red-letter day.

He held the scotch bottle up to the light; plenty there for a few healthy shots. Rossiter poured neatly, added a little water to his and filled Bud's glass to the brim. Serena had it wrong; Rossiter didn't plan to kill her father. But if Bud went, Rossiter wanted him to go happily.

"How's it going, Lourdes?"

Her eyes bulged. Of course, she didn't know if, having broken the ice, he'd leap on her, coarsely. Not such a bad idea, actually. How her body did push at her starchy white uniform. Lourdes was pint-sized, true, but she was all there. If he'd really wanted to, Rossiter bet he could've pushed her into the little bedroom next to the utility room and nailed her. She might even welcome it—*if* she believed he was up to it. With all of Serena's screaming, Lourdes could be forgiven if she assumed there wasn't a hell of a lot of *macho* left in Rossiter Addey.

"Okay, okay."

He was astonished. She had spoken. Had she actually understood his friendly question? He winked at her boldly.

"Hi, ho, Lourdes!"

Rossiter banged back through the swinging door and into the living room. Bud was lying as still as a mummy.

"Push me up a little, Ross."

The handle was at the head of the bed. Rossiter set down the drinks and cranked. Slowly Bud's head and shoulders elevated.

"Thanks. Now, pass me that drink, Ross. *I am ready!*"

Serena out of the room five minutes or less, and Bud was already better. A little color had returned to his cheeks.

He sipped. "Hey, Ross, the nectar of the gods!"

"The first of many more, Bud."

"I'm sorry about Serena, Ross. Sometimes—"

"Forget it. Doesn't matter, Bud."

"You've very patient with her, Ross. I 'preciate that," Bud slurred. Just the baby shot had hit him.

"Forget it."

What else could Rossiter say, that within weeks he was going to wind up his affairs with Serena, and the problem that had been worrying the back of his mind was that he didn't want to split his bonus with her?

"How in hell am I going to get back to Vegas?" *This* was Bud's salient worry. "Tiny won't drive me, that's for sure," he brooded. "You ever hear anything like that? Not letting me back in my own goddamn apartment? I could get a court order, couldn't I? Is it worth it?"

Trying to think optimistically, Rossiter suggested, "Maybe she didn't know what it was they were delivering."

Bud laughed mirthlessly. "You mean she thought they were delivering a load of hay . . . or horseshit? If it was a case of vodka, you can be sure she'd have opened up."

Rossiter chuckled politely. It was Bud's joke.

"Or a keg of her goddamn beer, you bet!" Bud guffawed. "Nah! She knew it was me, all right. The ambulance guy told me she said to take 'that asshole' to the city dump. So that's when I had to come here, Ross. Sorry."

"Hey . . ."

"You know I hate to be a burden on anybody, Ross."

"Bud . . . forget it."

How many times was he graciously going to tell Bud to forget it?

"But I gotta get back to Vegas, Ross. I can't stay down here forever. I got work to do. . . . We're getting together our Easter campaign."

"Who's coming in?"

Bud named singers, a couple of bands, and went on for a few moments about a new magic animal act wherein this Kraut fairy made elephants disappear into thin air. Pretty good trick if you liked tricks, which Rossiter didn't. He also hated Las Vegas, everything about the place, rejecting the notion that Vegas represented that which was best and brightest, the crowning glory, of American civilization.

"Aah, shit, Ross . . ." Bud stared at his glass. "I miss the old days."

Rossiter knew the next name out of Bud's mouth would be that of Shorty Estoril, deceased bandleader.

"Time was, Ross, when Shorty Estoril—I've told you about him before—Shorty was a standing feature at the Alhambra every Easter time. People say what Harry James was to the Paramount in New York, Shorty was to the Alhambra in Vegas. I've got every recording Shorty and the Royal Vibes ever cut, most of them thirty-sixes, natch. My collection is *also* complete," Bud went on spiritedly. "I think I'll probably will it to a museum, not give it to Tiny, the bitch. She'd just throw it in the garbage or give it away to the Salvation Army."

"It'd be worth a fortune, Bud."

"Goddamn right!" Bud fretted. "Maybe the Met in New York. I always liked the Met."

If memory of Shorty Estoril made Bud feel better, he'd let him go on, even though, sooner or later, Rossiter was going to begin screaming. Better get it all said before Serena came back.

But how could he have forgotten? Rossiter suddenly remembered MorrisCom. "By the way, Chet Arthur's going to lay down that bid next week."

Predictably, the deeply carved and illness-accentuated lines in Bud's face softened; for a second he looked like he might burst into tears.

"Do tell!" Bud clucked carefully; he didn't want to rip out his stitches. "On the strength of that, Ross, what say to one more course corrector?"

Why not? People didn't have all that much to celebrate these days. Why not, and let the chips fall where they might? Rossiter took Bud's glass and headed for the kitchen. Goddamn if Lourdes wasn't standing there still, peering out the window. What the hell fascinated her so? He followed her eyes . . . birds? Some guy flashing at her from garbage alley, that narrow roadway running between the blocks where the good people of Beverly Hills stacked their mountains of garbage?

"Hi, ho!"

Again, taken utterly by surprise, Lourdes leapt a foot off the floor. A small cry of alarm burst from her. She was shy, he appreciated, timid, like a bird, a nicely plump little Wetback Whitebreast. Grinning a little foolishly perhaps, Rossiter managed two more hits out of the bottle, then threw it in the trash. Lourdes watched him solemnly, as if he were doing something for the Holy Mass. Rossiter winked again broadly; this time she managed a brave smile.

"And I wouldn't mind throwing you an adult portion of *carne asada* either, honey."

Lourdes didn't get it. Why should she? She probably thought he was mentioning what he wanted for supper.

By now Bud was smiling beatifically. Rossiter wondered if they had valet parking at the Pearly Gates, because Bud looked like that was where he'd just arrived.

"Goddamn *good* news, Ross!"

"Yeah." Rossiter handed him the second, weaker drink. "Not a bad piece of news to end the year with."

"Shit, you say! Wonderful!" Bud beamed. "If I could just have a cigarette now, I'd have it knocked up."

Sure enough—Serena's word. *Knocked up.* It would have lifted her out of her grave.

Where the hell *had* she come from? She must have been in the upstairs hallway, listening, for at the moment she came tumbling down the steps. If her voice had been a knife, she'd have cut them to pieces.

"No! Goddamn it, Daddy, no! I heard you mention *cigarette*!"

Bud fenced pallidly. "Just kidding, baby, baby, wasn't I, Ross?"

"Of course you were."

She fumed. "A lot *you'd* care."

"Serena, I keep saying I do, I do, I do. Don't I, Bud?"

" 'Course you do!" With the two drinks inside him, Bud was a little sharper now. "Cut it out, baby, you're making us all nervous screaming like that."

"And another drink!" She pointed.

"The same one, right, Ross?"

"Yeah, right."

"Liars!"

Serena had changed costumes. When he'd arrived, she'd been wearing skirt and sweater, a half-dozen or so gold chains and medallions dangling into her roomy cleavage. Now she was in a jogging suit and Reeboks and had brushed her hair into a ponytail.

Coldly she informed Rossiter, "If you counted on us going out tonight, you'd better count again. The party scene is off—I just called everybody and told them we couldn't make it, due to circumstances beyond our control. . . ."

She glanced at her father, lips twisted in heavy sarcasm.

"Baby, baby, that's just silly. No reason for you not to go out. I'll just watch a little TV, then go to sleep."

"No way!"

"I shouldn't've come here."

"Oh? And where *were* you going to go, Daddy?"

"I dunno. I should've had those guys drive me straight back to Vegas."

"So *sorry,* Rossiter," she said with a sneer.

"Hey . . ." He shrugged. "Do I care? I don't need parties . . . do I, Bud?"

Bud shook his head unhappily.

"Besides," Serena said pointedly, "there's something I think you should do."

"Which is?"

"Go talk to *his wife* and find out her intentions."

"She'll never let him in, *the bitch,*" her father moaned.

Silently Serena went behind Bud's bed. She massaged his shoulders and ran her hands down his chest, through the top of his pajamas.

Rossiter nodded. Philosphically, he finished his drink and put the glass down.

"Good thinking. I'll give it a try." Serena expected him to resist, but he was at the front door before it registered on her that he was going.

"Now, Ross—" Her eyes bucked.

He flashed her a smile. "See you . . ."

Chapter Eighteen

*F*or a moment, ironically, Seth and Hildy were being invited to travel with the Betancurs on their plane to the Tennessee farm where Sol and Alice traditionally entertained their best political friends, principally the Occupants, as Katie-Corky Corcoran called them, on New Year's Eve.

But then it had occurred to Alice that this would be a bit much, more than unsubtle of her, considering her intimacy with Seth, the fact of which she was not sure she could conceal . . . and they were quickly disinvited.

Seth didn't advise Hildy of the invitation, or its reversal, doubting he'd have taken her with him anyway.

Hildy was digging deeply into New York City. Seth had expected her to be complaining bitterly about not having gotten back to Munich in time for Sylvesters Nacht, as New Year's Eve was called *auf Deutsch*, and he'd been prepared to tell her to go on back by herself, that he was stuck in Washington. But it was not necessary; Hildy was perfectly happy at Thelma's big place on upper Fifth Avenue, she said, adding, slyly, that Thelma did not always come home at night!

What did she mean? That Thelma was carrying on so openly with the financier Sandor Veruckt?

And now it seemed Seth might indeed have to make another trip to the West Coast. Madison kept muttering about a loose end out there—apparently the butler at Alex's place who had actually found the Ben Gazi body. Loose ends dangled, Madison said pallidly, and Nature abhorred dangling ends.

188

And, Madison insinuated, colorless eyes without hope, shouldn't Addey talk to one of the company psychiatrists about his dead Russian friend, Nick? Madison didn't want him out of his sight, Seth told Katie Corcoran bitterly; they figured he had to be in a stage of pre-crackup because of what had happened to Nick Kolhsa. In his own defense, Seth had become amazingly open with Katie; she was affectionate, sympathetic. Katie understood what to say when he awakened in a cold sweat, shaking from the nightmare, shown by the bad gods of his dreams what they had done to Nick. Katie held him to her generous body, comforted him.

But he couldn't tell her about Alice Betancur. Katie did not press him for information but she must suspect he had seen Alice again. She couldn't know why. She said nothing. And in the end, perhaps, Alice would make nightmares as bad as Nick's.

Alice mesmerized him, absolutely . . . there was no question about it. The sordid details of her relationship with Ben Gazi leaked out enticingly, like acid dripping on his imagination. Such a damaged woman! Scorched white, burned over the hot flame of passion, wasted by degradation; the bare thought of her made him tremble with a sick sort of desire. In his arms, in strange places, Alice mewed pathetically and begged him to do things he refused to do.

It was better, she said, that he not appear in Tennessee. He was so low when it came to the bureaucratic totem pole.

"I'd love to invite Corky," Alice wept, "but I can't—she's *press*! Do you like her? Is she your *mistress* now? Yes, I know it, how I die! And your fiancée, what about her?"

"In New York."

"Hildegard?"

"Yes."

"If you came, would you bring Corky . . . or Hildegard?"

It was freezing cold except where their bodies touched. Alice's skin caught fire; it burned, and she moaned painfully. Everything hurt her; surely, there was *something* wrong. But she wanted to hurt, wanted to be hurt. It was such a simple thing—but Seth would not oblige.

Sadism was not his bag.

But it did not hurt *him* to hurt her, so what was the difference? she asked.

"Wrong. It does hurt me."

"Masochist," Alice charged gaily.

"Neutral," he disagreed.

Alice was so strange, yes, unique, he had to admit it. He wondered how much Clara Addey knew. Alice's father had been an Air Force general. Even at the beach in California, Alice said, she'd enjoyed being fried by the cruel sun. . . .

"Violate me in different places," she begged.

"No way."

So, all in all, Seth was happy to be relieved of saying yea or nay to her New Year's Eve party in Tennessee. He didn't particularly want to see Alice again in her own milieu. Better that they should meet in the privacy of Washington. Alice had wondered if they dared use Katie's place. Seth vetoed that idea—he wanted Katie kept out of it. She was too good, too innocent. So it was strange hotels. Dumps Alice suggested, dives, ratholes, holes in the walls, dens of iniquity. It all went with the territory: punishment. Violate her, violate her. No. No.

Anyway, Seth had no desire to rub elbows with Kraszewski; surely, he'd be in Tennessee. Or to see Washburn again.

Katie? That would be all right. She was going back to Texas for a few days. And he'd be in New York—Katie knew about Hildy. Seth had leveled with her about *that* business right away. So he'd go back to his German, Katie summed up, and she wouldn't ever see him again.

No . . . *Yes*, he would have to see Hildy. But, believe him, that was all over. Hildy was headed in a different direction. Meaning? Meaning nothing.

"I've gotten to know you," Katie said, gazing at him, showing the big white teeth, without artifice baring herself to him, letting him stare at the big white breasts, so muscular, like all her body: big, brash, and open. The same way she made love.

He was a lucky man that way, Seth supposed.

Alice Betancur had apparently stopped worrying about Ben Gazi's disappearance. Explaining it away, she said it was obvious *Caz* was on a long mission somewhere. Which was the truth—he was definitely on a long mission. He could've made it to Jupiter and back in a lot less time. Maybe Alice didn't care anymore . . . Seth Addey was her new therapist. She adored him—at least she said she did. But Seth doubted adoration had anything to do with it, or simple love—Alice was merely dependent on whomever took over her mind.

Orchestrate . . . orchestrate. That was the secret.

Before she left, Alice told him there were black and white pictures and color film and books of names, and she was in all of them. Sometimes with men, alone, yes, she said, weeping into the pillow, begging him to whip her, presenting her back, her front, sides, upside, downside, wanting him to violate her in ways Seth was certainly not prepared to do. Yes, the pictures, Alice said, she with the men; or with the men and other woman. Yes, yes, the other woman, a close friend of Caz's, perhaps his cousin.

Her name was Mabel Harrey.

And so here he was in New York City. A couple of days' respite was a blessing. Seeing Hildy again after these last few trying and action-packed weeks was okay—though by now it was clear enough that their alliance was kaput. She didn't say it. But it was obvious. Hildy didn't bother to move back into a hotel with him; she stayed where she was, with Thelma.

The night was freezing, typical New Year's Eve weather. It had snowed, then rained, then frozen. Black ice surfaced the city. The wind howled down Fifth Avenue and they had to walk an uncomfortable distance for a cab.

He had picked Hildy up at his mother's apartment like they were going out on a date; the shared flat in Munich could be only a memory now. Seth wondered how he'd get Hildy out of there; she'd moved in one night, carrying a folding cot under her arm, saying unbelievably, that she was lonely but didn't want to "crowd his space."

There was no talk of resuming their love affair. Hildy was as cold and distant as she could be; gone were the days, Seth realized, of violent physical demand, even aggression—as Hildy would return from one of her photographic forays to the far corners of Europe like a wild woman, squealing and perspiring like a weight lifter, the fine film of upper-lip fuzz pearly with lust. God, he did have a memory of that; but didn't mention it now, as she trotted along almost primly beside him.

Comparisons were rude; comparisons of women *rudest*. God knew which of them suited him best.

* * *

To Seth's horror, Sandor Veruckt, his mother's barrel-chested capitalist friend, was dressed in a beautifully tailored black dinner jacket, ruffled evening shirt, and big, fluffy bow tie. Seth, of course, didn't have any formal clothes with him, and as he was apologizing for this, Veruckt waved his words away grandly, grabbed Hildy's hand and began kissing it in European fashion, starting at the fingertips and babbling at her in German.

"You're looking very fashionable, Mother," Seth said, bending to kiss her cheek. "I'm sorry about my clothes."

"Not to worry," Thelma said. "Sandor does love to dress up."

Sandor's apartment was splendid, high above the United Nations Plaza, with a view south, obliquely toward the East River, over the roof of the General Assembly Building. His arm around her waist, Sandor made Hildy go with him to the windows. Proudly, he began pointing out lighted objects of some small interest. After a few moments a middle-aged woman in maid's uniform hurried into the living room with a large tray upon which there sat the usual—an opened half-kilo of caviar, little forks and spoons, a plate of brown bread quarters, and dishes of sour cream, shredded eggs, onions, and lemon. Putting the tray in front of Thelma, the maid hurried away and returned with half tumblers of vodka.

Sandor muttered at the woman in Hungarian and rubbed his hands together.

"Now then, let us . . . *pitch in*!"

After they started on the caviar—Seth ate his unenthusiastically, with just a little lemon squeezed on top—and the vodka, viscous syrup, Sandor wanted to know all about Seth's work with the government. Thelma had evidently reported to him the bare outlines of the Moscow incident, which was no more, or less, than she knew.

"I am given to understand, *Seeth*, that you handled yourself very well," Sandor said warmly.

Seth delivered his minimal reply. "They nailed me, then let me go, that's about all there was to it."

All attention, Sandor nodded as if this were the most interesting story he'd heard in all three hundred sixty-five days of the expiring year.

"I remind you that the Secretary of State is a close friend of mine, Seth." Sandor's eyes rolled significantly. "He was in

Vienna in 'fifty-six, the year I slipped out of Budapest. I shall call him and tell him we've met.''

Seth's back stiffened. "No, no, please don't . . . bother.''

"No bother! When Dan joined the administration, I became one of the seeing-eye dogs for his blind trust . . .''

"Really, don't. Please.'' He glanced to Thelma for help.

"Sandor, *darling*, Seth is a boy who never—''

Sternly, Sandor held up his hand. "Say no more. I understand perfectly. I much admire young men who prefer to advance on the basis of pure ability. No friends at court—am I right?''

Seth made himself sound reluctant. "I appreciate your thought.''

He wasn't very good at smiling under pressure. About all he needed in the present circumstances was for somebody else to help him. Any problems he had right now had arisen entirely from the fact Tom Addey was a personal friend of Sol Betancur's.

"Such a coincidence for all of us,'' Thelma murmured, "that Rossiter works in Sandor's office in Los Angeles.'' Her pointed, painted, hawkish face was disarmingly serene.

"And a most promising young man he is!'' Sandor smiled at Seth cordially. "One son in the world of finance, the other in *diplomacy. Madame*, your sons have done very well.'' Sandor beamed while leaning forward to take another heaping helping of the Beluga. "When you tire of the world of diplomacy, my dear boy, *think of finance*! The two are not necessarily mutually exclusive, you know.''

Sandor dropped it there, this open invitation to Seth to apply for a job. It must be serious with Thelma, Seth thought cynically.

Thelma stretched her hand out for Hildy. "Come,'' she cooed, "sit here, darling!''

Obediently, Hildy moved from a big, puffy pillow-footstool to sit beside Thelma on the couch, which was upholstered in blazing red poppy-printed fabric. Loud, but comfortable. Thelma tapped Hildy's knees, then took her hand, almost lovingly. Seth hoped the change in relationship between himself and Hildy wouldn't interfere with Thelma's fondness for the girl.

"We get along so wonderfully,'' Thelma happily announced. "Quite like my own daughter, *at last*, to have Hildegard there in the morning when I awake.'' Thelma's beaky face colored.

"You know what I mean . . . *Sandy*, have I told you of this girl's antecedents?"

"No, you have not, so I remember, darling!"

Sandy? Darling? Very cozy, weren't they?

This, naturally, had to be the business about Hildy being a distant relative of Max Beckmann, the German painter. From this Max Beckmann, Thelma burbled, had Hildegard inherited her sheer artistry with the camera. Hildy accepted it; she had learned how useless it was to argue with whatever Thelma had seized upon as the truth.

"To have such a relative," Sandor yelped, "you should shout about it, not be so modest, ravishing girl!"

Thelma smiled indulgently. "The other part of my theory, Sandy, is that Herr Beckmann, of course, while he worked as a hospital aide on the Western Front, saved nasty little Herr Hitler's life. . . ."

Seth remembered that not all Hungarians necessarily harbored bad feelings about the Nazis of the 1940s.

"'I think you might have a little trouble proving this, my love," Sandor observed.

"*Oh, yes?* Perhaps." Thelma would argue about it on a night like this, would she? "Whatever . . . Sandy . . . it *is* interesting about Hildegard, is it not?"

"Very." Sandor stared keenly at Hildy.

"My dear," Thelma complimented her, "you look just beautiful tonight. Lovely. Just right. Not too formal, but *très chic*, doesn't she, Sandy?"

"She is perfection itself," Sandor said. He might have been drooling, his lips were so moist and red. Seth wondered if Sandor might be wearing just a touch of makeup? Hungarians, he recalled, had been known to do so. Somebody had told him once that the Budapest railroad station, *before the war* (Second, that is), had been a sight when the Vienna evening train rolled in.

"Hildegard will definitely be doing assignments for *Classics*," Thelma declared, her eye on Seth. "Isn't that good?"

"Terrific."

Hildy murmured, "It is more than I ever expected, Thelma."

"And I must say that we *pay* very well! And well above the average!"

"But the pay is not so important as the prestige, Thelma."

"Don't say that!" Thelma cried. "You're a professional, and for a professional it must be a matter of money!"

"Yes, yes, then I agree," Hildy stammered.

Thelma hammered away, nevertheless, in her fervor, stroking Hildy's bare arm. Hildy, ever a stranger to the cold, was wearing a sleeveless little black cocktail dress which hardly covered her. Sandor had noticed it instantly. His milky eyes stroked Hildy as surely as Thelma's hand.

Thelma laughed. "Heavens, I'm so pleased with everything, I'm seeing pink!"

"I, too," Hildy said.

"Soon we'll have a long discussion about *Classics'* editorial policy, little Hildegard. We will talk about our New Woman—"

Sandor interrupted with an oily chuckle.

"But not tonight, dearest. I believe, unless I am very mistaken, that the traditional *roasted goose* is ready! Hungarians, of course, are the best cooks in the world, and my cook, Katya—you have seen her—is supreme among the supremes."

As the women went inside to sit down at the sparkling, candle-lit crystal and silver-laden table, with the same spectacular view of the southern quadrant of the City of New York, Sandor nudged Seth with his elbow.

"My congratulations," he whispered, "this Hildegard is a *winner*! I admire her greatly. Women like this, ach!" His eyelids buckled. Then he said something which, if Seth had at the moment been very attached to Hildy, might have disturbed him very much. "She has tight buttocks, above all to be admired, my lad—she must be . . . *within* . . . like a tight shoe. A ballet slipper perhaps?"

Seth nodded, slyly agreeing. "Exactly."

Sitting there, then, while lascivious Sandor was piling the plates with meat, Thelma spoke up.

"Speaking of geese," she sang, her cheeks lit by bright red spots, "they're trying to cook *my* goose at Morris Communications—"

"Dear lady—"

She paid no attention. "Wilkey Morris Junior, a shadow of his beloved father, had the gall, the absolute gall—he made me see red, red, red—to suggest that my assistant be fired and that I, Thelma Drysdale, be replaced by a *man* as editor—even going so far as to accuse Esther Murat to my face of being a lesbian!"

Carelessly, for he was concentrating on the goose, Sandor said, "Actionable right there, I would have said."

"Incredible," Hildy said angrily.

Small wonder! Offered a job with the magazine, she now had visions of the offer as quickly evaporating.

Soothingly, Seth said, "Now, Mother, you know damn well they can't touch you. *Classics* is such a fantastic success!"

"Surely!" Hildy seconded the motion.

"Precisely." Sandor did too. "Dear lady, I shall not go into the details . . ." He marched his fingertips across the tablecloth in Thelma's direction, then cleverly twined his fingers in hers. "I will guarantee to you that before this is over it will be Mr. Wilkey Morris Junior himself who will be . . . totally humiliated."

"It would be beautiful to think so, Sandy."

"She doesn't believe me." Sandor winked at Seth. "But, we shall see—yes, *fraulein*?"

"Surely!" Hildy cried once more.

"The monster!" Thelma sniffed contemptuously.

Sandor waved his arms. He had had enough. He was pouring a red wine so thick it came out of the bottle like catsup

"Bull's Blood, my dearest friends, from the Hungarian *puszta*. . . ."

Wherever that was. Actually, Sandor told Seth, it meant the broad flatlands of Hungary, the central European steppes.

"Sweetheart! Beloved one! Thelma, my *princess*!" Sandor held up his glass. "Enough on Wilkey Morris Junior!" The command was unmistakable. *"A toast to us!"*

This was good, low-down strong wine, this Hungarian plonk, well-calculated to blur the edges of all but the most implacable hatred.

"All right," Thelma sighed submissively, "then just one toast: *Confusion to our Enemies!"*

"That I buy." Sandor's moist round face shone.

Seth had to admit that the goose was the best he'd ever had. This Katya, whoever she was, was supreme, as Sandor had boasted.

Hildy's face was flushed, like Thelma's, and her eyes gleamed with excitement. She was convinced that she'd made it. And why shouldn't she think so, sitting up here in the stratosphere looking down on the U.N. buildings and the whole East Side, a veritable Princess of New York?

As it must, the matter of his own extended stay in this country had to come up. Indeed, his mother said, was Seth not to have been back in Europe by now?

"I don't object, Heavens forbid!" Thelma said quickly. "I wouldn't want to lose my houseguest!"

"Well . . . I don't know what to tell you." Seth was being, he thought, uncharacteristically forward. "Something has come up—I may have to go back out to California."

"Really?" Thelma did a rapid calculation. "How convenient! Hildegard *will* be going with you—"

Seth held back, resisting. "It's really just for an hour or two. A flying visit."

"But Hildy *must* go with you!"

"Maybe not," Hildy murmured forlornly.

"Remember our story idea, Hildegard! The Great Houses of California . . . Are you going to Los Angeles?" she demanded of Seth.

"Maybe . . . probably."

"You see!" Thelma exclaimed. "Richlands! It does my heart good! I knew it! My intuition told me so—you're going to see Alex Spurzov, aren't you, one of my oldest friends! *Say hello!*"

"Not necessarily. This is a boring trip, some consular affairs," Seth dissembled.

It occurred to him that he had never really had it out with his mother. She could be very annoying; so sure of herself, with a superiority that set her apart. Her glittery eyes, her formidable features, put him off. So did the way she pawed at Hildy.

Not that he actually cared anymore.

"Hildegard! I want you on that plane!"

So saying, Thelma reached for Hildy's left hand. If she could have, Seth had the feeling, Thelma would have cut it up and eaten it.

Chapter Nineteen

*A*t approximately eleven-thirty Tom went to the kitchen for the second bottle of Dom Pérignon.

When he came back into the living room, Clara was standing by the marble mantlepiece.

"I think I'm going to bed," she said glumly, "I don't feel like waiting till midnight."

"Clara . . ." He'd known ahead of time it was coming to this. "That's strictly against the rules."

"Well . . . so it's New Year's—so what?"

"Goddamn it, Clara . . ." She faced him ceremoniously, one hand on the mantle, self-consciously poised, as if waiting for him to deliver the next line in a formalized drawing room comedy. Tom set the bottle down carefully. "Now just tell me what the hell's bothering you."

She heard him. And now she would say her line.

"I suppose I should tell you."

"Yes, you definitely should."

Maybe it would be something entirely different than what he expected. But, in his bones, heavy with the burden of déja vu, he knew it was about Martha, something over which he had no real control: Martha was rambunctious, but not serious, if the truth be known. There were so many other things . . . well, not many, but definitely a few that would better justify her feelings of umbrage.

Clara paused for so long that Tom thought he could maybe finesse her just a little, put her just slightly on the defensive.

"Clara—have you fallen in love with *another*?"

She looked startled, embarrassed to tell the truth. God, maybe he had hit on it, purely by accident. Maybe this wasn't about Martha after all. Clara didn't answer the direct question. Instead she leveled her own, the one he had expected.

"Have you started up some kind of an April-September thing with Martha?"

"What?"

"You heard me!"

"Don't be crazy."

"No, no!" Clara shook her head violently. "It was very plain . . . plain as the nose on your face up at the vineyard. . . . She's been chasing you for months . . . *years!*"

"No."

"No, what?"

"What do you mean, 'No what?' It's just ridiculous, that's *no what.*"

"Don't think I don't understand you, Tom," Clara said ferociously.

He shrugged, maybe too scornfully. "I have no secrets—I'm not a hard man to read."

"I've seen you operate, my friend."

"Really?"

He knew what was coming. She was sure to mention Bette Toland. At times of *extremis*, Clara usually threw that name at him.

"I know you've been to bed with Bette Toland."

"Prove it," he challenged.

"I have to prove it?" Clara demanded. "Are you saying we're going to court?"

He turned away. "Only if you bring it to that, Clara." Tom pointed at the champagne. "I'm going to open this bottle and have some more." He looked over his shoulder at her. "Do you want some?"

"No."

"Clara, it's getting damn close to midnight. So say your piece. I'd sooner the year didn't end like this."

"I've seen you look at her, Tom."

"Who? *Bette!* You know she's a tease—"

"I'm not talking about her. I'm talking about Martha!"

Already she was off on the wrong track and unsure of herself.

"If we live in the same house, it's kind of hard for me not to look at somebody."

"You now what I mean, Tom. I mean *look*."

"Oh," he said sarcastically, "you mean look *that way*?"

"Damn right!"

"No," he repeated.

"There's never been a time when you didn't look at women, Tom!"

"Including you, sweetheart."

He had the foil off the bottle, now was untwisting the wire around the cork. His glass was ready and waiting—so was he. Carefully, Tom pushed the lip of the cork upward; the trick, as he was always saying, was not to pop it explosively. That ruined the stuff. You had to ease it out with no more than a hiss of gas.

"We haven't forgotten about Ludmilla," Clara charged.

"Who has?" He'd done it. Puff! Fresh champagne gushed into his glass. "You weren't even alive then, sweetheart."

"Stop calling me sweetheart."

"What *should* I call you?" He held up the bottle. "Sure?"

"I know you find her very attractive!"

"Martha? You're damn right I do! She is attractive too! She's just like you . . . *ergo*, you must be damned attractive yourself . . . *ma'am*."

"You laugh at all her jokes—"

"So? She's a funny kid, so what do you want? She's good-looking and I do have thoughts that are normal for a horny old man such as myself."

"As I goddamn well said!"

Oh, boy, she was really livid now. Clara spread her feet on the hearth and planted fists on her hips, ready for a knockdown, drag-out.

"I want to know the truth—*has there been anything*?"

"You're crackers." He filled his mouth with reassuring champagne, swished it around in a way he knew would be infuriating.

"You won't tell me, will you?"

Tom stared at her amusedly. His reply had to be maddening.

"Clara . . . I'm a gentleman."

She let out a disgusted, furious snort, then impulsively

stepped toward him. But there was that self-conscious set to the corner of her mouth.

"Clara," he murmured lightly, "I hope you're not going to strike me."

She stopped. "You bastard! Give me some of that champagne!"

"Where's your glass?"

She glanced at the coffee table. Tom stepped past her carefully—she did have an unpredictable temper, he remembered. Retrieving her glass, he poured champagne in it, passed it to her, and offered a toast.

"Happy New Year, sweetheart."

Clara stared at him petulantly. "You still haven't answered."

"Nor have you. Didn't I just ask you if you'd fallen in love with another?"

Clara hooted. "With another? Another what? Water buffalo?"

"Old coot?" No, he hadn't forgotten what she'd said in the car on the way up to Morelli.

Clara adjusted her face calculatingly. Tom knew he shouldn't have asked the question. He was not going to get much of an answer.

"Maybe I have," she said, "but I certainly wouldn't discuss it. I'm *a lady*, and ladies are very discreet."

"Terrific . . ."

She smiled at him sweetly. "What time is it now?"

Tom glanced, as if nonchalantly, at his watch. He would never let on that he was concerned, or that he cared. So, he told himself, the chances were fifty-fifty—that's where he'd put them—that she had. He wondered who it was.

Biff Percy? It didn't seem Clara would have had time. Besides which, the uncouth and often slovenly artist was not Clara's type, not by any means. You could love the art, the work, without necessarily loving the artist.

"I make it midnight . . . on the nose," he said slowly, counting down the second hand of his watch.

"So," Clara said, "Happy New Year."

"Happy New Year!"

Gravely, Tom kissed her cheek. He wanted to put his arms around her and kiss her properly, but Clara slid away. She set her glass down next to the bottle on the hunt table by the dining room door.

"Well, now I am going. Will you come soon, Tom?"

He nodded. "I hate to let this go flat . . ."

"Bring it in, then?"

Her face softened. Maybe it was merely the light. But, at any rate, she seemed to relent . . . not forgive him, if that was what she had hoped to do. But maybe, what? Make the best of it?

He was not going to tell her about Martha.

On the surface everything *was* just wonderful. Christmas had been *beautiful*, Clara kept telling everybody. The weather had been very cooperative, you know, and they'd all had such a *marvelous* time together, just family, you see—Alberto, Clara and Tom, Martha, and Clara's brother Fred, and his wife and children.

In short, Clara had come away from Morelli in a terrible mood. Tom couldn't remember stickier times since those emotional days before their marriage when they'd become "inseparable," according to one of the Hollywood columns: the well-known divorce lawyer, they called him, and the northern California vineyard heiress, beautiful Clara Gates. Clara had been hell-bent to prove he needed her a lot more than she needed him.

Tom had the feeling now that he was closer to losing Clara than at any time since then. She had been bitten, he would've said, being rather an expert on the subject, by the bug of discontent, infected by a germ that set all her female genes a-battling.

Tom understood only too well that Clara was disturbed and frightened. With all the right instincts, she didn't know how to do battle with her own daughter.

Tom sat down with his glass next to the fireplace. Since they'd been out for a quiet dinner, just the two of them, their usual practice on New Year's Eve, he hadn't built a fire. The living room was chilly—a little ghastly and unfriendly, if the truth be told.

Christmas, as a matter of fact, had not been bad at all, leaving Martha out of it. It was a relief for him to be finished with all the business about Cazimir Ben Gazi. Tom had done his best, cooperated with those shadowy Washington figures . . . even then, the Ben Gazi bones had been lost in transit, like the most worthless piece of luggage. At least, Tom had told himself disgustedly, the powers-that-be might have had the sense to put

Ben Gazi on a military transport plane to save everybody trouble, and an ocean of potential embarrassment.

And then there was all the palaver with Alex and the witless butler. What did Alex actually know about Cazimir? Not very much, no more than Tom Addey, nothing worth reporting back to Washington. He'd left behind no letters, no known California bank accounts—not that Alex would've been aware of them—no address books . . . nothing. All Tom had found out really was that Ben Gazi had been Dick Richards's lover—for a moment, as unlikely a happening as one could imagine.

Tom hadn't even bothered to tell Seth.

So, being with Alberto for those few days at the vineyard had been pleasant, for him at least, never mind about Clara.

Yes, actually, never mind! Clara could be bloody tiresome sometimes.

Generally, the weather *had* been crisp and invigorating, perfect for long walks in the sleeping vineyards, or at the fireplace, the book, the bottle of peppy Morelli Zinfandel, and then the nap.

He had done his best to ignore Clara's irritable self. After all, a man could be held responsible for just so much. In truth, he could have argued, it was not his fault that Martha got it into her head to play games with him. Was it fair, Jury dear, that a man be held accountable for the actions of two perfectly mature but outrageous women?

Fortunately, none of them dared to show ill will in front of Alberto.

So Tom tried to stick close to the old man.

Alberto was not one of California's winemaking giants. His vineyard was of the boutique variety, which was to say that Morelli Vines produced a relatively small amount of high-quality wine, specializing in Chardonnay and that special California breed of Zinfandel.

Alberto had come out of the bottom of the heap in Italy, but in wide-open California he had prospered, as worthy immigrants were supposed to. What Tom liked about him—no, loved really—was that Alberto, whatever his background, was instinctive about what was best in the way of food, wine, and just plain living. Best of all, over his acreage he exercised a true patronship; he cultivated his land, nurtured it, improved it. As Alberto had been telling Martha, they would leave but the land would remain.

Alberto said Tom should work for the creation of special courts to deal with ecological banditry.

Clara's father showed no sign of slowing down, despite warnings of high blood pressure and a nervous heart muscle. Success always took its toll—how did a man go about trumping his own good work year after year?

That was Fred's bittersweet complaint. Fred wanted some time off. He'd come straight out of the University of California at Davis, the vinicologist's own school, to work for his father. Travel, he asked, *what's that*? No, no seriously, he wanted a year to take his family to Italy, to roam the vineyards in the old country. Why couldn't Clara and Tom come live here at Morelli for a year—just to be on the grounds, he argued. They understood what he meant; so did Alberto, though he'd never admit it.

"Women don't make winemakers," Alberto growled.

In a matter of years, a few or something longer than that, they would have to face it. Alberto was not going to be around forever. Fred was saying he wouldn't mind a few more brains in the business; it would be another fifteen years before he could count on his own sons for help.

Just think about it, he'd asked.

One afternoon, out for a walk with Tom, Martha tagging along just to get out of the house and away from Clara, Alberto had stopped and pointed his stick at the perfect rows of clipped-back vines.

"Straight, like an arrow! You see, Tom. Straight and honest. Beautiful, Tom, like God in Heaven. Like the law, isn't it, Tom?"

Like the law? He was still thinking about the vines and the law after Clara, too silently, her feelings so guarded, so mysterious, slipped out of the room.

The law was *not* like a vineyard with its straight and honest rows of vines, nothing like being aligned to the perfection of God in his Heaven. Tom understood what Alberto was saying— his own father had talked that way about the majestic redwoods, also in their logic and power related to the genius of the Almighty. But the law was made by men—and vineyards too. Alberto might like to believe his rows of vines were straight and true, but here and there they veered.

Alberto waved his Oakland A's baseball cap brashly in the wind, then pulled it down on his wiry iron-gray hair.

"See," he shouted, "all the way down there, past the vines to the clump of trees, all old cedar, *the road*! That's where your mother used to catch the school bus, Martha."

Alberto threw his arm around Martha's shoulder. The two were so unalike, one might wonder how they could be related. Alberto was dark and short, or seemed so because of his broad, muscled shoulders; Fred resembled him more than Clara did, or blond Martha.

Sometimes Alberto kidded them about that. They didn't look Italian; they looked like a bunch of Swedes.

"You'd like to get me here, wouldn't you?" Martha demanded of her grandfather. "You're too tough. I couldn't work for you."

Alberto only laughed and hugged her.

Sure, a likely story, Tom told himself, the old man merely adored her. He was allowed to. And Martha loved it. For a moment she could forget that Clara was giving her such a hard time. Hadn't Alberto noticed it too? There was not much that escaped his attention.

"You said women can't be good winemakers, Grandpa," Martha reminded him.

"*You could*. You could do worse too." Alberto looked gloomy. "And now *she's* talking law. Is that good, Tom?"

Tom grinned at Martha. She'd played with him so self-indulgently; his turn now.

"I'd give the law a wide berth if I was a *youngster* and stick to the land."

Sounded like the Old Coot, didn't he? When Alberto moved on, Martha gave it back to him.

"I'll stomp *your grapes*, mister!"

Then, later, when they'd finished the walk and returned to the main house and Alberto hustled into the big wood-beamed living room to feed the fire, and they were taking off their boots and coats, Martha did it to him again, slipped up beside him and kissed his cheek and hung on his arm, twisting his fingers in her hands.

Why?

Her scent by itself was enough to knock an Old Coot silly. She smelled like twenty, a good round figure, like the raw, moisture-laden wind, the bare earth.

Under her sloppy duffel coat, Martha was wearing those white cotton pants that ballooned around her hips and thighs and ran snugly to the ankle. She looked like a harem girl, all flushed and blond.

She hugged his hands to her breast, to the softness, no question about that: soft, giving. He did his best to keep cool.

"You've got to stop this, you're driving your mother crazy!"

"Is that why she's behaving so beastly to me? How could she notice? I never touch you . . . I don't get close. You don't let me."

"*She does notice.* Believe me."

Martha tossed her head. "Some things, you can't help—"

"Oh, yes, you can."

"Don't you believe people should let their emotions run?"

"No."

Of course he believed it but, as he considered the question now, only in the abstract. Tom tried his best to get a droll handle on this jagged and dangerous blade. He understood the world, after all, what a man could do, what he absolutely could not do. God must live in a state of deep ennui, having created such silly people and then being forced to watch them behave for all eternity with so little intelligence or imagination or respect. Run, Martha, run . . . *Run, Tom, run*, or Martha will catch you!

"Back off," he said gruffly. Alberto shouldn't come out of the other room and see them like this. "Unhand me, damsel!"

"Don't I mean *anything* to you?"

"He shook his head impatiently. "Don't be childish!"

"I know your problem. You're afraid of trouble . . . but I am *not* trouble."

"Oh, no? You *are* trouble—with a capital T."

But he couldn't budge her. Martha hiked herself up and kissed his cheek again, squirming against him, then forcefully got her lips to his mouth. As she had before, she seared him, like a branding iron pressed to his rump. Her belly swelled and she shoved her pelvis at him, whimpering . . . yes, childishly, like a child wanting something urgently. Ice cream, a piece of candy.

What the hell *was it* with her? Why this fixation? Clara had hinted at it—all the talk of Ludmilla had set them all going! The reminder of Tom Addey's wild affair with the Princess Spurzova had caused widespread aftershock.

"Hey! Tom! I'm opening the *vino*!" Thank God for Alberto!

Martha groaned with exasperation. So easily, then, could he

206

have put his hands to her in a going-away caress. He knew absolutely what he would have found, the shivering facts of flesh. Martha's face flushed and her lips became puffy . . . swollen with desire?

"I'm not attractive to you," she stated sullenly.

For God's sake, what was he supposed to say? He didn't want to put her off by telling her, no, she was a cow. On the other hand, he couldn't tell her the truth because that would only make matters worse.

"I refuse to answer on grounds of self-incrimination." No, too flip. She was ready to cry.

"Listen," Tom said urgently, "you're a very attractive girl—and you know it. If I weren't . . . well, I *am* married to your mother, for crissakes. If I weren't . . . But I am. Anyway, you're too young for me." He smirked at her judiciously, trying to put distance between them.

She was between crying and laughing. Tom pressed on.

"You're a bag of tricks I don't think I'd have the energy to open."

Martha grinned through tears, the sun through the rain. "Think of it as Pandora's *box*. . . . Age never bothered you with Ludmilla, *did it*?"

"She was older than me, not younger. See the diff?"

She was unconvinced, of course. Nothing Tom could say would deter her, which was nice, too, in a way.

"I told you before," she warned. "You just wait, Thomas Addey, you just wait."

Of course, Tom had ridden through the storm, whatever, due to his own good sense of balance, propriety . . . of the odds, most importantly. Yes, the odds were not good enough to let himself go with Martha Gates. It was too easy for a man to succumb to the primal urges, Tom thought he had learned. The odds, no no, they were not at all good for taking such a plunge and living to tell about it.

Better safe than sorry . . . that kind of thing.

Clara voice brought him back.

"Tom . . . are you coming? *I need you*."

Ah, Christ, he thought wearily, she had something else to say, another lightning bolt to hurl. Tom finished the glass of champagne, standing up then to take the bottle with him, yes, the Old Coot, to the bedroom. Pour champagne in her navel, that was an old Viennese idea. Perhaps such an old-world gesture would stave off the questions. He really had nothing more to tell Clara.

It was disenchanting, really, one of the great non sequiturs of life, that just when a man figured he understood a particular woman, something was always happening to make him realize that he didn't understand her at all. Ah, was this the sweet mystery of life, after all?

Of one thing, though, he was sure as he strolled into the hallway and past Martha's room—normally sensible men would kill to get at somebody like this girl.

"Tom? Tom . . ."

"Yes. Yes, Clara, I'm coming, Clara. I'm on my way, darling. . . ."

To his surprise, gratification too, Clara was in bed. She did seem to need him, very much so. Truce had been declared.

"Tom," she whispered, "don't turn on the light. Happy New Year. I'm sorry I was so horrible—"

"That's okay."

Biff? No, it couldn't be Biff. Whoever it had been, however, the experience must have been unsatisfactory. Clara was very unruly.

Afterward, she said, "God knows, I try. . . ."

"*Was* it Biff?" Tom asked her in the morning.

"Biff, what?" Clara was so innocent.

"The . . . water buffalo . . ."

Ah, a riddle. Clara laughed lightly. "Don't be silly. I'm trying to get *Martha* for Biff . . . not me."

"Old coot."

Clara leapt out of bed then and her rosy buttocks disappeared into the bathroom.

The telephone rang. Tom looked at his watch—eight A.M.?

"Hello."

"Hi, pal . . . Tom? This is Sol. How you doing? Happy New Year! Great party last night! You should've been here."

"We were not invited, Sol."

Just as well, Tom told himself briskly. To be in Tennessee with the Betancurs and their chums? No thanks.

"Well, you were, you know. Alice said she invited Clara—that's a fact, Tom!"

True? If so, Clara hadn't mentioned it.

"Well, you know, Sol . . . we always get bogged down with the family. . . ."

"Forget it, pal," Sol said breezily. "Best regards from George too, before I forget to tell you . . ."

George Washburn? Most unlikely, Tom told himself cynically. Regards from George were like the Christmas card from the White House—they only mailed a couple of million of them.

"Why I called, old buddy . . ." Betancur was positively singing with good humor. "I wanted you to be among the first to know . . . Our old friend Cazimir *has been murdered*! Yes, yes, don't say anything—very sad news indeed! Shot dead, Tom, our mutual friend. He'd been missing since he left L.A., if you remember—well, goddamn if his body didn't wash ashore in Spain. Near Malaga; the beach at the Marbella Club, as a matter of fact."

"My God!"

"Yeah. Everybody is very upset, Tom. Cazimir was a very good friend to this country, as you know. One of the Palestinian outfits must have gotten him, we figure—or possibly the commies."

"Sol . . . thank you very much for letting me know."

"Pal! Better you should know before the press gets it. Happy New Year once again, Tom, and many more. . . ."

The phone slammed down in Tennessee, where it would now be eleven, maybe ten in the morning, depending on the time zones.

So.

It was ended. The plan, evidently, had been to move the locale of Ben Gazi's death out of this country; it had something to do with turf. This had now been accomplished.

Clara reappeared as Tom lay there thinking about it.

"Who was that?"

"Sol Betancur. You didn't tell me Alice Betancur invited us to their New Year's party on the plantation . . . way South in the land of cotton, old times there are not forgotten—"

"Go away, go away—"

"*Look away*, Clara."

"Alice *did not* invite us, my foremost darling. . . ."

209

Foremost darling? What did that mean?

"Sol said—"

"Whatever he said, she didn't. Would I forget to tell you?"

"Yes, you might. There are things you don't tell me, Clara, *as I'm learning.*"

Then he remembered he hadn't told *her* about Ben Gazi. Well, he wouldn't now if she didn't ask.

Clara grinned playfully, hopping back beside him.

"There are things, leading man, it's better for you not to know."

Which meant? Yes, which meant *what*?

Slyly, Clara agitated him, with her mouth, her fingers.

"Shall we make it a memorable New Year's Day, Number One Husband?"

Goading, yes, teasing, taunting.

"You've been hanging around Chinatown again," Tom grunted.

Clara giggled happily. Happily? How could she be happy, keeping secrets to herself?

"It's the pills and powders. Maybe I'm turning nympho . . ."

At last! He had a shot. Tom smiled gratefully; the opportunity had come so soon in the new year to launch a good one.

"*I should get so lucky!*"

Chapter Twenty

Alex couldn't have been aware of it at the time, but Rose Richards moved into Richlands at approximately eleven P.M. New Year's Eve. She arrived carrying only that big sloppy pocketbook of hers, in a mink coat over slacks and a tight cotton ribbed shirt.

Rose . . . Rose. There was much more to Rose than even Alex had bargained for.

Rose, the Gypsy. Rose the passionate tramp. Alex had not seem her since the terrible Christmas luncheon fracas.

"Poor man, poor Prince," Rose whispered, "all alone on New Year's Eve . . ."

Alex smiled hauntingly. "Think nothing of it, darling. On such a night I prefer to be alone with my memories. . . ."

"Me too," she agreed. "Of course, we weren't going out. We *never* go out. Richards is already in bed."

"You *tiptoed* away?"

"Will he know? You don't suppose, Prince Alex, that we sleep in the same bed, do you? I could be gone a week and he wouldn't notice."

"Oh, Rose. Oh, Rose."

"Never you mind. I'm feeling fine—now that I'm here."

Having opened the door for Rose, nosy Peat lingered, lurking in the marble foyer overlooking the gallery. Quickly Alex had escorted her down there to get her out of earshot.

The man was behaving most strangely, Alex had decided.

Perhaps possession of fifteen or twenty *pounds* of Ludmilla's, and Alex's, gold had incited in him feelings of independence.

Tonight Peat was wearing a pair of riding breeches, veritable jodhpurs, shiny black boots, again reminding Alex of nasty things in Europe, as had the peculiar chauffeur's hat he'd worn Christmas Day. Was the man *all there*?

"Peat!" Alex turned, lifting his voice to echo through the gallery. "Bring us a bottle of Cristal in a bucket of ice, and glasses. And Peat," he cried gaily, for wasn't it nice after all to have such a guest, "put a couple more on ice. . . ."

Peat came to attention. For a second, suspiciously, Alex thought he would click his heels and salute.

"Yes, my Prince!" His voice crackled. "In a jiff."

"My God," Alex told Rose, "the man actually spoke. Usually, he is dumb as a post."

"He speaks to Richards all the time," she said.

Alex thought about that. Would Peat have told Dick Richards about the lad, how he had discovered Cazimir dead, a suicide, in Ludmilla's boudoir, then for some reason dragged him out of the house, and *then* stolen the gold, Ludmilla's treasure; correction: part of her treasure. No, probably not—for if Peat had told Dick Richards about the poor lad, then he might've been led to the gold . . . and was Peat going to split with Richards, who needed nothing? Not likely.

Chuckling acidly, Alex murmured, "And what do you suppose Peat will tell him about this?"

This being Rose here at Richlands with Alex Spurzov, who was even then in the act of elevating Rose's smooth hand to his lips, kissing her chubby fingers one by one, all the while gazing limpidly at her from out of the top of his eyes, dazzling her, as was his way. Women fell for Alex's smile, the slowly accelerating, searching, disrobing look. Of course, he'd already seen Rose disrobed. Nevertheless, he made the smile build, intensify.

"A Happy New Year, Rose, sweetheart."

Not at all shyly, eyes afire, Rose twisted her hand away to slip her arms around Alex and pull his skimpy body to her, hard against those ample breasts. She planted her large lips squarely on his mouth and kissed him generously, extravagantly.

"I hope you won't get bored with me, Prince," she gasped.

"Rose, Rose . . ."

Alex remembered, he couldn't help it, New Year's Eve, all

those years before in New York. The Stork Club at midnight with Ludmilla . . . Ludmilla had kissed all the bankers like this—plentifully, bountifully, as Alex, not far behind, gave his ardor freely to all the heiresses.

Peat had done them proud. The Cristal was wrapped in a white napkin. Two long-stemmed glasses rested beside it on a heavy silver tray.

"Peat, is it cold?"

"It is cold, my Prince."

"Then open the noble bottle! *Sesame!*"

Though Peat might not know it, Alexei was an expert at opening champagne bottles.

"You see," he murmured, as he monitored Peat's so-far impeccable maneuver, "Cristal was first served to the Czar. It was bottled, like no other champagne, in clear glass, by the famous Louis Roederer, precisely to be served in midsummer, at the Cristal Night party in Leningrad, Petersburg then."

"Oh, yes?"

But how would Rose know of such things, this American lass of varied ancestry?

Peat had done it! A bare pizzle of gas escaped the bottle.

"Well done, Peat!"

Something resembling a smile illuminated Peat's saturnine face—a fleeting expression of joy. He poured with care, passing one glass almost with reverence to Rose, the other to Alex.

"Ring when you're ready for the other one," he said.

Then self-consciously, for he must have known they were watching, he left, his boot heels clacking on the stone floor, up the steps, through the foyer and back into the butler's pantry.

"What's he gonna do now?"

"God knows."

Rose stared steadily at Alex, as if scheming where she would begin to dissect him. There was a single-minded focus in her eyes that after a time might unnerve a man. Alex must begin to wonder, eventually, what she had on her mind.

Unexpectedly, she said, "Prince, I'm sorry about the scene I made the other day . . . I just lost control."

"Rose . . . Rose . . ."

Of course, it didn't matter. Alex had been around ruffians all his life.

"It's water under the bridge," she said indifferently. "Dick can take it or leave it."

Alex remembered he'd already considered mounting a cuckolding operation against Dick Richards, and it did not seem now there would be much resistance from Rose to such a move. On the other hand, seeking such an adventure, one was by definition vulnerable. And Rose worried Alex; like Ludmilla, she could consume whatever came within her range.

Her full lips to the lip of the glass, Rose noisily sucked up champagne. Her tongue was a shocking red and she challenged him with it openly.

"I guess I was showing off." Rose laughed shyly; how different she was than on Christmas Day. "I should know better—I'm not built like a goddess anymore."

"Rose . . . Rose . . ." What could he say? Alex understood how women wanted never to change, always to be admired. How to tell her that a body was a body? "Rose, women don't remain girls forever, thank God! The body is admirable at every state of development."

Development? Or decline?

"You are speaking to a man who has always worshipped the female form."

"Ludmilla," she murmured unhappily.

"Now, now, Rose . . ."

She nodded. "You're right . . . I'm sorry. We shouldn't talk about Ludmilla tonight."

He squeezed her arm affectionately. How the skin gave, so softly, to the muscle far below. "We will not *dwell*, my dear. But if you mention it, then I should point out that Ludmilla did not end life looking as she did when I discovered her on the shores of the Black Sea fifty years ago. Or was it sixty?"

"Fifty years?"

"Which gives you some idea of my antiquity," Alex murmured modestly.

"Never! I would never think of you as an antique! You're the most attractive man I've ever seen! I mean it!"

Rowdily, Rose gulped champagne, then held her glass for more. Alex reached for the bottle, poured, stooped again to the hand that held the glass and kissed the soft notch where her thumb met knuckles. Rose melted groggily; how easily Alex could have spun her into shock.

214

Now was the moment. "Rose, sweetheart, I suggest we take the bottle upstairs . . ."

Her lips twitched, but not from recalcitrance. Rose nodded eagerly.

"Remember, Alex, I still haven't chosen my caftan . . ."

He laughed huskily. "*So you have not!* Rose, I yearn to look at you again," Alex whispered, so smoothly, so passionately. "Tonight! New Year's Eve! The very night to be inspired!"

Alex collected the champagne bottle and they proceeded. Rose gave him the railing side of the staircase, mounting beside him on the right, as if Alex had need of steadying, her fingers firmly set on his arm.

Suddenly she asked where Peat was. "You know, the little fart is going to squeal on me, Alex."

"Our errand is perfectly innocent, Rose."

She laughed derisively. "You know he was in love with the old lady . . . I mean Messalina Richards, the old man's first wife. They say he tried to kill himself when Messy died."

"She was called *Messy*?" Alex had to laugh. What a droll nickname.

They stopped on the staircase as Rose joined in his laughter. Just then the pantry door swung open and Peat scooted out. He lurched forward inquisitively, looking worried when he didn't see them.

"Peat . . ." Alex spoke quietly. Why not, he had nothing to hide. The butler's head jerked up. "Mrs. Richards and I are having another look at . . . Mrs. Richard's clothes, I mean the Princess's, of course."

Peat nodded anxiously. Maybe there was something he didn't like about it, but it was none of his bloody business. Realizing this, he turned abruptly and scuttled back into the pantry.

Alex put an arm around Rose's waist, the way a man should to escort a lady toward a boudoir, caressing a sweet roll of flesh at her waist and the distinct underswell of breast.

"Sweetheart, do you mean Peat carried on a romance with the first Mrs. Richards? With *Messy*?"

"All too true," Rose said spitefully. "Messy was very bored, Alex. Ask *me*. Dick and I were married a few years before she died."

Once again the theory surfaced—that the most unlikely of

men might turn out to be the greatest of lovers. For what could a woman find attractive about Peat, a creature who looked like he'd been grown in a sack of potatoes?

"The old man actually caught them," Rose elaborated deliciously, "down in the hothouse where he kept his stripling orchids."

"Incredible," Alex murmured. They were at Ludmilla's suite. "A wonder Rodney didn't kill him . . ."

Alex switched on the lights, batteries of strip lights exuding the softness Ludmilla had so adored, lights that made a woman look good whatever the hour of the day or night. He sniffed disgustedly.

"Holy God, the place already smells of decay and history."

There was a degenerating element in Ludmilla's perfume which palled within a week or two; the scent began to sicken suspended in dust and the stench of old candles. Ludmilla had burned so many candles—not to mention her own, at both ends.

Alex set the champagne down on the vanity where Ludmilla had performed her cosmetic artistry, more than ever in the final years.

"A little more?"

Rose shook her head. Her expression was solemn as Alex led her once again into the depths of Ludmilla's vast closet, the only place in the world where neatness had played any role in her life.

"A woman could go crazy in here, Prince."

"Go ahead! Take whatever you want!

"Prince . . ."

Rose hauled him up short. Again she placed herself squarely in front of him and kissed him full-lipped, boldly, more aggressively than before, if that was possible. She unsheathed her ravenous, red tongue and plunged it between his teeth. Her taste was a little sour—from the champagne, always a little acid, the one quality of champagne that was off putting. Rapidly enough, Alex felt himself aroused. He put a hand on each of her hips, aware of circular motion against him. Rose groaned as if saddled by a heavy weight.

"Prince, I can't, *please*!"

He understood. Rose could not bear to do what she was doing.

"Rose . . . Rose . . ."

"No, *please*, I can't!"

Prematurely, for he hadn't expected this so soon, Rose's hands dropped to his fly and violently unzipped. A ripping sound slashed the silence. Alex hoped it was the zipper and not his gray flannels. Rose cried out, Alex didn't know why. Why all the commotion? Her hot hands fumbled in his drawers, causing the welcome hot pulse to race up and down his spine, then center in the small of his back.

No, he had not lost it. Not yet.

"Oh, Prince, oh, *please*." Her breath was as laden now as the mistral with southern vapors. "Don't let me!"

Not let her? Sooner would he have tried to stop a two-horse troika.

Rose stared bravely into his eyes. "I want to kiss your penis."

He should tell her not to talk like that. He *would* tell her.

"Rose . . . Rose."

Rose pushed Alex back out into the more airy dressing room and down into Ludmilla's chair. Then, when he was comfortable, she dropped to her knees and extracted his manhood, as the penis was sometimes called in Moscow, in other places wolfhound or borzoi, the scourge of the steppes.

Alex should never have doubted himself, not for a second, for when Rose touched him with her lips, he came instantly, fully, thundcrously erect.

Voraciously, Rose proceeded. Still Alex had to ask himself, why him? Rose should have had other, younger possibilities. Perhaps she considered Alex safer or reckoned that at his age he would be more patient—tolerant, in fact, of the sound effects— the terrible sounds of chaos, of men slipping and sliding in mud, attack, attack!

Then, as she was in full flight—at the gallop, an equestrian might have said—Rose suddenly tore her mouth away from him and leapt to her feet. Quickly she kicked free of her shoes, ripped off her slacks and blouse.

At once Rose dropped to her hands and knees in the shaggy rug and clutched Alex's legs to her breasts. "Please . . . please, Alex!"

She dragged him down with her, pulling at his gray flannels, which Alex would have preferred to fold and hang up neatly. But before they were even properly free of his ankles,

Rose flopped over and gathered him to her. Her body was already in violent motion; she was as hard to control as the Ludmilla of old. Rose jerked and hopped and jumped in every direction, awash with juices, and before Alex really understood what was happening, Rose had whipped him into her, sucked him forward—like a stallion into its stall, Alex would have thought. And, God, the heat was tremendous, sure to bake his *comrade*, as Alex himself sometimes referred privately to his member.

It was best this way, to be taken in convulsive, mindless violence. He was not complaining.

Rose bucked and yammered wildly, enfolding him. He became part of her flesh. That was good too.

Yes, Alex had anticipated cuckolding Dick Richards, but he had never counted on the experience being quite so strenuous or fulfilling.

Except for a sudden rapping at the door, Alex might not even have survived it.

Rose yelped with dismay and alarm, and cursed like a cavalry officer. All motion stopped. She was becalmed, suspended.

As well she might be, for the intrepid Peat opened the door and stepped inside. He was carrying the second bottle of champagne.

Rose craned her head backward—she was facing in the wrong direction. Peat stopped in his tracks, frozen, transformed into stone. Struggling to get away, Alex was trapped between her thighs. Peat's face changed color, chameleonlike, from its normal ghastly white to pink—a greenish-pinkness, Alex thought.

"Put the bottle down, shitface," Rose commanded shrilly, "and get out!"

In all his years, Alex could not remember ever being caught like this, in flagrante. It was not as bad as he had thought it would be. Embarrassing, yes, his trousers tangled around his legs; he couldn't have gotten away if he'd tried. Imagine—fifty or more years of happy promiscuity and this had never happened to him before.

Peat did not heed Rose's crude instruction. He stood, like a bird, one foot in the air, staring numbly. Most likely he had never witnessed such an event.

"Just put the bottle down, Peat," Alex said softly, his voice like a cracked whip.

Whatever else time had cost him, Alex never lost his dignity. His tone brought Peat back. Peat stooped and set the bottle on the floor. Alex thanked him nicely, and in total confusion, Peat turned and exited.

Within moments, Alex calculated, Peat would have totally forgotten that the emperor was without pants.

"He's gone," Rose muttered angrily. "He'll go straight to phone Dick."

"About what? You having a look at Ludmilla's wardrobe?"

"Alex, the goddamn man is not blind." Rose shuddered as if chilled, shifting her body, flexing her legs. "Are you done for?" She stroked his back, his bare hips, tightening her arms around the waist. "I see you are not!"

Alex, amazingly, had maintained his integrity, never mind about nosy Peat!

"Isn't that wonderful!" Rose laughed hilariously. If Peat had heard her sounds before, he would certainly not miss this last exuberant blast of joy. Rose made smothering noises, wrapping Alex in her arms, sensuously jostling him with her hips. A powerful smell bombarded him; how had he missed it before? Musky, the odor of lust.

"Well," Rose chortled, "so that's coitus interruptus? Quite a little sensation."

With more measured agility, Rose resumed. The shock of Peat had served somehow to fuse them together, given the act more balance. The end, when it came, was not chaotic, even noisy, but smooth and almost anticlimactic, a pianist finishing an étude.

Like Ludmilla, yes, Alex remembered hazily, as he declined into a numbed trance, physical and mental. When the raging was done with, Ludmilla had always gone quietly.

And Rose seemed just as well pleased with him. Why shouldn't she be? Even out to pasture, Alex was more accomplished at love than any other Harry, Tom, or Dick who happened to tumble down the street.

Since there was nothing they could do about Peat, it seemed just as well to relax and forget it. If Peat telephoned Dick Richards, so be it. If not? Who cared? The die was cast.

Fatalistically, Rose, tensed down, sat in Ludmilla's makeup chair, careless how she revealed her body, one leg cocked up over the high back of the chair, all akimbo. Alex looked away.

"I seem to remember one of my grandmothers telling me Russian men were fabulous dolly-whackers. . . ."

"Not all of them, darling."

Alex was adjusting his trousers. He would have to get them cleaned.

"Very big *sputniks*, she said," Rose teased.

Patiently, chuckling fondly, Alex murmured, "A *sputnik* was the spacecraft, darling. What you are speaking of is a zee-zee."

Rose made a kissy-kissy face with her lips. "For inner space, then, Alex."

By and by Rose got up and casually wandered back into Ludmilla's closet. In the meantime, Alex thought, he would go into the bathroom.

While he was rummaging in the medicine cabinet for those pep pills Ludmilla had kept for such moments, Alex heard Rose's scream—it might have shattered windows.

He rushed out, post-coital fatigue forgotten.

Eyes popping, Rose was standing at the door of the closet. In one hand dangled a big red pocketbook. Rose was shaking squares of paper in the other.

Pictures, Alex saw, a handful of Polaroids.

"Jesus! What the hell!" Rose shook the pictures at him. "I don't believe it!"

Alex saw why. Flesh, bodies, pink and tanned, all manner of limbs; at first one might think they had been taken at the scene of an awful accident. But, *no*. Finally Alex identified one of the men as the poor lad; the other was Dick Richards! What they were doing to each other was indescribable, guaranteed to make a man like Alex Spurzov sick to his stomach.

Rose was in shock. "Dick Richards! I never . . . I didn't . . . I thought he was boring—but *this*?"

"Where did you find these?" Alex demanded.

"In that red bag . . . Alex, *who's the other guy*?"

A good question. Was he going to answer it?

"A friend of Ludmilla's . . . I *thought* a friend. His name is . . ." Or was that *was*? "Cazimir Ben Gazi."

"Do I know him?"

Alex shrugged and shook his head. Now he was very weary. The world could be a tiresome sort of place; ugliness piled atop lunacy.

"You might have met him here. Cazimir was here sometimes."

"Holy Christ," Rose gagged, "this is the father of my children!"

Yes. And Cazimir Ben Gazi, the poor lad. Alex hadn't known he was poor *that way*. Very disillusioning—hadn't Ludmilla had *any* clue Ben Gazi bounced both ways? If so, she'd have kicked him out long ago. What had Tom Addey been asking—what more did they know about the poor lad? People, places, bank accounts, where he arrived from and where he went when he left Richlands? Pictures? Why? And why in Ludmilla's closet?

Of course, Alex understood . . . everything. The poor lad had merely hidden them in the closet as a temporary measure. Was that what he'd been doing all that night? Not mourning for Ludmilla but assembling his cache of blackmailing material? But it seemed a bit stupid to stash them away in very lurid red pocketbook. Why not in an old shoe? Or under a stone in the garden?

But then he remembered another of the old rules—the safest place to hide something was very often in the most obvious place.

God knew the police had combed the room; they'd been over everything twice. Then Tom himself had had a good look around.

Had Ludmilla known anything about it? No, she had not been close to the poor lad; the fact that Cazimir hadn't been into her hiding place proved that.

On the other hand, Alex could just as well imagine her studying the pictures, lying in bed with the horrible poor lad and screaming with laughter. Ludmilla had been perverse too.

"Destroy them, Rose!"

She looked at him as if he were mad.

"Destroy them? Alex, don't be crazy!"

"Rose, sweetheart, burn them and forget."

"In no way!" Rose's face hardened maliciously. "Don't you understand? Now I've got him . . . right by the balls! What's Richards ever going to be able to say, ever again? About *anything*?"

Dismally Alex stared at her. Yes, so it would be. If the lad had had blackmail in his heart, which Alex thought was very likely, Rose would take over the game as his proxy.

"So," Rose said coolly, "this *guy* took the pictures and hid them in Ludmilla's closet. Will he be back for them?"

"They're vile, Rose."

Vile of Cazimir to take them. Vile to keep them. Vile to use them in such a way. Of course Cazimir would never be back to claim them; she could rest easy about that.

"These little items are my ticket out," Rose gloated. "I could never leave him before because everything is tied up—I wouldn't get a nickel out of that goddamn foundation. I couldn't prove two cents worth of property. Do you see?"

Despairingly, Alex nodded, and wondered if Ludmilla would have been more generous. Was Rose speaking of more money—or her actual freedom?

Rose marched back and forth, waving the pictures.

"For starters, Alex, just for goddamn starters, I'm not going home. No way! Do you suppose I'm going to go back *there* and live in the same house with *him*? After seeing *these*?" She laughed loudly. "Like hell! I'm staying right here, at Richlands."

Rose's eyes had fired up; she was a Gypsy in full flight.

"*This* is my new home! I'll have it in the settlement anyway, along with enough money to run it. What do you think of that?"

What would Ludmilla have advised?

"Sweet Rose," Alex said sadly, "I've been thinking the time has come for me to return to beloved Paris."

Rose grinned, nodding violently. "*With me*, Alex! God! Paris! A new life *together*, Alex!"

Alex prepared his evasive smile. He was not completely sure of Rose yet. Lips tingling, he stunned her with charm. He was not ready to say yes . . . or no . . . or even maybe.

Softly, he said, "I was educated in Paris, Rose. My family came from Berlin in the twenties."

"From Russia?"

She didn't understand, did she, about revolutions and fleeing?

"First from Russia . . . after the Bolsheviks."

Face anxious, Rose tried to understand. She wanted to be part of his entourage, didn't she, his baggage? Ignorance was not a serious impediment; ignorance, of course, wasn't bliss either. In a few months, if it came to that, Alex could teach her everything she needed to know. As he'd taught Ludmilla, his

Bulgarian wanton—what had she known about the world, or society, or love?

Rose glanced behind him at the littered vanity.

"My God, Alex, it's ten after midnight! The new year! *We missed it!*" she wailed.

Alex smiled. "We were *rather busy,* sweetheart. But not to worry! Ludmilla always kept her clocks fifteen minutes fast. She liked to say it's never what time you think it is—there's always fifteen minutes more."

Chapter
Twenty-One

When he made his move, Chet Arthur did so hard and fast. On the first business day of the New Year, Chester Arthur Ltd. began buying MorrisCom shares on the open market; by closing time the price had advanced from its fairly constant forty to forty-two fifty. At the end of the week, when Chet Arthur made the announcement, in accordance with SEC rules, that he'd assembled an eight percent stake in Morris Communications, the price jumped to forty-eight. The following Monday Arthur's holding increased to ten percent and the price went above fifty. The Arthur people then stated, as expected, that they were ready to pay sixty to win control of the company.

Chet Arthur had already put something like two hundred million dollars into the effort; the remaining forty-some percent he'd need for control would cost him an additional plus or minus nine hundred million. Half of that would go to Wilkey Morris Senior, who owned the biggest block of stock, some thirty percent, and at this point the Morrises would effectively be out of their company.

Said the pundits: The days of the family-owned conglomerate are numbered.

As always, Chet Arthur had prepared his game plan with great care. Of course, there were always wild cards involved. One was the SEC. The government conceivably could object to the merger on anti-trust grounds. But Sandor Veruckt, for one, considered this unlikely—you couldn't ignore Mr. Grassroot Republican's political clout.

It was taken for granted that the Arthur move would bring the nation's arbitragers out of the woodwork—notable among those mentioned was Sandor Veruckt & Associates. Indeed, if Sandor had *not* dealt himself in, there might have been serious doubts about the credibility of the whole deal.

For the record, Chet Arthur had stated in many in-depth profiles that he hadn't much respect for the arbitraging art. He described the likes of Sandor Veruckt as sharks and parasites feeding on the capitalist system. In rebuttal, Sandor sneered that the system was a big overfed, overweight, vomitous giant whose only hope of survival was to be stirred into action by the shark teeth of takeover . . . and the arbitraging that went with it.

Harsh words, also for the record. Though actually he and Chet were rather good chums, Sandor claimed.

"Rossiterre," he informed his West Coast employee, "it goes like clockwork. You see now—Sandor knows exactly when to strike."

With the MorrisCom share price headed toward fifty-five, who could disagree?

"We will buy more," Sandor forecast. But to buy at fifty-five and sell at sixty was no big deal unless Sandor committed many more millions.

"Price adjustment is not impossible," Sandor crooned.

Rossiter couldn't decide what he meant. This was the sort of loaded comment Sandor was so fond of making; he meant to scare the hell out of him, or reassure him, he couldn't decide.

Sandor went on to tell Rossiter that his group—Thelma and Seth, himself and Hildy Beckmann—had celebrated a magnificent New Year's Eve. Sandor had so much enjoyed meeting Seth, such a dignified and modest young man, and of course the fraulein, she was simply edible. It sounded like Sandor had had several bites out of her Bavarian body.

"And you, Rossiterre? Your own celebration was fine?"

"Very quiet, Sandor. Very, very quiet."

"And your dear wife? Serena, is it not? Is she well? I'm led to believe . . . maybe something Fraulein Beckmann said . . . Is she ill?"

Question after question fired at him like rifle shots. What was Rossiter to tell Sandor? It would've been nice to be able to confide in somebody that Serena was unhinged. Bud Slagger's presence in their house had set Serena back twenty years. Serena was Daddy's little girl again, sitting with Daddy, lying next to him, stroking him, caressing him beyond any decency, driving him around the bend. . . .

"Oh, no, Serena is fine," Rossiter lied. "She's just had a little cold."

"Good, Rossiterre, good. Sandor worries . . . I take you to my heart, Rossiterre, you realize this?"

The great financier needed constant reassurance that yes, he was a gracious employer, a fine citizen, a man of integrity, the salt of the earth.

"Come east, young man," Sandor proposed. "Maybe when . . . this business is completed, we will get together. Bring her—"

"Who?"

"Your wife, Rossiterre, your wife! Perhaps Seth will be here still. He mentioned he might have to return to California on some consular business or other."

After Sandor hung up, Rossiter sat quite still for several minutes, staring at his computer screen. With this wondrous gadget he could call up at will the current market status of any and every stock trading anywhere in the world.

He did so now, punching in the MorrisCom code. A few clicks and clacks later, the information flashed up. The price had gone to fifty-six and a fraction.

In the mid-afternoon these days, Rossiter preferred to go anywhere but home. As one worthy pretext for putting off the moment, Rossiter had taken to stopping at Tiny Slagger's condo.

Never mind about Serena and Bud, Tiny was pretty much of a mess herself. Her alienation from her husband and daughter was more or less total. When Rossiter first visited her in Century City to ask why she'd sent Bud away, Rossiter had found Tiny loaded—if not drunk, then soggy with vodka, "her drink," she liked to call it. Tiny seemed able to remain drunk for long periods of time, floating along the hazy line between lucidity and incoherence. Tracking through the swamp of her mind, Rossiter learned in a few days more about the Slaggers than he'd ever known before, or wanted to know.

Did Rossiter realize that Bud Slagger was a mere cog in Lorenzo Diamond's machine? Lorenzo Diamond, the Devil Incarnate? When Bud told everybody he was only an organizational spear carrier, he was telling the absolute truth. The fiction was that Slugger Slagger directed public relations at the Alhambra Hotel and Convention Center. According to Tiny, everybody knew the office was in reality run by a tough little bimbo named Abby Basilica, who also happened to be Lorenzo Diamond's mistress. Nobody dared cross Abby Basilica—or to dare anything else with her unless they yearned to test the steel of Lorenzo Diamond, the D.I.

D.I.?

Devil Incarnate, what else?

The force of this revelation boosted a set of burps into Tiny's upper digestive tract and encouraged her to go on. Wickedly, she ventured that despite Diamond's doing everything but locking her up, if Abby Basilica had been a church, then surely she'd had a lot of dicks in her apse—among the most recent of which was none other than that of Bud "Slugger" Slagger.

If there was anything wrong with Bud's heart, Tiny held that it had been caused by pure fear—the understanding, too late, that he had gotten himself in the wrong with Lorenzo Diamond.

At a certain time of life Tiny must have been a striking woman. She was tall, broad-shouldered, and, even in *extremis*, she had a sense of humor that apparently had bypassed her daughter. A former chorus girl, Tiny had legs that were still very good. Also her shape had lasted even if it had collapsed a little. Sadly, her hair, metallic red, had lost its luster—due to the booze, Rossiter supposed. But all in all, a week or two, maybe a month on the wagon, would put her right. Tiny had not quite lost it; somebody should talk to her abut the Betty Ford Center in Palm Springs.

Tiny was worth saving; peculiar that Rossiter tended to think in those terms: saving and losing. His mother had reminded him once that many of the previous Drysdales had been ministers.

Poor Tiny.

Rossiter leaned back in his chair, wondering for a second if *he* happened to be worth saving. He closed his eyes, pinching the pressure point between his eyes, pushing back a headache, careless of the fact he could be seen like a fish in a bowl by all his colleagues, sitting in their own glass cubicles. Rossiter's assistant was no more than twelve feet away.

As he passed into deep brood, his phone rang. Rossiter dropped his feet off the desk and prepared for business. In fact, it was his assistant, Marjorie. He watched her mouth words as he heard them in the telephone.

"Your wife."

"Hell!"

Marjorie was a genius at covering. Oh, he's just stepped out; he's gone downstairs for a newspaper; he's in conference with a client.

"Oh well . . . okay."

Marjorie put Serena through.

"Rossiter!" No preliminary, of course. "We have a crisis! You have to come straight home!"

Her voice said she was out for blood.

"Serena, I'm in the smack middle of my day."

It was two o'clock. New York had just closed, but that didn't stop business being done in California.

"I don't give a shit! You've got to come home. *Right now!*"

"Serena . . . give me a clue, will you?"

It couldn't have been a life or death problem to do with Bud's health or she'd have been screaming, not yelling. Therefore, the crisis had to be of a psychological sort. Perhaps there had been a stressful argument; maybe, he thought idly, the delectable Abby Basilica had blown in from Las Vegas to claim her one true love.

"I'll get there as soon as I can."

Best not to put it in a time frame. But this wasn't good enough for Serena.

"You bastard! You are so *insignificant!*" Serena said insultingly. "I tell you there's a crisis and you tell me you'll get here as soon as you can?"

"Listen, Serena," he barked, "cut the crap. I can't get there any sooner than I physically can!"

"Oh, no?"

"I don't have wings, Serena," Rossiter said sarcastically. "Tell me something—is there an ambulance outside?"

"No!" She was boiling. "But that doesn't mean I don't have a crisis on my hands. If you cared one iota about anyone except yourself, you'd get here quick!"

"Attend to your crisis, Serena," Rossiter told her. "I'll be there soon."

He mumbled a good-bye and hung up before she could say anything else, glancing ruefully at Marjorie.

The status quo was getting very hard to hold.

Rossiter might have closed things up right away without doing severe damage to the American economic system; but, out of meanness, he hung around another half hour, then slung on his jacket and made for the freeway.

"So long, Bernard Baruch," Marjorie said as he left, one of her ways of bucking him up to face going home.

Marjorie was discerning; she had her own brand of wit, a cynicism he liked, a lightness about things. He'd been thinking of Tiny. Marjorie was tall too, as well as a good bit younger and better preserved. She wouldn't have been half bad, he suspected— definitely a person with whom another person could come to grips.

That made him think of Clara. And he was instantly depressed. Their secret, he promised himself, would go with him to the grave. That was the best he could do. But it wasn't good.

Rossiter exited the Santa Monica Freeway at Robertson Boulevard and drove north into Beverly Hills. At this time of the afternoon the traffic was still manageable, one advantage of working on a schedule geared to New York. If a man lived a normal life, he had time, if he was so inclined, for a game of golf, or tennis, or to play with his children, if he had any, before dinner and darkness.

Nothing looked out of the ordinary at the house. Rossiter pulled into the driveway and parked behind Serena's Mercedes. Bud's Seville was on the other side of the security gate.

Rossiter took his usual shortcut across the lawn and no one screamed at him. That in itself was an encouraging sign. Nevertheless, there was a crisis. Serena had heard the car and had assumed her posture of fury. Plainly she had been addressing emotional words to her father—the room was dead quiet when he came in.

Bravely, Rossiter said, "Hello, everybody. What's up?"

Not turning, Serena repeated his words. "What's up, he asks!" She spun at him like a dervish. "What's up is that *he*"—she cocked her thumb accusingly at the dumb figure in the bed—"*he* has gotten hold of cigarettes and he's smoking again!"

Bud knew better, too true. Nine out of ten doctors said taking up the filthy habit again would drastically reduce his five-year survival rate.

"Bad, Bud, very bad. Very, very bad."

"So what are *you* going to do about it?"

Serena's face was twisted out of recognition. It wasn't that Serena was angry at Bud, or even at Rossiter. She was angry at *everything* and *everybody*.

"There's not a hell of a lot I can do about it, it seems to me. If Bud is going to smoke, then he's going to smoke."

Serena nodded, impatient for him to finish. Bud might as well have been out of the room. "I'm going to have the dumb son of a bitch committed. How do I go about getting somebody committed?"

Rossiter smiled at Bud reassuringly. "Smoking is not a certifiable offense, Serena."

"No?" Her eyes narrowed. "Anybody that smokes has got to be crazy."

Finally Bud blew. "I'm not crazy! Ross knows I'm not crazy and so do you. Sometimes, the way *you* act, a man would think *you're* crazy."

Serena responded by speaking to Rossiter without looking at him.

"Now my own father is calling me crazy. Did you hear that? Me? Because I love him"—her voice dropped piteously— "and I want him to get well, he calls me crazy." Tears ran from her eyes, making muddy channels in her pancake makeup. "I guess I am crazy to care anything about him . . . or *you*, you inconsiderate, insignificant—"

Serena whirled around again and swung out blindly at Rossiter. He dodged her and she began to howl, then flung herself down into one of the chairs by the fireplace.

"All right," Bud whined, "all right! I'm going to quit again. I promise."

"Liar!" Exchanging a look, Rossiter and Bud recognized the tantrum for what it was. Then Serena screamed again. "Do you know how he got those goddamn cigarettes? Do you?"

"No."

She pointed toward the kitchen.

"He gave that little *whore* money and she went out this morning and she bought them!"

Sternly, Rossiter said, "I don't think you should call Lourdes a whore, Serena."

"Yeah," Bud agreed, "not just because she did me a kindness."

Serena shrieked, "Kindness? Is it a kindness to buy you the stuff that'll kill you if you start on it again which you did and don't talk to me about quitting again because you won't once you start!"

"Look, Serena . . . even so—"

"Well, if she's not a whore, then she's a *killer*. How do I go about getting her deported?"

Rossiter drew a deep breath. Whimpering pathetically, Bud made it worse.

"Ross, Serena's locked the little thing in her room."

Serena croaked, "So what? She's locked up and I tied her hands so she can't do any more damage."

"You tied her hands?"

Bud whispered, "I didn't know."

"Serena, you cannot do that! Haven't you ever heard of false imprisonment? Jesus, she'll sue our ass off! Goddamn it, Serena," Rossiter yelled, "sometimes I'd like to—"

"What?"

"Me too," Bud muttered. "Sometimes this little girl of mine behaves like a—"

"What?" Serena blasted a second time.

Bud faded fast. In truth, he looked terrible, and that couldn't be credited to a couple of illicit cigarettes. Serena was driving him nuts. Serena was bad medicine, *heap* bad medicine.

Leaving them at a stand-off, Rossiter hurried to the kitchen. Past the utility room he could hear Lourdes sobbing. Her door was locked from the outside. He turned the dead bolt.

"Lourdes?"

The crying increased, doubled when he opened the door and stepped into her room. Lourdes was crouched on the narrow bed, her hands secured behind her. In her struggle to get free, Lourdes's white uniform had twisted, buttons popped open down the front, exposing firm brown breasts. Naturally, Rossiter couldn't look, not there nor where the skirt had ridden up her thighs.

"Please, Lourdes. Be calm."

Serena had tied her cruelly, very cruelly, with a thin piece of cord, wound many times around the girl's wrists and much too tightly. Lourdes's fingers were already swollen from loss of circulation.

Rossiter muttered disgustedly and Lourdes flashed him a grateful, pathetically grateful, look.

"Wait a minute."

She would understand he needed a knife. Rossiter made a cutting motion with his hand and went back to the kitchen. Finally, carefully, he cut the cord with a little paring knife.

Lourdes moaned as the blood rushed back into her fingers, rubbed them vigorously and finally smiled at him with the same helpless gratitude.

"All right? *Okay*?"

She remembered about the uniform, embarrassedly pulling at the disarrayed top and straightening the skirt.

"Lourdes, I promise you this will never happen again."

Did she understand? No. She shook her head bewilderedly, puzzlement on her face. No, Rossiter couldn't explain either why Serena had done such a thing. What he most wanted Lourdes to know was that she shouldn't worry.

"No mas," Rossiter said awkwardly.

He meant *never again.*

"No. No more," Lourdes murmured.

She knew that much English!

But he was not referring to her cigarette-buying mission, if that was what she thought. He meant that the bitch, the she-devil Serena wouldn't pull another stunt like this and get away with it. And he wanted her to realize that whatever Serena had done had nothing to do with Rossiter. *Please,* he thought, *don't mention me in the law suit.*

Clumsily, Rossiter patted her shoulder. Lourdes smiled so trustingly that, impulsively, he bent over and kissed her cheek.

Instantly, she tensed. Lourdes must have suspected this was part of the plot. But just as quickly she sensed otherwise, and what she did next startled Rossiter completely.

Lourdes reached all the way up to his cheek and gently put her fingers to it, caressing him for just a second. Then she looked quickly away.

"Well . . . okay, then. Okay," Rossiter stammered.

Chapter Twenty-Two

"**Y**ou really believe Ludmilla was murdered too?" Seth asked. Well, what did he expect? After all, two people ordinarily did not die of unnatural causes in the same house within twenty-four hours of each other without provoking a certain amount of talk.

"Yes. God knows why."

And Spain? The fact Cazimir Ben Gazi had come to ground, so to speak, on a beach at the exclusive Marbella Club near Malaga was another turn in an already quite twisted tale. According to first reports, the Ben Gazi remains were so badly decomposed that had it not been for waterproof packets containing a treasure trove of documents, the body might never have been identified at all.

"At least," Madison murmured delicately, "he resurfaced in the Mediterranean. What if he'd gone to Scotland after visiting Detroit? Kind of a distressing thing for a corpse, wouldn't you say, Addey?"

Yes, Seth realized Madison would have dearly liked to blame the Detroit foul-up on Tom Addey—hire a non-pro and what did you get?

Well, everybody knew about Ben Gazi by now . . . including Alice Betancur, evidently. Katie Corcoran had called him at the crack of dawn—Alice had been in touch with her. She desperately wanted to see him.

"Seth, what the hell is going on?"

"I . . . Look, I'll explain everything. I don't want you dragged into this, Katie."

He knew what it was about: Ben Gazi. The President had even issued a statement the evening before deploring "the brutal murder" of this true friend of America "and champion of freedom in the political cauldron and slaughter house of the Middle East. Our sympathy goes out to Mrs. Gazi and all the little Gazis. . . ."

Madison laughed about that. Well, he said, in the spy-counterspy biz, you took what you could get.

They were riding together in the padded backseat of Madison's company car. Nondescript on the outside, inside it was air-conditioned, humidified, soundproofed, and most likely bullet-proofed too. It rode heavily and quietly.

Madison was on his way to Dulles Airport. He was making a quick trip somewhere or other and wanted to see Addey before Seth went back to California.

Seth wasn't ready for him. Madison's call had been unexpected, peremptory. He was worried about Alice—would she be able to hold up under the shock and strain of the Ben Gazi news? Or was that why Madison wanted to see him? Maybe she'd blown already. And why had she called Katie, not Seth directly? Above all, he didn't want anything screwing up his relationship with Katie Corcoran. He believed in her, he who believed in nothing much these days.

Life was becoming very confusing again. Hadn't Seth seen more than he needed in the way of intrigue and deceit during his months in Moscow? Was it possible Washington was as bad . . . or worse?

Madison admitted that there had been a terrific foul-up in the drop. Yes, Ben Gazi had had a ticket for Cyprus. Don't ask him what happened. Anyway, the mistake had been compounded by winter winds and currents.

Not that it mattered. The important thing was all the paperwork Ben Gazi had been carrying—to the point, somebody remarked nastily, that it was a miracle the corpse didn't sink off the coast of Egypt or wherever it had finally been dumped by submarine.

What mattered, according to Jim Madison, was that all the documents blazed a trail straight to the Kremlin gate.

"If that hit wasn't ordered by the KGB," he gloated, "then my name is Gordon Liddy."

Sure enough, by morning authoritative sources in Europe had pinned the deed on the Soviets, saying they were up to their usual dirty tricks: destablilizing the Middle East and making it clear in brutal fashion that it didn't do to be a great and good friend of America.

Such bold stuff, Madison predicted, would scare the hell out of the European neutralists, scatter the incense of holy anti-communism over the whole civilized world.

Madison was interrupted in his exposition by the beep of one of his car phones. He picked up the red one.

"Jimbo here," he announced. "Oh . . . Yes, good morning, Krash. True, we're getting word in on retaliation in several hemispheres for this Soviet outrage. . . ."

Madison winked broadly at Seth. This *was* enjoyable.

"Krash, their pissant embassy in Aden was bombed. And Vladimir Churlovsky went to Heaven from Bonn, Germany. Your friend Caz-bubby is finally paying his freight."

Seth turned his face away, pretending he couldn't hear, wasn't listening.

Outside, the Virginia countryside slid past. Here and there a white barn stood out starkly in the brown winter landscape. Puffs of smoke rose from chimney tops. Serene and reassuring, wasn't it, all the gentlemen farmers snugly in residence.

He could hear Kraszewski's rumbling. Whatever the old general was saying made Madison chuckle warmly. Yes, Madison agreed, rarely did such an operation work so perfectly.

After he'd gotten Kraszewski off the phone, Madison reminded Seth that people had often tried to pull off this sort of thing. The best-known and maybe most successful use of the ploy had been when the Allies had floated a document-laden stiff into the English Channel to throw the Germans off the scent about the location of the D-Day landings in 1944.

Madison stared at Seth unsympathetically. "This is *part* of the reason for my trip to Europe, Addey. All the *more reason* not to let it come unraveled in California."

That was the point—there were people in California who could blow them out of the water.

Madison's eyes danced the macabre.

"Alex Spurzov thinks the *butler* done it."

235

Seth's heart sank. "Killed *both* of them?"

Madison nodded, almost indifferently. "Seems too good to be true, doesn't it?" He laughed thinly. "Of course, we'll want to know who he's working for. I don't need to tell you to be careful. Do you carry a weapon?"

"No."

"Well . . . this son of a bitch could be very dangerous."

Seth's facial expression must have been the equivalent of a groan, for Madison looked at him sharply and said, "You know, we're all trapped in a web of circumstance."

"I wish I was back in Munich."

"*Everybody* would rather be in Munich, Addey." Ominously, Madison added, "Don't imagine I like this. I was a lone wolf for too long myself to have a good feeling about other lone wolves on the loose."

"I'm flattered, thank you, sir."

Madison tapped his knee. "The most important thing is to find out who hired him, my lad! Remember that—this butler, Peat, is an insignificant tool—"

"I understand that."

"Want some coffee?" Madison asked companionably, "We've got a machine in this marvelous car . . . someplace."

"No thank you. Don't go to any trouble."

Madison leveled another surprise barrage at him.

"By the way, I want you to straighten out your personal affairs."

Perhaps there was an ejection mechanism also built into this *marvelous* car—one flick of Madison's wrist and Seth would have been propelled into a muddy Virginia ditch.

"Well, that, sir . . ." He'd known, of course, they were bound to find out. "We were talking marriage, but the way it looks now, that's off." Madison's interest was probably, he thought sorely, due to the fact Hildy Beckmann was an alien.

"You and *Mrs. Sol Betancur* were planning marriage?" Madison asked coolly.

"No! I mean—"

"Addey . . . Addey, I know all about the German. I'm talking about Alice Betancur."

Seth was destroyed. He felt like a mouse being teased by a cat; no, the mouse swallowed whole by a cobra.

"The woman is unbalanced, Addey," Madison went on

scornfully. "Betancur's got to do something about her, I don't know what. It's gotten to be very risky . . . security-wise."

Seth's mouth was very dry. Did they know about Alice's concubinage with Ben Gazi? Did they also know about Seth's small adventure with her, not of his own planning, to be sure? *Did* they know that?

Madison's eyes drilled into him. A man would be unable to lie to such eyes.

"How much does Alice Betancur know?" he demanded testily.

Seth wiped perspiration from his forehead; he wouldn't try to fool Madison. He was sweating like a pig and his stomach was all knotted up. This was not the third degree—it was the fourth and fifth as well.

"She came to Ben Gazi's apartment when I first got there . . . I never expected to see her," Seth told Madison guiltily. "At the time I convinced her he'd gone on a long trip."

"She won't think so now." Madison's lip curled.

"No, not if she's seen the paper."

Which she had. Why else was he meeting her at Katie's?

"What I'm saying," Madison said churlishly, "is that we know whose little *pet* Ben Gazi was—Sol and Alice Betancur's. *What happened?*"

"How? In what way?"

"Well . . . when she got to the apartment?" Madison smiled, like the same cobra that had just swallowed the mouse. "Did she hit on you?"

Seth understood what he was saying.

"Um . . ." He gulped.

Madison nodded knowingly. "Say no more. Alice was quite a number when she worked over here . . . *pre-Sol*. She gets *very emotional*; she falls in love rather too easily, if you see what I mean."

Seth was perspiring freely and the car was not that warm. He hated this and Madison too, for bringing it up so cruelly.

"I . . . uh . . . I have a high regard for her, sir."

Madison's eyebrows, what there were of them, rose.

"Do not get involved there, Addey. As I've told my men . . . *over and over* . . . it's not worth it. You've got to be very careful of Sol Betancur. He's a power in this town."

"She's such a beautiful and elegant woman—"

"Beneath that?" Madison suggested thinly. "Alice is also what we'd call an intelligence groupie. She can't keep her hands off my agents! The work has such cachet. My men are intolerably romantic, reflecting the glamor of derring-do . . . danger . . . wiggling out of tight spots . . ."

All that? Madison must be making it up.

Madison continued amusedly, "My Albanian friends used to say that making love to an overly emotional or hysterical woman was like shoving your johnson bar in a buzz saw."

"I—" No, he was demolished; there was nothing Seth could say. Madison, with a few words, had turned Alice into a harridan.

"Well, Addey," he concluded, "do you have any final thoughts on the matter of *La Morte de Cazimir*?"

"I think you've said it all." One did not have to pretend it was pleasant hearing Madison's lectures.

Seth's boss sighed profoundly and went quiet as the car moved slickly through the maze of approaches to Dulles departures.

"I'm taking the Concorde to Paris," he remarked offhandedly.

Christ, like they'd been talking about the weather all this time. Madison was a cold fish. People said so repeatedly. But they had no idea of how cold was cold. You were talking here about Absolute Zero. Abrasively, sardonically, Seth wondered about throwing him a Madison-style curve—ask him to be best man when Seth got married, when he married Katie Corcoran, that is.

But Seth hadn't time, even if he'd been so daring, for Madison startled him again.

"By the way, we've just had more news of your friend Nick K. . . ."

Why did Madison always save that part of it for last—because he didn't like telling Seth, or wanted to save the *best* for last?

"We heard he'd been executed, you remember. It seems not. He died finally of *other causes*."

"You're saying he was . . . tortured."

Madison nodded regretfully. "This was *not* your responsibility. I stressed that before."

Seth wondered about life again—who, why, where, what? Mainly *why*. But *what* . . . what had happened to Nick was not something he could dodge.

238

"I'm all right."

"Look—" Madison started, then stopped. In the meantime the car drew up outside an anonymous door in a long concrete wall. Madison put out his hand and Seth shook it numbly. Madison said softly, "I don't know that I understand you, Addey. You seem absolutely cold-blooded. . . ."

Seth glanced at Madison. Cold-blooded? Madison must have realized Seth was thinking the same of him, for he slid that familiar pained smile across his face.

"Or maybe you're just operating on some kind of stored-up hatred."

Hatred of what? Seth didn't understand that.

Miserably, he said, "I like to think the former, sir."

"Yes, all right. Well, good-bye." Madison shut down his human side. He pushed the car door open and began to step out. The man in the blue suit who'd been driving was standing there, holding a small flight bag.

"All the same, Addey . . . all the same," Madison muttered. "Do what's necessary."

Chapter
Twenty-Three

*I*t hardly mattered how Nikolai had died once it was done. Dead was dead. Seth assumed Madison had been telling him that Nick had been put through the mill: The competition would have wanted and needed to know how much had been passed along to Seth Addey.

Seth understood now that he could, for all practical purposes, kiss good-bye any hope of reassignment when the time came, to somewhere like Prague or Warsaw. The other side would simply not allow it. Seth Addey was too dangerous. . . .

Seth had Madison's driver drop him at Dupont Circle. From there it was an easy walk to Katie's place, and he had time enough, as it turned out, to dawdle. Seth dreaded this meeting. There was nothing he could say to Alice; he *had* deceived her. And he didn't know what he was going to tell Katie Corcoran.

Seth stopped opposite the Dupont Circle Metro station to study the window displays in an antique shop. Casually, he had a look over both shoulders. Weird, wasn't it, but he'd gotten in this habit in Moscow.

Nobody seemed to be on him, but he'd stroll a little more and stop again farther up the street, where pedestrian traffic was thinner.

Seth didn't think Katie had any idea of what was going on . . . not unless Alice had spilled the beans—which was possible. He couldn't forget what Madison had said about hysterical women. But whatever had happened at Ben Gazi's flat and in the three or four times since then had not definitely been in the nature of love freely given. Alice Betancur had simply taken it for granted that Seth would step into the Ben Gazi role. Coercion, pure and simple, for how was he expected to find out more about Ben Gazi without playing along with Alice Betancur?

But try to explain that to Jim Madison . . . or Katie Corcoran, for that matter.

Seth stopped once more for a look around, then watchfully circled the block before hopping into the doorway of Katie's building and ringing the bell where it said Corcoran.

The door buzzed him inside. So far, so good. Katie was waiting upstairs. She was dressed to go out. Seth kissed her cheek guiltily. She wasn't much interested in being kissed. "What's happening?"

Seth tried to worm out of it. "I'm not one hundred percent sure . . . I'd rather tell you about it later."

"Thanks a lot!"

Unwillingly, knowing he didn't want to ruin it with her, he said, "I wouldn't tell *anybody else* . . . I hope you realize that."

"So far you haven't said anything."

"It's about this Arab. You must've seen it in the paper. The one who washed up on the beach . . . Ben Gazi."

Katie's eyes widened, gleaming. "*Very good*. You *will* tell me later?"

"Cross my heart."

"Okay, I'm gone." She kissed *him* this time. Trustingly. Trust me. "You know how to open the downstairs door."

Seth didn't have to wait long. Just before noon the bell sounded and in a couple of minutes Alice stood before him.

Yes, you knew it when you saw her—Alice had been kidding herself, saying Ben Gazi was still alive and on a long trip. The kidding was over now. She had been hard hit, no less than he'd feared. Her fragile face was drawn. There were deep circles of shadow under her eyes. With the sloppily applied dash of lipstick across her mouth, she looked ghostly.

"Hello, Alice."

She said nothing, walking unsteadily past him into the studio. Seth closed the door. Huddled in her fur coat, Alice remained silent for a long time, then finally spoke.

"Once upon a time I was in love with a man, you see. Shall I tell you about it?"

241

"If you want to, Alice," he said softly.

"Mr. Ben Gazi did something for me . . ." Then her eyes cleared; anger leapt forward. "Why didn't you tell me?"

"I didn't know, Alice," he lied. "Not until yesterday."

"That he was already dead?" she asked incredulously. "He'd been dead days . . . maybe weeks, when they found him. *You did know*, and you didn't tell, *you bastard*! You let me make a fool of myself. . . . You men *always* lie to me and laugh!"

She moved aimlessly across the room to the window, parted the blinds with one finger and peered outside.

"Alice, take off your coat and sit down so we can talk. I wanted to ask you—what has Sol said about it?"

She turned around, laughing bitterly. "Sol? He brought the paper to me this morning and pointed at the story. And then he hit me—"

"*Hit you?* My God . . . *why*?"

She shrugged, hugging her fur coat around her. "Because he knew about Caz. He knew Caz was my *dear* friend. He hits me where it doesn't show. He hits me in the arm or stomach or my breasts. He likes to bruise them. . . ."

Seth stared at her. Should he believe this? Was Sol Betancur such a brute? If so, no wonder Alice needed to go outside for love.

"Should I show you?"

Seth shook his head. No, no, he couldn't stand it. Did the omniscient Jim Madison know all about this too? It was easy enough to blame Alice for everything—but maybe they should look a little more closely.

"You knew, *didn't you*, that Caz was in serious trouble?" Alice demanded. "And you didn't say anything. That doesn't surprise me—you bastards have always lied to me. You talk about love and kisses, and the next thing I know it's 'Get away, don't bug me, Alice, you're embarrassing me in my career!'"

"Alice," he exclaimed, "I never said any such thing."

If she wouldn't sit down, he would, feeling deflated. Yes, she was right: Madison had warned that she would do him damage; and if she didn't, then Sol Betancur would.

"They say the Russians did it," Alice muttered angrily. "That the Russians killed the only man who never lied to me—"

"Never lied to you? Alice . . ." He didn't believe she could still think so, after everything she knew.

"And I say: *Sol did it*!"

"Sol? That's ridiculous, Alice."

She shook her head. "Do you want to see my bruises? Proof?" He shook his head. "If Sol knew, then *he* had it done. There's no doubt about it," she said emphatically. "And next— he'll have me done. First he beats me up; then they kill me!"

"I don't believe it," Seth said slowly. "He wouldn't . . . He's not that kind of man."

Scornfully, she asked, "What do *you* know about him? Why do you think he had Ben Gazi imported here in the first place? Only—he didn't think Caz and I would get so friendly. . . ."

Seth had began to perspire again; it wasn't especially warm in Katie's apartment either.

"What are you saying? *Why was he imported?*"

"He was brought over here to kill people," Alice whispered.

Now she did come and sit down beside him on the couch, still holding the coat closely around her.

"Alice, I don't believe *any* of this."

"Why should the Russians kill Caz?" she asked cleverly, staring at him from those frightened gray eyes. "Caz was friendly with them."

Seth was stopped again. "Why do you say that, Alice?"

She shrugged disdainfully. "I know he was sometimes invited to their embassy, for small parties, he told me. Caz would brag about it: *Everybody* loves Caz!"

Nervously Alice let go of her coat and grabbed Seth's hands, pressing them to her.

"Touch me! Put your hands where it hurts!"

Seth felt himself stiffen. The horror of it was heart-pounding, tension-producing. More than ever the lost girl in Alice fascinated him. Despite his resolution, in a wink of an eye, the fragile flower, petals trembling, swept him away. If Betancur was the monster she described, then what had transpired between Alice and Seth was . . . what? Deadly business! Russian roulette of the worst sort, played with six slugs in the chamber.

"Darling," she breathed, panting convulsively, "I'll confess something to you because I may never see you again."

"Don't say it!"

Careful. Remember what Madison had said. Madison was

probably halfway across the Atlantic by now, leaving Seth behind to face . . . this! Hysterical, yes . . . maybe also very
imaginative, Mrs. Alice Betancur.

"I know," Alice whispered, "that besides being a wonderful lover, Cazimir was not a nice man. But then, wonderful
lovers are often not nice men. Rather the reverse: The worst of
men, conspirators and killers, are the best lovers!" Alice tried
to smile, but she looked very weepy and afraid.

Here was an opening. "Alice, didn't you ever get the
feeling Caz was *using* you?"

She flinched. "No! I was the one person he did not use. He
did not lie to me. I know what he did. I knew the connections—
where Sol sent him!'

"Where?"

"To the gangs, my darling," she cried softly. "Connections . . . everywhere. Chicago . . . Las Vegas . . . Caz told me
where he'd been. *Almost everything.* Not the worst of it—he
thought that would hurt my ears. And anyway, what about it?"
she asked scorchingly. "Sol had his girlfriends. His *mistress*,
you know who. She carries her money, in cash, in brown paper
sacks!"

Numbly, Seth listened, anxiety piling on anxiety. Did she
have any conception of what she was saying, what an explosion
such a revelation would cause—if it ever became public, if she
ever talked? What had Madison said? If Alice blew, Sol might as
well move to Antarctica and join the penguins.

Very carefully, he said, "Alice, these things are scary! You
know what would happen if—"

"Do I know!" She laughed recklessly. "I'm dead meat!"

"This is incredible! What you're saying is that Caz was a
. . . hit man—"

"Yes . . . in effect. He did a lot of work for *governments*,
though. I don't think governments call them hit men. People like
Caz do 'special activities. . . .' "

"Alice . . . *this is awful!*"

He could not believe what she was saying. Did she *really*
understand the implications? Or was she making the whole thing
up? That was what would be said if it ever came out—"Mrs.
Betancur has a very vivid imagination!"

"Of course it is. That's why you were such a godsend on

the scene, my good boy! A pure and innocent lad—such a balm—"

"Alice, I'm not innocent, *you know that*."

She grinned archly. "Then why are you so shocked?"

"A good question."

"Will you?" Alice put her long arms around him and kissed him lingeringly on the mouth.

"Alice . . . I'm just . . ." Weak, he should have said.

"I need you very badly . . . I'm a wreck. I need you to bring me back down, darling, I'm so high! *Help me down!*"

"I can't, Alice! I can't help you."

It was too late, he thought, too far gone. But Alice was running to her own tempo now. She began pulling at his belt, certainly not what he wanted.

"Give me your body?"

Alice was wearing a loose blouse and skirt under the mink. She slid to the side and tried to pull him on top of her.

"Alice . . ."

"Will you, my Black Knight?" she demanded fiercely. "Will you jump the White Queen?"

"No," he said.

"I thought you were my friend, a friend in need, a friend indeed!"

"I am your friend." He grabbed her hand as she slapped at him. "Listen to me—goddamn Ben Gazi is dead and I'm trying to find out what he was up to. So . . . just level with me!"

"Level?" she drawled contemptuously. "Horizontal? I know what you want, goddamn you! You want the pictures, don't you?" Alice reached down to the floor where she'd dropped her pocketbook, opened it, and took out a fat envelope. "Here!"

She threw the envelope across the room, then crossed her arms on her chest and waited for him to get up and retrieve it.

Seth walked behind her. There were a couple dozen of the pictures, not in terribly good focus, but nevertheless clear enough for Seth to be dismayed, shocked if not sickened—though Alice seemed nonchalant enough about it as she sat and watched him.

Some of the faces had been blacked out with a sticky pen, but there couldn't be any doubt about the women in the pictures. One was Alice, and the other the woman Katie first pointed out to him as the mysterious and sordid Mabel Harrey. Most of the shots had to do with Alice and Mabel, twined in lurid and much more than suggestive poses or entangled in even more complex ways with men, one or sometimes two.

It was the expression on their faces which made him gasp, the smirking wantonness, particularly Mrs. Harrey's. Yes, she had to be the ringleader.

"Well," Alice asked coolly, "do they do me justice?"

"I think," he replied, "the worst of it is that you look like you were having such a wonderful time."

"I was!"

"Who blotted out the faces, *you*?"

"Yes, to protect the guilty."

Seth stared at her. He liked Alice much less than he had. She was rapidly losing her power to mesmerize him. Stripped of her various layers of sophistication, Alice finally did reveal her true colors. She was a selfish, self-destructive woman.

"Now who are *these* guys?"

"You don't need to know."

"You're quite proud of yourself, aren't you, Alice?"

She smiled sweetly. "Just because I like men so much? Exciting men, like you?" She extended her arms toward him, as if to pull him back to her. "They're just like you, big man. Come on," she urged, "I'll make it up to you. All that training shouldn't go to waste."

"For crissakes, Alice!"

"Oh, come on! I can't remember all of them, Seth!"

"Doesn't it bother you? People seeing you like that?"

"No!" she exclaimed angrily. "Why should it? I'm more interested anyway in sexual position than I am in social position— don't you know that much yet? Didn't anybody tell you that yet? Didn't *Corky* tell you?"

"Corky? No, she'd never say a thing like that about you!"

"Oh, *come on*! People talk about me all the time, and I don't give a damn," Alice exploded defiantly. "That I never muss my hair and I'm shaven clean at the armpits and I'm willowy and gorgeous, like a swan in heat, and I never make animal noises. Is there anything else, Mr. Detective?"

"That's enough! It doesn't help to talk like that!"

"Go to hell!"

Alice put her face in her hands and began to sob in earnest. Then she muttered, "I'm sorry, I'm sorry. You've been so nice to me and now I've hurt your feelings so much." He went back to the couch. Eagerly, Alice pulled him down beside her.

"Let me kiss your skin?" She yanked his shirt out of his belt and put her lips to his bare belly. "Soft . . . kissable . . . more like Caz than you know . . ."

Seth put his hand to her shoulder and stroked. He didn't know whether to pity Alice or scorn her. He could not make her out—was she telling the truth, any of the truth, a little bit of the truth? Or was it all lies, lies, lies?

Alice turned her head up toward him and, amazingly, she was smiling radiantly. She laid her head down in his lap and pulled up her blouse, revealing her girlish breasts.

"Look . . . see! That's what he did!"

She was right about that. Black and blue marks clustered around the rosy nipples.

"Make the bad marks go away, darling. You can . . . *like Caz*. Caz cured my scar."

"I, uh . . . I don't think I've got that kind of power, Alice."

"Kissy, kissy?"

He lowered his head, touching each nipple with his lips. Alice closed her eyes and squirmed.

"What'll happen now?" she asked in a low whisper.

"I don't know. I've got to go to California again . . . and then, I hope, back to Europe."

"I mean right now. Will you slip it to the White Queen?"

"Alice . . . what will you do?"

"Me?" She was taken aback. "You mean *afterward*?" She chuckled excitedly. "I'll just go along, singin' my song . . ."

"No, Alice. I mean, drastic changes—"

"Never mind drastic changes! How can I say?" She stroked his face fondly, drawing him down, kissing him again, using her tongue to arouse him. "If you stayed here, we could keep on as lovers. Strictly sub rosa, we'd have to be very careful because of Sol . . . Stop frowning like that, dear boy. Or I could run away from Sol. Couldn't I?" she asked hotly. "If you'd agree, yes. I'd make it good for you, Seth."

But he knew better, and she must have seen the doubt in his face.

"Here I am, defenseless before you, and all you do is ask questions?" she began her ritual pleading.

"I haven't asked any questions. Look, what about the pictures? Shall I get rid of them?"

There was no reason he could think of to pass them along to Madison. The Ben Gazi dossier would not rise and fall on a few sordid orgy shots.

"Do with them what you will," she muttered. "Keep them around, if you like. Don't you get a little buzz-on looking at them? That's what they're for . . . and for me to remind myself how *bad* I was."

"Alice," he said finally, "I cannot figure you out."

"My dear, *what* is to figure out? I want you, that's all."

She touched him, everywhere, but Seth was beyond it now.

Rather stupidly, he supposed, Seth muttered, "You're going to get over this, Alice."

Coldly, she asked, "You mean get over Cazimir, I suppose. Is that what you're saying—that I'm in a mad depression because of Cazimir, that I'm not behaving like myself. That I'm acting like a *madwoman*?"

"Alice—did I say that?"

"I thought I might get over Cazimir, with your help. Now it appears not."

"Look, Alice, I'm really sorry. I wish it could be different."

She lay inertly now, half on him, half off. Her legs moved, fluttered slightly, like a bird's wings.

"I suppose being in Corky's apartment throws you," she said. "I think maybe you're in love with Corky Corcoran."

Seth didn't answer.

Slowly Alice pulled herself together, then got up. She picked up her fur coat.

"Well . . . good-bye."

Was that all?

Alice walked to the door, then turned back a bit, smiling in a strange way.

"Well, back to the social whirl, my dear. I did try my best. I am sorry, Seth, so sorry. But I guess this was not meant to be. Good-bye."

And then she opened the door and left. Seth wasn't sure yet why she had really wanted to see him so badly. He sat, unmoving.

Fifteen minutes later the phone rang. Katie.

"Well?"

"She's gone," he said.

248

Katie Corcoran's voice was very cold.

"You screwed her on my couch."

"I . . . what? I did not!"

"Bastard!" She hung up.

So, *Alice*, was that it? Alice had called Katie and told her that? Alice was a liar; she'd lied about everything.

Chapter
Twenty-Four

*T*he heart of the matter was that Alex had begged Tom to come back down to Los Angeles, and Clara and Tom had had a nasty little quarrel about it.

Worse, it happened at the gallery and while Biff Percy was there. Poor Biff—he hadn't known what was happening.

Life, Alex Spurzov told Tom when he phoned, had reached a very delicate state. He confessed to a bizarre, if not byzantine, development in his own affairs. It seemed that Alex had allowed himself to become involved with one of the daughters-in-law of Ludmilla's deceased last husband, Rodney Richards. This woman, this pursuer of geriatric Lotharios, had moved into Richlands and intended to divorce her husband, Dick, for Alex.

And people said nothing ever changed? On the contrary, the variables of life, as opposed to the *facts* of life, changed drastically, surprisingly, unexpectedly.

Martha had learned that Stan Gates's lover, Will Sorge, had *unexpectedly* died, and she had taken time off again from school to go to her father in Palm Springs.

Of course, Alex would be flattered by the attentions of Rose Richards—she was quite young and, he reported, not unattractive. But Alex was also a little frightened. Rose was a determined woman, a perfect example of Woman, the Predator.

They'd been sitting back in the office, drinking a little Morelli Chardonnay.

"Tom likes to think," Clara said, "that there's a tiger in every woman roaming the jungle of male-dom."

"Not in you, darling," Tom said. "You're a very wifely sort of wife."

"Oh, yes?" she fired back. "You mean submissive? Don't kid yourself."

Biff looked embarrassed and scratched his two-day-old beard. "I like to think it's the other way around—mad-dog males searching the jungle for women," he muttered.

Tom just looked at him. Clara knew the argument, that Biff Percy's modus operandi in women-chasing was to run them over with a car.

"Rose," Tom said thoughtfully, "is going for the *whole enchilada*, and on top of Richlands she's going to ask for twenty million to run it. Alex has convinced her I'm the very man to arrange the whole thing neatly . . . quietly."

"We know the family is very rich." Clara sipped some wine. "I remember from the days I helped at the Music Center."

"Ah . . ." Tom drawled. "Those halcyon days lived ever so briefly in Los Angeles. . . ."

She paid no attention. "I thought you were through with divorce work."

He laughed archly, maddeningly, and said, "Though I am extremely wealthy, both materially and in the love of my dear ones, I wouldn't turn down a half million or so."

"Ten percent for me," Biff grunted. "I was here when you took the phone call."

"The point is," Clara said irritably, not able to stop herself, "do we have to go down to L.A. again so soon?"

"We?" He stood up and walked over to the bar, pouring himself a hefty one. "You don't have to if you don't wish to. You can stay right here—*with Biff*."

"Hey, babe! *Awright!*"

They both ignored Biff.

"How long does Alex figure it'll take you to work your magic this time?"

"Impossible to say."

"You know I'm not crazy about running down to L.A. every time Alex Spurzov gets on the telephone," Clara said stolidly. "I've got a lot of things to do here."

"*Biff?*" Tom growled. "Mr. Terrif-ic?"

"On the other hand . . . if Martha is going to be in Palm Springs, maybe—"

"What?" Tom turned around angrily. "You think you should go to the Springs too and help comfort Stan Gates?" Frowning ferociously, he said, "Wonderful! Why don't you?"

Biff stuffed his cigar in his mouth and began to climb out of the rickety chair which he'd parked so casually on one side of the desk. He wanted no part of *this* family fight.

"I guess I'll be . . . meandering—"

"Sit down and drink your wine, goddamn it!" Tom exclaimed.

"Yes, sit down and shut up!" Clara added.

Biff sat down.

Clara was not intimidated or impressed with Tom's fury.

"I've said before I don't think it's fair on Martha to bear all this. I think Sorge was already sick at Christmas time and that's why she was so depressed."

"Depressed? I didn't see she was very depressed."

"Oh, no? You were too damn self-absorbed!"

Tom said, "Then go, for crissakes! Look, if everybody is so goddamn worried about Stanley, great! But I've got news for you—there's nothing much you can do or say that's going to help. . . . Am I right?" he asked Biff.

Biff shrugged. "Aren't you always?"

Tom glared at him. "I understand you'll always take Clara's side. I know you love her."

Biff smiled cagily, not taking Tom seriously. He shook his head.

"Nope. Clara's too old for me—the one I'm crazy about is Martha."

Tom looked darkly at him. "Well, *you little bastard!*"

So what was Clara? Chopped liver?

He'd had enough. "Listen, Clara, I've said it before and I say it again—if you feel like going to Palm Springs, then go! If you don't want to come to L.A., then don't! Stay here with this fat little lecher, the Picasso of North Beach—"

Biff interrupted huffily, "Not Picasso. Modigliani . . ."

Tom stared. "Well?"

"Well . . . what?" Clara was furious at both of them. Tom had the nerve to accuse Biff, obliquely to be sure, of playing around with Clara, and how did Biff react? He'd made a joke of it. Was the possibility *so* outrageous or unlikely? So it seemed. Neither of them took her seriously, that was what it amounted to.

"Well, *what* what?" Tom barked self-consciously. "I'm not even one hundred percent sure I am going to L.A., for God's sake—before you get all out of joint, Clara—"

"Thanks a lot. I'm going for a walk. Maybe I'll see you both later."

Despite the pain Stanley had caused her—this was what was in Clara's mind—despite that, she didn't wish him unhappiness. Perhaps Tom couldn't appreciate her true feelings. The process of forgiveness had been long and tedious, but in the end Clara had forgiven Stanley, and she did thank him for finally being honest with her.

So, she had to wish him well. And she could sympathize with him, for Martha's sake.

On the other hand, mention of Martha still made Tom nervous. See how he'd gotten riled up at what Biff had said . . . that *Biff* had the hots for Martha! Clara believed Tom would have killed Biff if he'd thought there was anything to it.

"You're too nice a person," Tom said later. "I'm sorry. You're a lot nicer than the rest of us."

"Not necessarily, Tom." He should be careful not always to expect the best of her. She was not Mrs. Pushover; not as pliant as he'd come to take for granted. "Some day you might be very surprised."

"I know, I know," he said, but he wasn't listening to what she said. "I feel sorry for Stan Gates too, and I've never even met the man."

"Well . . . we'll see." She wouldn't commit herself to going . . . yet.

"The thing is, Clara," Tom muttered, "I did promise Alex."

"I thought you said you were thinking about it." She sighed wearily, out of patience now. "All this for some dumb divorce. You couldn't say no, even if you wanted to."

Well, perhaps some renewed legal *heat* would divert him. God knew Tom had reached the point where he needed some sort of diversion. Getting his teeth into another messy divorce action would surely make him forget everything else.

Playfully, he kissed her. "My dear, don't tell me you're not just the *tiniest* bit curious about Alex and Rose Richards. . . ."

*   *   *

And once they were on the scene, Clara couldn't say honestly that she was indifferent about having the chance to visit Richlands. People had never stopped talking about the place, although through the years, relatively few people had actually seen it. During the declining days of the first Mrs. Rodney Richards, there had only rarely been afternoon charity tea parties at Richlands; nobody could remember an evening dinner party there. And Messalina Richards had been so sickly, seeing no one, so the stories went, except Rodney and the faithful young butler.

Then, during Ludmilla's brief reign, both Ludmilla and Rodney had turned increasingly anti-social.

Driving through twenty-foot wrought-iron gates and up the narrow, curling road sided with overgrown forest, then across several acres of cosmeticized hills, you might feel you had stepped back in time to the glory days of Hollywood. Indeed, Rodney, in the old days, had flirted with the high and mighty of show business, also of politics and big oil. Legend had it that Rodney had rushed completion of the Richlands ballroom so as to host a Herbert Hoover victory party there in 1932; the ball room went unused until 1952, when General Eisenhower finally won the White House for the Republicans. It was even said that Eisenhower had danced there with the first Mrs. Richards, though people claimed that Ike had hated dancing.

The gardens at Richlands had been much discussed too: hedges, sylvan galleries of topiary, palm-tree oases built into the hillside, miles of gravel paths, and the Olympic-sized pool in which Richards had once floated an entire symphony orchestra in real Venetian gondolas. The pool was fed by an artificial fifty-foot waterfall. And the Richlands garage was spoken of only in passing—it was large enough for a dozen full-sized cars and God knew how many coupes or economy-sized vehicles.

Nobody had ever counted how many servants could be housed at Richlands.

But now, so it seemed, they were down to one: only a butler named Peat.

It was Peat, dressed oddly in black jodhpurs, shiny black boots, and a soiled white ticking jacket, who led them to the fifty-yard long glassed gallery.

In France, Clara supposed, such a room would be called the

Orangerie, conceived as an ornate hothouse, filled with exotic flowers and plants of local and tropical variety. All it boasted now were a dozen or so bedraggled palms, underwatered azaleas, and on an oversized round glass table in the center, pots of half-dead ivy. Above this hung an art nouveau chandelier with sweeping metal arms, looking like nothing as much as a nightmarish man-eating spider.

Clara still didn't really understand why Tom had consented to take this job. But now she was glad that he had. But she also could not help wondering if he had already met Rose Richards and was here because of her.

Rose was a woman who would be called "very put together." Her jet-black hair was freshly trimmed in a short, sculpted Vidal Sassoon style, sideburns pointed and black locks brushed boyishly across her forehead. Red lipstick lighted her darkish skin, and the color of her cheeks was just so. Rose might be a little heavy, Clara thought, but the weight was well concealed. For this "evening at home," as it was billed, Rose was wearing a freely flowing caftan made of gauzy silk; it was bright red, the color absolutely glowing against her black hair and eyebrows. Underneath the drape Rose seemed to be wearing undergarments . . . wasn't she?

As they were introduced, Clara saw how Alex beamed. He nodded dotingly. He might as well have said it outright: Rose was *his* creation!

"I'm so pleased to meet you, Mr. Addey," Rose said gravely, shaking Tom's hand. Her fingernails were of the same subtle red as her lips, not so scarlet as the caftan, or perhaps the woman. "And Mrs. Addey."

"Clara," Clara said.

Tom introduced Seth and Hildy.

"And," said Rose solemnly, "you see your other son is already here, Mr. Rossiter Addey."

"We've met." Clara couldn't resist. She smiled at Rossiter a bit cruelly, took his hand, kissed his cheek. She felt him twitch. His eyes darkened with hurt. "How are you, my child? And dear Serena?" She might have pinched him; his reaction was as pained. And she did have to mention Serena, didn't she? "How's her father doing?"

"Better."

"And now, please," Rose said, "you must meet *Prince Alexei*!"

Alex Spurzov seized Clara's hand, rushed it to his mouth. He kissed her fingers. His lips felt feverish but his eyes jumped and skipped with energy. Yes, Clara could imagine that this particular old coot would still be doing very well that way. He had that look; he stared at Clara shrewdly. She wondered what he read in *her* expression.

But Rose was the star attraction. Alex seemed very proud of her, as he would have a dear child. And Clara watched Tom *watching* Rose Richards!

Make no bones about it, Rose was the new mistress of Richlands!

What role was she playing? The liberated woman . . . a 1920s flapper . . . Isadora Duncan? All Rose lacked was the yard-long ebony cigarette holder. She greeted her guests warmly but with a curious indifference, as if she wasn't quite sure why they were there, or that they were, somehow, interfering with the fascinating rhythm of her private life. Her manner with Peat was unusual too, as if she had chosen him as a sounding board by which she would establish her rule over the estate and all who lived with her—including Alex Spurzov, though Rose treated Alex with great respect.

"I would like for you to see my gardens," Rose announced, making no offer to show them anything else—the long gallery, the reception and dining rooms, the spectacular ballroom. Rose went on grandly, "I wish to have the light turned on outside so that I may show my guests the gardens and the pool with its spectacular waterfall spilling in one end . . . *that is, if Mr. Peat can remember where the switch is*?"

"In the kitchen," Peat muttered.

Fortunately they'd not come for dinner, only for coffee afterward. Rose offered, "We'll have a brandy or port from our extensive cellars. *I'm sure* Mr. Peat can find his way down there."

"Can do," said Peat sullenly.

The butler unlocked doors on one side of the gallery to let them out on the terrace which ran across the back of the house. From crusty balustrades, the whole length of the pool could be seen. And, as Rose had promised, when Peat pulled the switches, the fountain at the north end of the pool was activated along with the lights and creakily began pumping rusty water.

For a few moments they all gazed at the well-lit scene. There was no question about it—Richlands still warranted its description as a showplace.

Hildy felt obliged to comment.

"This is like one of Ludwig's castles in Bavaria," she announced. "I think it reminds me most of the one called Linderhof."

"Oh!" Rose spoke quickly, her voice cutting. "No, Richlands is modeled on the Palace of Versailles."

Tom grunted in amazement. Versailles? That was going some.

Even so, Clara appreciated seeing Hildy knocked down a notch or two. During dinner she'd exhibited a tendency to be *too much* family—certainly not because Seth showed her any great devotion. On the contrary, he'd been subdued, his expression muted. He took notice of Hildy, yes, he didn't ignore her, but he was far away. Clara thought if Hildy was still thinking *family*, then it must be because she'd made a great hit with Thelma Drysdale.

As far as Seth and Hildy were concerned, Clara would have said they were done for.

This thought made her wonder about Washington and prompted her question.

"Seth, did you see Alice Betancur and say hello for me?"

He glanced at her quickly, his guard down for an instant. And he realized Clara had caught the flicker of surprise, dismay, anxiety.

"Oh, yes," he muttered. "I did."

"And you *kissed* her for me?"

"Yes, I did. Has she been in touch?"

"No, no, I haven't heard from her again."

Clara wondered why he was so sensitive about Alice. What, in fact, had happened? Perhaps they'd clashed, like hostile colors. What did she know anymore about Alice? Being old friends was not the same as being good friends. There had been stories. Sol was so much older; everybody said also so ugly. Clara wondered, but she hadn't the nerve to say anything more to Seth.

Being honest, Clara was pleased Seth and Hildy were finished. Now she could be freely irritated that Hildy had spent so much time with Thelma, no doubt discussing her in broad and narrow outline. And then, there was the fascinating news Seth carried—news that didn't disturb him—that Thelma Drysdale was contemplating remarriage, to Rossiter's employer, the Hungarian financier Sandor Veruckt.

Tom's eyes had sparkled maliciously. "At last!" he cried.

Naturally, he would overdo it. As if to incite her more, impulsively, or so it was supposed to seem, Tom clapped his hand down on Hildy's, running his fingers over her smooth knuckles and the wrist covered with a shadow of sensuous dark fuzz. Tom patted her knuckles, stroked, then in a blur of action stroked, patted, and stroked again before picking up his wineglass.

Maybe he'd sensed it too—that Seth had turned his back on Hildy, that now she was fair game. Certainly if Seth had noticed anything of the foreplay, he gave no sign.

Tom had better be careful. Even now, on the terrace, he was standing too close to Hildy, one arm, thoughtlessly, caught lightly around her waist. He couldn't help himself, could he? He had to dazzle, to do his best to knock a girl like Hildy off her pins.

By now Rose had had enough of the great outdoors.

"It is *very cold*, Peat," she said, as if he were to blame. "We'll go back inside. Close the doors, Peat—and bring the drinks."

"Yes, madame!"

Clara drew Rossiter away. It was not difficult. He was alone. More than that, he *looked* alone, and lonely, at odds with the world. Like Seth, he was unhappy. The two Addey boys were not doing very well, were they?

Seth remained outside, pacing the terrace by himself, studying the pool, the scene of the crime—or suicide . . . or misadventure . . . while Tom and Hildy huddled with Rose and Alex next to the potted ivy.

Though she'd been rebuffed, Hildy couldn't stop talking about the magnificence of Richlands, even then making her pitch to Rose for a picture-taking opportunity. It seemed *Classics* was planning a series on classic California houses. When Rose heard this, she warmed considerably toward Hildy.

"Peculiar we're all together again," Clara murmured to Rossiter.

"Not all."

258

"No. Serena's with her father and so is Martha—she's in Palm Springs again, with Stanley, the gay blade."

"Yes."

"Well, you *could* sound relieved," Clara said boldly. She didn't care if anybody, anybody at all, noted the confidential nature of their exchange. "Are you pleased about your mother marrying the Hungarian?"

"I think Sandor will be a match for her," he said.

"Tom wasn't?"

"Sure. At the time." Rossiter shrugged. Clara moved closer; she rested her hand on his arm. Rossiter tensed and backed away. "She's grown since then. It'd take a Sandor to keep her in line now—he's more brilliant than she is."

And Tom wasn't? Was Tom some kind of a dullard? What did that make Clara, then, some kind of a stupid slut who didn't come close to measuring up to the exquisite Thelma?

"What's cooking with you and Serena?"

He just shook his head.

There had been a suggestion, quickly squelched, that Seth and Hildy might stay with Rossiter and Serena. Of course, this had been impossible with Bud Slagger still in residence. Now, if Seth had been willing to confide in Rose—as he'd evidently been with Alex—that he was out here again to look into the circumstances of the death of Ludmilla Spurzova *and* her last lover; and if Rose had known then what she had just learned, that Hildy wanted to take pictures of Great Houses, for the prestigious *Classics*; they'd have been invited straight away to stay at Richlands, a convenience for all concerned.

Now the invitation did come, flying. Of course, Hildy would want to do the house and its art treasures, which had yet to be catalogued but included, principally, Rose said, with a dutiful look at Alex, the renowned *Spurzov Egg* which *our dear prince* intended soon to remove from its bank vault in order for it to be viewed at Richlands by the crème de la crème of the art world.

"Isn't that so, Alex?"

Alex smiled the smile of a cornered man, but did not in fact say yes or no. Judging by Tom's quick attention, this question of the Fabergé egg could be one of Alex's prime worries vìs-à-vìs his new relationship with Rose Richards.

"Wunderbar!" Hildy cried out in joyful German, startling

them all, especially Peat, who by then was taking their drink orders. His head snapped up and he stared at Hildy rivetingly, all but clicking his heels. Who'd once said, Clara tried to remember, that Peat was some kind of a neo-Nazi nutcase?

"Agreed, then?" Rose asked eagerly. "I think you and . . . Seth . . ." She found his name, but where was Seth? Still outside but just then opening the terrace door and coming in. "Ah . . . here he is. Peat will prepare a room." One room? What of sin? No, Rose was a modern woman. "I think Seth and Alex have something to discuss—"

"We have a mutual interest in communist affairs," Seth muttered blackly. "A day or two here would be convenient."

"And then?" Alex asked intently.

Seth shrugged. "Who knows?"

His answer didn't please Hildy. Sullenly, she frowned and looked away. Given their attitude toward each other, it was hard to imagine them sharing a room.

"Tom . . ." Alex spoke loudly and cordially, getting away from the matter of his Egg, "I've seen your sons separately but not together, the three of you. The similarity is striking, if I do say so!"

Then Alex held out his hand. "Sweet Clara, come sit next to Alex!"

Clara had gotten what she hoped for—a balloon of very mellow brandy. Rodney Richards must have put the stuff down fifty years ago.

"Is it good, darling?" Alex asked solicitously. "If I dared, I would have one too."

"It's beautiful, Alex."

Alex would not remember that they had never met before, not that it mattered: It seemed to Clara she'd always known him.

"*So are you*, Clara Addey." His jaded old eyes sparkled. "My Tom is a very lucky man!"

"Oh, *now*!" she objected.

"We will be friends."

"We *are* friends!"

Alex played provocatively with his cravat, passing his hand over his slickly brushed hair.

"And your daughter is a very beautiful girl!"

Yes, he *had* met Martha. The day of Ludmilla's memorial, Martha had driven Tom and Alex back to Richlands.

"In fact, your daughter looks exactly like you. You might be twins."

"I'm a little older," Clara said wryly.

"No, not so! Twins, I say. To Clara and Martha!" Alex toasted them gravely. "Well, Clara, what do *you* think of this old place? Richlands is not what it used to be, we might as well admit it right away."

Looking around, following Alex's eyes, Clara wondered if the place had ever been what it used to be. Someone, whether Richards or his wives, had impressed a barrenness of personality on the house. One had only to see the litter of worthless knick-knacks interspersed among the pots of ivy, on the big glass coffee tables and the white mantle. Hopefully, Clara thought, Ludmilla had not brought this collection of junk to Richlands.

"I know what you're thinking, Clara," Alex whispered. "But when they finally sell it, Richlands will bring millions. It's the last of the big Bel Air estates."

"I'm sure," Clara said. "But it's such a barn. It's so cold, Alex."

"Rose will bring new life to the place, Clara. *Isn't she wonderful?*" Alex smiled fondly and gulped icy vodka.

"She is a very striking woman," Clara admitted. "She has a beautiful face."

Alex looked terribly sly and whispered, "Do you know who she looks like? Guess!"

That was easy. Looking at his face, watching Tom watching Rose, the answer was apparent.

"Ludmilla, am I right?"

He nodded violently. "I look at her sometimes . . . and I see Ludmilla. She has the same spirit, Clara."

Whatever else Rose was up to, she was very possessive of Alex. Noting how intimately Alex was speaking to Clara, Rose hurried across the room. Exercising her claim, she crouched on the footstool across from Clara, put her hand on Alex's arm, then quite blatantly rubbed his thigh. There couldn't be any doubt Rose was having her way with the old prince, and he with her.

For a second, then, everybody was quiet, motionless, as if they had been warned of an impending shock.

Rose responded first. "What the hell—"

Peat appeared at the top of the short flight of steps leading down to the gallery. He had exchanged the ticking jacket for a black shirt and a black uniform jacket, one sleeve of which bore the distinctive and frightening swastika armband. With the shiny black boots, black britches, and his sallow and emotionless face, Peat was the exact image of Death and Destruction.

"The Nazis have landed!" Alex yelped. Was he hallucinating? But that wasn't all. Peat had an announcement.

"Mr. Richard Richards is here and would like to be asked in."

Rose jumped up. "Tell him to go home! And *you* get out of that goddamn outfit!"

But it was too late. A female figure appeared next to Peat, this person in a flowered dress and high heels, with a pink pocketbook under one arm.

"I want to talk to you!" Richards squeaked.

Alex snorted. "Madame Hitler, I presume!"

Clara looked at Tom. No good—his jaw was slack. Rossiter stared. Hildy looked very embarrassed; she must have assumed this entertainment had been designed for her. Her face flushed angrily.

Dick Richards, as might be expected, blushed bright red. Under an unruly blond wig his blotchy face looked like one huge freckle. The voice was so soft and reedy, it barely carried across the room.

"I didn't know there'd be people here."

He didn't look at anybody directly. He gazed around people, through them, over them, to the side. But shy? Maybe what appeared to be shyness was actually arrogance. But how could a man dressed up like a woman pretend to arrogance?

Rose yelled, "You're disgusting! You'd better go, Dick!"

But he came on down the steps, Peat at his side like a faithful escort.

"Hello, Tom."

Tom didn't even blink.

"Good evening, Dick," he said. "I'd like to introduce you to my son Rossiter. This is Hildy Beckmann. There's Clara, my wife, sitting with Alex. Alex, you know . . . *and Rose*. You know Rose."

Dick Richards nodded haughtily, stroking his pocketbook. "Yes, I know Rose. If you knew Rose, like I know Rose—"

"Get out!" Rose shrilled.

"Your daughters are asking for you."

"Oh? And what are they asking?"

"Where their mother is!"

He seemed to have no conception of the irony, the contradiction in the statement. Rose might have retorted that Dick should be mother enough for both of them. But she was tongue-tied, struck dumb.

She finally stammered, "Well, I'm here, am I not? There's no doubt about where I live. At Richlands, my new home."

Richards repeated that. *"Your new home?"* He turned and looked inquiringly at Tom for a moment, then said, "I read in the paper that our friend Cazimir Ben Gazi is dead."

Tom nodded. "I saw that too."

"He was here and then he was gone and now he's dead—just like that? As simple as that? Have we no better explanation?"

"It's generally agreed," Tom said uncomfortably, "that it doesn't take very long to kill a man." Seth had crossed from the windows to stand beside him. "And this is my other son, Seth."

Seth showed no emotion, no interest in Richards's unusual appearance. "How do you do?"

Dick Richards responded dryly, "Pleased to meet *you*."

"Dick was asking about Cazimir," Tom said.

"Yes. Are we really *so sure* of the chronology of Cazimir's trip?" Dick Richards inquired pettishly.

He gave it away by glancing at Peat. Peat, on the other hand, stood stoically, his arms crossed on his puny chest, the horrible swastika facing out for all to see.

"I heard." Seth kept his eye on Peat. "We don't know *when* he got to Spain, if that's what you're asking." Richards's eyebrows rose. Who was Seth to have a comment? "I happen to work for the State Department," Seth said. "Cazimir Ben Gazi was a valued friend of America."

"Then what are you doing here," Richards demanded sharply, "if he was murdered in Spain?"

"We're tracking him back—"

"Tracking him back . . . where?' Richards laughed shrilly. His voice had quite gone. "To what end?"

Seth's voice was very deadly. "This was his last stop in the United States before he flew to Europe. . . . We're very interested in his *California contacts*. They might give us a clue what happened in Spain. *Do you see?*''

Richards's bravado had noticeably faded. ''We were *casual* friends—''

''Casual?''

''Oh, yes . . . Peat can confirm that. Can't you, Peat?''

The butler looked confused. *''I confirm nothing!''*

Richards began to look uncomfortable. ''Well, confirm it or not—it is a fact!''

Rose cast him a belligerent look, then cried out, ''Why have you come here to tell us these stories, Dick? You're beyond patience! What do you *mean* by busting into *my* house like this, dressed for a costume party which we are *not* giving!''

''Your house?''

''Yes. You bet!''

Richards's lips shook but he managed a smile. ''Rose is no Ludmilla, Prince Spurzov!''

''The hell I'm not!'' Rose cried.

Peat drew himself up erectly. His eyes blazed, for a second almost fanatically. Then he spoke in resonant tones.

''Hail Ludmilla! Beauty is Truth. Truth is Beauty. *Ludmilla* is Truth *and* Beauty!''

The words boomed. Who could say that Peat wasn't crazy?

Alex Spurzov turned white, then red. He stared as Peat did an about-face and practically goose-stepped across the gallery, his boots drumming on the stone floor. Dick Richards in his heels clattered behind him.

Alex came half out of his chair, then fell back. ''What have we done?''

Chapter
Twenty-Five

*T*he point, Rossiter assured himself, was that the Vegas crowd could have sold their Morris Communications holdings at any moment after Chet Arthur began buying and made a very handsome profit. The day the price jumped past fifty-five, fifteen dollars a share better than their buy, would have been a perfect time to bail out.

But no—Lorenzo was a gambler. He'd want to let it ride, at least to the sixty dollars a share Chet Arthur had pledged, Bud said stubbornly. They were going to wait it out.

Rossiter always underestimated the power of greed. Diamond and company were gamblers, sure, but they didn't understand the first rule of the market: smart men *got out* when they were on solid ground, *before* the sand began to slip from under their feet.

Was this day in Rossiter's personal history book to be written as the time when all hell broke loose? On Friday Rossiter phoned Bud at the Addey homestead to urge him to persuade Diamond to sell.

"It's fifty-six, Bud," he said. "The time has come. . . ."

Again Bud refused.

"No, no, Ross, I can't. There's something else . . . never mind! Ross, you *said* it's going to sixty!"

"Yeah, but what if it doesn't?"

"You promised, Ross!"

Slowly Rossiter began to understand. Bud was afraid to call

Lorenzo Diamond; he wondered immediately if it had something to do with what Tiny had told him about Abby Basilica.

"Bud," he said patiently, "even if you've got something else on your mind, you've got to give this some attention."

"Ross, I can't even think about calling him!"

Did it matter that Rossiter had a very funny feeling in the pit of his stomach? No, he couldn't tell Bud that. Stockbrokers were not supposed to operate on the basis of funny feelings—hunches were okay, but funny feelings were things that came to women, not men.

Once more he tried. "Bud, now *is* the time! People shouldn't wait till it tops out. Take the money and run!"

Bud heard what he said, or did he? *"Why?"*

Serena burst into their conversation; she had picked up the extension, the goddamn little spy.

"Stop badgering Daddy!"

"Serena, baby, you shouldn't . . . This is between—"

"Shut up, *you!*" This had become Serena's customary way of addressing Daddy. "Ross, I don't want you bothering him with all that stock-market stuff. Leave him alone! Every time he hears the goddamn phone ring, he lights up a cigarette!"

Bud's pledge, his heartfelt promise to quit again, had gone up in smoke, so to speak.

Rossiter patiently said, "This is an important business matter. It has nothing to do with you, Serena."

"The hell it doesn't! No more, Daddy. *Hang up.*"

Bud's despair was palpable. "Thanks, Ross," he whispered, "but—"

"Get off the fucking phone!"

Serena slammed her extension down and began rattling the hook. Rossiter simply hung up.

At approximately five minutes after the market closed in New York that day, the something Rossiter had felt in the pit of his stomach, the unforeseeable something, did happen.

In a brief announcement Chet Arthur Ltd. told the world it was withdrawing its offer for Morris Communications and would immediately begin selling off MorrisCom shares accumulated during the last couple of weeks. It seemed that certain unexpected and untoward developments in the takeover process were worrying enough to cause Chet Arthur Ltd. to rethink the whole situation. No details were given, no clue as to what these adverse developments might be.

The announcement had the effect of a nuclear blast on the value of MorrisCom shares, and the fallout was just as bad. Rossiter was covered in cold sweat. His fingers commenced to tremble at such a rate that it was impossible for him to operate the keyboard of his computer.

What in the hell could have happened? The MorrisCom share price went into a sickening spin. In the three and some hours left of Pacific-time trading, it was established that MorrisCom would open on Monday morning, "when traded," at forty-five or under, a drop of more than ten dollars a share from the Friday high.

Of course, this was not the end of the world. Oh no? If not, how much worse would the end of the world be?

What had happened to scare Chet Arthur off? *Surely not* the Diamond group's minor investment; there was no way Arthur would have heard about that. Even if he had, so what? Was the feeling between Chet Arthur and Lorenzo Diamond so bad that Arthur would withdraw from a perfect deal merely to punish his Las Vegas enemy?

For punish Diamond this certainly would.

Rossiter had had tense moments during his days with Veruckt & Associates but this took the cake—for once he was *personally* involved in the disaster. The shit had hit the fan. He was in deep, deep shit. He was up Shit Creek without a paddle.

For the first time in his career, at about three P.M., Rossiter had to go outside to be sick. He puked his heart out and when he came back to his office he must have looked so terrible that Marjorie asked if maybe he should go home and lie down?

No. Grimly, stomach churning in the place where, in the morning, he'd had that funny feeling, Rossiter had to call Bud. There was still time to salvage something from the deal and perhaps make a small profit.

At first Serena wouldn't let him speak to Bud, but Rossiter was so curt and ugly that she caved in. Bud came on dully— they'd probably been having another one of their father-daughter discussions.

Rossiter drew a breath, working to steady his voice. "Bud, you have got to call Diamond."

Reflexively, Bud began to sputter.

"MorrisCom has nose-dived, Bud. Chet Arthur cancelled his offer."

Bud shrieked. His smoke-raw voice rose to a cracking pitch of pain.

"No! Not possible!"

"Afraid so, Bud." Once said, it was not so hard to repeat the bad news. "I did have a feeling . . . I tried to tell you."

"No! You didn't tell me."

"I told you about two hours ago to get out."

"You didn't!"

Of course Bud would deny it, wouldn't he? He could never admit Rossiter had advised him to speak to Lorenzo Diamond.

"Rossiter . . . *don't tell me this!"*

Serena must have heard him wailing. She tried again to cut in. This time Rossiter would not put up with it.

"Serena, get off the goddamn telephone!"

Bud ignored her cursing and name-calling. "Ross, where's it at right now?"

"Forty-five, Ben, and sinking—like the barometer."

A sob, such a terrible, terrified sound, trickled through the phone line. "What the hell we gonna do, Ross?" Bud's residual vitality was waning. "Lorenzo is gonna kill me. He's *really* gonna kill me now."

"No, no . . . these things happen," Rossiter said, trying to reassure him, but not so sure himself. "Something happened, I can't figure out what." Listening to Bud groaning, Rossiter began to feel like a tower of strength, a man of decision for the darkest moments. "Bud, you can still get something out of it."

"What?"

"I don't know. Monday morning is going to be fierce—it'll probably drop to below forty. Maybe we could arrange a block sale now and break even. Maybe take a little loss."

What he was saying was that taking a little loss might turn out to be the best they could do.

"Oh . . . my . . . God. It's the end, Ross. Forget it. I'm all washed up now—for sure."

"Hey," Ross exclaimed, trying to cheer him, "it's only money."

Bud whimpered.

Serena might have shut up for a while but she hadn't stopped listening. Now she interrupted in a fresh fury.

"Goddamn you, Ross, you're so sick, what are you trying to do to Daddy, kill him? Which you'll succeed in doing if you keep this up over some dumb stock!"

Bud's voice pitched upward. Unsteadily, he screamed, "Baby, will you get *the fuck* off the fucking tele-*fucking*-phone!" Serena gasped. "Can't you understand, *you bimbo*, there's more important things going on than your hair and nails and nose and tits—"

"What are you saying?"

Yes, what *was* Bud saying?"

"Didn't I pay for all that?" Bud yelled hysterically, "to have all your goddamn parts remade? So will you, for once, leave me alone and shut your trap!"

"You . . . you . . . you . . ."

Total shock closed down Serena's repertoire of scathing rebuttal.

Again, ignoring Serena, Bud demanded, "Ross, what am I going to do?"

"You've got to call him, Bud. Do we sell or do we stick it out . . . and hope?

"He's going to kill me now—for sure."

"Come on, Bud—not for losing a few bucks."

Well, yeah, more than a few bucks. Calculating rapidly, Rossiter figured Diamond and his boys would be out more than a quarter-million dollars for every dollar MorrisCom dipped below forty.

Bud sounded as though he was struggling for air, working to keep his renovated heart pumping. Rossiter could almost smell the devastation.

"That's not all," Bud whined noisily. "Children . . . children, there's more."

"More what, Daddy?"

"The dame . . ." Bud began weeping. "You heard of Abby Basilica, you know, Lorenzo's bimbo."

"She works for you in the PR—" Serena began.

Bud bleated, "She works for me—*for shit!*"

"You're her boss, Daddy."

"No, baby, you never understood that, did you?"

Rossiter did, though. He remembered what Tiny had divulged—that Abby Basilica actually ran the Alhambra's public relations department. Bud was only a front man, a handshaker. And *he* had been stupid enough to put the arm on her; even more stupid when he'd allowed Abby to succumb to his charm.

"Daddy?" Serena voiced a big question mark. She'd just caught a whiff of something rotten in the State of Nevada.

Bud stammered, "We had a little . . . deal."

Serena made a gagging sound. "What you're telling me is—"

"Yeah," Bud screamed, "we made out and Lorenzo knows about it! You ask why I got the screamies, why my nerves are shot?"

He'd get no sympathy from Serena. How could Bud betray her at a time when she was so defenseless? Her voice was bruising. "And you're sick and on my hands to take care of and worry about and that's what you do behind my back, not to speak of *your wife's*, who's sitting up there waiting for you, and that's what you do, you bastard, you fucked the Mafia princess!"

Rossiter heard, listened, said nothing. A mere son-in-law was not justified in interfering. This matter was between Bud and his daughter, between Bud and Tiny, between Tiny and Serena, whatever; it had nothing to do with Rossiter Addey, innocent bystander.

"Yeah, thanks," Bud moaned weakly, "the way you scream and yell at me, it's hardly worth living."

"Well, you dumb shit!"

"Thanks, again," Bud muttered. "Lorenzo turns off my water, a lot you'd care."

"You're right! A lot I care! Are you *hearing* this, Rossiter?" Serena demanded. "And what do you say, Mr. Smartass Stockbroker, now that Daddy's going to be blamed for losing Lorenzo Diamond's money because you didn't keep him properly advised at a time when Lorenzo is also very unhappy about Daddy screwing his girlfriend?"

"I had nothing to do with that last part of it."

Serean howled wildly. "We'll go away, Daddy. He'll never know where you are."

"Such as?"

"Hawaii, we'll fly to Hawaii."

"Oh, sure," Bud snarled. "We'll stay at the Kahala Hilton, he'll never think to look for me there. . . . Aah, you wouldn't know, would you? You're just a baby." Bud's body temperature had dropped below normal; fatalism took over. He accepted that his future was hopeless. "I suppose you didn't see in the paper about the guy they found dead in Spain a couple days ago."

"So?" Serena retorted. "So? A lot of people die in Spain."

"Of bullet holes?" Ben demanded. "A guy who did business in Vegas? With Lorenzo Diamond?"

Serena hesitated. "Well, you don't have to die just because you did business in Vegas with Lorenzo Diamond."

"You float up on the beach with bullet holes and lead poisoning?"

"Daddy, what are you saying?"

Rossiter began to see a faint glow of light under the thick door of Bud's mind.

"Happens this guy, besides doing certain confidential business with Lorenzo over the last few years . . . happens this same guy also got into Abby's panties. And Lorenzo found out."

Serena said, "We'll go further away, Daddy!"

"*Further than Spain?*"

Bud might straighten out Serena's appreciation of the length of Lorenzo Diamond's arm. But Bud and Serena would've been even more terrified if they'd known the truth—that Ben Gazi had in fact been bumped off in California, not Spain. That was why Seth was out here again—to ensure the cover-up, to protect the fiction that Ben Gazi had been murdered by the Russians in Spain.

"His name was Ben Gazi," Rossiter said, somewhat calmly. "And Washington says he was killed by the Russians."

Bud Slagger said feebly, "*Russians, my ass!*"

"What was Ben Gazi doing in Las Vegas?" Seth might be interested in Bud's answer. "What'd he have to do with Lorenzo Diamond? This is all news to me, Bud."

"Who the hell knows?" Bud replied angrily. "Does Lorenzo tell me anything? They had business. The Arab was supposed to have high-up contacts—bankers and politicians and guys in intelligence. He was a *fixer*," Bud muttered. "They'd sell their goddamn mother for a pork barrel. There never can be too many guys like that in Lorenzo's pocket." Bud pondered all this information, then added, "But this Arab made one small mistake."

"Which is?"

"He slipped it to Abby."

Serena cut in crudely, "You'd think by now she's banged so many guys, Lorenzo wouldn't care anymore."

"He cares, baby," Bud muttered. His courage dipped again. "So *what about the stocks*, Ross?"

"Bud, do you want *me* to call Lorenzo?"

This was a terrible question, a terrible decision for Bud to make.

"No, no," he finally said, "I've got to call him myself. I got to take my lumps, bite the bullet."

The Saturday after Black Friday was little better. Rossiter had to accept that he was screwed out of a hefty commission—something on the order of three- or four-hundred thousand dollars.

Chet Arthur had dumped on Rossiter Addey as well as Lorenzo Diamond.

Much more potentially damaging to Rossiter, however, was how Sandor Verucket would react. Rossiter had expected to hear from Sandor apoplectically the previous afternoon, but all was silence. Gone home? No, Sandor would be acutely aware of the situation. He had bought into MorrisCom at least partially on Rossiter's say-so, and even though Sandor had presumably checked it out for himself, Rossiter's little piece of intelligence was in Sandor's memory bank.

All this did not make for a thrilling end of the week. Newly ambulatory Bud, and Serena, thank God, had gone out—where, Rossiter didn't know and didn't care. In an old sweater and banged-up tennis shoes he was out back indolently raking soggy, rotting greenery. Stopping to drink a beer, Rossiter leaned on the rake and stared at the back of his little house, this dump which in spirit he'd already sold. Now, thanks to Chet Arthur, he was stuck here awhile longer; or, at least, was stuck here as long as he *stuck with* Serena.

The house had been thrown together. Sloppily built, circa 1940, like so many of the outrageously expensive houses in this part of town. Stucco was piled on a jerry-built frame; half the studs were missing, and you hardly dared hang a heavy picture for fear it would pull down a wall. But the house had recently been painted, the trim cheerful.

The garage was probably better built than the house—not surprisingly, cars being more important in southern California than people. They'd get about five hundred thousand for it, when and if they sold. Facing him was the kitchen window and the little wing that stuck out toward the garage and contained the utility room and Lourdes's cell. Upstairs a bank of windows defined the master bedroom; to the left of where he was standing was the bath. The sewer ran from behind the pool and under the house and out to the street. And it was horrible when the thing backed up—Serena had a habit of throwing nondegradable trash into the toilet, then blaming it on Lourdes.

Still, Rossiter supposed it was not a bad house. If somebody had children, it was perfect because the school was only four or five blocks away. That one feature would help move the dump when the time came. If you didn't happen to have any children, well . . .

On the other hand, Rossiter dejectedly told himself, it was perhaps lucky for him Serena had lost interest in playing the pregnancy game. Though she'd teased Bud with the possibility of a grandchild, Serena showed no further sign of being that way. No, she wasn't pregnant; if she had been, she'd be screaming nonstop about miscarriage and blaming Rossiter and her father for every fit of nausea.

No, Serena was too close to Daddy anyway to become pregnant by a man so distantly related to her as a husband. Was there something about this relationship between daughter and father that should, as a matter of fact, cause Rossiter anxiety? Their fighting and making up had a lover's ring. Could he mention the word *incest*? Serena didn't try to hide the caresses, the passion of their kisses, even when Rossiter was sitting right there in the room. And when she didn't think he could see or hear, well, that was something else again. Maybe it was dormant now, but at one time, in the past, he was sure there must have been unnatural and noxious doings between these two Slaggers, Serena and Bud.

When Rossiter had finally come home the night before, Serena's thin lips were set in an even thinner, but thank God, more silent line than usual. Bud, in a sorry state, turned in early, and Serena went to "sit with him," leaving Rossiter in the den downstairs with several heavy drinks and then alone in bed, where he passed into a deep and blessedly untroubled sleep.

That morning Serena announced she was taking Bud shopping. If Rossiter was lucky, by the time they got back he could be half loaded again and ready for another night of deep sleep.

Of course, if it was Serena's intention to whisk Bud Slagger out of the way of Lorenzo Diamond's revenge, they might not be back at all. If she was smart, she wouldn't give advance warning to anyone . . . including Rossiter, hopefully. That way the information couldn't be tortured out of him.

Rossiter laughed aloud as he raked. No, better not tell *him*. He'd squeal immediately. Gaily, he arranged a little pile of manure-to-be on the far side of the dinky pool, next to a particularly diseased-looking orange tree. It was covered in aphids and badly needed spraying, he thought. But the soil here—the vast bean field that had become the incorporated City of Beverly Hills— was rich, fertile, or seemed so to Rossiter, uneducated in the way of the Earth. The soil was dark red, with a high clay content, thick—*fecund*, the very word.

Fecund, wasn't that a lovely, suggestive word? It did not make him think of Serena. Clara, yes. Marjorie, his secretary, perhaps . . .

"Señor!"

Lourdes! But, of course . . . *fecund*!

Rossiter turned in time to see a bare arm thrust out the kitchen doorway, then a little of the rest of her. Lourdes was clutching a skimpy cotton robe to her buxom figure. Of course, she'd be getting dressed up for her day off, her night out with her friends.

"Telefon!"

Lourdes waited for him inside the door, pointing the way to the telephone, in the hallway by the front door. As usual, she acted as if he'd never been inside the house before, as if he'd get lost if she didn't direct him.

"Thanks, Lourdes."

For a split second he considered giving her a little pat on the bottom.

"Nada." She spoke self-importantly but smiled. It was her way; the telephone was important! But she'd been smiling at him more readily these days. She was grateful to him still for rescuing her from Serena.

"This is Ross Addey."

Rossiter announced himself formally. It was a weekend, but you could never be sure who might call.

Sandor's voice was so clear and sharp, he might have been

in the next room; it eased up to Rossiter, pressed against him like a body in the subway.

"My boy, how are you? I trust I'm not disturbing—"

"No, I was just fiddling around in the garden."

Like Nero . . .

"The garden ," Sandor murmured, "one forgets how warm is California when one is so cold in New York. In New York, Rossiterre, a day for staying home and reading learned articles."

"I was going to call you yesterday, Sandor. . . ."

Sandor laughed, like a man squeezing a sponge. "Ah, yesterday, Rossiterre, a *very* busy day. *Capitalism—I love it!* The rich get richer, you know what they say."

Rossiter tried to feel encouraged. All must *not* be lost; why else would Sandor speak so graciously?

"You know what they say in Vienna, dear boy? We say . . ." He laughed broadly. "The situation is desperate . . . but not serious."

"Morris dived, Sandor," Rossiter cried. "I thought there'd be smoke coming out of your ears."

"Nonsense!" The dead certainty in his voice was like thunder. "Never! Sandor Veruckt is never surprised by this market. Sandor is ever in control, fine-tuning the laws of averages, ever-diminishing returns, and even gravity. A daring young man on a flying trapeze, is your friend, Sandor Veruckt!"

"Maybe I don't understand," Rossiter humbly suggested.

"We buy more, my dear! Yes, yes, others sell, retreating in confusion, but Sandor slips in with the very few wise men . . . *to buy!"*

"But Chet Arthur withdrew, Sandor!"

"Ha, ha! Rossiterre, remind yourself of what that ancient Hungarian philosopher Confucius says: Where there is *retreat* on one side of the coin, the reverse says: *attack!"*

Sandor did not have to explain. Rossiter understood now that Arthur had pulled back in order to smoke out the speculators— also, not just incidentally, to buy more MorrisCom at greatly reduced prices.

And Sandor had deciphered Chet Arthur's strategy! The man *was* a mastermind; it *was* true what people said about him. Or? No, he didn't want to speculate about that; it was not possible that Sandor had peeked.

"Yes, my boy," Sandor said, "we are in the market for

more MorrisCom equity. To me, it matters not a whit whether Chet Arthur rebuilds his merger offer. Morris is worth the price on the basis of its own assets. In my calculations, Morris is worth well over *eighty dollars* a share. *Don't tell anybody!*''

Rossiter faltered. "I . . . see."

"*Do you understand* what I'm saying?" Sandor asked, a harder tone to his voice. "People will be cutting their losses— am I right? Am I telling it like it is, Rossiterre?"

Now Rossiter understood. He had been sentenced. He had only to wait for the axe to fall.

"We buy up what they sell, Rossiterre," Sandor hissed. "There is one block of stock in particular that I know of . . . and I *expect* it to become available. It is the law of the weak and frightened that it *will* become available."

This was the end. Now Rossiter better understood how Bud had been feeling.

"I want *you* to take care of that for me, *Rossiterre*."

A reprieve? A very *slight* reprieve? Rossiter's cheeks and armpits turned from cold to hot. Was Sandor being generous, letting him keep his job? His life?

Quavering, Rossiter asked, "What price are you thinking?"

"Forty. No higher. Thirty-nine would be good. Thirty-eight, exquisite."

Rossiter didn't know what else he could say, except to mumble, all right, he'd try his best. He could not acknowledge in any way that he was being forgiven for his mortal sin; if the words were spoken, Sandor would have to send him to the block. Notice, Rossiter told himself pitifully, it wasn't even necessary for Sandor to mention the party or parties who owned the block of shares to which he referred.

"By the way, my boy . . . I think I should tell you something very important."

He was not out of the woods. There was something else. Being a Hungarian, Sandor really knew how to twist the knife.

"Yes, Rossiterre, your mother and I . . . well, we are speaking of merger too. Did you know?"

"Seth . . . Seth suspected something was up."

Sandor laughed. "I do hope you will approve. As oldest son, you are responsible for your mother's well-being."

"I am . . ." Rossiter was so grateful he almost sobbed. "I do, yes. I approve one hundred percent."

*   *   *

Uncanny, the effect on a man when the certainty of ruin is unexpectedly reversed. Rossiter was so relieved that he immediately began to loathe Bud Slagger and Lorenzo Diamond, in an instant had identified completely with Sandor against the Las Vegas bandits who were trying to take advantage of the MorrisCom-Chet Arthur situation. Rossiter was ready, willing, and, he prayed, would be able to throw Diamond to the wolves.

To be sure, no more than a half hour after Rossiter had finished with Sandor then made himself a huge scotch and water and was sitting in the den, thanking his lucky stars, the phone rang again.

"Hello, this is Ross Addey."

He recognized the voice. Diamond had called before, to inquire after Bud's health.

"You're the guy Slagger got to buy that stock, right? You're his son-in-law, *right*?"

"Yes . . . that's right. I advised him of—"

"Sell it!" Diamond's voice rattled the connection. Diamond didn't mince words; he chopped them up brutally. "How much can we get?"

"That depends. The MorrisCom market has gone to hell."

"I *know* that. We paid forty," Diamond snarled. "Get us out!"

Rossiter thought he had to ask. "You *are* Mr. Diamond?"

The response was a tight laugh. "Who'd you think? Liberace?"

"I need to be sure."

"How much can I recoup out of this catastrophe, Addey?"

Hesitantly, Rossiter said, "It could go up again . . . it might go down even more. Right now, I think I've got a buy offer at . . . thirty-eight. . . ."

He held his breath. Would Diamond go for it?

"Two dollars under what we paid."

"Yes. Arthur knocked the bottom out."

"That son of a bitch!" Diamond's gravelly voice was like a big shoulder muscle, a fist in motion. "Okay, do it! I want out! Don't ever put me into anything with Chet Arthur again— *remember that!*"

"I will. What should I do about the proceeds?"

"You don't worry about that part of it, Addey. . . . I'll get the money out of New York. See . . ." Diamond didn't finish.

He seemed to know what he was doing. "And listen, Addey, do me a favor—don't tell Slagger I called, okay?"

Chapter
Twenty-Six

"**P**rince," Rose Richards muttered sleepily, "I dreamt the whole night through of thrones and slaves and knaves with golden staves and of me and you under an ermine bedcover, making love. . . . God, Prince, your body is as thin as Christ's when they took him down from the cross. I can count your ribs with one finger. . . ."

Rose would not stop. She simply would not stop babbling, never mind that Alex was tired. But he was smitten too; he didn't really want her to stop. Alex Spurzov, being what he was, liked love; he loved to love and to be loved. He was a romantic, in fact—that was his weakness. He had always been the romantic partner in his pairing with Ludmilla; romantic still, Alex knew they would be reunited—but only in death, toward which Rose Richards was unrelentingly pushing him.

Dear little chatterbox that she was, Alex listened with only one ear, half an ear, smiling and nodding against the pillow, as if filing her every word, while the dear child fondled him with flying fingers as she might have a flute, tickling the tip until it grew numb and smarted—he couldn't decide which—and, every now and then interrupting her narrative to duck down and take the bud in her mouth and feed on it, tossing it back and forth from cheek-right to cheek-left with her tongue.

Rose seemed to come unhinged just in the vicinity of a man's penis. Alex didn't have to ask himself why, considering that she'd been married—still was—to Richard Richards, a badly dressed transvestite.

"Alex," Rose said, "could you think of me as Catherine, the great one?"

"I'm not so old as all that, honeydew," he purred.

"She had a good many lovers, I know that."

"Catherine was one of the great romantics."

A true Russian Catherine had been, even if she'd come from Germany to be married to a decadent son of a czar. Germanic and blond had Catherine been; not a dark-haired Bavarian, blood shot through with Slavic impurities, like Seth's pretty little girlfriend. Or Tom's wife, Clara, the blond Italian.

But Rose . . . Rosita . . . Rosa, this parlor maid from Odessa, what of her? So base in her desires, so eager to please the Grand Seigneur. She made him feel young again—and wasn't that what it was all about?

"And when she tired of them, she had them killed, am I right, Alex?"

"Not precisely, my Rose-hips. She killed them with love—"

"I'll kill *you* too—the same way!"

"Oh! Have mercy!"

Rose bobbed down again, making uninhibited sounds of passion spent. It was Heaven.

Alex remembered, yes, how he remembered! Ludmilla had been fond of this too. It was how she got her vitamins, she'd chortled, and in the process kept her neck from going flabby. Avoid the double chins at all costs, darlings!

Ludmilla . . . Rose . . . Ludmilla. Rose was so like the young Ludmilla, fresh out of the Bulgarian cow pasture.

Alex couldn't think what they'd do about the revolting Peat. It was fairly obvious Peat couldn't hang around Richlands dressed like an SS chieftain. Perhaps he should ship him to the other side of Bel Air to keep the lovely Dick Richards company? After things had finally settled down a few nights before, Rose had begun making noises about taking her children away from the Richards house . . . and how would Alex feel about becoming a father overnight?

Not too bad, actually. Alex had detected something of worth in Rose's daughters. Would it be so bad? There were things Alex could teach them.

But Peat? Alex had thought surely Peat would reveal the truth about Ben Gazi when Dick Richards put him on the spot.

But he hadn't; like the cleverest of scoundrels, he had refused to talk.

The vital question was what Peat had meant by his explosive announcement about Ludmilla's close alliance with Beauty and Truth. Peat's very vehemence suggested to Alex something he didn't want to think about—but had to! Was it possible that during her final months Ludmilla had taken on this excuse for a man? Was Alex not enough for her, or if not Alex alone, then Alex and Cazimir? Had she needed the butler as well?

But Peat was a man. That would've been all the qualification he needed.

And what had Rose told him? Yes, that Peat had been madly in love with the first Mrs. Richards too, with the oddly named Messy?

Alex suffered dire and dismal thoughts.

Fortunately there was Rose. And Rose was a rose was a rose.

Her cheeks puffed and she made a rude farting sound, then happily laughed. Wonder of wonders, she had succeeded in dragging him to half-mast; instantly she spread-eagled herself upon him.

"Do I satisfy you, Prince, the way I envelop you in my skin?"

"You make an old man young again."

"Oh, sweetheart Jesus!"

Love would never disappoint a man. It was a sure answer for a troubled century. Ask Alex what time it was and he'd say, Time for love. A man could grow old and disillusioned with many things, but Love would never let him down. It was a diversion, an art, a career . . . and also an excuse for doing nothing else.

Rose had progressed to her rutting sounds, one of the mannerisms he liked least about her lovemaking; indeed she did sound like an excited porker reaching a climax, grunting. Not pretty, Alex told himself, not pleasing.

But inspiring, in a way. Alex flexed his loins, providing her incentive enough without overexerting himself, at the same time hefting on his fingertips the veined weight of her breasts. He floated them like big balloons of Rodney Richard's brandy.

"Prince . . . oh, Alex!"

Rose freely screamed his title, and the royal sound must

ricochet off the walls of all the rooms in Richlands. Rose didn't care. Why would she? She was the new mistress of the place. If she wished to shock the ghosts, that was her privilege.

Besides, Alexei thought spitefully, let Peat hear, the emaciated bugger!

All right, so Peat *had* had Ludmilla. Now Alex had Rose—and Rose despised Peat. *She* would not act out the role of the third Mrs. Richards.

Rose proclaimed her Victory over Death in another way, appropriate to the grunting. Flatulence trickled through the rumpled bedclothes, like poison gas through the trenches in the Great War. Fortunately this was not deadly stuff; but a trained chemist could have analyzed Rose's last three or four meals on the basis of a single whiff.

Alex loved it! Again he was reminded of Ludmilla. How close to Turkey a Bulgarian was! The Turks considered belching and burping the supreme compliment to be paid a good meal. So in Bulgaria, said Ludmilla, après-lovemaking was best celebrated by a resounding fart.

Now Rose was wheezing and coughing so violently he had to slap her on the bare back. Her skin was like silk. *He loved it.* She tilted toward him and he gathered as much of the right breast into his mouth as he could without choking himself.

Rose snorted, expiring lust, and thumped down on his bones several final times.

"My God, I can't believe this, Alex!"

Rose exulted in orgasm, crying out like a Wagnerian maiden caught between rocks. She tumbled forward, burying her sweaty face in his neck. The movement uncorked her, and Rose vented more air, this time in the form of a whistle as it rushed out of her vagina.

"Peter was great," Rose exclaimed loudly; "but better than Peter was Peter's peter." Her face within inches of his nose, Rose stared deeply into Alex's eyes.

"What do you see far back in there, my perfumed daisy?"

Rose straddled him comfortably. "Alex, when are you going to bring the Egg home?"

"Dearest, lovelips," Alex whispered, "it is not so simple as it seems."

"But an egg is an egg, Alex. It *is* a Fabergé Egg, isn't it, like I told Hildy?"

"Yes, yes . . ." He wondered how much he would have to reveal. Alex hated even to talk about the Egg. "It cannot really be seen in public, you know—never mind about how much the insurance would cost, Rosita."

"Why is that, Alex?" she pressed, great disappointment in her eyes.

"It is . . . improper. Very rude, the tableau—"

"I don't understand how that could be," Rose whispered, her mouth against his. "All is permissible in Art, you told me so. As in Art, also in Love, everything is permitted, whatever I like to do."

"Yes, yes, that is true," Alex said, trying to find the verbal formula. "But you see, it is a matter, darling Rose-bud, of my own ancestors depicted . . . performing, well, within the Egg, there is a harem scene of unimaginable decadence. Yes," he added with a smile, "but of such craftsmanship . . ."

"Art—" she began to argue.

"Luscious one, sweet tunnel of love, *Rosita*, believe me that I had to promise my father on his deathbed never to show the Spurzov Egg. Could I break such a promise?"

Alex saw tears in her eyes—would he break *her heart*?

"But, surely, *I* can see it, Alex. *Me*."

Alex managed his little laugh, the nervous irritation of a man trying to squeak out of a tight corner.

"Yes, precious, and you will when the time is right. *Rosita*, you must understand, the Egg is a heritage. It is without value, as valuable as it is."

"All right, Alex, whatever you say."

He couldn't believe it. She was so trusting; was she so childlike? This was hard to believe, having observed how brutally she'd treated her husband. But remember, Alex, he told himself, she was grateful for a port in the storm.

Rose kissed him warmly, grinning with joy, her Gypsy eyes dancing, then jumped off the bed and pranced across the long room to the window.

"Don't you love to look at the garden?" she cried, peeking through the shutters. Then her voice dropped. "Oh, there's Peat. He's down at the pool. Alex, do we give him permission to go swimming in the middle of the winter?"

"I think," Alex mused exhaustedly. "I don't know, Rosa, maybe in his free hours. . . . Why? Do you think he's going in?"

Maybe, yes, maybe the insolent fascist bastard would conveniently drown. It was a pity Alex hadn't been able to retrieve Ludmilla's little automatic.

"Alex," Rose mused, "how long do you think it'll take Tom Addey to arrange my divorce?"

"Everything is in motion, my beloved beaver."

"I want to get this show on the road."

She had begun talking about Paris. Rose seemed to take it for granted Alex and she would go to Paris, to France.

"There's no way Dick can fight us, Alex."

"No . . . no way."

Rose fiddled with the shutter, opening one slat just a little bit wider.

"And what is the varlet doing now, Rosie-posie?"

"Staring at the pool. He took off his Nazi jacket . . ."

Standing there, where Ludmilla had died. Was Peat paying some final respect before he was packed off to care for Richard Richards, the transvestite?

Timidly, not daring to look at him, Rose murmured, "Alex, we've never talked about marriage."

"No, we haven't, Rosalee, my darling. And we cannot! Not seriously, my sweet. It would not be fair to you—I'm far too old for you, let's be frank."

"No! Oh, no, Alex, I do not admit that!" She whirled briefly to show him a tear or two. "I *want* to be the Princess Spurzov!" Her voice was plaintive, yearning.

"Spurzo-*va*!" Alex corrected her absently. Since it was only hypothetical, might as well get the name right. "In Russian it would become Spurzo-*va* to express the feminine—and you are so feminine, after all!"

"Spurzova, isn't that the most beautiful sound . . ." Rose purred with pleasure. It would've been so sinful to hurt her. "I see myself as the Princess Spurzova, and you and I ensconced—yes, that's the word—here at Richlands. What would *that* be in Russian?"

"Oh, sweetness, we wouldn't change—"

Rose didn't hear him. "The silly fool is going in, Alex. He hates me, you know, Peat does." Her voice dropped. "He takes Dick's side, and *you* heard how he talked about Ludmilla. . . ."

The minx—she'd learned soon enough how sensitive Alex was about that.

"And we know he made out with Messy Richards. . . ."

Alex closed his eyes painfully. "Does all that matter now, Rose?"

"I'm like Catherine," she said. "I could easily order the bastard killed . . . drawn and quartered, boiled in oil."

"Rose, Rose, you're too cruel!"

"Not to those I love, Prince Alex," she cried softly. "To those I love I'm the soul of generosity . . . I will do anything for them. They may use me as they wish. . . ."

God, he couldn't keep his mind off it, the difficult picture of Peat in Ludmilla's all-encompassing embrace; how did such a dried-up cadaver interact with a woman like Ludmilla the Magnificent? But then Alex remembered how she'd been capable of drawing ecstasy out of a stone, as the sword Excalibur out of rock.

"Alex, I think Peat is going to go swimming. He's sitting down . . . he's pulling off his awful boots . . ."

"Jackboots, sweetmeat. The Germans wore them . . . still do, I suppose."

"Alex, Peat is getting undressed. I think he is going to go swimming. He'll freeze!"

Hopefully, Alex told himself bleakly, hopefully.

"Alex . . ."

"What is it, dark-eyes? Is he sinking? To the rescue? We don't have a lifeguard, you know."

"I think the man is deformed, Alex."

"How so, Rosita?"

Slowly, Rose announced, "I said drawn and quartered, Alex . . . I should have said *hung*. I doubt if there's a bigger one than that in the whole Western world, Alex."

Alex's eyes popped open. Gone, sweet relaxation, gone wholesome post-coital slump.

"*Goddamn son of a bitch*! You mean the man is not wearing a bathing suit? This is some sort of nudist colony here at Richlands?"

Of course, Ludmilla, careless of all eyes, had bathed in the nude for years. Peat had caught the habit from her.

"My God," Rose said quietly.

Alex was aware of his heart. He had tested it, defied it in the sweet fury of his service to Rose. Now his heart seemed to

285

bleed. This was too much! Would Alex never escape men like Cazimir . . . and now pendulous Peat?

"Rose," he groaned. "Rose," he begged, "come back to me . . . I want to kiss your sweet bunnies. . . ."

Rose chuckled thickly. "Well, you know what they say, Alex, you've seen one, you've seen 'em all."

Willingly enough, she did come back and sit down beside him. Thankfully, Alex drew circles with one finger around her large brown nipples.

"I wanted to tell you more about the *Spurzov Egg*," he whispered. "You know, it was made for my family by the famous Fabergé, working at the express wishes of the czar of all the Russias."

"Yes," Rose sighed, her eyes closing, her head nodding with the pleasure of a child being told a story. "Could I be the Princess Spurzova? And this is my Egg?"

Her house, her egg . . .

"It could be *ours*, Rosita."

What else did he have to offer? Money, yes, but not as much as Rose would have when Tom Addey was finished with Dick Richards. What of value? The Egg.

Rose laughed again, shaking her head in wonder.

"That Peat is something else, Alex, I have to tell you—"

"Rosita, Rosa, Rosalee . . . Rose . . . *Don't tell me*. Just speak to me of love."

Rose's look again became alive with desire, maybe even lust. She dipped her head, gathering *his* cock and saggy balls in one hand and sticking her nose down, sniffing, tasting.

Well, it was the only way. Must he buy Rose's kindness and good faith? Yes? Then he would. Thank God he had the Spurzov Egg to use in Love's own barter.

And so the Spurzovs had preserved the Egg from the bloody Bolsheviks and passed it down to Alexei, the son. And the son of the Spurzovs would pass it to Rosita, Rosa, Rose. . . . Was this possible?

Well, Alex smiled, at least it would be of some use. Maybe it was better this way than having it tarnish in a bank vault. Rose, yes, Rose. Was she worth the Spurzov Egg?

It was entirely possible.

Chapter
Twenty-Seven

*H*ad Clara known all along that something so shattering was going eventually to happen?

She had begun to dream a lot, surely a symptom of big trouble in the subconscious. Most of the dreams she'd forgotten by morning, but there was a recurring one in which she and the beautiful Stanley flew side by side over the hills and vineyards, zooming and swooping, diving and pulling up, like God's angels over God's vineyards without end

When Tom hustled into the hotel after seeing Dick Richards, Clara was still lethargically sitting at the table by the window, drinking cold coffee and glancing at the morning *Times*.

"What?" he demanded good-naturedly. "Still there?"

"Still here is right! You know, we could buy a condo for what we're paying for this suite."

"Just money!" Tom snapped his fingers.

"Martha called," Clara told him.

"Ah—that's why you're still sitting there. So, how's everything in Palm Springs?"

Clara shook her head. "Not good. What happened is—Will Sorge, Stan's lover, killed himself."

Tom was impressed, as he would be by such news. "But I thought he was sick."

"He was," Clara said briefly. "Martha says everybody's talking AIDS but Stanley says no, Sorge was some kind of a manic depressive. Anyway, he went outside and hung himself among all the decorating props. . . ."

"Jesus . . . That's kind of hard to swallow."

True enough. Sorge's last unpleasant act, killing himself within range of a loved one, a nasty thing to do.

"From what they say," Clara said, "Will Sorge was a real son of a bitch. He did it that way just to demolish Stanley."

Tom nodded. "I think that would tend to do it." He grunted. "Lousy goddamn business for Martha to be involved in."

"It never was fair," Clara reminded him. "Stan always took advantage of her."

"You should get her the hell out of there," Tom said. "She's too young to have that kind of stuff loaded on her."

His tight-lipped disapproval depressed her all the more.

"Tom, I know that . . . He'll be weeping and doing mea culpas, expecting Martha to sit there and listen."

"Well, then?"

"It's not that easy, Tom. It's the same as if somebody's wife dies . . . or husband."

"So they say."

"Well, it is! We know that, don't we . . . don't be so goddamn . . ."

"What?"

"I don't know," she said hopelessly. "Insensitive, I suppose. I don't want to fight about it."

"Who's fighting?"

"Goddamn it, Tom!" she exclaimed. "I'm not some kind of an ogre. I was *married* to the man, you know!"

"Do I know?" he retorted. "Sometimes I think you never got over it!" He jumped up and strutted angrily. "I thought we'd settled this, Clara."

"We have." She felt beat upon, very much so.

Tom stared at her. "I don't know what the hell is ailing you. If you need to be the Angel of Mercy, go ahead!"

"I can't just tell Martha to leave," Clara said. "Anyway, she wouldn't—especially if *I* told her. She's too stubborn."

"Like you," he muttered.

"That's right," Clara said sorely. *"Maybe you've noticed*: Daughters *are* like mothers. They make the same mistakes . . ."

"So *you* behaved like Martha when you were her age?"

A tricky point. "In a way, I suppose."

Tom came to the table and sat down. He touched the coffeepot.

"This stuff is cold. Do you want fresh?"

"No, no," she said quickly. "Well . . . let's not talk about it anymore. There's very little we can do. . . . How did it go with Richards? Was he wearing a different dress this morning?"

Tom chuckled. "No, he was wearing a stunning little three-piece suit. He screamed like hell, but I guess he realizes there's not a hell of a lot he can do . . . just try to keep Rose from absolutely cleaning him out."

"Would she?"

He shrugged. "She *could*." Tom sipped some of the cold coffee and made a face. "Yummy!" He leaned over, his face close to her ear. "I shouldn't tell you this, but Rose also found some pictures—of Dick doing nasty things with Cazimir Ben Gazi."

"The late Arab."

"Yes, the late Arab blackmailer. He had them hidden at Richlands. Anyway, Rose has really got Dickie-boy over a barrel. She gets her kids, which I guess is obvious enough. And the house and . . . I don't know. Twenty million is what she wants. She could go for a lot more . . . I mean a *lot*. I advised fifty."

"Fifty! Jesus, Tom!"

"That's a bargain, and Dick Richards knows it. She could sue for a hundred or more, plus the bad press. The company is worth close to a billion."

Clara touched his face curiously with her fingertips. "Unscrupulous boy! Who gets custody of the butler?"

"Ah! I think Dick will get custody."

"And the pictures?"

Tom shook his head. "I don't think so. Seth has got the pictures. From what I can get out of him, Ben Gazi collected pictures in the East too. He had quite a little operation going, aside from his primary career of Mr. Fixit and Hit 'em, money laundering and arms trafficking."

"The bastard! No wonder he was murdered." Clara grinned. "Maybe Dick had him killed."

Tom put one finger to his lips, then kissed her cheek.

"Darling, the walls have ears," he drawled.

"It all stinks, doesn't it?" she asked moodily. "What about Alex?"

"Merely in clover. Rose wants to be Princess Spurzova."

"Would he? The poor guy!"

"Poor? He sure wouldn't be poor, Clara, my sweet."

She wished he would stop endearing her. Clara didn't feel darling, or sweet.

"So, *sweetheart*, what are you going to do today? I've got to go over to Richlands this afternoon to see the party of the female part."

"I may just drive out to Venice and see a friend. On the other hand, who knows? You won't need the car, will you?"

"I never drive in Los Angeles, you know that, angel. Where else might you go?" he teased clumsily. *"Palm Springs?"*

"That's not impossible."

Tom nodded, then said, "I knew we'd get to that. I'll tell you what's wrong with you: Clara, you're behaving like a woman. *You're jealous of Martha.*"

"That's a stupid thing to say."

"Stupid? I don't think so," Tom said coldly. "You don't want to let her go—"

"Ridiculous."

"She's a carbon copy of you . . . and you of her," he continued caustically. He walked to the window and looked out—weak sunshine was beating through a metallic layer of clouds. "Pissy weather. I hate it when it's like this in Los Angeles."

Defensively, Clara said, "Stanley is very messed-up father-figure for a girl like Martha, you know that, Tom."

"But he is her father."

"And you're not exactly what they'd call a good father-figure replacement!"

"What the hell do you mean?" He whirled around. "Whatever you mean, I hope I'm *not* a good father-figure!"

Clara sniffled. Maybe that was the trouble—she was catching a cold. She stared at her hands, her wedding ring—thin and gold and old—the nightgown and robe she hadn't changed from, the slippers on her feet. She had so much to do, so little time . . . and she didn't feel like moving.

"So . . . *go!*" Tom came from the window and put his hand on her shoulder. "I'll be back about five-thirty—after I see Rose, and Alex."

Clara looked up at him. "You know, I'm not deserting you," she said in a small voice.

Tom just lifted his black eyebrows and headed for the door. He didn't even say good-bye.

If she had been younger, as young as Martha, she might have done something drastic, like run off to a foreign country and worked in the Peace Corps. But she had nothing to offer the Third World, no skills, no words, no advice. She'd been caught up in the wrong generation, a greedy and warped generation. She'd run off with Stanley, then made Tom Addey her profession. And now, at this late date, had she finally discovered that men were not a full-time occupation?

If so, then why was she thinking about driving to Palm Springs to see to Stanley Gates, a man who had done her wrong—did that make any sense?

If she needed a man to care for, Alberto Morelli was the best candidate. But that wouldn't be any good either—Alberto wouldn't stand for it. He'd kick her out.

Angry with herself, with Tom too—he was so sure of everything, that he had her absolutely figured out down to a T, about Martha . . . about himself—Clara finally roused herself.

The first thing she did, surprisingly, in light of what she'd been thinking, was to call Rossiter.

"Hellish," he said as soon as she asked him how everything was. "How's with you?" He could afford to be a little forward; they were separated by several miles of Wilshire Boulevard.

"I might have to go to Palm Springs," Clara said. "There's trouble about Stanley—his boyfriend committed suicide. I don't like Martha being alone with it."

He sounded anxious. "I'm sorry." He was much too nice for Clara Addey. "Anything I can do?"

"Could you—" Clara stopped herself. Where could such an idea have come from? Had he some inkling what she would ask of him? "Well, I was thinking you might drive down . . . but I suppose you couldn't. It's midweek . . ."

She would scare poor Rossiter to death. But nimbly he asked, "Where will you be?"

"I don't know!" she said, "Not at Stanley's house. . . . *Maybe* at the Sheraton there . . . *maybe* at the bar at the Sheraton, the one downtown, at eight o'clock tonight . . . *maybe*?"

291

He surprised her mightily. "I'll try, Clara . . . I know you're depressed. I'm not surprised."

She nodded tearfully. What did *he* know? What *could* he know?

"Somebody to talk to would be nice for a change . . . *you know*. Tom's got a lot on his mind."

"Sure. Clara, look—*I'll be there!* If I can. Like I said, it's hellish. I can't explain."

She did understand. He did not equivocate or dissemble. What Rossiter said, Rossiter meant.

"We'll leave it at that."

What was she thinking of? Did she really want to run off with him now? Knowing all the trouble it would cause? Had it come to that? No, she wanted to talk to him, that was all, to be reassured. What had gone wrong that she couldn't talk to Tom? But it *was* possible to talk to Tom. Clara's problem was she didn't know what questions to ask.

People said: Women sometimes did wild things like this, without conscious decision or consideration of consequences, women threw themselves into unlikely adventures—not even in the service of lust, as a man might, but out of a need for pure, low-down adventure—or romance.

Clara went into the bathroom, pulled off her robe and the nightgown, turned the water on . . . turned the water off.

She went back to the telephone. She had written the Palm Springs number on a hotel pad.

A man's voice answered. Clara was stricken. Stanley?

Clara put her hand to her mouth, half over the speaker of the phone.

"Please let me speak to Miss Martha Gates."

There was a pause, an intake of breath. He knew it was her. But he didn't let on.

"Just a minute. I'll get her."

Chapter
Twenty-Eight

*I*t was not a big deal to transfer the MorrisCom shares from the Diamond group to the Sandor Veruckt & Associates account. Veruckt bought and sold every day, and being arbitragers, he and his associates always had a bulging portfolio of investments. There was nothing about the transaction to cause the Stock Exchange to blink.

Veruckt was only doing what came naturally—averaging down his per-share cost. There were people who would say Sandor was taking a big risk now that Chet Arthur had backed off, but Sandor was unconcerned; his studies showed that once a company had been bid for, even after the bid was withdrawn, sure as shooting another bid would follow. What some of his competition deemed a foolhardy act, others called brilliant investment procedure.

Morris Communications was a tasty morsel, Sandor argued, regardless of what Chet Arthur did. If liquidated, Morris assets would add up to about eighty dollars a share; not the least of these assets, remember, was the brilliant editor Thelma Drysdale and her brilliant magazine *Classics*. But even Sandor could not be one hundred percent sure. In the final instance his shirt was just as much at risk as everybody else's.

That morning, when Rossiter tested the market, MorrisCom was weak enough to make him sick: thirty-seven and a half.

He had pledged Diamond thirty-eight.

Sandor would take it out of his hide—but watching Bud Slagger tremble and shake was about all the convincing an

293

intelligent man needed that Sandor's icy scorn was preferable to Diamond's anger.

Bud and Serena had stumbled downstairs before Rossiter was out of the house, about seven. He was late. Maybe they figured he'd already gone. Bud was unshaven and in pajamas wrinkled from a long night's anxiety, and Serena wore a transparent negligee that showed everything she had and then some, too much altogether. Pretty obviously, Bud's presence had short-circuited Serena's sexual equilibrium.

Rossiter was no longer shocked or dismayed to come upon Daddy and Serena having a little nap together in the guest room. Lourdes, with her own powerful intuitive gift, wouldn't even go upstairs when Daddy and daughter were up there alone. Serena in her gracious manner had a habit of screaming at Lourdes to "be gone!" when the diminutive maid chanced to surprise her *au toilet*, and that accounted for some of Lourdes's recalcitrance, but not for her nose-out-of-joint, eyes-cast-prayerfully-heavenward grimaces when other noises and voices—Bud's growling, Serena's cries—trickled downstairs.

"I'm just leaving," Rossiter had said. "I didn't hear you get up."

In fact he hadn't heard or seen anything of Serena all night. After several stiff ones, Rossiter had gone upstairs, as had become his routine, undressed and dropped into an emotionally drained sleep, pummeled by badly lit dreams which fortunately he couldn't remember in the morning.

"I've been . . . talking to Daddy."

"Talking, what do you two have left to talk about?"

"Many things."

"Name one," he said.

Bud groaned eloquently, lowering himself into a hard wooden kitchen chair. He put his hands to his face, rubbing desperately.

Serena smiled at Rossiter. "Like what a pain in the ass you are."

"Oh, come on, baby, it's too early for that," Bud whined.

"Only joking." Serena flung open the refrigerator and peered inside. "Where's the goddamn orange juice? Where's that little . . ."

She looked around, even under the kitchen table.

"She's not up yet," Rossiter muttered.

"Why not?"

"Because she's never up this early, Serena," he said matter-of-factly. "It's just seven. You can't expect to work her more than twelve hours a day."

"Amen," Bud muttered.

"Oh, shut up!" Serena went on rummaging in the refrigerator; now she couldn't find the fucking cereal.

"Feeling okay this morning, Bud?" Rossiter asked.

"Lousy, Ross."

They'd spent a good two hours the night before discussing Bud's prospects vis-a-vis Lorenzo Diamond. Rossiter wasn't supposed to have told Bud that Diamond had called, but he did owe Bud that much.

Okay, so there was going to be a loss of more than a half million dollars, but Diamond hadn't seemed all that hysterical about it. In fact he'd been more concerned about getting himself out of a situation where he didn't belong in the first place. It was business, pure and simple. Nobody was particularly to blame. Bud had alerted Lorenzo to the opportunity to make some money, but it hadn't worked out that way. Period.

No, Rossiter didn't understand. The simple basic fact was that Lorenzo *hated* to lose money as much as he liked to make it.

"Guys like Lorenzo don't even play the slots because losing a quarter drives them crazy—a friend of mine saw Lorenzo break up a slot machine in his own casino because it didn't pay off," Bud told him.

Serena parked her hips against the sink as she peeled apart an orange. The negligee fell against her thighs; if you looked you could see the shadow of pubic hair which Rossiter tried to remember, oh yes, reached all the way to her belly button.

Bud stared at her, absently tapping at the breast pocket of his pajama top. Realizing he was looking for a cigarette, he jerked his hand away.

"Near a million," he gulped. "Might as well be a trillion."

Serena bit into the orange. "Please *forget* it! You're not going back to Vegas. You're resigning, for health reasons."

"*Health reasons?* That's a good one."

"Retire, then."

Bud laughed hoarsely. "Retire? Just like that?" He closed his eyes and licked his lips. Rossiter realized Bud had lost all his desert suntan. "I could use a drink."

"At seven o'clock in the morning? Are you crazy? The cigarettes and the whiskey—"

Recklessly, Bud yelled, "And don't forget the wild, wild women!"

"Shut up!" Serena turned her fury on Rossiter. And Rossiter wondered if anybody had ever thought about ripping her clothes off and kicking her to death. "You! And I suppose you'd give him one?"

"Not necessarily . . ." Had he not done his best? "On the other hand, I might."

Bud looked hopeful for a second, then folded. "I know. never mind. God . . ." He rubbed his red eyes. "Man, I am beat, just beat."

There were tears in Bud's eyes "Everything's changed so much. In the old days I had leverage. I was a good baseball player and had the respect of a wide circle of friends. But friends die, or go away. I can remember the days when Shorty Estoril was big, big, big in Vegas. But who remembers Shorty Estoril? *Who? Who's Shorty Estoril?*"

Serena belched scornfully, "Yes, Daddy, *who is* Shorty Estoril? You know who? Nobody. Because he'd dead, Daddy. Live in the present, not the past! Shorty's dead as a goddamn doorknob!"

"Jesus . . . oh, Jesus, do I need a smoke!" Once more Bud groped his empty pocket. He pulled out an imaginary cigarette, so powerful was his memory of habit, put it to his mouth and blew a cloud of smoke. "Shorty was my best friend, my very, very, very best friend, and as long as he was alive, I was *big time*, a lot bigger time than I ever been with Lorenzo Diamond and his dirty bastards."

"But Shorty *is* dead, Daddy!"

Awkwardly, Rossiter tried to soften the truth for Bud. "When did Shorty die?"

Serena snorted impatiently. She was now eating a half of a seasame-seed bagel dripping with jam. Still leaning on the sink, she crossed one woolly slipper over the other and insolently answered the question for Bud. "Before you ever knew me, Mr. Nosy. Shorty got blown up. His wife used to start his Lincoln in the morning—like in that old joke. *Boom!* So Shorty figured her little Mustang must be okay. *Boom!*"

"Jesus, baby!"

"Face it, Daddy."

"Baby," Bud whimpered, "if Lorenzo ever heard you talking like that . . ."

Serena laughed contemptuously. "I never said Lorenzo did it. All I know is Shorty and his Royal Vibes had a contract at the hotel and Lorenzo wanted out of the contract. That's *all* I know."

"All . . ."

"It's all you ever told me," Serena added wickedly.

"Me? I never told you any such thing."

Serena shrugged. "Maybe it was Sammy who told me, then. . . ."

Sammy, the weirdo, who'd been Serena's first husband.

Bud began to cry. He hid his face in his hands, elbows on the table, shoulders shaking. Serena glanced at Rossiter bitterly, then without saying anything took Bud's hand and made him stand up. She led him out of the kitchen. Rossiter heard them on the stairs.

Then he left for the office.

Serena called a little later, just ahead of Clara Addey . . . and Sandor. Was Bud all right? he asked. Bud was as good as he was ever likely to be, Serena told him, and still had not forgiven him for whatever it was he was supposed to have done. Then it occurred to Rossiter he didn't have to ask. He knew. The bitter juices poured into his belly. Rossiter struggled to keep his voice flat, like unstirred water.

"When he wakes up, you can tell him the shares are sold . . . I got thirty-eight, which was the best I could do."

Serena's voice was dull, lifeless. She was guilty and she knew that Rossiter knew it too. But did Serena understand that such guilt had a stench all its own?

"So Diamond loses five hundred thousand?"

"Plus fees. So tell Bud . . . *or not*. Suit yourself."

Serena was not really there. "We're going out." Hesitantly, for she hated to confide in Rossiter, she mumbled, "We may just go away, Daddy and me, till this thing blows over. I need some money, Ross, *this afternoon*."

This hit him. Rossiter had not considered the money part of their difficulties. "How much . . . what about Bud?"

"I need ten thousand."

That stopped him . . . stumped him. How was he going to

put his hands on ten thousand at a time like this, when everything had blown apart?

Angrily, Rossiter said, "Well, I don't have it. Use your goddamn cards."

"I will. I need cash too."

His nerves began to unravel. "Goddamn it, let Bud pay!"

"Rossiter, Daddy can't get at his, the way it is. He's losing money too, you know, because of the mess you made of the stocks."

"Me?" Unbelievable! "Listen, Serena, *very closely*—I am not responsible for these guys losing their money . . . I told Bud to get out, and he wouldn't."

"It was your idea."

"Listen . . ." He began again, then quit.

"You . . . insignificant . . ." She mouthed the magic word, but not tellingly. "I'm just going to go to the bank and take out whatever's there. How much *is* there?"

"About eight thousand . . . *Take it and shove it!*"

Well, there. At last he'd told her. Not well, not completely, but enough for starters. They'd have to split everything anyway. Might as well get that started. What Serena took now, he'd get back later when the house was sold, the furniture, their crummy art, the garden chairs, the hose . . . what else? Rusty rake, old magazines, garbage . . . They'd split it down to the last five cents!

"I will take it," Serena said bitchily, "but not shove it. I've got better things to do with it than that. *Good-bye!*"

Down went the phone. Rossiter laughed out loud. Just like that, it was over. His eyes met Marjorie's. Did she realize he was a free man?

Next came the call from New York.

"The top of the morning to you, Rossiterre!"

His stepfather to be, Sandor Veruckt, sounded extremely cheerful; that was also a plus.

"I did the deal, Sandor," Rossiter said.

"Yes, so you did."

Sandor didn't even sound interested. His swift mind must already be into a new money-making situation. Sandor was easily bored by the past and present; the future tickled him.

"For thirty-eight."

Rossiter could almost see Sandor's ears flatten against his head.

"It was thirty-seven and a fraction, my boy—"

"It jumped in the process."

"No, no, the needle wavered . . . no more than wavered, dear boy."

"Well . . ." Rossiter began to retreat, aware of the smell of his own fear. "I bargained with Diamond for thirty-eight, Sandor, and for two hundred fifty thousand shares, you know—"

Sandor's voice was veined with disbelief. "You paid this man Lorenzo Diamond *a bonus* of roughly a quarter-million dollars? Rossiterre! Sandor Veruckt and Associates is paying *a reward* for selling to us when the market is *sinking*?"

"But I got it two dollars under the forty, Sandor. You told me thirty-eight would be . . . exquisite."

"I don't care what I said."

"Sandor, I was committed!"

There would be no sympathy from the Hungarian mastermind. Rossiter was going to pay. What and how much, he didn't know yet. But he knew he was not simply going to walk away. He had sinned against Sandor Veruckt in a very explicit way. The competition would laugh and say that Sandor was getting weak in the head!

Suppose *The Wall Street Journal* got its paws on the story? What a wedge to drive under the rock-solid reputation of Sandor Veruckt & Associates. Wizard indeed!

"Two hundred and fifty thousand shares, Sandor!"

"A quarter of a million dollars, Rossiterre!"

All right, Sandor would say, there are ten million Hungarians in the world—do you suppose the ten million of us keep afloat in hostile environments by being *stupid*? By being generous to people who do not need or deserve generosity?

"Lorenzo Diamond will not thank you for the gratuity, dear boy, I can assure you of that."

Rossiter's glands pumped shame. In this business, people said, guys could sweat right through the soles of their shoes and make damp marks on the floor.

"He said—"

Sandor cut him off. "I think that is all, dear boy." There was resignation in his voice. Yes, he'd given up on poor Rossiterre.

Sandor hung up. Rossiter felt himself walking toward the void.

That was when Clara called.

Chapter
Twenty-Nine

*S*eth was already wide awake by the time the morning sunlight crossed the carpeted bedroom and came to rest on the too-busy Richlands wallpaper next to the bathroom door.

Across from him, fortunately in the other single bed, Hildy slept on soundly, silently. In sleep she looked like a baby, her calculating face for the moment at peace. One bare arm lay atop the sheet; a bare shoulder met tousled head and pillow and disappeared under the cover.

Seth thought of Alice, the lady of angst, her willowy body, how entranced he had been by her very flaws, her sordid history. And of Katie Corcoran, the primitive, beloved savage; and had no inclination whatsoever to slip into Hildy's bed before she was awake enough to push him away.

It was final—he and Hildy were splitting, veering in opposite directions. It seemed to Seth now, sadly, that he'd never been deeply, deeply attracted to her; certainly they'd never been in love, whatever that was, nor as riotously aroused as he was by Katie Corcoran. No, there had always been a restraint about Hildy, a refusal to abandon herself to passion. Even in the hurly-burly of lovemaking Hildy remained on guard. She seemed always to be thinking about something else, to be flipping through a mental ledger of things done, things still to be done. Making love was good exercise, Hildy had even said so, like cross-country skiing.

Her long sigh escaped the covers. Dreaming . . . but of what: money, career, fame? Not of Seth Addey, that was for sure. He'd often wondered what Hildy did on her travels, but he had never asked. Part of her wandering had been in the communist east—perhaps she'd had a Russian lover or two that he'd find out about in due course from Jim Madison.

Betrayal came to mind.

They'd made a peace of sorts, one that would last through the duration of the California trip. It would have been awkward to announce the breakup now.

Hildy had her work to do, after all. Thelma had given her instructions.

Her California assignment on the great houses was, as they both knew, a cover for the other thing, Thelma's scheme to do a final job on Ludmilla Spurzova. Hildy had argued that the story would be larger than that, and that it would not be unkind. Besides, how could he doubt the editorial intuition of a Thelma Drysdale? Seth's retort was nasty; he'd been thrown into the embarrassing position of criticizing his own mother.

Speaking of courtesans, he'd said, had it occurred to Hildy that Thelma fit the bill of particulars pretty well herself? Witness her pursuit of Sandor Veruckt.

But he regretted the comparison. Thelma Drysdale was a professional woman. She did not need a Sandor Veruckt to survive.

This was Hildy's test! She would deliver brilliant pictures of Alex Spurzov, of Tom Addey . . . *and* of Ludmilla's successor at Richlands, Rose Richards, Alex's paramour . . . and of the house. . . .

And there was more! What about the mysterious Lebanese, Ludmilla's last lover, the man who interested Seth so?

It would not, Seth had told her, be a great idea to mention Ben Gazi in such a story. God, he worried, how embarrassing if Hildy Beckman stumbled on the truth of it; Madison would never believe Seth hadn't tipped her off.

And the butler Peat, what had the butler seen?

As far as Seth was concerned, this butler had merely found the body. That was all. He would not buy Alex's speculation that Peat had killed Ben Gazi. Seth Addey would eat his hat if this cringing creep had the gumption to kill anybody.

But . . . how could he know for sure?

Suddenly Hildy was wide awake.

Cryptically, she muttered, "Two days . . ."

"Yes?"

"In two days my work is done at Richlands. . . ."

"Wonderful," he said. "As far as I'm concerned, mine is too."

As a matter of fact, what Seth had started thinking of as the Cazimir Ben Gazi dossier seemed to have come together—not, to be sure, due to any back-breaking work of his own. Try as he might to fend them off, new bits and pieces of information kept flowing in. The infallible Jim Madison, it seemed, had been right to send him back to California.

But Rossiter's report of Ben Gazi's linkage to Las Vegas was positively a bombshell. It confirmed what Alice Betancur had told Seth—that her husband had put Ben Gazi in touch with the shady elements.

However, was this the sort of rip-roaring scandal Madison would be looking for? Seth doubted that very much. Something like this, if sourced and developed, why, it would be enough to shake the Washburn administration to its foundation!

Thus, what Madison had called Project Loose Ends took on greater importance. Next, Seth told himself acidly, they'd be covering up Sol Betancur's connections to the White House.

So what if Ben Gazi had practiced his allures on the Lorenzo Diamond mistress? He did not believe it had been Diamond who'd ordered him put out of the way. And not the Soviets . . .*not* that shadowy Middle Eastern group that so badly wanted the credit . . . *not* Sol Betancur . . . *not* even Dick Richards, who had a helluva motive—all you had to do was take a look at those pictures.

It was enough to make a man shake his head and quit.

Wasn't it possible that Ben Gazi had simply killed *himself*? That was a mighty convenient explanation—the gun that had fired the shot had been clutched, after all, in Ben Gazi's hand.

"No. Madison would dismiss it as too neat . . . too easy.

Hildy yawned, turned her head, and smiled at him. She looked dewy, like the morning; her eyes glistened. For a second she might have been in love. But only for a second.

"Good morning, Seth."

"It's very early," he said. He really had nothing else to say.

Hildy said, "It's best to rise early and get one's business done before the world intrudes."

Business? *Exactly*. She'd never even kiss him before they had brushed their teeth.

"Will it be so easy to say good-bye?" she inquired, holding the smile. "But maybe we won't—"

"Yes, we will! You're going to be in New York, working for Thelma. It's over, Hildy."

"You did not love me."

"Or you me."

She sat up, chuckling, and stretched, deliberately flashing her rusty-nippled breasts. Hildy had always been good at that. But the gesture was sexless now.

"The trouble," she said, "is if I am to see the so-called *Spurzov Ei*—Egg—Rose must make Alex bring it from the bank. Thelma believes the Spurzov Egg is a fake, you see. The experts have never examined it closely—"

"So? Who cares?" Seth stayed where he was, hands clasped under his head. "What's the point of the whole thing? You think anybody is going to remember who Ludmilla is, or was . . . or care?"

Sternly, Hildy said, "My German readers are intrigued by all stories of royalty . . . although Thelma believes that Alex's title is as fake as his Egg."

"As far as I'm concerned, he's a prince, and to hell with what Thelma thinks," Seth stated blackly.

Hildy stood up and reached for her robe. Her body shone like Meissen porcelain. Sleep did her wonders.

"Your opinion is that I should not do this story for Thelma, isn't it?"

"I personally do not give a good goddamn if you do it or not," Seth said harshly. "I just don't think it's honest to sneak pictures like this."

Hildy flushed angrily.

"I will, therefore, *not* make love to you one last time," she announced. "Because you are so cruel, I will not do what I had planned to do, to give you a finale—"

"Break my heart."

Hildy tugged on the belt of her robe. "I should tell you now—"

"Go ahead."

"I never made orgasm with you. . . ."

303

He heard, nodded, and slowly said, "I'm not surprised to hear that."

"Or with any man," she said coolly. "I do for myself."

"Wonderful! Congratulations on being self-contained."

"And speaking of honesty," Hildy said bitingly, "are you so pure, after all?"

He didn't reply. She was hitting home, below the belt. Hildy knew just enough about what had happened in Moscow to hurt him when she needed to.

Betrayal came to mind for the second time.

But then such dire thoughts were interrupted by a loud knock on the bedroom door.

"Washington, D.C., call for Mr. Seth Addey."

This was when the day began going downhill. . . .

Katie Corcoran told him, "Sol has stuffed Alice into a clinic in Virginia." Seth's mind flooded; he was that surprised. "Did you hear me?" she asked.

"Yes. Yes, I did. I . . . well, I don't know what to say. *What* happened . . . *why?*"

"Goddamn if I know. Sol is afraid she's been talking to me. What about, I don't know. . . ." Ah, yes, but Seth knew, didn't he? "Sol warned me off. I'm to understand whatever Alice might have said, any dirty rotten stories or rumors or whatever, it's all lies and hallucinations. Sol said Alice is in the middle of a nervous breakdown. She's driving with her top down, Sol said. But I never thought so, Seth. Did you?"

"She was not in good shape, Katie."

"Did Sol call you too?"

"No, but it's still early out here."

"Sorry—"

"Never mind."

"Listen . . . Seth." Katie stopped and took a deep breath. "The rest of it is that Mabel Harrey was killed."

"For crissakes!"

"Yes," Katie whispered. "During a burglary, they said, shot and killed by persons unknown. . . ."

Grimly Seth said, "That wipes it!"

"Seth, I get the feeling this is a story and a half!"

Boy, did he have a scoop for her!

"Katie," he said softly, "do what Sol says—for the moment, anyway."

"Alice never told *me* anything!" she exclaimed angrily. "I don't know what the hell Sol's talking about. He wants me to stop the story. How could I? Even if I wanted to?"

"Not the Mabel Harrey story?"

"No, no, he didn't mention that. Just about Alice. You talked to her. Do you have any idea what this is all about?"

All he would say was, "I'll tell you . . . *when I see you*?"

"Oh," she said blankly, "yes, forget what I said about . . . you and Alice. She made that up."

Urgently he said, "I'm not going to be here much longer. I'm about done. I . . . well . . ."

She waited a moment, then laughed briskly. "You're to come straight here."

"Oh . . . good." Seth was warmed, relieved. Better already. Life had changed, so nicely, like turning the tap from cold to hot. "I really . . ."

Again, she laughed. "Don't try, Seth."

It was amazing. As much as Hildy thought she knew, how little she or the rest of them did know. Hildy's journalistic nose was twitching all morning, but she didn't dare ask about the Washington phone call; and she was so busy bustling around with her camera that she wasn't aware of the next one, from Jim Madison.

Madison would be calling about Alice Betancur . . . or Mabel Harrey, Seth thought. Not at all. The call was to inform Seth that a "couple of guys" would be coming along to pick up Peat. He was there in the house, was he not?

Was he ever! As Hildy went about the tedious business of setting up her equipment for interior shots of the long gallery, Peat fiddled about maddeningly with a long-handled feather duster, tripping over cables and bumping the rickety metal light stands and reflectors.

"Yes, he is here. What're you . . . on what grounds, I mean . . . exactly, sir?" Seth asked.

"Income tax evasion," Madison said blandly. "The neo-Nazi bastard has not paid a dime of taxes since 1960."

"I'll tell him to get dressed," Seth muttered.

"No, do not tell him anything! Just make sure he doesn't leave."

Madison hung up as Rose was ordering Peat to get the hell out of the way and stop bugging them. And then Peat came trotting down to where Alex was sitting and watching all the activity, for some reason on fire to tell Alex that indeed he now remembered what their Lebanese guest had been doing on the evening of the last day of Ludmilla's life.

"Didn't I see him follow the Princess out there? And didn't I see him with her on the diving board!"

"*On the diving board* . . ." Alex jumped up. "Fool! You're dreaming!"

Angrily Alex marched out of the house, Seth following. For a while they strode back and forth on the terrace as Alex cooled down.

Finally he said, "I think we are going to have trouble with this Peat creature. I am at the end of my tether with him."

Seth wanted to tell him to stop worrying. But he couldn't.

At lunchtime Peat started up again. Perhaps he had a premonition that the men in the white coats were coming for him—as they already had in Washington for Alice Betancur. But at least Peat was back in his own white jacket, serving seafood salad and fresh asparagus from some warmer clime.

Peat chose that moment to make the announcement. He would be leaving Richlands and going to work for Mr. Richard Richards on the other side of Bel Air, where he was, at least, appreciated. Not like here.

Rose glared at him nastily. "Good! You can leave right now!"

Peat turned up his rodent's nose. "There are trashy elements—"

The bad side of Rose Richards's nature exposed itself. To everybody's horror, including Peat's, she heaved a Lalique candlestick at him, missing Peat but taking a deep chunk of decorative plaster out of the trim around the dining room door. Peat leapt back into the pantry, Rose's voice ringing after him.

"I'll kill you with my own bare hands, you ugly rat!"

The atmosphere remained tense for all of two and a half minutes. Then the good-natured Rose laughed and said she was sorry.

"He makes me so mad. I keep seeing him standing next to Dickie in that silly uniform."

Then she and Hildy went back to the picture taking.

"Oh, God, oh, God," Alex murmured anxiously as he led Seth back to their spot in the gallery. "It is a horrible mess, my dear, all of it."

"Well, it'll be over soon, won't it?

Alex stared at him closely. "How? How so?"

"Well . . ." Seth hesitated. "I'm finished here, and I guess Hildy will be too. I'll probably leave tonight, or tomorrow."

"But did you find what you were looking for?" Alex murmured. Seth shrugged and Alex added, "Did you *know* what you were looking for?"

Seth smiled and shook his head. "Not really, I guess. Ben Gazi didn't leave many clues behind. The trail was very faint . . . but enough, Alex, enough."

Alex nodded shrewdly. "But not back to Moscow, I take it."

Seth shook his head.

"I do know about your trouble there," Alex said. "Was it bad?"

Seth was a little surprised at the blunt question. "Yes, but not so much for me." It wasn't too difficult to say this to Alex. He was older, vastly experienced. "I was grilled a few hours, then released to a consular officer. You know the drill." He shrugged. "The fellow I was . . . talking to, well, he was hauled away. I never saw him again. Now we hear . . . he's dead. I, uh . . . don't like thinking about it."

Alex nodded sorrowfully. "You had become friends."

"Pretty friendly, yes. You get to know somebody fast in a situation like that. He was a wonderful man, Alex, a brave man, I can tell you. . . ."

His voice dropped away.

"My dear boy . . ." Alex put his hand on Seth's shoulder. "You have got to understand that this chap knew exactly what he was doing and what the risks were. *Another hero*, and the world will never know his name!"

"I know his name," Seth said.

The phone rang again. It was just two P.M. Peat probably wouldn't bother to get it, he'd be in such a stew. Seth started for the end of the gallery. But Peat popped out of the butler's pantry.

"Urgent call for Mr. Seth Addey . . . again!"

This time it was his brother Rossiter. Something terrible had happened, something to do with Serena, Ross wasn't able to say precisely what. But could Seth meet him there, please, at a certain supermarket in Beverly Hills? Ross would be coming as fast as he could.

Alex brought Seth out to the garage and gave him the keys to the Ford Mustang parked on the other side of Ludmilla's mint-condition Mercedes. The smaller car was gassed up, easy to handle; Seth preferred it. He wouldn't be caught dead in a high-visibility car.

As Seth climbed in and put the key in the ignition, Alex bent down and spoke into the window.

"We may yet discover, my boy, that *our Peat* is merely very jealous about the *third* Mrs. Richards." Alex smiled sardonically. "I hope that is the simple fact of the case."

"What right does he have to be jealous?"

Alex shrugged. "Madmen have no rights?" He glanced up at the gray house. "*Bedlam*—Peat may well be in charge!"

"I gotta go, Alex." Seth still couldn't tell him that the problem was soon to be solved. Whatever they got the crazy butler for—murder, wearing a Nazi uniform, indecent exposure— he would soon be gone.

Seth ran the little car down the driveway and slowed to allow the wrought-iron gate to open ahead of him. He drove through, speeded up, turned and turned again into Bellagio Road and headed for the west exit of Bel Air into Sunset Boulevard.

Seth wanted to get back to Washington quickly. He'd had enough of California to last him a long time.

Unaware of the Sunset traffic, Seth drove east to Doheny Drive, then down the long hill into Beverly Hills.

From a block away he counted as many as a half-dozen black-and-whites drawn up at the entrances and exits of the supermarket parking lot. An ambulance, its lights flashing, was just pulling away.

Chapter Thirty

*S*erena Addey had managed to throw herself in front of Bud Slagger, or so several confused and shocked eyewitnesses told it, in that final split second of time when life became death.

The shotgun blast caught Serena full in the chest, tearing away the left of her reconstructed breasts, simultaneously blowing apart Bud's recently renovated heart valves.

Why Serena? This seemed the most tremendously puzzling question, and the answer was simple—what she'd done was instinctive. Numbly Rossiter told Seth if it had been *him* under the gun, Serena would have ducked the other way. Whatever the motivation, the police said Serena was some kind of a heroine, though admittedly a dead one, and it didn't help much to praise the dead. Serena and Bud were dead before they hit the ground—gunned down, the papers would say, in a supermarket parking lot, a favorite place these days for such assassinations.

"Bud must've been going in to buy himself some cigarettes," Rossiter suggested.

The police were busily trying to sort out the violence and get a line on the victims. The perpetrators had disappeared into thin air. According to the witnesses, two nondescript white men had just walked away from the carnage.

One hand playing with the radio aerial of Serena's Mercedes convertible, Rossiter heard that the victims had been hauled off to Cedars-Sinai and that it didn't look very hopeful with wounds like that. The police wouldn't say that Bud and Serena were already dead.

Robbery? Possibly—the man's wallet, if he'd been carrying one, was gone, and that was the reason they hadn't known who he was until Rossiter arrived. Serena's pocketbook, on the other hand, hadn't been opened. Her identification was inside, as was Rossiter's phone number, which explained how they'd gotten in touch with him, and six thousand dollars in cold cash.

"His name is . . . Bud Slagger," Rossiter stated. "He was a baseball player."

The policeman wrote down Bud's name, and Rossiter added that Bud's wife would probably be at home right now at their condo in Century City and her name was Tiny . . . Tina Slagger.

The policeman looked interested when Ross mentioned Bud's home in Las Vegas, but what really had caught his attention was the money.

"Any particular reason your wife had six thousand dollars in her pocketbook? If the two men were following them, they'd have seen them go to the bank and they'd have made sure to get the money—"

"*If* she went to the bank today," Seth said quickly.

"*She went today,*" Rossiter said. "She told me she was taking the money out of our account."

"Why would that be?" the cop asked curiously.

"Serena," Rossiter said cautiously, "was taking Bud off on a vacation. They were probably on the way to buy tickets—and Bud had to get his cigarettes."

"What did . . . Mr. Slagger do in Las Vegas?"

Rossiter began reciting Ben's history, in some detail, too much detail, about Ben's ball-playing days, his friendship with bandleader Shorty Estoril, and how, after quitting baseball, he'd landed a job in public relations at the Alhambra Hotel and Convention Center.

"P.R.?"

Rossiter shrugged. He thought it was a silly profession too.

"I'll have to take the money in. I'll give you a receipt. They'll want to check the numbers and all. You understand?"

Could Rossiter *not* understand? The money might be marked.

"Did you say, Mr. Addey, who Mr. Slagger worked for at the Alhambra Hotel? Who can we call, if necessary?"

Rossiter sucked air, giving it away that this was not his favorite question. "The man he worked for? Lorenzo Diamond."

Yes, Seth recalled, Lorenzo Diamond—whose mistress Bud

Slagger had boffed. Whose mistress Cazimir Ben Gazi had also boffed, according to Bud Slagger.

Then, suddenly, the police didn't need them, or want them around anymore. They'd be in touch. Men were taking pictures, blood samples, and, Rossiter was told, they had to impound Serena's Mercedes for fingerprinting purposes, and so on.

"C'mon," Seth said, "I'll drive you down to the hospital. My brother's going to leave *his* car here for a while," he told the cop. "That Ford."

The cop said they'd watch it.

Rossiter squeezed his long legs into the front seat of the borrowed Mustang. He threw his head back against the leather headrest and began to yawn, eating oxygen. Seth had seen men do that. They weren't bored; they were unsteady and scared.

Seth took it easy and didn't say anything, waiting for Rossiter.

Finally Ross muttered, "I don't see why Serena."

"Probably because she saw them up close," Seth guessed.

Rossiter glanced at Seth, his eyes strained.

"You think Diamond did it? Just because the takeover thing went sour?"

Seth shrugged. "Or because of the bimbo?"

"No, no."

"It wasn't the girl . . . *or* the money," Seth said thoughtfully. "There must've been something else. . . . You think Slagger was maybe supposed to collect something from Ben Gazi?"

"Like?" Rossiter asked in disbelief.

"I wonder. Maybe he was Diamond's courier. It looks like Diamond and Ben Gazi were mixed up in lots of business." Seth was smooth at the wheel; he felt Rossiter's eyes on him, doubtfully, watchfully. "Look, I don't have any answers, only questions. Maybe Diamond just got up on the wrong side of the bed," Seth continued. "It's either *nothing*—or the trail leads in every conceivable direction. I don't know which."

Rossiter shook his head. "I don't see it. Serena and Bud getting killed because of some connection to Ben Gazi . . . who killed himself?"

Seth said harshly, "Wrong! Ben Gazi was murdered, big brother, in Spain!"

"But we know different, don't we?"

"No!" Seth shook his head violently. "We do not! I'm

pretty convinced by now that Lebanese bastard was a double agent. . . . I think he blackmailed info in Washington and out here too. He got close to people inside the intelligence community and there's no telling how much he passed across—up to and *including* the stuff that got my ass in a sling in Moscow and in the end killed a good friend of mine!''

Rossiter didn't buy it. "Give me a break."

"I'm not saying that's it in toto," Seth said. "Just admit that the tail of coincidence has a whiplash effect—we learn that over and over!"

Viciously Seth slammed the Mustang into an invalids-only parking place. Well, they *were* invalids, weren't they?

"I'm telling you more than I've told my own bosses, Ross," Seth hammered. "Ben Gazi had a connection with a crooked banker in Maryland and both of them tied into Las Vegas and Washington. Ben Gazi had a pipeline into the Cayman Islands, the banking paradise of the Western Hemisphere. . . ."

Rossiter's face was sullen. This wouldn't interest him. He didn't have that kind of a mind.

Seth slammed his door, as tellingly as if he'd had Ben Gazi's balls stuck in there and was giving it to him good.

"The son of a bitch worked both sides of the street," he charged. "He helped us in the Middle East, I don't doubt it, and then he used that as his door opener in Washington. Like a goddamn snake . . . he slithered into powerful company . . . and that's how he *betrayed* us."

Rossiter stumbled along beside him. "And from all that we get to Serena and Bud? This schnook Bud bumped off in a stinkin' parking lot?"

"That's it. Think of it, big brother—the mightiest machines fail because of one small cog. . . ."

At the Emergency entrance Seth pushed back the door and held it for Ross. Inside, phones were ringing off the hook—not because of Serena and Bud, you could be sure of that.

Rossiter was terrified. He stopped and grabbed Seth's arm. "We better call the old man." He blinked at Seth fearfully. "I don't even want to ask. You know they're dead." Rossiter shook his head. "Do you believe in . . . in *retribution*? That's what you've been talking about—Ben Gazi, Slagger. But Serena? You don't understand me, do you?"

Seth shook his head gently. "No. Better not to dwell on it. . . . Let's get this thing over with, what do you say?"

Rossiter grabbed Seth's arm. "Wait a minute . . . Bud and Serena were committing *incest*. I know they were, I got this feeling, though I couldn't prove it."

"Oh, come on, Ross, that's bullshit!" Seth said sarcastically.

Rossiter stared at him bitterly. "Why are you so ready to believe in your own goddamn plots . . . but not this?"

"Are you trying to be *funny*?" Seth drew Rossiter to the side of the big, noisy room. "You ask me to believe those two morons were punished from on high—not by Lorenzo getting even with Bud for losing his money and screwing his girlfriend?"

Rossiter shook Seth's hand loose. "You're the goddamn *paranoid*, Seth! You see a plot everywhere . . . I'm telling you this is God's plot, pure and simple."

Chapter
Thirty-One

*O*f course they were dead. One needn't be an expert anyway to know that the survival rate from a sawed-off shotgun blast at close range was very small indeed. A very sordid way to die too. Fortunately it was only necessary for Rossiter to identify the faces, Bud's contorted with fear, Serena's strangely, well . . . serene, more so than she'd ever been in life.

Seeing her dead, and looking so calm about it, Rossiter felt a strange sense of peace himself. Was he not half crazed with grief, at least all broken up? Seth was waiting for him to crack, he knew it. But he wouldn't crack. He could be a cold fish too. Rossiter couldn't be overjoyed that Serena had passed on in such a way; but she didn't look unhappy about it either. And for Bud Slagger he had no special feelings.

Bud had already died, in a way, when his baseball career ended. Yes, Bud had been dead on arrival for some time now.

And Tiny?

Seth said he'd go call their father. That was when Rossiter gave him the slip. He caught a cab back to the supermarket, retrieved his car, and drove to Century City.

Tiny let him in without a word, perhaps even suspecting from the look on his face that something terrible had happened. She could not have known . . . had there been something on the radio already? Did she even listen to the radio?

"I've got bad news, Tiny, *very* bad news."

Why did Rossiter have the feeling that he wanted to laugh? In high-heeled red sling-back shoes Tiny tottered across the

314

living room to a pair of chairs by the window. The view was angled toward the Century Plaza Hotel. Not speaking, she pointed at a bottle of Smirnoff vodka sitting next to her on a cigarette-scarred coffee table. Rossiter went into the kitchen and got a glass. He took ice from the refrigerator, then sat down in the chair facing hers. He poured vodka on the ice and held the glass up in a makeshift toast.

She beat him to it. "Slagger finally struck out, didn't he?"

"You might say that."

Tiny said, "It was only a matter of time. Such a dummy. He gets fixed, then starts up right away smoking again."

She had that part of it wrong, though the cigarettes were at least partly to blame, in the sense that Bud had been gunned down on his way to buy a carton of Camels.

With little emotion on her florid face, Tiny threw one long leg over the other. She was wearing a tomato-colored pants suit to go with the ghastly shoes.

"He was shot, Tiny," Rossiter said gently. He couldn't be totally sure how she'd react, especially when she heard about Serena. "Both of them—Bud and Serena. They were at a store down in Beverly Hills and somebody shot them."

"Both?" Tiny's glass stopped at her lips and she lowered it. *"Serena too?"*

"Yes, both of them. I'm sorry."

Tiny swigged then, emptying her glass. Rossiter took it from her and went to the refrigerator for more ice, leaving her alone for a couple of seconds. When he came back, Tiny still didn't show any agitation, only puzzlement.

"Why would Serena be caught in it?" She took the glass, pouring a huge dollop of vodka over the fresh ice. "Him, I understand. Slagger ran out of luck a long time ago. Why her? She didn't do anything." At last there was a crack in her voice, in her composure. She stared at Rossiter bleakly. *"Those bastards."*

Rossiter didn't bother to ask who.

"The cops told us . . . she kind of . . . threw herself in the way of—"

Tiny interrupted emptily. "The shotgun has a spread of pellets."

"It was instinctive. She tried to shield him."

Sticky tears ran out of Tiny's puffy eyes, down both wings

315

of her nose. She shook her head, putting the glass to her lips, then, without drinking, set it carefully on the table. "Why? He wasn't worth shielding—or loving, that's for sure, the big swaggering fake. So? He went too far and Lorenzo had him nailed." She looked at Rossiter for an answer. "Would you say he was especially *lovable*?"

"Well, I don't know," Rossiter said uncomfortably. Tiny must have loved him once.

She reached for the glass. Her hand stopped again. He wondered if maybe the tragedy would put her right off the booze. "You know, it is true, they do have their own code of rules. But it doesn't include killing innocent people. I'm going to have a little talk with Lorenzo about that."

Tiny was crying, but she didn't take any notice of the tears, now dribbling off her chin.

"The police will be coming to talk to you," Rossiter said.

She shrugged. "They can come. I don't know anything to tell them. I'm just a broken-hearted old mother and widow now." Tiny's eyes were small and angry. "I guess I'll move to Florida. I hate Vegas, always have, ever since I went there to dance in that goddamn club. The Fifth Ace was the name of it. I came from Atlantic City, did *she* ever tell you? 'Course not. If they'd had casinos there then, I could've worked at home."

Rossiter sipped his drink, all attention. What could he tell her? That there was no good reason why she should cry over Serena, that Serena had never cried over her?

"Come see me down there." Tiny's voice was rough-edged. She'd be showing it now; she'd have to feel bad about her daughter, if not Bud. "The only reason I ever stayed in Vegas was because of him. Now I'll have what's left of his pension and some savings and I'll sell all the property and I'll move to Palm Beach. I've always loved it there. You can watch the vultures circle over the Breakers Hotel, waiting for the old people to drop." She laughed raucously, mockingly, then sobbed freely for a moment. "And Lorenzo will throw in a little too, you can bet your bottom dollar—"

"The code."

"Yeah," she hooted. "God, country, and colleagues—as long as the colleagues don't deceive you. Country, always. God, forever."

There was one important thing he had to ask Tiny.

"In the way of . . . well . . . burial, or what?"

Tiny waved one hand dismissively. "Have 'em cremated." Finally, and he waited, a little worried for her, Tiny went for her drink, hoisted it to her mouth. "Suit yourself about Serena." She thought about that for a moment. "Bud? I think what he'd really like is if you sprinkled him around left field down in Dodger Stadium."

It was so quiet at home. Not again, ever, would Serena's voice by way of greeting yell at him not to walk across the grass. Ahead of him, in the half-open garage, Rossiter was struck by the sight of Bud's baby-blue Seville. No more Bud either. It was so peaceful as Rossiter unlocked the front door and stepped inside. Never again would Serena's sharp words crash down the stairs like breaking glass.

Alone at last. Rossiter drew a long and contented breath. Try as he had, and would, he could not dredge up any grief. No, he was not going upstairs to cry his eyes out.

He was not *happy* that Serena was gone. But he was relieved. Though maybe it was a dream. Her voice, any second now, would come flying to destroy his equilibrium. Well, maybe Serena *was* still alive and well, elevated to another plane of existence. But she had definitely left this one.

Above the hall table next to the door, where Serena had always meant to keep a little bowl of welcoming flowers but didn't, there was a mirror with a scalloped wood frame, and in this Rossiter inspected his face. Yes, he was alive and not any the worse for the shock, it had to be said. A smudge of new beard was showing on his chin, but his skin was fresh and smooth and healthy . . . in fact, beautifully alive and well-preserved, the widower Addey!

Rossiter glanced toward the upstairs, thinking he had, after all, heard a noise. No. She *was* gone; the only thing left of Serena would be her clothes, the lingering scent of her cloying perfume.

But then, Christ! A door did open and slam and there was a sound of footsteps out of the bedroom and into the upstairs hallway.

Rossiter stared. For certain, Serena's unmarred chest would precede her onto the landing.

No.

Lourdes. She was carrying an armload of rumpled towels and sheets and didn't see him standing, tall and silent, at the bottom of the stairs.

But when she did, she gasped and blushed.

"Hello, Lourdes."

She wouldn't know yet what had happened. Even if the police had called here first, she wouldn't have understood.

"Hallo . . . señor."

Lourdes came down the steps, clutching the bundle of linen, and in a confusion of shyness banged into the kitchen.

Rossiter followed her. Should he try to tell her what had happened, or let her find out for herself? Her friends would hear soon enough; they were better informed than the natives. Forget it; he was going to have a drink.

This, Lourdes did understand. Gravely she handed him a glass and swung open the refrigerator door for ice.

"Thanks, Lourdes."

As she watched Rossiter poured himself truly a half glass of the brown stuff—a bereavement-sized portion, he'd tell anybody who asked—then added a touch of water. Lourdes said nothing.

"Thank you, Lourdes."

What to do now? He could go anywhere in the house he wanted and not be bothered. Taking his time, looking the dump over, Rossiter strolled through the living room, kicking at Serena's chairs, and into the study. He sat down in a fake leather wing chair next to the French door that opened into the unkempt backyard.

There was a telephone on a table next to the chair. Rossiter knew what he had to do, wanted to do, first. He tapped out the number of the Westwood Marquis Hotel.

"Mrs. Addey, please."

The phone rang in the suite. Well, he had to tell somebody.

"Sorry, sir, there's no answer in the suite. Would you like to leave a message?"

Hell, then he remembered. Clara was on her way to Palm Springs. Rossiter looked at his watch. Hell! She might be there already. It was four o'clock and he had practically promised he would meet her there. But he had plenty of time, didn't he? What had they agreed? Eight? Four hours to Palm Springs, easy. There was time to finish this drink and hop in the car and go.

Just like that—who was going to yell at him, or scream, or shout, or do anything? Nobody.

But he'd known when he agreed to meet Clara that it was a bad and unwise thing to do. Until now their chance encounters had been accidental—he could always say, hell, I just stepped off the curb and got nailed by this determined woman, not my fault. Not my fault! The flesh is weak. Tom Addey should understand well enough.

No, definitely he should not go. Going had meant sweet escape just a few hours before . . . before this had happened, by Act of God, to Serena. Now, what was there he needed to escape from? Nothing, not a blessed thing. He had escaped; it was done.

Rossiter luxuriated, flexed his liberated muscles, felt his groin. All there, raring to go.

Exhilarating, that was it. Murder was an exhilarating experience, especially if you were not the one murdered.

Rossiter stared outside at the windswept back garden, the inadequate pool. It was stuffed with leaves and battered palm fronds. The filter would be clogged. By and by he'd go and clean it. Yes, dear! *Maybe*, dear. Probably not, dear. No, piss on this house. He'd sell it immediately and get out of Beverly Hills. Screw Beverly Hills; he was sick of the place, sick of the goddamn pool and the goddamn lawn and all the nosy neighbors.

Bye-bye, Serena. Rossiter lifted his drink.

The phone rang. That was nothing new, and he'd be damned if he was going to answer it. He didn't wish to talk to anybody about Serena. Most likely it was for Lourdes; her friends called during the daytime, when it was likely neither he nor Serena would be home.

Or maybe for Serena. Sorry, Mrs. Addey is not available, thank you very much.

The ringing stopped. Lourdes had answered in the kitchen. Blessed silence returned. No one would ever be able to say that Rossiter Baker Addey had not been a good husband to Serena Addey. He had been patient with her, understanding, kind; he had endured her insults and anger. He had been at his best with her when she was at her worst. And he had been faithful. Hadn't he? In spirit? No, not at all.

Well, they couldn't shoot you for trying to be a good guy.

Rossiter savored the whiskey. When he looked up, he saw Lourdes standing in the doorway, her face dead white.

Her trembling lips invoked Spanish words. Rossiter understood. One of her friends had called to tell Lourdes that Serena Addey, her less than beloved employer, had been blown away.

Rossiter nodded confirmation. "Yes, Lourdes, she's dead. Dead as a mackerel. *Muerta*!"

He wasn't sure that was the appropriate Spanish word, but it was close enough. Or was the word the equivalent of *merde* in French? No, he thought, *dead*.

Lourdes shook with fear, her bosomy chest heaving with sympathy. She was muttering words Rossiter interpreted as *poor lady, very very poor poor little lady dead, dead, dead!*

Of course, for purposes of her own earth-bending sorrow, Lourdes had to believe that Rossiter had loved Serena madly and probably would not survive without her, that he was torn by sadness and sundered by despair.

Whereas, if the truth were known, all he could think about was how quiet the house was.

Lourdes was somehow invisibly tethered in the doorway, unable to get at him, keening in incoherent grief. She looked about to pass into some kind of fit.

"Lourdes!"

He spoke sharply to snap her out of it, not so sharply as to offend.

Lourdes reacted as if the bond that had held her back was suddenly cut. She plunged across the room and dropped down on her knees beside his chair, grabbed for his hand—the one not occupied with the glass of whiskey—and squeezed it to her breast, such round, plump softness encased in the cheap white uniform.

Eyes fluttering at poor Rossiter, Lourdes sighed tremulously and an astonishing thing happened. She slipped his hand under the stiff front of the uniform, pressed it against the bare skin of her breast. His fingers parted around the small, stiff nipple.

A terrible, frightening, unbereaved sensation tore through him.

But this was not possible. It would not be a good or wise thing. Rossiter fought for control.

Losing the fight, he set his glass down blindly and, ignoring shoulds or shouldn'ts, fumbled with her buttons, roughly pulled tiny Lourdes up into his lap, and buried his face in her softness. Her breasts were far more delicious than anything he could imagine. For one thing, they were for real. How often had he considered taking a handful of these and then never dared.

Lourdes bubbled with compassion for his sadness; he could smell it, taste it on her skin. She surrendered to him in sympathy, her mournful groans doleful enough to lift him out of his shoes. Rossiter ran his fingers up her leg, so smooth, and all the way to her perfect hip. Lourdes moaned. Not pausing long enough for her to get used to the idea, he shoved his hand between her thighs. She resisted for the full count of ten expected by the rules of etiquette, then dropped her legs open so he could fully admire the welcoming warmth of her sopping crotch.

Lourdes was quick, he would give her credit for that. With Serena foreplay would have eaten up half a weekend and even then might have led nowhere.

Rossiter's own passion was huge and undeniable. It erupted within him, shaking his body inside out. A terrible need took him by the throat and he startled himself by gasping, begging, pleading; for Rossiter, by and large, was a silent man. Before he could stop himself, he had stripped her bare and himself, and there in the den, he fell upon her. How could she survive? He was huge when he entered her, she built compactly as a mouse, he, by grief engorged, a King Kong. . . .

Lourdes took him in stride. She gritted her teeth and growled but certainly survived. Not only survived. Prevailed. She handled him like a toy, chirping little yipping noises, meeting each of his power thrusts with a powerful reply, blunting his fierce aggression, her body seemingly hinged or mounted on ball bearings, achieving such a whipping, twisting effect that it would have been enough to throw out the back of a lesser man.

There were so many lessons to be learned.

Never, Rossiter realized in a delirium, had he experienced such exaltation of purpose. Like all men, Rossiter had heard of women like Lourdes. Men talked of such women as the ancients had of all-powerful gods, gods of thunder and lightning and cyclone. But, in the normal course of life, they seldom met such a woman.

But Lourdes did exist. And Serena was gone! Lourdes made love to Rossiter in a way that Serena would not have conceived or that he imagined possible. Amazing—for Rossiter could not believe Lourdes was a woman of very wide experience. No, she had definitely not learned these tricks from previous lovemaking. This intense reaction came naturally, Rossiter knew, but only when the chemistry was exactly right. It was a rare thing, very, very unusual.

It struck Rossiter like a revelation that in order to make love like this a person had to be *in* love.

Lourdes was *in love* with him! And had been for many months!

When it was done, she lay with him on the Chinese cotton rug, exhausted, her eyelids beating, her cheeks flushed, breathing deeply, her belly rising and falling, the muscles in her loins twitching.

And the phone rang again . . . the goddamn telephone!

It had to be answered. With great effort Rossiter heaved himself up and toward the ceiling. In his body there was such lightness. He thought of covering his nakedness with his hand—Serena had always turned her head away—then didn't.

"Hullo," Rossiter said.

This *was* his voice, but he sounded wrung out, like a sopping towel.

"Ross . . . it's me. Your father."

Guilty? Yes, your honor. No, your honor! He wouldn't be going to Palm Springs.

Tom Addey spoke slowly, sounding perplexed. Maybe he thought Rossiter was drunk. No, he didn't know what he should say, that was it.

"Are you okay?"

"All right, yeah . . ."

Lourdes was watching him so soberly, and it occurred to Rossiter that she couldn't even speak English. How were they going to communicate, to talk intelligently of important things?

Such as? And who *needed* to talk?

He smiled back at Lourdes and she blushed, then went on watching him earnestly, finally stretching her arms over her head and squirming, like a cat, feline, shyly but at the same time signaling with her body, causing him revived desire.

Lourdes blushed again at the sight.

Yes, *blushed*!

His father said something but Rossiter wasn't hearing properly.

"I said, 'What a day,' " Tom Addey repeated.

"You can say that again!"

Chapter
Thirty-Two

*T*his was unquestionably the culmination of something very rotten. How could it be otherwise? The murder of such a classic has-been as Bud Slagger, and his daughter along with him, could only be a gratuitous expression of annoyance over a plan gone awry.

Tom Addey felt for Rossiter. What did a father say to his son in such a situation as this? Ross's marriage had not been the stuff of dreams and it had probably not been the greatest thing either to have Bud and Tiny Slagger for in-laws. But it would have been crass to congratulate Ross for being well out of it. Too bad Ross didn't have a bit of the hatefulness of his brother Seth, the secret agent.

Tom hadn't been aware anything was wrong until he arrived at Richlands in mid-afternoon, having finished with Richards, then Clara, and finally lunch by himself at the Regency Club.

He'd taken his time over the meal, grateful for the chance to be alone. A little solitude was to cherished. As for Clara, well . . . she was impossible lately. Something was sour; he didn't know what. Of course, Clara was always nervous and out-of-sorts when they visited Los Angeles. L.A. reminded her too much of the past—*his past*, and of Ludmilla. Ridiculous, but Clara remained jealous of Ludmilla, even in death. And what about *her* past?

And now the news that Thelma might remarry disturbed her. Tom couldn't understand that either. Clara apparently believed that Thelma was such a bitch that no man would ever again ask for her hand. It was almost as if she expected Tom would be called upon to give Thelma away when she married the greasy Hungarian.

So . . . well, Clara went on these emotional binges from time to time. She'd recover; she always had . . . so far. A drive to Palm Springs would do her good.

One did have to be very patient with women.

Tom enjoyed his drinks and the food, cold salmon and cucumber salad. He ordered a nicely dry gin martini, straight up, as martinis used to be made before on-the-rocks was discovered.

On the rocks used to be how they described a marriage gone to the dogs—like his? No, he thought, things hadn't gotten that bad. Though Clara had told him just the other day that he grated on her nerves. He had only to cock his head and say something flippant and Clara went just plainly . . . berserk.

Tom sat for a while, preoccupied with thoughts of Clara and the changing view of Westwood, from little old Mexican village to college town to business crossroads whose skyline was being poked to pieces by high rises.

But what the hell did he care? He didn't live here anymore. Once the Rose Richards business was settled, he wouldn't be back for months. And he wouldn't let it matter to him at all that Clara was in a huff. Of all people, Tom admitted, he tolerated her best, but at the same time he was not going to hold himself ransom to her moods. He had not a great deal of time for moody people, particularly women.

Actually, most of the trouble in Tom Addey's life had come because of his foolishness with women. But that was over now. He had grown up. He was immune.

Or so, at least, he was telling himself when he arrived at Richlands.

Hildy Beckmann, it seemed, had been appointed guardian of all the news—bad, mysterious, or otherwise. As soon as Tom had paid off his cab and come inside, she reported that Seth had received a very urgent phone call from Rossiter right after lunch and had had to rush away. Now Seth was on the telephone from a hospital, she didn't know where, and said he'd be calling again in a few moments. Seth was terribly angry, Hildy reported, her face flushed and excited. She was the more attractive for it.

"Didn't he give any clue?" Hospital. "Probably Ross's father-in-law. He had some bypasses. Where's Alex? And Rose?"

Smiling proprietorially, Hildy said, "They are upstairs . . . resting." Oh, yes, in everyman's language, resting meant you know what. "We worked very hard this morning."

Taking advantage of the opportunity, Tom walked Hildy down the gallery, his arm paternally around her waist. She seemed comfortable with this intimacy—why not? He was being extremely casual, friendly—*paternal*.

Hildy smiled at him engagingly. "The morning," she said, "was one of dramatic scenes. . . ."

"Besides Seth rushing out?"

"Yes." She chuckled significantly. "Peat hints of very strange things, upstairs and downstairs—of sexual doings between the prince and Rose. Rose tells him to shut up. Peat threatens to leave Richlands to go to the other side of Bel Air to the service of Rose's husband, Mr. Richards. Rose throws an *objet* at him, not striking Peat but making a hole in the wall. It is a shattered Lalique candlestick. . . . The phone rings. Seth leaves. Furiously, the prince orders Mr. Peat to visit the Richards family doctor, who will prescribe for him some tranquilizers. . . ."

"Lots of fun, it sounds like." But Tom didn't care anything about that. "And what were you doing the whole time?"

"I?" She laughed breathlessly. "Listening . . . watching."

And she hadn't quite finished her report.

"Mr. Peat accused the guest, Ludmilla's lover, the man who was murdered in Spain, of making love to the princess on the diving board. The prince was very upset."

Tom grinned. "I don't believe that either," he told her, speaking softly. "I can tell you about Ludmilla—she would never have allowed herself to die in the middle of it—maybe afterward, but never in the throes."

"Ah, yes," Hildy insinuated, "Tom Addey would know, as her lover. *Were* you a good lover?"

"Very good," he said.

"You think me a nasty child for asking. I am sorry."

"No, I definitely do not think of you as a child."

"I apologize . . . I kiss your hand," she muttered.

"Don't be silly!"

But she grabbed his hand and held it to her mouth, moving

provocatively close. Tom began thinking about the odds. Hildy had turned the tables on him—no worry about Tom Addey being too forward. She was way ahead of him. She came up on her toes and kissed his cheek, startling him even more with the pressure of her body.

He must have drawn a gaspy breath for she chuckled knowingly.

"You are a very fascinating man," she murmured, smiling at him.

"Not hardly."

"Please! With your experience as a famous solicitor . . ."

"Solicitor?"

"So Seth has told me!" Her eyes sparkled. "So many scandalous divorce cases to your credit . . . and now Rose's against the peculiar Mr. Richards . . ."

"I wouldn't talk about it," Tom said, already backing off. "Besides, Hildy, in this country you're an attorney, or a lawyer. Not 'solicitor'—that's British talk."

She didn't let go. Frankly, she pushed against him.

"I must have some pictures of you, Tom."

"Me? I've got nothing to do with the stately homes of Bel Air."

"But I would be grateful if you would permit me a few pictures." Hildy shook his arm insistently. "Should I tell you why? Seth made me promise I would." Fearlessly, or so he was supposed to think, she stared him in the eye. "I am to do a photo-reportage on Ludmilla Spurzova, and for this I need shots of the principals, including Tom Addey."

Impossible. Ridiculous. He would never agree to do this.

"I thought you were doing something about the house."

"That too . . . for a German magazine. This other story of which I speak is to be the life of Princess Spurzova, the last of the great courtesans."

"For *Classics*," he said, "for Madame Drysdale?" Of course. It wouldn't be for *Life*. "She wants a picture of me? She must have plenty of those around."

"Not recent."

He smiled at her, using the patronizingly quizzical expression that drove Clara wild.

"I find this very amusing. What could it all matter now? Who cares?"

"It is madness, I agree," Hildy said, "or would have been. But now the story is a little different. We have the butler, Peat. Obviously he was in love with Ludmilla too. And the Lebanese . . ."

"Nobody will thank you if you drag the Lebanese into it."

"So Seth remarked. Why is that?"

"Because . . ." Why indeed? "He was so much younger, it'd make Ludmilla look bad."

"Did Prince Alexei hate this man called Cazimir Ben Gazi?"

Her question introduced something very troubling into Tom's head, a flash of doubt or uncertainty, like a dent on the smooth surface of his thought process.

But he said, "Alex was completely indifferent to Ben Gazi. He didn't like Ben Gazi much—but who did? I didn't at all."

He couldn't tell whether Hildy accepted this version of things. She hugged him clumsily; she couldn't seem to get close enough. What about Seth?

"And this Peat," she whispered, her face close to his. "He is a *very* strange man. *Is he a Nazi?* I do not understand."

Tom shook his head. "Don't worry about that. Peat's a nut. He forgot to put his sail up." He certainly wouldn't share with her Alex's theory that Peat had killed Ben Gazi out of jealousy. "Where?" he asked.

"Where?"

"Where do you want to take my picture?" he teased. "And you can tell Thelma that if she runs this story *without* my picture, I'll sue her! After all, I'd feel very slighted if I was not remembered as one of Ludmilla's lovers. . . . Let Thelma chew on that."

Hildy brushed her smooth cheek against his. "I am very grateful," she said. "Most grateful. I do not think Thelma has in mind to humiliate you—I would not agree to that."

"Oh, you wouldn't?"

"You should know"—Hildy sighed—"I do not want to give a false impression . . . or be disloyal. *It is this*: Seth and I will go our own ways now. . . ."

"Splitting up?" Tom interpreted. "Well, I'm very . . . sorry to hear that. I had an idea you two might be getting married."

"Oh, no," Hildy disagreed. "That was never—" She stopped herself, then went on. "Career. Always this *verdamnte* career . . ."

Seth's career—*or hers*?

"Should I speak to him?"

"No, no! It is useless! I will stay in New York . . . for the time being."

"Working for Madame?"

She smiled tremulously. "I have been staying with her, as you know. . . . Will you visit me when you come to New York City?"

Tom was amused. "At Thelma's? That'd be something!"

"Or call?"

"I say, Thelma dear," Tom drawled in falsetto, "kindly let me speak to the beautiful and desirable Hildy Beckmann. . . ."

Irritably, she laughed. "You make fun of me, Tom!" She kissed him fiercely on the lips. "Older men *are* more fascinating!"

"I've always thought so." Tom held her to him gingerly; she had begun to breathe a little erratically, as women did. He gazed at her attentively, searching for motive. "Hildy," he said, "if you want the picture, you've got it. You don't have to offer yourself on a platter."

She jumped back, gasping in outrage.

"But I am not. The two things are not related, Tom. It is not nice of you to think so!" Reprovingly she muttered, "You are like Seth—more like Seth than Seth knows how to be."

"I'm his father."

Annoyance compressed her lips. Now Tom was seeing a Hildy Beckmann so far kept under wraps. Meet Miss Trouble. If he wanted trouble, or needed it, here it was, all wrapped up and ready to take home. A lightning-fast flash of lust came and went. And stayed . . . gone.

But she didn't release his hand. She held it to her, gripping his thumb, pricking the end of his thumb with a fingernail, putting the thumb in her mouth.

"It is not nice to be rejected." Shuddering, she pulled on his thumb with her lips, then greedily whispered, "Some men are naturally attractive to women."

"And some are not."

Hildy laughed at him harshly and proceeded to an analysis he hadn't yet considered.

"When we do our story in *Classics*, women will discover how much you pleased Ludmilla, such a demanding *exotic*, this

328

love machine. Even in death she transmits her charisma to her men. Women will come to beat at your door, *my Tom!*"

"Your Tom?"

Hildy, he decided then, was *too* insistent. In truth, Tom had become a little tired of this game.

"You have only to touch me, Tom, and all my nerves start to shake. . . ."

"Bloody nonsense!"

She rubbed his ill-used thumb along the line of her jaw. It would have been churlish to stop her.

"Just there, you see. The spot."

"The jaw spot?"

"Yes."

"Hallo!"

Alex! Tom was saved. Saying *shit* in German, Hildy dropped his hand and moved back to a properly social distance. Alex's jovial voice echoed down the gallery to where they were standing, half concealed behind bedraggled potted palms.

"*Tomasso!* What news from the Rialto?"

"I'm not sure, Alex. Hildy tells me Seth just called from the hospital. . . . Something must have happened."

"Oh, Christ! Is it that? I put Seth in a car. But what?"

"We don't know," she said curtly. "Seth will call again."

It seemed to Tom that Alex looked exceptionally frail today, especially if he'd just had a nap—if indeed he'd been able to nap. He feared Rose Richards was wearing Alex to a frazzle. There was a limit even to Alex's endurance; all the same, it was amusing to think Alex was taking his turn at poetic justice.

Alex's eyes flicked toward the stairway. "I am feeling quite . . . washed out, my dears. I think some tea would be in order." He threw back his head and roared, "*Peat!*"

"Prince . . . Alex," Hildy muttered, "I don't think he's back yet."

"Back from *where*?" Alex demanded haughtily.

"The doctor," she said sharply. "You sent Peat out to the doctor, to get medicine for his . . . nerves . . . his *hallucinations*."

"Nerves? Hallucinations?" Alex snorted. "The fool goes to the doctor for sex treatments. He goes for hormone shots, I swear to you, can you believe that?"

Tom did his best not to laugh. "A most eccentric gentleman is our Peat."

"Eccentric! The man is totally mad, Tom."

The phone rang.

"Seth," Tom said.

"*I* will answer," Hildy said. She trotted to the phone, said hello, then held the instrument out toward Tom Addey.

Tom was unprepared for Seth's outburst of pure anger.

"Have *you* talked to Ross?"

"No. Seth, what the hell is going on?"

Seth came down a little. Even he could not hold his father responsible for something he knew nothing about.

"Slagger was shot to death. And Serena with him. Shot and killed, both of them."

"I see," Tom said slowly. It was strange, wasn't it, how different people reacted to different news. Tom had always taken shock in slowly. "Say that one more time."

Seth's voice was hostile.

"Serena and her father were shot and killed, outside a supermarket this afternoon. Two guys with a shotgun."

"My God . . . *where's Ross*?

Seth became angry again.

"Ross was here . . . at the goddamned hospital. He ran off. What the hell am I supposed to do? I don't have any *instructions*, for crissakes!"

"Seth, take it easy."

"*Goddamn it,*" Seth stormed, "Slagger was involved with Ben Gazi—at long distance, sure, but *involved*, via that bastard in Las Vegas, that Diamond character . . . and they were both *assassinated*."

"Oh, yeah?" Tom grunted. "That's a loose connection if you ask me, pal." His son, the secret agent, was inclined to read too much into simple situations.

"Dad! We know Diamond—"

Tom interrupted him harshly. "Not on the telephone, Seth! You ought to know better!"

Tom had caught him out and he'd hate it.

"Yeah," Seth said slowly. "I'm saying I don't know where he went . . . maybe to see Slagger's wife?"

"I'll call him at home," Tom said. "I'll keep calling."

Seth slammed the phone down. Tom did the same at Richlands, then he turned to tell Alex and Hildy.

"The problem . . . the trouble . . ." He had trouble himself, stating it with composure. "The reason Seth rushed away is that Ross's wife and her father were shot . . . *and killed.*"

Hildy seemed also take the news as a personal affront. "*Gott!* Here in this peaceful country. Two innocent people. You have terrorists. *Just as in Europe!*"

Tom frowned. Seth *was* right to dump her.

Alex was stunned. "*More deaths!* My dear, I am so sorry for Rossiter! I did not know the girl . . . did I? Or her father?"

"No, you didn't know them, Alex."

Tom thought he'd better get back to the hotel so he could be available for Rossiter. And he wanted to tell Clara. He missed Clara just now. At such times, in moments of crisis, a man needed to talk to somebody he trusted.

Alex wilted, lowering himself into a chair. Fearfully, as if she expected the terrorists to burst into Richlands, Hildy sat down next to him, close enough that Alex must smell her too, her special scent of photographic chemicals and drenched rose petals, blended to attract the aging satyr.

She looked at Tom skeptically. She was dismissing him.

For wasn't it true that the oldest men were most interesting?

Chapter Thirty-Three

*M*aybe Clara was not meant to live in a world like this. A couple of months earlier, a couple of weeks earlier, reality had not seemed so oppressive. It had never occurred to her then that her life must change, should change—actually that it was *bound* to change whether she liked it or not.

And what had happened to throw all the remnants and debris of existence into such high relief? Why had her life become so chaotic? In the normal course of human events, people came and went, they were born and died, history proceeded smoothly—or did it? No, the tiniest shock was enough to throw everything into disarray—the well-worn puzzle was torn apart and a new picture painted over the same old pieces.

It had started, it seemed to her, that early morning in San Francisco when Alex Spurzov had called Tom to tell him Ludmilla was dead. That had been the starting gun.

Clara had never expected that a few weeks later she'd be on her way to Palm Springs to see her first husband, Stan Gates. This was, indeed, a weird turn of events.

But it wasn't fair to blame everything on fate. Discontent had arrived a good deal earlier; the trouble was, Clara had not recognized it, this discontent, such a stranger to her. Ludmilla's death had turned all the lights on, illuminating the darkest corners—Clara's own tensions, the business with Rossiter, worry about Martha . . . a new awareness of Tom.

The fact was, she did not get to Palm Springs.

Clara had driven sixty or seventy miles from Westwood,

past San Bernardino and Cucamonga, past the halfway mark, thinking furiously, not really aware of passing time or territory, in fact thirty miles farther after being shaken by the certainty she'd spotted Martha on the other side of the freeway, pointed in the direction of Los Angeles.

Why was she going to Stanley? Or did she intend to see Stanley at all? Wasn't she merely going to meet Rossiter? But why? Hadn't Clara been buffeted enough by her men? Was she so stupid that she'd offer herself all over again for a repeat of the same? Stanley was not going to change, revert to the good old days, just because Clara materialized in Palm Springs. And Rossiter? No, if Clara really needed help, a far more daring and radical revision of lifestyle would be necessary than either Stanley or Rossiter could provide.

This revelation came to her with great force.

Rattled now, Clara turned off the freeway in the vicinity of a place called Beaumont, deciding she'd better stop, for coffee, something, then remembering she hadn't had any lunch. She was hungry, at the same time quite light-headed, and peculiarly happy. Along here only a few houses speckled the desert; early spring rain had turned the land green. Maybe Clara should drop out of sight, settle in a place like this . . . raise cactus for a living. Open a truck stop, like the one she saw ahead, joke with heavy machinery men, find her salvation with the tattooed driver of a trailer rig, christen herself with a CB moniker: *Dirty Clara*.

People would laugh, and cry, and point. But maybe life would have some richness, some earthy quality at least.

The name of the place was Jack's. A roadside diner.

Not feeling embarrassed or even nervous, but instead like she belonged there, Clara got out of the car and went inside. Jack's was nearly empty. Clara took a seat at the counter. A highway cop was sitting down at the end, a dozen seats away, next to the window, his Stetson beside him. A girl and boy occupied a booth to her right.

The counterman came bearing coffee.

Clara studied the menu, standard Low-Desert fare, typed on a sheet of paper in a cracked plastic folder.

The counterman and cop resumed their conversation. Laconically, the cop was telling a story about a fire—a derelict barn or house had burned down the night before out in the desert. People had seen the light of the flames for miles around.

You forgot this—once you turned off the freeway, real life went on. There had to be a message there somewhere for Clara Addey.

The old house or barn had burned for hours; you wouldn't expect dried-up old wood to burn as long as it had. But maybe there'd been something else there burning, something they didn't know about, the cop admitted. Who knows? Damp paper, or coal or old rags . . . A body or two, the counterman remarked ghoulishly.

"Decide on anything?"

"What's the Hungarian omelette like?"

She'd have that in honor of Rossiter, whom she would not be seeing, and his Hungarian boss, soon to be Tom's ex-wife Thelma's new husband.

"Goddamn vandals." The cop pronounced judgment. "They come off the road and drive down there and get drunk and set the place on fire. Bastards!"

It was a big omelette. When the counterman said *big*, he meant big. But she had time, lots of it. Clara ate slowly, chewing at length, breaking hard-crusted bread.

Weird to be sitting in the middle of nowhere, *between lives*, alone in every way, as if she'd taken herself out of circulation, unplugged from the world. There was a certain satisfaction in it too, having done it.

Clara thought about Tom. It would be evening before he got back to the hotel. Maybe later than that if he got tied up with Alex again. Clara could have driven straight back to San Francisco right then, today, and gone on up to see Alberto, and nobody would have known she was gone. Clara wanted to be somewhere, she didn't know exactly where—a hole in the ground, a place where she could hibernate, sleep through the winter of her particular discontent. And in the spring, recovered, venture forth.

Clara ate more of the omelette than she'd expected. In fact, after a time, the counterman turned to look and seemed surprised at how much she'd eaten. But couldn't he tell Clara was a lady of appetite?

Some people were reminded by certain foods of sex. Perhaps the mixture of green and red pepper with the egg batter had a certain effect on her. The feeling of warmth and sustenance received gave Clara courage.

The trouble with this place called Jack's was that there was nothing else around here: A couple of frame houses attached to permanently placed mobile homes, a gas station down the road next to the freeway off-ramp, hardly a settlement, nothing more than a wide spot in the road. How did people end up in places like this? Surely, they hadn't started here.

Desolation. It could have been a spot on the map of Africa, no more than an hour's drive from L.A.

If there'd been a motel, Clara thought, she might have taken a room and gone in to sleep, or maybe invited the cook over, this obviously impressive man who produced truly gigantic Hungarian omelettes.

Martha. Had the blonde she'd spotted in the blue sports car really been Martha or a desert mirage? Perhaps Clara expected in her mind to see Martha driving toward L.A. Whatever . . . it didn't matter now.

Clara finished as much as she could eat and laid her knife and fork down on the plate.

The counterman strolled toward her, smiling grotesquely, his Daliesque moustache jerking.

"He's gonna be sad you didn't finish."

Clara smiled back. "I couldn't eat another bite."

"*Nobody* ever finished one of those things. I keep telling him!" The counterman called out, "*Raoul!*"

He waited, drumming his fingers on the counter until the swinging kitchen door flew open. Out bounded a very short man, a tiny man.

Smiling broadly, he exclaimed, "*Si!*"

The counterman stared at Raoul impassively. "Our short-order cook, see?"

"*Si!*" Raoul said again.

"Look, Raoul, the lady couldn't finish . . . what do I tell you? You make the Hungarian omelettes too big. Nobody ever finishes them."

Raoul had the face of a child, big round eyes and heavy cheeks. But he couldn't have been more than four feet tall. A short-order cook, what a joke, it could not be intentional.

Anxiously, for Clara didn't want to hurt the feelings of such a small man, she said, "But I liked the omelette very much. It was delicious!"

Raoul glanced at the counterman.

"I'm only kiddin', Raoul."

"Are *you* a Hungarian?" Clara asked.

The counterman answered for Raoul, who he said didn't speak much English. Raoul was a Basque, the counterman said. From the old country. He couldn't herd sheep like normal Basques do because the sheep dogs—were *they* Hungarian pulis?—were bigger than he was. If they could've saddled the dogs, the counterman joked, then Raoul might have managed as a short cowboy . . . or sheepboy. As it was, Raoul had taken up cooking.

Yes, yes, that made a lot of sense.

There was something about Jack's that was entirely too surrealistic. She felt as if she'd come from outer space. She had to be careful what she said or the cop and the counterman, with Raoul's assistance, would throw her in the back of the car and take her away to some lonely place from which she would never return.

They were all so close to oblivion. Think about it! Only the car outside and what she had in her purse stood between Clara and nothingness.

The bill came to four and a quarter.

In a moment of self-induced panic, Clara convinced herself she hadn't any cash in her pocketbook, then that Jack's didn't accept credit cards. What then? Take it out in trade . . . Raoul first. Raoul watched her closely, an enigmatic smile plastered across his face. Was he thinking what Clara was thinking? Yes, that just then she could have dragged him to the motel room.

Clara slid a five dollar bill across the counter, adding a quarter to cover a very generous tip. Of course she would pay. Clara Addey was a citizen of good standing, a wife and a mother.

So much for rebellion and desertion. Clara was stuck with herself. Maybe that was the simple message of the desert! She was herself, nothing more, nothing less.

"*Merci mille fois,*" said Raoul.

Ah, Clara thought, French.

"*Hasta la vista!*" he added.

Spanish.

The counterman grinned. "Come see us again."

He was missing a tooth in front, and Clara was jolted at the sight of the gap. Suddenly he seemed to turn ugly with waxed moustache and thin, tooth-gapped, insinuating face; and the highway cop masquerading in a starched beige uniform and heavy gun belt hanging off his middle; and even the little couple slurping soft drinks.

"Good-bye," Clara said meekly.

Outside, the heat of the sun only increased her anxiety. The emptiness terrified her. She was alone, *on her own*. She was, Clara told herself again, finally responsible for herself, for however she felt, for whatever she wanted to make of it. Her understanding of this was huge, yet dwarfed by the vastness of the surroundings; she was in control, but at the some time she was totally insignificant.

"Drive careful!"

The Daliesque counterman stuck his face out the doorway of Jack's and grinned. Clara's fright vanished. He was being friendly, that was all.

"Have a good day!"

"You too," Clara called back.

He waved at her joyously, really, genuinely joyously, and Clara wondered why, or how. She didn't understand how he could be so happy, living and working like this, in a desolate wilderness.

Or maybe everybody lived in a desolate wilderness, never mind about their opulent trappings.

She was in the car and driving slow-motion through the desert winter sunshine.

Why *was* he so happy, this toothless man?

And was she suddenly happy too? It seemed like she could be, if that was what she wanted. And then she thought of Biff again, and the gallery. *Her* life. If that's what it was.

Chapter
Thirty-Four

*H*ildy jumped up, her face flushed and aggravated. "Prince, you should not do that!"

But he had done only what she'd obviously planned that he should do. "I'm so sorry, fraulein. Forgive an old man."

"I . . . well, never mind," she said tersely. "Prince, I can make the argument for taking pictures of the *Spurzov Ei*—if you wish to listen. Or are you being a serious fellow?"

"Darling, never more."

"Such an object . . ." She thought about it, then continued fervently. "It is a treasure for all mankind, one of the great artworks. It is sinful to hide it away in a bank."

Alex had heard this same lecture before.

"Why? What is so wonderful about mankind that it deserves to see everything? I do not find *mankind* such a great work of art!"

Hildy's mouth dropped open, then closed. Of course, there could be no reply. His charge could be substantiated. Mankind was on the rocks. The thing was *to save* art from chaos, not to *expose* it to chaos. Should he feel any obligation to let *them* view the Spurzov Egg?

Besides which, in the way Alexei reasoned, the Egg was quite possibly worth more to him unseen than seen. Suppose, as some unpleasant people charged, the Egg was a forgery, though a treasure in its own right, maybe even more beautiful than the genuine Fabergé article . . . but *not* a Fabergé?

What then? People would shriek: Spurzov's Egg is a fake! And the man who owns it, also a fake!

There was no question in Alex's mind as to its authenticity, but that was beside the point. Over the years the Egg had served as Alexei's leverage, his handle on the world. Without it, real or fake, where would he be? For example: One good reason Rose adored him so was, simply, the Egg! Seventy percent was his charm, savoir-faire, his special talent for delighting. But thirty percent was the Egg.

Alexei stared at Hildy and sighed. She was pretty, but not a Rose.

It came to Alex again that the Egg must go to Rose. This was only just. For years he had expected that upon his own death, which was unthinkable, the Spurzov Egg should be returned to the Russian people, all the Russians—not the goddamn Bolsheviks; he had hoped they'd be long gone. The Egg *belonged* to the Russians, Great Russia. Then, for a time, giving up, he had decided to bequeath the Egg to Tom Addey, possibly his best living friend despite the fact Tom had cuckolded him with Ludmilla—even though, strictly speaking, Alex hadn't been actually married to her then. But it had unquestionably been a spiritual cuckolding—not that this mattered now.

Next to Rose, Tom still deserved the Egg more than any other person.

He would have to get Tom to draw up the papers. This was the least he could do for Rose, who adored him so. It would represent justice done, he told himself, remembering back to the centuries of bad treatment his ancestors had wreaked on hers.

Yes. Dear Rose would be custodian of the Spurzov Egg until it was returned to his people!

Sheer genius. Sheer irony. Sheer theatre!

"My darling fraulein," Alex said lightly, "we cannot talk of the *Spurzov Ei* in relation to Richlands. What connection has this montrosity of a house with the art of Fabergé? Nevertheless, perhaps you and Rose and myself will arrange a visit . . . *at the vault.*"

Her eyes lit up. She could not hide the hope that danced through her eyes. Yes, there was still a possibility of a photographic coup.

"Perhaps *one* picture and one picture only," he qualified the offer. "I require absolute control."

"Of course. Naturally, Prince."

"We could not open it," he cautioned. "The scene within is so shocking . . ."

She began to protest, then seeing his look, stopped.

"My father made me pledge. It would bring dishonor to my family. Personally . . . I . . ." Alexei smiled and shrugged. "In this day and age . . . But I did promise."

"The scene, Prince?"

"Of an orgy, can you believe?" Of course she could. "My father used to say that the orgy scene should have been included in our coat-of-arms, instead of chains and riding crop. At a certain time in the last century," Alex continued comfortably, for he liked the story, "we Russians were much taken with romantic notions about the Arabian Nights—dancing girls and the likes of Mussorgsky's operas—so did the Fabergé workshop concoct a harem scene complete with all manner of activity, the likenesses of all my family on the faces taking part . . . and the completed Egg was presented to my grandfather by the czar."

With stony logic, Hildy said, "No one would have any idea now who they were."

"Exactly . . . but I did pledge. It is the most marvelous tableau, fraulein. You can study it for hours and find still other depraved things happening."

Hildy's eyes darted as she imagined the Egg. But he had to finish with her quickly. Rose would be coming soon. She usually did not nap so long. Indeed, Alex thought he heard a door slam.

"Was that Peat finally?" Alex asked rhetorically. "Tea would be nice. Peat must be back *soon*." He was determined to change the subject, away from the Egg.

"You and Seth will be leaving. Seth told me he is finished here."

She stared at him coolly. "I will have finished too when I have seen and photographed the *Spurzov Ei*, Prince Alex."

"But have no fear. You . . . and Rose . . . and I . . . will go to the bank and deepest vault . . ." He winked. "My terms."

Hildy's head jerked in agreement. She had no choice.

Myriad thoughts filled Alex's head. Yes, he should visit the bank again. Ludmilla had left certain valuables, and instructions that had vital importance for Alex. He was to have everything she'd amassed; but it was not possible yet to say what all that was. And, of course, he remembered bitterly, the Peruvian gold jewelry was missing.

Well, yes, then, in the process he could provide Hildy a single, enticing look at the Egg, perhaps even one quick picture of its enameled, bejeweled, and golden exterior. A mere look would serve his purpose—for Alex and Rose would be going to Europe soon, and a reminder of the existence of the Spurzov Egg was, by itself, reason for doors to be opened. Yes, yes, Prince Alex Spurzov was still patron of the Egg!

Alex touched Hildy's burning cheek with gentle fingers.

"What are *you* doing in the orgy scene, Alex?" she asked.

"I? But, darling, I was not yet born!"

"Well . . . as in family resemblance?"

"I can tell you where I would *like* to be in that family tableau." Alex chuckled. "In the very center of the scene, spread upon a tiny divan covered in silk, is a dark-haired *houri*, and at the *very moment* of entry, caught in that split second of time, is my ancestor. . . ." Alex paused to smile at her; she looked as though she would burst, so total was her attention. "The very *instant* of coupling, it is breathtaking. I think it was meant to be my uncle Vladimir, in the act of ravishing this girl of unimaginable beauty and total submission. . . ."

Hildy murmured.

"Imagine," Alex continued dramatically, "to be hung like that in full erection for centuries to come. A person might well wonder which is the real world and which is the dream."

Alex might have said more, but it was too late. A volley of laughter ripped through the upper stories of the house.

"Oh, my God! Peat!"

The voice, such a high-pitched joyous bugling, was Rose's.

"What has happened?"

Alex tried to struggle out of his chair. Hildy lent him a hand, and as he came up and forward, he pitched conveniently into her arms. She laughed breathlessly and jumped out of the way, in the nick of time. Rose bounced into the Gallery of Mirrors, as she had begun to call the garden room, after the palace of Versailles.

"My God, I don't believe it!" Rose pealed another girlish scream.

"Rose! What in the world is wrong?"

"It's Peat."

"So the fool is back? Finally, we can have our tea!"

Rose raced forward eagerly. She put her arms around Alex and snuggled close, bringing him life, and not shy about it, either, in front of Hildegard Beckmann.

"Rose, what has he been up to now?"

"Alex, Peat is running around upstairs with no pants on."

Alex shuddered. But Rose continued to laugh madly. What was so funny about it? Not again, Alex thought, please not that.

"Rosa," he said, fury rising, "this awful chap must go!"

Chapter
Thirty-Five

"Are you okay, Ross?" Tom Addey asked his son.
"Yeah. I'm okay."

Rossiter didn't sound okay—naturally enough. For regardless of what one thought of her, Serena had been murdered, and her father too. Whether he was ever in love with her or not, Serena's death by violence must have come as a shock.

Relieved? That was also possible. It wasn't all bad to have somebody like Serena out of the way. Not a terribly nice thought—but Tom wasn't saying it out loud.

"Do you want me to come over? You want to come here?"

"Oh, no! Not necessary! I'll be fine. I just need, uh . . . to be alone for a while."

"Will you call me if—"

"Sure, I will," Rossiter promised. "I'll call you later. I'm, uh . . . just absorbing it . . . having a drink . . . you know."

"I understand, Ross. . . . Ross, *I'm sorry.*"

"Yeah." Rossiter made a whooshing noise. *"Helluva day!"*

Tom glanced at the bedroom door. "I haven't told Clara yet. I think she's asleep." He spoke quietly, not wanting to disturb her if she was napping. More than likely, though, she was in there sulking.

Tom stood, indecisively, waiting for . . . what? Staring out the window, he sniffed. Some of that distinctive photographic darkroom smell of Hildy's had caught in his nose, a sickening reminder of high school chemistry. Or was it German girl-in-heat? He removed his jacket and went into the bathroom. A

shower would rid him of the smell of Hildy; it also was something to do if Clara was indeed lurking in the bedroom. But to
hell with it, Tom thought. He was tired. How come she hadn't
gone to Palm Springs? As he'd hoped . . . and expected.

Tom took his clothes off and slipped into the hotel terry-
cloth robe. A little after-shave slapped on his face woke him up a
little, improved his outlook just that extra bit.

The bedroom was dark. But she was there, as he'd figured, a
lump of body on the near side of the bed. He heard measured
breathing, but that didn't mean she was asleep.

Tom slipped in on the other side of the bed and lay there
quietly, eyes closed, thinking about Serena and Hildy and his
poor sons. *Rest.* The time had come to get away from it all . . .
to rest. Finally his body began to relax. Gentle sleep would
come.

But then, startling him, she flounced over, her naked body
thumping his ribs, giving off sweaty welcome. In this Tom could
silently wallow, no excuses, no apologies. She didn't speak
either, only breathed explosively and shoved against him. He
wouldn't tell her about Serena yet, so as not to ruin the reunion.
The sweet mouth nibbled his cheek, his lips; she tongued him
lavishly, and Tom felt the fuzzy patch of her crotch urgently
against his hand, her hand seeking him.

Her smell rose tantalizingly to his nostrils; not like Hildy's,
not like anybody else's. Clara's scent was pungent, aggressive.

Obligingly, Tom slipped his hand along her thigh. The heat
was intense; she was slick with desire.

She hardly paused. Eagerly, without further prelude, she
pulled him on top of her and guided his penetration smoothly,
frankly exuding satisfaction. There was such directness about her
today; yes, she had been having second thoughts about herself
. . . *and him*. She had been unreasonable and was acknowledg-
ing it, making up for her petulance. She had found this wonderful raw eagerness to please. How generously she absorbed him,
how expansively she performed, all her muscles laboring, blood
pounding, limbs clutching.

Too soon, Tom began to peak. He tried to slow himself but
it was impossible. She kissed with such abandon! She was out of
control! Fingers digging into his back, she heaved wildly and
cried out as she climaxed once and then, a few seconds later, a
second time. She had overtaken and passed him.

Yes, she surely had been thinking seriously about their relationship.

Then, surprisingly, for serious Clara did not often do so in moments of passion, she laughed. An exhilarating sound, that frothy giggle, burst from her.

And Tom realized he was in bed with Martha. He could have stopped then, on a dime. She laughed again, excitedly. Of course! The laugh was all Martha, never mind about the rest of her—the rest was Clara, could have been Clara, should have been Clara.

It was not too late. He should stop. She had deceived him, brutally . . . even cruelly. He should have stopped then, leapt away, up, out of the bed, raging. He should have known. Martha was not *precisely* her mother; close, but no cigar!

Now was the time to stop if he intended to stop. He had not much time left if he was going to stop. The young body leapt at him, devouring, like fire, greed, but generous too.

But was he sure? Perhaps he was wrong—this *was* actually Clara. How did he conceive the idea it was Martha? Whoever it was, this *she*, she forced him to focus on the one thing. This. Now. It didn't matter, then, who she was.

She, this woman, must have felt the surge, maybe his last ever. She gasped, devotedly countered, grinding down, delivering to him and taking from him every vestige of vigor. He had handed over his sword, surrendered. She laughed again, triumphantly, rocking back and forth so that he was aware of every square inch of the firm, fresh body so alive beneath him. Tom knew all about the missionaries, but how did they make a go of it with a woman who never stopped laughing?

Then, wonder of wonder, she did stop and go silent, her hard-soft belly heaving. She was peaking again, like a freight train coming from miles away. Elemental sounds, reminding him again of the beginning and end, of men and women beginning and ending it in the damp, cold caves of pre-history.

It took her a while to finish. Only very slowly did she come down.

Cryptically, Tom whispered, cleverly, he whispered, "So you didn't go to Palm Springs after all."

This time her laugh was explosive, astonished, rather insulted. "*Don't you know who I am?* Jesus, Tom, you big boob!"

345

"What!" He feigned total shock, made his body jerk and recoil. *"Martha? Martha!"*

"Well, yes, for God's sake!" She clutched at him violently, squeezed with her legs, held him tightly with her arms. "I told you, didn't I? Didn't I warn you?"

"Martha! You must be joking—this is terrible! How in the hell did you get in here?"

"I said I wanted to go up and wait for my mommy—they know me downstairs by now."

She kissed him longingly, still not ready to release him, as much as he squirmed, which he did . . . half-heartedly. What was he going to say? Martha arched her back, rubbing her breasts on his chest, terrible girl. Yes, of course, shocking, but among other things, she had this insatiable sex drive. How could he resist it?

"Was it . . . okay?" Martha asked him softly.

What a question? Okay? Tom felt himself coming loose; he groaned inside.

"I'm so surprised . . . I don't know what to say," he lied.

She kissed him again, her lips hot and wet. "Well . . . I can't get enough of you, Tommy, and I don't notice you running for the hills."

"You deceived me, Martha," he said severely, "and I don't like this."

"Yes, you do!"

Yes, he did. It was unbelievable. The body didn't lie; the body was honest. After the heat died down, the passion receded, you felt the body against you and it didn't lie.

"You knew right away it was me—and don't say you didn't!"

Was this for the record? Was there a witness for the defense in the next room, ear to the door—though the door was half open? Clara, for all he knew, having come back after all and crept into the suite without them hearing.

Martha sighed tremulously. "I knew it would be like this. Don't you love me? Could you? Do you?"

"This is a little sudden," he said.

Martha let him go, then. Tom rolled over, endeavoring to be grim, but she tucked herself into him, slid under his arm, put her mouth against his shoulder. She must be joking, he told himself. This was madness, or a grand old joke. But, as a matter of fact, well . . . he shouldn't say so, even think it, but what difference did it make? Weren't such moments, such adventures, to be cherished, regardless of risk? When all was said and done . . . well, weren't they all finished? They were not going to survive forever. Make the most of it.

But he said, "It's also a little risky, wouldn't you say?"

In fact, he was thinking, they had better get the hell up—right now!

"She's in Palm Springs by now," Martha assured him nonchalantly.

"You're so sure of that?"

"She called this morning and said she was coming."

"And if you're wrong?"

Martha worked herself against him, ignoring such a possibility. "If we smoked, now would be the time for a cigarette," she said, then added in a wounded tone, "How could you have thought it was—"

"Clara?" He supplied the name. "You might as well say it. *Your mother?* You wanted me to think so, didn't you?"

"Are we so much . . . alike?"

"What have you got against her?"

Another question that had to be asked. She couldn't answer. She squirmed.

About the only thing he had learned, as a matter of fact, and he wasn't going to say that either, was that Martha had not been a virgin. Still, he didn't believe she indulged very widely. A man could discern this. Martha was squeaky new, malleable, adaptable to a single lover, like a good hat to be molded to its owner's head, a piece of living leather with a memory.

"She's in for a big shock," Martha muttered, with a satisfaction in her voice that was very annoying.

"Who is? Clara? How? Only if *you* tell her. . . ."

Martha tried another kiss. She stroked his back and tried to hold him. But Tom felt cold now. He was fading. They were suddenly not in good spirits. Her intensity made him uncomfortable; he could feel the vitality and that made him uneasy too. Martha was not much short of overwhelming—in mind and body, especially the challenge of the body of which he was so conscious.

He moved to the side and Martha clung to him. She didn't want to let go.

"Does this mean you won't run away with me . . . *Tommy*?"

She was teasing, trying to tease, hoping he would think she was teasing.

"Not this month, sweetheart."

How did he manage to edge away from her, to make distance between them? He was so aware of her warmth, the electricity of the blond skin. He had no excuses now. He wanted to touch her. Christ, to be young and rightfully able to enjoy her. Martha had fooled him, for there was no way he was entitled to this. But to be honest, and why not, he had fantasized her; and it had actually happened, like discovering the whole of life all over again.

If you loved life enough to want it all over again, was that a sin against God? One wouldn't suppose so—after all, it was God who'd created the Garden in the first place and dropped Man into it.

"I finally found out what happened in Palm Springs."

Tom said nothing. If she wanted to confide in him, intended to confide, then she would.

"*Sorge . . . Will Sorge*. The name means something like *sorrow* in German. Very appropriate, actually. Sorge hung himself in Stanley's workshop, as we knew, but it wasn't because he was sick or anything—no, the reason was that Stanley found a new guy. Everybody always said Sorge was such a shit—and he did the last nasty thing he could, hanging himself fifty feet from the house—to inflict the maximum hurt."

This reminded Tom of the other, awful business. Poor Serena, he'd almost forgotten, and Bud Slagger.

Tom turned on his side, facing Martha again. In the dimness he could almost see her body, fancied he did see her. Yes, well, so Clara had gone to Palm Springs. Maybe that was her signal of the end. He strained to see Martha but didn't touch. The long slim body gleamed. He was driven by desire.

Soft flesh brushed his chest and he started.

Martha laughed.

Grimly Tom said, "I was saving this until later . . . another piece of not-so-nice news. Serena was killed this afternoon. And her father."

Martha reacted predictably.

"Holy cow! In a car? Where was Ross?"

"No, not in the car. They were . . . what they call 'blown away.' Guys with a shotgun."

"Jesus!"

She was impressed. She lay silently. Tom felt the flutter of her fingers against his leg. He could hear her heart beating in the silence, the batting of her eyelashes as she struggled to see him.

"And what about me?" she asked in a small voice.

"*About you?*"

Hesitantly she put her face against his shoulder. She seemed to be crying a little.

"Yes . . . Poor little me."

Deliberately, Tom misconstrued her little effort. "I've got no complaints about you. You might possibly be a little too active for an older man."

Her laugh was quick, again surmounting gloom. It was said, Tom remembered, that certain girls had laughter of champagne grade. Ludmilla's, too, had been a fine old vintage.

"Well, I was going to tell you that Stan booted *me* out."

"Good for him."

"Sure," she said dryly, "but now what?"

"Back to school, ducky," Tom said, "study hard and save your money."

But that was not what he was thinking. God, could he get away with it? Carry it off? Older man and young chick? Young chick only too obviously *adoring* older man, young chick laboring under the heavy burden of father fixation? It was truly not often that a man walked into the forest and stumbled over a beautiful wild flower! And what did he do? Pass it by? No, he stopped and stared, not believing his good luck, marveling at the symbolic meaning of such a personal message. The man might even pick the flower and stuff it in his pocket, intending to preserve it.

Pity him if he passed by and the next time he came to this place the flower had turned brown and shriveled into dust.

And so there always did have to be a first and a last time.

"I'm your slave now. What are you going to do with me?"

Put you in a bottle, tuck you in a drawer, press you, like that flower, between the pages of a big fat book.

He said, "I don't keep slaves."

But consider the options. Run away with her, far away, and begin a whole new life. Pretend you're twenty-five again. It was not as though Martha was some dumb girl he'd be bored with in a few weeks or months. She was just young . . . only young . . . too young. Say, Good-bye, Clara! People would be very shocked . . . but he'd shocked them before—nobody should ever take Tom Addey for granted, that was the thing.

"She knows I'm in love with you," Martha said matter-of-factly.

As if *that* mattered.

"Come on, now! She doesn't . . . and you're not!"

"All right," Martha compromised. "So I'm infatuated."

He'd be very wrong to accept anything about Martha at face value. She was serious—but not serious at all. She was sincere, but at the same time unthinking and insincere.

"Okay," he said, "so what do you expect me to do?"

Fingers stroked his thigh. No, *he* would not touch her. He could bear it; he was a brave and disciplined man.

"Now that you've seduced and ruined me?"

Casually she shifted her body, as if she weren't aware of what she was doing. Soft breast jostled his arm, the dagger-sharp point of nipple.

"I'm not improvident, you know," Martha murmured lazily, breezily. "You could rent a little love nest in Berkeley when you go teach and I'll meet you there. I'll play mistress." She put her face close to his; lips sought his, the tongue, hot breath tickled. "You don't have a mistress just now . . . *do you*?"

"No," Tom grunted. She was playing with him, he realized that. He must take great care. "You would do that, wouldn't you? And it wouldn't mean a goddamn thing to you."

The casual girl of the eighties. Casual about everything, all the arrangements of life. And of course it was gruesomely predictable that an old man named Tom Addey would fall horribly in love with this fragrant flower, this *young thing*, only in due course, predictably, to be thrown over, devastated, destroyed . . . driven to *what next*? Suicide? Murder? Yes, perhaps to a delicious crime of passion.

It happened. It could happen. He had seen it happen. But mostly it did not happen.

"From such sordid imbroglios, O Lord, please deliver me."

Martha pinched crudely, cruelly. "It would scare you, wouldn't it? Not such a fearless old brute after all, are we?"

She was too intelligent, too discerning. *Old?* She also had a great talent to annoy. Like Clara, Martha understood instinctively where to dig at an exposed nerve.

"Sure, so I divorce your mother? I've done that before, nothing new to me. And marry you? Will you marry me? *Would you?*"

If he'd expected the raw question to floor her, he was wrong, Martha chuckled throatily, as if she knew everything. Well, she did know him too well. Throwing one arm around his shoulder, she tugged herself even closer, smack up against him, truth against truth. The skin was enough by itself to ruin him; the body, soft, hard, soft, round, flat, muscular, registered itself square inch by square inch on his imagination. He would never forget it. The temptation . . .

"What if I said yes . . . what would you do then, *Tom?*"

Run like hell? Take to the hills? What?

"I don't know," he answered.

"Anyway, who says it's necessary these days to marry? The best of people don't these days. Marriage just seems to make trouble, wouldn't you say? Don't people tend to get very possessive?"

She was asking him? Since when was he the expert?

"Where did you learn to be so cynical?"

"At college. School is not a total loss," Martha said flippantly.

"Tramp!"

"Tramp-ette, buster!" She hugged him boisterously and tried to draw him over, moving her legs, wanting him again, he knew it. This was how she'd learn the sad truth—he needed more time in the recovery room. Martha whispered, "I don't know if I'd marry you anyway. You know why? Because I don't think you treat your wives very well. It would have to be pure sex between us. Do you agree?"

Yes, well, slowly, in a way amazingly, he did begin to agree. After a moment he agreed very definitely, emphatically, even stridently he agreed. Tom was astonished, but he did agree.

"You'll see," Martha said. "I improve with age."

Chapter Thirty-Six

*F*inally they came downstairs.

Clara had positioned herself where she could see everybody getting on or off an elevator. The concierge at the desk had informed her that her daughter had arrived, and a little later, Mr. Addey.

Clara bought an afternoon paper and simply sat down to wait.

Certainly Martha had every reason to think Clara was in Palm Springs, and Clara was not going to go upstairs and into the suite without knocking and, perish the possibility, surprise them in the bedroom. There they might be, with the door half closed, muttering at each other, talking things over, having a few laughs, thinking they were in the clear.

Eventually they would have to come downstairs. And if they didn't finally come down, she'd get on the phone and say she was on her way back, calling from Cucamonga, and would be there soon. Then watch them scramble.

Just by the way they walked out of the elevator, one might *possibly* be led to believe something had happened, though it was not possible, on the other hand, to know just what. Martha had always treated Tom in the same familiar, half-teasing, intimate way, and now as they emerged from the elevator, she wasn't acting any differently, only more so . . . *very* familiar in what might be a slightly different way. Or maybe not.

Tom looked his usual self—half amused, but aloof, distant, slightly miffed, as if Martha, as usual, had said something as annoying as it was funny.

Martha was a child. Clara had to remember that.

Tom saw her first. He stopped short and did seem for just a second to reel back in proverbial amazement. But did not follow through; and why should he? There shouldn't be anything surprising about seeing his wife at their hotel.

Martha smiled broadly, nothing embarrassed about her. Brazen, shameless bitch that she was, Martha strutted toward Clara, upon her face that sated, slightly squashed look some women got after sex.

"Hey! I thought you were going to Palm Springs, Ma."

"I was. I changed my mind halfway there and came back." Too late?

"Well, why are you sitting down here?" Tom inquired, so indulgently. "We've been upstairs . . . waiting."

"For what? I told *her* I was driving down to Stan's."

Smoothly, Tom took up the slack. "For you to call?"

Martha stared at her, genuine sympathy in her eyes. Sympathy, for what? Was Martha preparing an announcement?

Sorry, mother, I'm taking Tom. . . .

"Well," Tom said, shrugging, "let's go in the bar and have a drink . . . now that we're all here."

"I'm driving back north," Martha offered.

"I didn't know you were leaving the Springs," Clara said.

"I've had it with Palm Springs and *that* scene. Good thing you didn't get there, Ma. Quite a story. I'll tell you about it some time."

They got a table next to the window. It wasn't five yet, and still not too crowded.

"True to form," Tom stated prissily, "I'm having a gin martini, straight up, with two olives."

Martha ordered an orange juice. Think of it—she was still too young to drink in a bar, but old enough for everything else.

"I'll also have a martini," Clara said.

When the waiter had gone, Tom leaned back in his chair for a moment, looking bad-humored and unprepared.

"I have something to tell you—not good news, I fear."

He glanced at Clara, frowned at Martha. What was coming now, not another declaration of intent?

Sorry, Clara, I'm running away with Martha, your daughter.

"I have an announcement to make too," Clara said. It was about fighting fire with fire.

"First things first, Clara," he said smugly. "Serena and her father were bumped off this afternoon."

Clara felt her blood reliquify; had she been so frozen with hostility . . . fear?

"A joke of some sort?" she murmured. "Ross . . . ?"

"No joke. I've been on the phone all afternoon: To Seth at the hospital. Ross is home—in *deep shock*, as you can imagine."

"What happened?" She forgot about Martha.

He shrugged irascibly. "People keep asking and I don't know, not for a fact. Seth has already turned it into a Mafia-style execution, two men with a shotgun and all that," Tom continued gloomily, "which I suppose it was, given what we know."

Clara shook her head dumbly. *Poor Rossiter!* So he wouldn't have gone to Palm Springs after all. He'd stood her up, due to circumstances beyond his control.

"Why Serena?" she asked. "I can understand her father. But—"

Martha, as always, found the appropriate comment. "Maybe they didn't like her nose job."

"Oh, Jesus! *You!*" Clara's voice rose furiously. She forced herself to stop. Just now she'd have liked to kill Martha too. "Poor Rossiter . . . the poor, helpless thing."

Tom looked at her askance. Calling Rossiter helpless? He *was* a helpless soul. But it wasn't Clara's function to say so. Frustrated, Clara turned on Martha.

"What right have you got to say things like that?"

"Sorry."

"Look . . ." Clara drew a nervous breath. "I'm sorry too. Very sorry. You just get to me. Your comments stink!"

"All right!" Martha said sharply, briskly, "I said I'm sorry! What I wanted to tell you—it's a good thing you didn't get to Stan's. You'd have discovered the truth of the matter which I *finally* figured out." Martha spoke embarrassedly, erratically. "The reason Will Sorge hung himself was not that he was sick, unless you call sick at heart being sick. What's happened is that your *former husband* is weaseling around with a new boyfriend, and Will couldn't take it."

Delivering the unwholesome report like an ultimatum, Martha stared with bitter defiance, daring her to object.

Clara carefully said, "*My* former husband . . . *your father*."

"Don't I know it?"

354

Disillusion sounded in Martha's voice like a crack in a bell, and instantly Clara was sorry she'd been so nasty.

"Look . . ." Clara did have a good point to make. "Nobody ever said Stan had to stick with that prick Will Sorge. If Sorge killed himself, well . . . so what? That's his responsibility. Am I right, Tom?"

"One hundred and ten percent right."

Clara tried to smile at Martha. What a lucky break she had not gone on to Palm Springs. How embarrassing—Stan wouldn't have thanked her for showing up to stare at his new boyfriend, would he? *Really*! Heading off in aid of the stricken Stanley only to discover that he'd once again perpetrated havoc.

"He's a cute little blonde with the tightest little ass—"

"Martha! Goddamn it!"

That was Tom speaking up, at last. But Martha merely guffawed, recklessly, loudly enough to make the bartender pause over his bottles, a man passing the bar-lounge door look inside for the party.

"Rossiter needs us," Clara said quietly. "That's much more important right now."

"No, leave him alone," Tom advised. "He sounds okay. I hate to say it . . . *He sounds fine!*"

Nevertheless Clara tried to remember proper protocol, assuming there was sorrow or sadness involved.

Martha sucked back orange juice, looking at them disparagingly. "If you ask me—"

"Which nobody did!"

"Let's face it," Martha said, undeterred, "the woman was an asshole."

Tom snorted laughter. Clara wondered how she could have forgotten that they were in league, these two. Upstairs, alone for at least the hour or so Clara had been waiting, they'd been plotting. Tom said he'd been on the phone—and what else?

"Not to speak ill of the dead," Tom drawled.

Clara didn't care for Martha Gates, not at all. Martha reminded her too much of Clara Morelli. Brilliantly, as if looking into the distant past and picking out faraway peaks and valleys of angelic performance *and* misbehavior, *brilliantly* Clara remembered when she'd run away with Stan Gates and, ultimately, produced this blond baggage . . . this Trouble . . . this daughter.

"Sometimes," Clara said quietly, "I don't like you at all."

Martha shrugged. "Be my guest."

"Now, listen," Tom intervened archly. "My sadness is too vast to tolerate you two bickering."

Martha slapped his knee boisteriously. "Not to worry, Tommy!"

"Curb your daughter, madame."

Martha made a face and grinned at him. She was a preposterous character to have for a daughter. Clara had to wonder, where had this teasing and mocking bitch come from? Was it fickle Stanley's blood surfacing? Clara was the soul of propriety compared to their daughter. Whatever had happened, that which made Clara so suspicious, perhaps had not happened at all. Everything was so confusing. Watching Tom and Martha grimacing at each other like a pair of schoolchildren, it was not possible to judge. Grinning slyly, Martha caressed her lips with the tip of her rouge-red tongue. What was this meant to convey? Nothing, by the look of Tom. He bared his teeth in a silly Charlie Chan look.

Something had happened, yes. Nothing had happened, no.

"When are you leaving?" Clara asked Martha.

Naughtily, Martha said, "In a few minutes, don't worry. I'll drive through the night!"

"Not by yourself!" Instant Mother materialized.

"Why not?"

Gloomily, Tom muttered, "Go in the morning."

With no warning, Martha's jocular mood left her. She spoke at Tom directly. "No reason for me to hang around here, is there? I want out. *Out!*"

Tom barked back. "Then you should go. *Go!*"

"Done!" Clara realized with a shock that Martha was in the process of telling him off, telling him to get lost, telling him not to bother to send flowers. "I'm going," Martha repeated, softening her own tone just enough not to leave them limp. "I like to stop in San Luis Obispo." Chuckling bitterly, she added, "Who knows—maybe I'll get lucky."

"Very funny. Jokes galore!" Tom reacted in a disapproving, disappointed, disillusioned way.

Martha stared at him and finally managed to produce a wounded smile. What had she realized just now—that whatever had happened or hadn't happened upstairs, whatever Tom had said or hadn't said, all that was cancelled?

Sorry, little Martha, but I will not run off with you.

What *had* Martha learned, or maybe more importantly, unlearned? Did Tom come out of his shell for just a moment, then quickly retreat?

Blithely, Martha murmured, "You just remember . . . *Tommy* . . . you'd just better watch out. . . ."

Tom smiled a little and nodded. "I'll be on my guard."

"I *will* grow up one of these days." Martha said.

Revelation . . . or comprehension, flashed, like a glare from distant lightning . . . then faded, as instantaneously as the weather. A line had been drawn, a mooring cut. . . . The cord? No, Clara and Martha were past that. This was different.

Again Clara asked herself what Martha had learned . . . or unlearned?

No, mother, I'll not be taking Tommy away from you after all.

But, darling daughter, would I deprive you?

Tommy? Tommy looked very uncomfortable. After Martha had gone, he realized, Clara would have questions, many questions, questions as galore as Martha's bad jokes.

Martha finished her juice, then abruptly pushed herself out of her chair. "Much as I hate good-byes . . ."

"Dear," Clara said mildly, hopefully, "when you get back, would you mind . . . Would you please check on Biff? Tell him I'll . . . *we'll* be back in a few days? Soon?" She looked at Tom.

"Yes," he said. "Soon, within a couple of days. I hope."

Martha mocked. "Oh, yes, *darling* Biff. Of course I'll let him know, *darling*," she growled, in the worst humor.

Nonetheless, Martha bent over quickly to kiss Clara's cheek, the very minimum in the way of a good-bye kiss. More delicately, she said her good-bye to Tom, turning her back a bit so Clara could not see the kiss . . . on the mouth, ritualistic, emphatic, Clara had no doubt. Tom's toes might have curled for all Clara cared.

So. So? Whatever had happened upstairs had . . . simply . . . happened. Or not. It was too late now; too late for anything to matter.

People should remember the big lesson. Nothing was for

nothing. You paid. Martha wanted to be gone, yet she didn't want to go at all. She wanted to fall into Clara's arms and weep over *Tommy*, and Clara wanted her to as well. But she wouldn't. Martha wanted somebody to hug her . . . Tommy. But he was not going to. Not Tommy; not in front of Clara, perish the thought!

Martha was going to cry all the way to the freeway; then she'd straighten out. She was young.

The question was whether Clara was going to straighten out.

"Will you please call . . . when you stop tonight?" Clara asked.

"*Yes . . . Okay . . . Ta!*"

Shoulders hiked up tensely, Martha marched away. Tom made no move to go outside with her to the valet parking.

Something *had* happened. But what? Chances were Clara would never find out. She didn't know what to say when they were alone—should she apologize for Martha? Or face Tom with the big question?

"I wouldn't worry about Martha," Tom said awkwardly. "She'll be okay."

"Oh, yes? Are you so sure?"

Whatever she meant by that, she meant in spades.

Suppose the worst had happened? Suppose Tom had made love to Martha there in the darkened bedroom? Suppose he'd come back and Martha had been inside, and without knowing it was her, Tom had slipped into bed with Martha and made love to her, discovering too late this was Martha and not Clara, his legal wife?

Suppose all that . . . Did it have to be so terrible? You could hardly blame Tom. Martha, yes. But Martha was her daughter; if Martha fell in love with Tom, you couldn't really blame her either.

"So . . . what now, brown cow?"

He was startled. "*What now?*" Tom shrugged wildly. "I thought everything was all wrapped up, until this murder business. I've finished with Dick Richards. The deal is struck."

"I was hoping we could get out of here." No, she was absolutely not going to rush across the city to be at Rossiter's side. Love? No, it made Clara tired to think about love. She had a huge feeling for Rossiter, poor, dumb, helpless Rossiter, but it wasn't love, and there was no use playing that it was.

Tom grumbled, "People like Serena and her father are programmed to be destroyed.

"Is Seth right? Has it got something to do with Las Vegas?"

Tom shook his head disgustedly. "According to Seth, *everything* that happens anywhere in the world is connected— like the knee bone is connected to the ankle bone. There *are* people like that. They see a plot in everything. For me, though, it's kind of hard to imagine Bud Slagger mixed up in gun-running and money-laundering. But . . ." He shrugged dismally. *"Who the hell knows?"*

Reflexively, he signaled for the waiter. Yes, Tom would want another drink, wouldn't he? He was on trial now, and nervousness told.

"But what about Rossiter?" Clara asked, putting it off.

"I don't know. He's got to deal with this himself," Tom said. "Nothing we can do."

The moment had come.

"Now . . . about Martha," Clara said conversationally. His eyes came up, darkly, defensively. But Clara had a surprise for him. "You two don't seem to be getting along very well . . . I think she ought to move out of the apartment, get her own place—what do *you* say, Tom?"

Thoughtfully, he replied, "You may be right."

"The time has come for her to leave home. She and I are on each other's nerves too. What do you think, Tom?"

He was totally unperturbed, as crystal-clearly transparent as arctic ice.

Clara let a few beats pass. "You know, I *was* going to Palm Springs."

"And?"

And? Did he want to know that she'd invited Rossiter to meet her? Of course, she wouldn't be there for the rendezvous, nor would Rossiter if he were home trying to absorb the fact of Serena's death.

"I'm not sure. My idea was to stay as long as Stan needed me."

"Needed you? Well, now you've found out he didn't . . . at all!"

"It could have been otherwise."

'So?'' he said calmly. "You were leaving me."

Candidly, she nodded. "In a way, I suppose I was. But I didn't have it in mind not to come back . . . *sometime*." She smiled, self-mockingly. "I didn't even take a bag with me."

He nodded tolerantly. "Which suggests you didn't intend to go at all."

"Do you really think so? Do you have it all figured out so well?" she asked.

"Well, you did come back."

"A good point," Clara admitted.

She noticed something—he didn't ask *why* she had come back.

Inconsequentially, he said, "'We live a fairly nice life."

"Yes, we do. No arguments about that."

"We take a few trips, we see people, we get along . . . don't we?"

He said that so often—*we get along*. Great! Better to get along than not to get along. Was that *all*? Clara paused, taking her time, trying to keep her voice from cracking. She was feeling very emotional.

"I turned around and came back *because*"—she would answer the question herself—"it occurred to me it was a stupid thing to do—driving to Palm Springs because I had some crazy idea Stan would need me. Why me? Why would he suddenly need *me*?"

Tom was embarrassed for her, realizing, as she did, that they were only talking around the subject; but then, they didn't want to talk about it, did they? Far too dangerous to do that.

Stoutly, he said, "What's so weird about *assuming* somebody might need you?"

Clara lifted her shoulders hopelessly. "Does it make any difference if I'm here or not?"

"Well, *of course it does*. . . . You think I don't need you—is that it?"

"We go on . . . day after day . . ."

"Well?"

"I'm like a clock. Wind me up and put me on the mantle and I tick away. When it's time, wind me up some more."

His lips firmed impatiently. But then he joked, "So now you're a *clock*?"

"That's right. I tick away," she repeated. "The point is, what difference does it make if you wind me up or not?"

"Now, Clara . . ."

"So, what *does* it all amount to?" She stared at him accusingly. "You're not all that satisfied with the way things are—you're going to teach your course. That shows *you* need something else, maybe a contact with *youth*."

Tom smiled knowingly. "Now we're growing old, is that it? Feeling sorry for ourself."

He made her angry. He was always so goddamn sure of things, patting her on the head as if she were some poor, half-mad, misguided slut.

"Martha!"

"What about her?"

"Your contact with youth!"

"What do you mean?"

"Nothing." But she did mean a lot more than *nothing*, and she might as well say what she meant. Without being explicit; there were ways. "She's your contact with youth, that's what I mean. You laugh at all her jokes, you think she's so goddamn hilarious—because you want your *youth*!"

Tom looked relieved. Was that all there was? This very blunted accusation, if it came to that? Was that all she was worried about—his fixation on youth? Was that all? No—Clara plunged ahead.

"Martha is very lucky. I've been thinking about the mistake I made with Stan . . ."

Now, finally, would he get the point? Would he understand and at last begin to squirm? Not if he could help it.

"You think Martha is so much like you," Tom said analytically, "but she's not. She's a lot different. She's not such a sentimentalist, for one thing."

"I hope not," she said sternly.

"Don't you believe, anyway, that things happen as they're meant to happen?"

Did she have to thank him outright for not running away with Martha and ruining her life?

Oh, thank you, kind sir, for your nonbinding educational effort.

"I hope it is fate,' Clara said. "I'd hate to think I've done all these dumb things on my own hook."

Tom frowned. "I don't think it's such a dumb thing . . . you and me."

His hand shook a little as he lifted his second martini. Oh yes, he'd be projecting now, a few more minutes of confrontation and he'd walk out of the room a free man. But Clara was not going to let him off so easily.

"I can't keep offering myself up," she said. "It's no great career just being somebody's mistress."

Stiffly, stung, he said, "As I recall, we got married."

"So what's the difference?"

As far as Clara could see, she had undertaken to be there when he wanted or needed her, promised to do his bidding, and so on, all the things any good mistress contracted to do.

"All right," Tom said curtly, "so what's the answer?"

This is where he had her.

"If I said I just *finally* have to start being me, you'd laugh."

Tom shook his head patiently. "No, I'd think it was a little strange. But I wouldn't laugh."

"Maybe I should be more like Ludmilla was, Ludmilla, who didn't give a goddamn about anything and *always* did her own thing. Am I right about her?"

He tried a little laugh. "I . . . don't think you know what she was really like."

"I think I have a good, general idea."

He paused long enough to let her see what was on his mind. "Are you thinking about all her men, her promiscuity?"

Men? Not necessarily. Not primarily. No, Clara had truly been thinking more about the reckless abandon with which Ludmilla had apparently lived her life—with no regard for the consequences, or really, if it came to that, of the effect her actions had on other people. That was a good part of it: Clara had always been too concerned about other people.

With deadly, killing calm, Tom added, "I'm not as dense about women as you might think. I am interested . . . in being nice, in treating *other people* well."

"I'm sure you are—in theory. *Academically.*"

"Now, Clara! Goddamn it—be fair!"

"I am. I'm trying to be. Look . . ."

An idea was forming, out of nothing it was coalescing within her mind. Yes, she'd been sure that if she thought about it

long enough, some kind of plan would emerge. Out of the blue
. . . no, not exactly, because the elements had been there. But
he didn't have to know how improvised it was.

"You see, Tom," Clara said slowly, "I've been thinking
about this for quite a while. I think I'm going to go back up to
the vineyard for a while. . . ."

He was truly dismayed. His face showed it. Nothing she
said could have caused him more discomfort—to leave, but not
to leave. To go away but not to run away.

"To do what? Why?"

"Well . . . You remember Fred's idea? I'd try to take up
the slack as best I could."

"But what the hell would you do?" Now he was disgusted;
the idea appalled him. Obviously it wasn't what he'd had in
mind for an answer. "And the gallery? What about that?"

Clara shook her head impatiently. "It runs itself . . . practically. I'd come down a day a week, maybe two. Biff can handle
it. I'll get *Martha* to help. And there's a lot for me at the
vineyard, more than at the gallery. Alberto has never been
comfortable working with the advertising people, for one thing."

"Sure," he grunted, swiftly polishing off his second drink.
"Sure, you can make a good case for whatever you want to do."

Strictly speaking, however, it was not required that he
agree, or even sympathize. At a certain point a person had to be
brutal. This was part of personal responsibility.

"Tom," she said patiently, "it may not sound like much,
what I want to do. But it's very important to me."

"And that's what counts, isn't it?"

"Now, Tom . . . try to follow me. You're going to be at
Berkeley—"

"A couple times a week, Clara!"

"It's as easy to commute to Morelli as from the city."

He began to understand. No, he was not totally dense.
Slow, yes, but not dense. "So—you expect to see me from time
to time?" he asked ironically.

Clara smiled at him, ever so gently, ever so understand-
ingly, ever so . . . patiently. Just a little bit *patronizingly*. "Up
to *you*, Tom."

He nodded, eagerly, like *a little boy*. "You're right. It's
not a bad drive . . . and I'd only be down there, like I say, two
or three days a week. But what would I do at Morelli?"

Clara shrugged indifferently. "How should I know? Write a book. Your memoirs. *Memoirs of a Casanova . . .*"

Tom left instructions that they be paged in the restaurant, but by the time they finished dinner and went back upstairs, there was no word from Rossiter. Or Seth . . . or Martha. At nine-thirty he called Richlands. Peat, the butler, answered, and Tom asked if Seth Addey was in the house. Well, was Prince Spurzov there? Alex came on abruptly. From across the room Clara could hear him baying. Like many older people who are slightly deaf, Alex tended to shout at the phone. Next Tom punched Rossiter's number. Clara eavesdropped with more care. The phone rang for quite a while, long enough for Clara to suggest that maybe Seth had come by to take Rossiter out to dinner . . . or something.

But then he did answer.

"Ross? Me again. Are you all right?"

As rapidly as Alex had run on before, Rossiter picked his words deliberately. Tom talked to him gently—how carefully, respectfully one treated a person in Rossiter's situation.

"Clara's *very worried* about you, Ross—you're sure everything is okay? We can get over there in a jiffy." Tom glanced at Clara. What was Rossiter saying?

Tell Clara I'm free!

Tom turned from the phone. "He says you shouldn't worry. He's fine . . . just a little tired. It's been a hell of a day. . . . Rossiter says he hopes he'll get to see us before we leave for San Francisco."

"Well . . . we should, shouldn't we?" Clara looked out the window, having heard the helicopter. No, the emergency was over.

"I'm kind of tired myself."

Tom would want to read a little and probably watch the local TV news to see if there'd be anything on the bloody end of Serena Addey, wife of a local stockbroker. And then to bed. The maid had been in while they were downstairs, the bed was turned, and back from where Clara sat, it looked crisp, pristine, unmussed by moist, drenched, wet exertion.

Tom came to stand beside her at the window. Tentatively, gently, he put his arm around her waist.

"To hell with it," he muttered. "Ross'll be okay. We can't worry about him. That doesn't help."

"No, not at all. Of course he'll be all right. And think—it turns him loose. He'll be able to do anything he wants," she said, sort of wistfully. But not sadly, or even more than moderately wistfully.

"I think I'll read the paper," Tom said.

No, Clara shouldn't wait for him. She undressed and climbed into bed nude, thinking she'd put him to the test. She had a book too, and as he sat outside making a crackling racket with the newspaper, Clara read, tried to read, made believe she was reading, and finally turned off the light and lay there thinking about what she'd told him.

Already, she realized hopelessly, the importance of what she'd said would be sliding away.

Oh, Clara was just talking, you know; by morning she'll have forgotten the whole thing.

Wrong.

It occurred to her again that he hadn't been interested *at all* in why she'd come back, *why* she hadn't continued on to Palm Springs. So *why* had she come back?

Thinking of that, and the other, what had happened here in this bed, or what had not happened, Clara willed herself to fade away. Forget him, it, everything, and sleep. But then she couldn't fall asleep either.

Finally Tom finished the paper and went to the bathroom, and *finally*, muttering to himself, came into the bedroom, sighing so ponderously you'd thought the world had fallen on him.

But it hadn't. Mercilessly, wide awake, Clara rolled over. How awful she could be. But stimulated, inspired, aroused, she would make her point. She could have gone for his jugular first. But did not. She grabbed a leg, a piece of his tail, chuckling fiendishly, knowing he wouldn't understand.

"I'm Clara!"

Chapter
Thirty-Seven

*I*t was all over now but the denouement. Rossiter congratulated himself that he'd handled the whole messy business with the greatest of aplomb, as people might have said.

When the authorities had finished with the remains of Serena and Bud, a cremation was arranged—he wondered if they did them as one lot or two—and now Rossiter was the proud possessor of two urns full of ashes. Strange, when the human body was thusly reduced, it resulted in so little, ended, as it were, in such insignificance that even the slight decoration around the lip of the pot was more impressive. In volume Bud didn't appear to take up any more space than his daughter, and the two urns weighed precisely the same, within a couple of ounces either way.

The main thing was that it was over. The police hadn't come up with anything more brilliant than their first finding—that father and daughter died by shotgun blast at the hands of assailants unknown.

Rossiter placed the two urns in padding in the trunk of his car and drove away, into the future—or back to the past, if you wished to consider that the few years with Serena represented only a peculiar time warp.

Moving slowly, contemplatively, back uptown with his cargo, how grateful Rossiter was that the family had left him alone in his grief. Thankfully, they had not insisted on overwhelming him with sympathy or being there to share his hour of sorrow, as so many families expected to do.

This *hour* they were talking about . . . well, dare he say her name without beginning to shake, the Maid of Lourdes had absorbed the whole hour and then some. The only time Rossiter had been out of bed in the last two and a half days was to take a leak or answer the phone . . . and now to make this sad journey.

Tom Addey had called a couple of times and then given up.

And, of course, his mother, but she had not been as brief. Thelma was dreadfully sorry about it, sorry for Rossiter, but, to be absolutely frank, she had never much cared for Serena, as Rossiter probably knew.

"So I feel no great loss personally at her departure from the planet, Rossiter. My emotional reaction is somewhere between a neutral brown and gray."

"Taupe?" he suggested.

"Exactly."

His mother went on to say that Sandor Veruckt sent his deepest sympathy too, even though, as Thelma was quick to inform him, Sandor remained greatly miffed at Rossiter, Rossiter would know why, would he not? Yes, Rossiter did know why, he told her, and wasn't that just too goddamn bad! But he was not to worry, Thelma said, unhearing, for she had saved him.

Well, as a matter of fact, Rossiter was also greatly miffed at Sandor. For it was a remarkable, if depressing, fact, he learned from his secretary Marjorie as she read him his messages, that the Chester Arthur bid for Morris Communications had been reinstated. No sooner was the Diamond group out, in fact, than the deal was back on.

This was enough to make you puke—*if* you really cared that much.

But it was nothing to Thelma.

"My sons, my *worthy* boys. Forget your dear, dead wife for a moment, Ross—are you aware of a significant triumph your mother has enjoyed here in New York?"

"How could I be?"

"Rossiter! The dear man, Chet Arthur, our new leader, has let it be known that Wilkey Junior has six months to clean out his desk. My position at *Classics* is as solid as the Rock."

"Congratulations."

Rossiter wondered how this snobby woman, this conceited person he had trouble recognizing as his mother, would react to Lourdes . . . if it ever came to that.

"Thank you, darling. I owe it all to Sandor, everything—bless his soul!"

It was obvious that Thelma was in a jolly, almost giddy mood; she was a rainbow of spring colors. Confidentially, Thelma lowered her voice.

"Are you aware, Rossiter, that your brother and dearest Hildegard Beckmann are breaking up?"

No, Rossiter was not briefed on this matter.

"Hildegard will remain in New York . . . *working for me*," Thelma confided happily, "and Seth—I don't know if I'm at liberty to tell you—Seth will be appointed to a new, high post in Washington."

"Is that good?"

"Of course it's good, darling! Your brother will be in a position of great influence . . . I cannot tell you *where*."

Thelma commenced to bubble and lisp a soprano of joy over the phone. "I'm seeing such pinks, darling, pink, pink, pink—"

"Pink elephants, by the sound of it," Rossiter muttered.

"Don't be gauche! Tra-la, darling! Our wedding bells are in the offing. The tintinabulations of the bells, bells, bells—"

"Is somebody getting married?"

"Rossiter!" she barked. "You know very well Sandor and Thelma are to wed! And we expect you in New York for the event."

"I'll try to make it," he had said automatically.

"We do not take no for an answer, Rossiter!"

Actually, Rossiter had been thinking more in terms of Mexico. Those hours in bed with Lourdes had brewed exciting visions of exotic, erotic adventure south of the border. Lourdes spoke the language. . . . They would drink the beer and eat the food of life . . . tamales and chile relleno and guacamole and rice and chicken and fresh fish of every description . . . and they would *breed*. Rossiter would sell his house, the expensive cars, Serena's life insurance policy—if there was one, he didn't know—what about double indemnity? Think, he could have taken out a million dollars of insurance if somebody had tipped him off! Another great opportunity gone to hell—Lorenzo Diamond *could* have signaled . . . just a word!

Unfortunately, Rossiter had already discovered, the shapely little Hispanic sexpot wouldn't hear about Mexico, or anywhere south of the border. The farthest south she was willing to go was Disneyland. Lourdes actually began to tremble when you mentioned to her the great historical names of Mexico: Guadalajara, Baja, Merida . . . the Yucatan, Tijuana, Mazatlan.

When Rossiter said chicken and rice, Lourdes said hamburgers and french fries. God, life was sad; nothing was simple! There were cultural differences, to be sure. But in matters of the mattress, sheets, pillows, they were as one. Did it really matter that they didn't agree about food? Was food important to Rossiter when weighed against the violence, the acrobatics, the teeth-chattering totality of her embrace? No! Well? No . . . His mind became confused when he thought about Lourdes. She had great moves, his buddies would have said.

But what about her *eventually*? Of course, there was another reason she didn't want to hear about Mexico. Suspicion that once he got across the border, he'd dump here there like an unwanted animal. Would an intelligent man do a thing like that? Get rid of the hen that laid the golden eggs?

Rossiter remembered Clara only vaguely. But Mrs. Addey was his father's wife, was she not? There had been a moment, though; a window of opportunity had briefly opened, then closed.

Bang!

Speaking of which, Rossiter remembered just in time he'd promised Lourdes he would stop along Third Street somewhere and pick up some burgers and fries.

Out of the Frying Pan: not a bad name for a barbecue joint.

It was two P.M., more or less, when Rossiter pulled into the driveway and parked behind Serena's Mercedes convertible, spared by the Almighty from flying buckshot, and now returned, heavy with fingerprinting dust. And Tiny said she didn't want Bud's Cadillac. She was going to buy a new Porsche.

Rossiter wondered if the neighbors were peeking at him from behind their curtains or through the slats of their micro-blinds as he carried the cartons of food across the lawn, suddenly remembering, *Shit*, he'd forgotten the Cokes.

What is going on over there in the Addey house? He's alone there now, since she was murdered by the Mafia. They were always suspicious people. . . . 'Course he's got that maid, if she is a maid and not something else. . . .

Lourdes would be waiting for him inside the front door. No more white uniforms for her! No more clothes at all for her!

She'd let her black hair down—it hung to her waist—and her eyes would be shining humility and simple adoration.

Rossiter opened the trunk to take the ashes inside first.

Behind him a voice said, "Hey!"

Bud jumped out of Rossiter's hands and the urn shattered on the driveway. Gray matter spilled all over the concrete.

"Christ, Seth!"

"Brother Rossiter." Seth grinned at him in that sinister way of his. His nice smile was another guy's frown. "Sorry, I made you drop that. What was it anyway?"

"Bud."

Seth nodded suspiciously. Then he got it. "Oh, for crissakes, Slagger's ashes? Shit."

"It doesn't matter. Either here or Dodger Stadium."

Rossiter remembered about Lourdes being inside. Would she have seen Seth or was she already half undressed?

"Come on in," he said cautiously. Rossiter handed Serena to Seth, then kicked the shards of Bud's pot into the grass. The powdered ashes, on the order of flour, he sort of spread around with his foot. The sprinklers would finish the job; Bud would wind up as part of the topsoil—was there anything particularly wrong with that?

"I brought back some food . . . for the maid and me," Rossiter stammered. "Are you hungry?"

Seth shook his head. Rossiter took out the burgers and fries.

The moment they stepped into the house, Lourdes popped out of the kitchen, and wouldn't you know? At least she'd slipped on one of Serena's cotton dresses, but sure as hell, the top of it was all unbuttoned. Seth couldn't miss her firm, fine breasts.

A piece of limp black licorice hung out of Lourdes' thick-lipped mouth.

Seth stopped in his tracks, consternation breaking in his throat.

Lourdes emitted a little shriek. She was back in the kitchen so fast, you couldn't be entirely sure you'd seen her at all. But Seth obviously had.

"The maid. Her name is Lourdes."

Rossiter shrugged and smiled at Seth. It didn't really matter much; let Seth think what he wanted to think. Who cared? Whose business was it? So Bud had landed on the sidewalk, so

370

what? So Seth had seen some of Lourdes's stuff, so what? It was more interesting than Serena's; Seth was lucky he hadn't seen *those*.

Rossiter continued on into the living room. "Sit down," he told Seth. Rossiter retrieved Serena from Seth and, for want of a better place, he put her remains on the mantle, shoving the clock over a little to make room.

Nice jug, singular, Seth might have said, but he didn't have the wit. Instead, he remarked. "That's your fucking maid? Does she always walk around like that?"

"No, no, of course not." Rossiter wasn't required to explain. "So what's up, Seth?"

Seth wandered around, practically sniffing the place like a dog before settling down in the easy chair by the entrance to the little den.

"I'm leaving tomorrow. I came to say good-bye. And to see you're okay . . . which I guess you are," he said grimly.

"Yeah, I'm doing just fine."

"The old lady called you, didn't she?"

"Yes, yesterday . . . *I think*. I've been so busy. So you're finally going back. How long have you been here now?" Rossiter asked politely. He had to take the food out to the kitchen, but didn't know how to get from here to there. "It seems like a good long time."

"The longest month in historical time," Seth agreed, somehow angrily. He removed his glasses, put them back on. "Did Thelma tell you I'm not going back to Germany—as I told her to keep her mouth shut about?"

"Well . . ."

"Of course she did. Well, I'm being reassigned to Washington."

"Isn't that wonderful? What about a drink? Shall we drink to it?"

Seth nodded, relaxing a fraction. "I'll take a scotch if you've got one."

Rossiter smiled confidently. "Does Lourdes cook Mexican jumping beans?"

"And, do I . . . get to meet her?"

"If she'll come out. She's shy, like a little . . ."

"Mink?"

"No, not like a mink," Rossiter said. "I'll be right back. . . ."

Lourdes was standing by the sink. She'd buttoned up her dress and seemed to have slipped on a bra. Rossiter put down the burgers and fries and came up behind her, slipping his hands around her little body. She stiffened. Did women always have to react as if the worst had happened?

"It's my brother, Seth. My brother . . . *hermano* . . ." He chuckled. "Not Herman, *Seth*. My brother. Understand?"

She nodded and turned, eyes flighty with anxiety. Rossiter kissed her.

"Two scotches . . . coming up," he called.

Lourdes got the ice out. Rossiter loaded two glasses with it, then poured in two long shots of the best stuff he had in the house, which happened to be a Glenfiddich malt that he'd splurged on in a quick resupply expedition the day before.

"And you, Lourdes?"

She shook her head. "No, no." She didn't like hard liquor; he should've remembered a bottle of tequila.

"Come on." Rossiter gave her one of the glasses to carry and took her other hand and led the way out of the kitchen and into the living room, where Seth was standing again, inspecting without touching the urn of Serena's last hurrah.

"Lourdes," Rossiter said, "my brother Seth. Seth, this is Lourdes."

Meeting Lourdes was probably the last thing in the whole world that Seth wanted to do. But too bad. They'd have to know her eventually. Why not start right now?

Solemnly Seth took her tiny hand and shook it carefully, like it might break.

"How do you do?" Seth said mechanically, not a ray of sunshine available. "I'm very pleased to meet you."

Lourdes might have surprised Seth if he knew how little English she spoke. "I am happy to meet you," she said haltingly.

She did not have a bad voice, Rossiter realized for the first time, not bad at all. It was soft, a little husky from living in the wind too much, but clear, like a bell. Tintinabulations. When Lourdes had learned more of their lingo, she would be a verbal knockout, as well as an oral specialist.

Seth accepted his glass and Rossiter said, "Well, congratulations, little brother."

"Little brother?" Lourdes repeated worriedly.

"Yes," Seth said. "This one . . ." pointing at Rossiter, "very old!"

"No, no," she said gravely. "Not old. Young, like a boy." She nodded for emphasis, then said, "Excuse me."

As Lourdes left the room, Seth pointed. "You don't let her wear shoes?"

Rossiter laughed. He hadn't noticed. Lourdes was barefoot.

"That's what they say," Seth observed dryly. "Keep 'em barefoot and pregnant, old boy!" he added with a nasty laugh.

"Hey, hey, buster! Take it easy! She'll bring us some tortilla chips," Rossiter muttered uneasily. "So, *where were we*? You're staying in Washington."

Seth nodded. "I think they want me where they can watch me. I know too much."

"Cut it out! They want you there because you're a valuable man."

"Bullshit!" Seth was obviously not at all convinced of that. "I'm going to be working for Krash Kraszewski—keep that under your hat. The famous old spy master," Seth added maliciously. "Everybody calls him the President's polack."

"And Hildy?"

Seth's information trickled like a hoarder's gold. "She is staying in New York, working on Thelma's magazine. Then I dunno, she'll go back to Munich . . . or whatever."

"I'm sorry, Seth. Is that bad?"

"Bad?" Seth blinked in surprise. "Shit, no! It's fine! I don't trust her anymore. And I can tell you exactly why. Never mind. Look, I've still got my apartment in Munich." His eyes slitted. "Why don't you hop over there for a while? Take a vacation. Get away . . . cool off. It's in a beautiful spot right in the middle of town . . . *very secure* too."

Rossiter's heart leapt. Why not? What had he to lose? He had only to pack a bag and be on his way.

"That is . . . unless I'm too late." Seth glowered toward the kitchen. "I hope I'm not. *Devoutly* . . . Ross, *who is she*? Some goddamn Sandinista? *Probably* a Sandinista. How'd she worm her way in here?"

"She's a Mexican, Seth. She's the maid," Rossiter said patiently.

"A plant! What does she know *about me*?"

Rossiter grinned at him soothingly. After all, Seth was his brother.

"She hasn't got an idea *in the goddamn world* about you. Until I introduced you, she probably thought you're an insurance agent come to hand me big money, double indemnity for the murder of my beloved wife."

"Bad joke, brother," Seth said tersely. On the mantle, Serena's urn seemed to hop—were they *all* going mad? Rossiter half expected her to pop her cork and materialize above them like a big, bad genie in a puff of sour eau de cologne.

You insignificant son of a bitch, you are so insignificant to say a rotten, fucking thing like that!

Heavily, daring Serena to do her worst, Rossiter said, "Lourdes is ten times smarter than Serena . . . ten times better. . . ."

"Yeah? And ten times what else, Ross?"

"Never mind! Why'd you break up with Hildy, then? I thought you were supposed to get married."

"Bullshit! That's what everybody thought. It was *never* in the cards, in retrospect. She's a golddigger with *career* branded on her ass. . . ." Seth peered around bitterly, swung his eyes again toward where Lourdes had disappeared. "Can't we go outside and talk? I hate closed rooms."

Rossiter couldn't conceive of anybody wanting to bug a house as insignificant as this one. But if it made Seth happy . . . He took him out the French doors into the garden. Seth didn't speak again until they were standing on the other side of the pool; he stared at the swirling activity at the filter—dead bugs, a handful of leaves, a skim of scum out of the southern California skies.

"Hildy's left for New York," Seth said. "Alex took her and Rose down to his bank vault for a look at the famous Spurzov Egg. *She saw it!* It does exist—the old lady is going to be mightily pissed off. She always claimed there was no such egg, or if there was, it was a fake."

"How's anybody supposed to know for sure? Alex has kept it such a secret."

Seth nodded amusedly. This would please him. "The bank wouldn't allow any pictures, though. Hildy's already renamed it—the Lost Egg of the Fabergé Workshops!"

Seth sipped carefully, as if he wasn't quite sure of the drink.

"That's malt whiskey, Seth. You better like it!"

"I do, I do," Seth said absently. Now he was staring down at a spider with long willowy legs. "Hildy's a disloyal bitch. . . ." He glanced at Rossiter. "You know, working for Kraszewski is kind of a political appointment. When the administration changes, I'll probably be out on my ass." His lips pulled back in another hateful smile. It wasn't his fault, Rossiter warned himself; Seth's sense of humor was simply twisted. "I guess I'll have to go to work for Sandor if that happens—he more or less invited me."

Rossiter shook his head. Best not to encourage that idea.

"Sandor . . . is a *pisser*," he muttered. What else nice could he say?

"Well, don't worry—I couldn't *stand* doing that job of yours. Jesus!"

"Not that bad," Rossiter said.

"Counting beans . . . moving sand? No, thanks." Seth glared at him in a fairly friendly way, then suddenly got to the point. "My ass got kind of burned in Washington, big brother," he confided. "There's this woman. Sol Betancur's wife—you heard us talking about her, Clara's old friend . . ." Sure, Rossiter had heard; he did pay attention. "I don't know what's happened to her. She had a really sick relationship with that goddamn Ben Gazi." Seth seemed to recoil from the mere memory. "Now Sol has put her away. Supposedly she's flipped out. I'm not sure of that, see? And I don't know what to do about it."

Rossiter was hearing more than he wanted, or should know. "What *can* you do?" he asked slowly.

Seth scowled. "That's it. *Nothing.* Understand, I'm not in love with her or anything. We just got . . . close. I could've gone hog wild but didn't . . . thank God," he mumbled worriedly. "Why am I telling you this, one good reason why?"

"Because you want to tell *somebody*."

Seth nodded. "That makes a certain amount of sense. You can *never, never* repeat any of it, though—remember."

"Would I?"

"The problem is I have no way of knowing whether everything Alice Betancur told me was true—or any of it—about Sol and Ben Gazi and the whole crazy thing." Seth kicked at the daring spider. "Goddamn daddy longlegs. That's one of the things I never liked about California, goddamn bugs!"

"Most of them are harmless," Rossiter pointed out quietly.

Seth glanced at him again, his eyes for a second frightening.

"Maybe I'm telling you . . . well, if anything happened to me . . . you understand?"

"*In Washington?*"

Seth snarled, "Don't be stupid. It can happen anywhere."

He strolled stiffly from the pool, toward the back gate which led into Garbage Alley. "Sol Betancur is a very powerful man, Ross. Alice Betancur told me really dynamite stories and, well, if there's any truth to it . . . You never know."

"So?" What was the sensible thing? "Tell your boss."

Seth shook his head. "Forget it. I think he already knows—he won't want to hear it from me. Then he might have to do something about it. We're talking high political stuff, Ross!"

Seth remembered about Lourdes again; his eyes swept the back of Rossiter's house.

"Anyway," he continued, "keep in mind what I've told you. . . . We'd better go back inside before your tootsie gets on the phone."

"Goddamn it, Seth! I wish you'd stop—"

"You think I'm crazy, don't you?"

"No, not crazy. *Paranoid*, like I told you before," Rossiter said irately. "Forget about Lourdes—she's as harmless as a duck."

Seth didn't take offense this time at being called paranoid. Altogether, despite Hildy's departure, he was in a happier mood, if such a thing were possible.

"I mean . . . I want some of them tortilla chips," Seth grinned. They strolled back into the den. Seth even put his arm around Rossiter's shoulder in the most brotherly of all possible gestures. "I've got good reason to be paranoid, I can tell you."

"Maybe."

"That goddamn day in Moscow didn't help—I don't think I told anybody, but the guy I was meeting, he's dead. They fixed him good, Ross." Seth flopped down in the leather chair and stared intently at Rossiter. "You know how it was?"

"No. Not at all," Rossiter murmured.

"Simple enough," Seth said. "Nick—that was his name—and I would usually go for a little stroll in Red Square—I always figured the best place to meet was right out in the open. A thousand people could see us, including the guards in front of Lenin's Tomb, if they wanted to look. As if by accident, we run into each other. Not impossible by any means—he worked nearby and I was usually down at the GUM anyway, seeing what they had in the way of fur hats and canned goods and imports from Red China. Part of my job. So we'd just happen to bump into each other . . . once a month or twice, maybe stroll over and watch the change-of-the-guards goose-stepping. It worked well. . . ." Seth's eyes turned dark and guilty. "Until one day we got rushed by a dozen KGB guys. I got hauled in one direction . . . the last thing I saw of Nick was a white face being pushed into a black car. *And that is it.*"

Rossiter nodded. "I'm glad you told me. I'm . . . flattered you've told me."

Seth scowled. "Don't be silly. I'm just saying . . . *so you see*?" He pointed at himself. "And now, I'm into the same shit *here*?" He shook his head and shrugged. "Forget it. But *don't* forget it. . . . Say, where's the goddamn tortillas? My ice is melting. . . ."

"I'll get some more."

"No, no, I've got to get going anyway." Seth's eyes were blurry. "I'm sorry about what I said. I'm sure she's terrific. Anyway, there's something else I wanted to tell you. I've got somebody . . . somebody . . ."

Rossiter smiled. "Yes, yes? Christ, it's like pulling teeth—do I dare ask her name or is that strictly confidential, top-secret stuff too?"

"She's a journalist and I'm crazy about her," Seth growled, "and her name is Katie Corcoran."

"And she works in Washington."

"Yes."

"And?"

Seth looked puzzled. "And *what*? Oh—*and* I trust her."

"*You* trust a journalist?"

Astonishingly, almost frighteningly, Seth laughed, openly, freely, without reservation or qualification or suspicion.

"Yes, I do. That is weird, isn't it?"

Lourdes came to the door so quietly—remember, where she'd come to commiserate with him all those days ago, beyond recall. She was carrying a big bowl of tortilla chips.

"Ah," Seth sighed, "there we go. Thanks, little lady, I sure do 'preciate that."

"Clown," Rossiter said. "I remember—you used to be a goddamn clown, didn't you?"

"Still am, big brother, underneath all the layers, playing goddamn clown games."

Chapter Thirty-Eight

With the tip of her carefully crafted fingernail Thelma Drysdale turned the pages of *Classics* from personal shopping hints to Horoscope and studied the prognosis for her sign.

Aries, a child of the light and the wind. All well with personal relationships . . . Career blossoming . . . Good news from faraway places, whatever that meant. By and large, yes, the outlook for February was acceptable; it matched the facts.

Chet Arthur, Thelma's new best friend, was taking control of Morris Communications, and dear Sandor had seen to it that Thelma Drysdale would not suffer in the process. Chet was a reasonable man. Of course, the *outlook* for Wilkey Morris Junior, creature of the cusp, was far from optimistic—*poor* Wilkey Junior, Thelma told herself gleefully, victoriously, vindictively! Bright reds and yellows!

Well, then, other things had become less important. One in particular—the idea of the Ludmilla Spurzova takedown had lost much, if not all, luster.

What, indeed, would the New Woman really care about an old lady of undoubted ill virtue? Thelma was sorry; but that was what she'd have to tell Hildegard Beckmann upon her return from the coast with her pictures and all the gossip.

Thelma had laid down a streamlined new editorial policy for a recent meeting with beloved Chet Arthur; she and Esther Murat had worked it out. The entire strategy was reducible to three quarters of a page of Thelma's rose-colored office stationery.

Classics policy is crystal clear, yet always open to discussion, debate, and revision. Our reader is the New Woman, she who is in control. Our New Woman invariably has a career of her own; she also, beyond question, manages a home and a family of (whatever number of children: one point eight, two point two, whatever). Men like to think women are not capable of such organization, of delegation of time and energy. But women are most definitely capable of that . . . and much more.

Classics editorial policy, though it would not be stated so outright, is that women are superior to men in every intellectual and many physical respects—it is, after all, the women who guide husbands and children, cook the meals, do the household chores, and transmit themselves and what is left of the husband to the next generations. . . .

But physically, Hildegard had observed one night, men were the stronger.

So were horses and oxen stronger than women . . . and so? Women used horses and oxen . . . and men . . . to pull things, lift things, and plough the fields; mammals of a different number of legs. It could be argued that women were of a different and superior species altogether—as different from men as men were from chimps. Women had graciously consented to breed with this inferior species. Eventually in this way, thanks to woman-kind, the world would be populated by intelligent beings.

By the end of the present century, women would pretty well be running this country—a woman president could not be more than twenty years away. Very soon women would be handing down the important legal decisions—of course! Women had better judgment than men. Remember, we see it every day, the sculpture of Blind Justice—always a woman, blindfolded, holding the scales. Never a man, and why should this be? Because, if not blindfolded, a woman would deliberately tip the scales? Because Justice should be blind and a woman? Or because Justice, like a woman, is fickle.

No! The answer was that *even blind* the Lady of Justice is fair.

And so, fair was fair! At the moment, beautiful victory over Wilkey Morris Junior was far more satisfying for Thelma than rubbing Tom Addey's nose in it once more, especially if, as Hildegard had insinuated, Tom was so willing, if not eager, to be included in any exposé they did of Ludmilla Spurzova.

The message to women was that if it didn't hurt, there was not much point in twisting a man's arm.

Of course, it was a rare pleasure to torture Wilkey Junior. Just then if somebody had rushed into Thelma's office to report that Wilkey had jumped to his death, Thelma would've been disappointed. Suicide was too easy a way out for the scarlet-faced little pipsqueak. Humiliation was only meaningful if the Humiliatee was around to suffer; and the Humiliator there to observe him suffering.

The only thing that would have made it any better for Thelma was if Wilkey Junior had rushed hatefully into her office to try for a last word. Thelma could dream him there, create him in imagination, a red carnation stuck in the lapel of his best gray suit, a canary-yellow tie against a two-toned blue-white shirt, his chubby face inflamed with the inverse passion of defeat.

Well, I suppose you're happy now that you've been able to stick the knife in my back, cut my throat, and snip off my balls, Thelma!

I beg your pardon, young man?

She would have stared at him like a high priestess down the length of her long nose and told him with the greatest dispassion that she viewed his debacle with the greatest of indifference.

You old cunt, the only reason you got away with this was because you let that filthy fucking Hungarian slip you the salami, that's how you did it!

And in reply to such vileness one simply stared, as if at a half-dead worm.

You're just an old hooker like all the rest of them—so he would've screamed, had he been there, prostrate before her, at Thelma Drysdale's mercy, the poor, dull lad.

Fortunately the phone rang before Thelma could conjure up more unpleasant sightings of Wilkey Morris Junior.

It was Sandor. His buttery voice lit the late afternoon gloom. He was confirming that they would meet later. They had a date for six P.M. at a Fifty-seventh Street gallery. Sandor had invited Thelma to pick out a few pictures. He was undecided: Did he want the A. S. Breslauer *Choppy Seas off Cap D'Antibes* or L. Radley's impressionistic *Young Girls Frolicking Around at Lunch Under the Trees*?

"Sandor, I'm expecting Hildegard back from California. . . ."

He sighed deeply. "Darling, bring her along, if you like. That would be nice, yes. . . ."

Thelma was not so sure. Sandor had shown an interest perhaps too intense in Hildegard Beckmann. When the two of them began rattling away in German, God knew what they were saying.

And then, suddenly, Hildegard was there, knocking timidly at Thelma's office door.

"Come in, come in," Thelma cried out. "My . . ." Hildegard looked worse for the weather. Her loden coat was shiny with damp and her cheeks were red, even more inflamed than by natural shyness.

"Delightful girl!" Thelma almost distrusted her own pleasure at seeing Hildegard Beckmann again. "Sit down! Tell us about California!"

Us? Hildegard looked around.

"I mean the *imperial Us*." Thelma smiled, so strenuously that she felt her noontime makeup cracking.

Hildegard unbuttoned her coat, and without taking it off, sat down opposite Thelma in the chair reserved for employees.

"Was it a trying time?" Thelma demanded, leading her to speak, to tell all. Hildegard shook her head. "And Seth? Is it over, you and he?"

"Yes, it is so," Hildegard said. Her face showed no emotion. "But . . ." She twisted her shoulders, minimizing any pain. "So be it. Besides, I must say I do not feel badly for it!"

"Oh, no?" Interesting, Thelma thought. She tried to remember how she'd felt about Tom at the time of rupture. More of a burning desire for revenge, it would have seemed, then abject misery . . . or both.

Whatever feeling of sadness Hildegard might have had, she shook off with ease. "Well, then, I may report to you now, Thelma, that I have seen the Egg, the Spurzov Egg!"

"*Have you?*" Thelma nodded; but really, as she'd been saying before, it didn't much interest her anymore. "And the Prince? How is the *old rogue*?"

Old rogue, yes. Indeed. There was no other way to describe the aging roué, the lady killer. . . .

Hildegard smiled guardedly. "I think you would probably say: he has not changed in the least."

"And you passed him my best regards? Did he remember

me? What did he say?" Thelma was very interested to hear about this part of it.

"He said to give you a large kiss for him," Hildegard said slowly. "He wanted to know how you were getting on—and were you as lovely as ever?"

"Old rogue," Thelma murmured, "delicious old liar and flatterer. A devil with the women, Hildegard."

"And with you too, Thelma," Hildegard recalled slyly.

Yes, well, Thelma had made a mistake, hadn't she, hinting at lunch that day that she'd dallied, ever so briefly, with Prince Alexei.

"There was a short and tempestuous affair, Hildegard," Thelma stated, making it clear she was not going to elaborate. "You're aware of what was going on at the time."

Why did Hildegard bring it up, then? And why was Thelma even willing to discuss such old business? To prove that she was a woman of great experience with men? Surely Hildegard would have gleaned that from Thelma's affair with Sandor Veruckt.

But Thelma was still not entirely convinced this was the right thing to do. Thelma had some doubt about Sandor. Hildegard, naturally, was aware that Thelma overnighted now and then at Sandor's, he once in a while at her place. But Hildegard couldn't know all the circumstances—though they kept to separate rooms, Sandor made a practice of slinking in after lights-out attired in a silk dressing gown much like Noel Coward's—though Sandor was not as skinny as Noel had been; he was a porky Central European. Perhaps it had to do with the paprika. Sandor, at the age of sixty-two or whatever he truly was, was as active *sexually* as a thirty-year-old Ivy Leaguer or yuppie careerist. It was possible, Thelma would have to admit—she had experienced more in the way of *rapture* with Sandor that she ever had with Thomas Baker Addey, or even Alex, if it came to that or had ever come to that, or the one or two others Thelma had taken on since Tom Addey as a means of staying au courant in the ways of the New Woman. After all, Thelma had always rationalized, one could not advise the New Woman on the facts of life if one didn't know about them from experience.

Poor Hildegard. Thelma wondered if she'd understand.

"The Prince would not open the Egg, however," Hildegard complained, "so there is no way I can tell you about the workings of the inside—though he *told me* it contains an intricate scene of Slavic orgy, a clockwork orgy including the faces of all his family.''

"Indeed.'' Thelma smiled scorchingly. "I never saw the Egg, never mind about a 'cock-work orgy,' Hildegard.''

"Clockwork, Thelma,'' Hildegard corrected her humorlessly. "But I am not some expert, so whether this Egg is genuine or not, I could not say.''

"*It is a fake*, Hildegard,'' Thelma said loftily. "That goes without saying—as fake as the Prince himself. But . . .'' Now she would hand out the bad news. "It matters nothing now, dear. . . . We've decided to spike the Ludmilla Spurzova story for the time being, maybe forever. I'm sorry. I know you'll be disappointed.''

Hildegard shrugged. "No, not especially. I was able to take many pictures of the house, Richlands, and to talk at great length with Rose Richards—''

"Rose Richards?''

Hildegard smiled in her secretive way—an evil little smirk on her face.

"Rose Richards is the wife—separated—of Mr. Richard Richards, whose family owns Richlands. You see, Ludmilla was married to Mr. Richards's father, Rodney Richards, And so—''

"*I see*,'' Thelma said crisply, "so this Rose Richards has taken Richlands. And wherefore, then, Alex Spurzov? Is he to be thrown out?''

"No.'' Hildegard shook her head wisely. "Rose Richards is the new *inamorata* of Alex Spurzov. There is talk of the two marrying.''

Thelma's face must have fallen a good six inches.

Very carefully, she said, "That *is* . . . a news item.'' Hildegard seemed to enjoy reporting it too. "And how old is this Rose Richards?''

"I would say thirty-four or thirty-five, at the very most, Thelma.''

"My dear! That . . . old rogue,'' Thelma murmured. "I am quite . . . *devasté*!''

Hildegard laughed brittlely. "It is a relationship of some great passion, I think, Thelma—but then, who can say with any exactitude? The whole house, Richlands, reeks of depravity. Bedlam, the Prince himself calls it. The butler is mad, and Rose, if I may say so—''

"You may!"

"Rose is an innocent. You would not believe, Thelma, that such a young woman can be so in love with such an old man—it is remarkable," Hildegard cried.

"Perhaps there's a story *there*, darling," Thelma said acidly.

"But," Hildegard thrust ahead warmly, "I, for one, am pleased to be away from them *all* and back here . . . with . . ." She lifted her head and stared directly into Thelma's eyes, directly, searchingly, but at the same time, so very vulnerably. "With . . . *you*," she completed her sentence.

"Ah . . ." What to say to that? How to handle Hildegard Beckmann, surely a descendant at least in emotion of the great artist. "And, well, Hildegard, I'm so happy to have you back here . . . *with me*!"

She had to be careful. *The walls were glass.* Unaccustomed languidness came over Thelma's legs, a logy sense of sinking toward the very molten red-hot, vermilion center of the Earth, where dwelt the Devil himself. The feeling was of delicious, all encompassing dread, but abject fascination. Thelma had never *really* been sure about Hildegard, what with Seth mixing up the logic.

"I . . . I have a date with Sandor at the Keating Gallery on Fifty-seventh, darling," Thelma said softly, her voice not quite as powerful as it had been. "He is choosing between a Breslauer and a Radley for the house in the country. . . ."

Perhaps, one weekend, how delightful, they could all drive up to Sandor's place on the Hudson. . . .

"Rose Richards also owns a Breslauer," Hildegard murmured huskily. "She made a great to-do about it—it is a portrait in gouache: *Rodney Richards with Carpenter's Awl*. Richards, of course, was a big builder of California homes, post-war—"

"Yes, yes, I understand, Hildegard, I do understand. At any rate," Thelma said breathlessly, "Sandor says you should come along. . . ." Thelma couldn't stop herself now. She stood up and came around her desk, reached to lay two fingers along Hildegard's flushed cheek. "Oh, you are quite warm. Are you chilly, feverish? Perhaps we should put off the rendezvous."

'No, no, Thelma. It is just the cold, from cold to very warm in here."

"And hot to cold," Thelma muttered. "How familiar . . . unfamiliar . . . everything is. . . ."

385

She felt so warm herself, Thelma did, uncustomarily dopey, as if, in a weird way, drugged.

"I will be so pleased to see Sandor," Hildegard murmured. "And with you. The three of us. Such fun! Such fun?"

Thelma nodded shyly, feeling a trifle frightened. "It will be fun, won't it, darling, the three of us, like old times. Such fun! Yes!"

Chapter
Thirty-Nine

*T*here was a story—Rose Richards recounted it later—a legendary story or a myth, that if another man—one of the servants, for instance—sees the king's wife naked, he has to be killed; either that, or he kills the king and takes his place. Peat had seen Rose naked as a plucked chicken, she admitted to Tom Addey, and more.

Maybe, or maybe not. Maybe the story had relevance for Peat.

When Tom arrived at Richlands that day to pick up Alex for their private business lunch, an orange-and-white ambulance was drawn up at the front door. Inside the house, in the foyer, two men in jump suits of the same color mixture were in the process of loading Peat into a wheeled stretcher and tying him down. Rose stood to the side with Alex, her hand to her mouth nervously, weepily.

"What's happening?"

"Peat has had an accident," Alex said glumly. "We may have . . . *just barely* saved his life."

"Accident?" An echo. It seemed to Tom for an instant, a discouraging point in time, that there had been little around here recently but accident and sudden death.

Unfeelingly, Alex said, "The stupid fool was in the butler's pantry playing with the toaster and came within a whisper of electrocuting himself."

"Poor, poor Peat," Rose whispered.

"Poor, poor idiot," Alex said stuffily.

One of the ambulance attendants turned to remark jarringly, "Do you stick your hand in cold water and try to grab a piece of toast at the same time?"

"Suicide?"

Alex stared at Peat's inert body. "Who knows?"

The other ambulance man said, "We got his heart going. But no way of knowing how long he was out."

"Where are you taking him," Tom asked, "so we can check on him later?"

One ambulance man, heavy, with a florid face, stared at Tom Addey as if he were missing a link. Under the jump suit, Tom noticed, he was wearing a button-down shirt with a striped tie; there was a pair of power shoes on his feet, oxblood cordovans. Something odd in that.

"Off to the, uh . . . Hospital of Heavenly Termination," he finally said.

"A Catholic place," Alex explained.

"Well, there we are, all zipped up!" The other ambulance man was more jovial, thinner, and clearly the boss. "We're on our way, folks. He'll be fine, just fine . . . not to worry. They'll buzz you later as to his condition."

The two men wheeled Peat out the door, and efficiently, since Peat was not a heavy man, slipped the stretcher into the back of the ambulance. They slammed the doors and a second later were on their way down the driveway.

"*Well!*" Alex shook his head grimly.

Rose said, "I think we should let Dick know. Will you call him, Tom?"

"Okay."

"Dick will want to make sure Peat is okay—Peat was going to move over there anyway."

"Rose," Tom said, "I can tell you that everything's been worked out with Dick."

"Oh, good." Rose flattened herself against Alex's thin frame, hugging him for security. "Then *we* can begin making *our* plans . . . *at last*. Yes, darling?"

"Yes, Rosita . . . yes, yes." But Alex's mind was in the ambulance with Peat. "Do you know, Tom, we found all Ludmilla's gold jewelry—all the things I bought her from that Peruvian maiden . . . we found all of it in a laundry bag in Peat's closet. The *thieving scoundrel*!"

"Yes, and now this," Rose seconded.

"Now this?"

"The accident." She pouted. "Very inconsiderate. Do you think he *was* trying to kill himself?"

"I wouldn't know," Tom said.

"Nor I!" Alex exclaimed. "My little darling, as you know, Tom and myself are off for a business conference. You understand?"

"Sweetie," Rose said brightly, "I've got to get on the horn to arrange a maid or two . . . with Peat gone now. And the handyman is coming over. I have a little work I want . . . Lance . . . to do."

"Must get my jacket," Alex said. "I'll be back in a *mo*—"

Tom watched him take the staircase. He supposed that Alex, if he'd wanted to, could have done it two steps at a time.

"He's amazing," he marveled.

For answer, out of gratitude, Rose kissed his cheek. Her eyes filled with tears.

"He *is* amazing!" She snapped her fingers. "*He's special!* You know, Tom, lovers are a dime a dozen. But on a scale of one to ten, you see, Alex . . ." She laughed mischievously. "Alex is a *twelve!*"

"Good," Tom said, "good."

Too bad he wasn't more like Alex, more ruthless. For example, did Alex feel for stupid Peat? Was there any sympathy there? No, no more than Alex would have felt for a stray cat hit by a car, maybe even less. Martha, he thought to himself, feeling weak, Martha, save me! Come and get me, Martha! But Martha had said good-bye and Tom Addey was out in the cold. No more to stretch himself alongside that fragrant, surprising stranger. No more . . . He could look at the bright side—he'd had her the once at least.

Rose put her arm in his. She moved him out of the foyer, down the steps, and began to promenade him down the long gallery. It had surely become a familiar thoroughfare.

"I'm glad Dick is going to be reasonable," she remarked companionably. "I feel a lot better about him already. I shall have the girls, of course, my daughters, shall I not?"

"He's not going to fight you."

"The oldest girl was premature, you know," Rose said. "If

she'd been a boy, I'd have called him Peter. After the rabbit test. That's how I came to marry Dick. He wasn't always . . . *funny-peculiar*, you know.''

"No? I wonder what changed him?''

"I think he's simply a bisexual,'' Rose declared, then continued with a giant non sequitur; perhaps it pleased her to hop around like this. "By the way, we're planning the first of our afternoon charity things—I've been in touch with my people. The first at Richlands in years, God knows how long.'' She shook loose another idea. "Maybe that's what bothered Peat, the thought of all the work. But that's what we have a . . . handyman for. You and your wife are invited, of course, if you're still here.''

"We'll be long gone.''

"Two hundred fifty a couple—in aid of the Los Angeles Baroque Music Ensemble, surely a worthy cause. . . .''

Oh, yeah, Tom was tempted to say, for a couple of lousy glasses of wine and canapé or two or three? Not on your life!

"I'm so sorry about your son's wife,'' Rose suddenly remembered, "and her uncle . . .''

"Father. Bud Slagger. Thanks, but, well . . . that's life. And death, I guess.''

"You're thinking about poor Peat. He's been acting very strangely, you know, Tom. I should tell you so you'll know. . . . Alex, dear heart, he gets so angry, really livid, about it. Peat had taken to flashing . . . exposing himself. What would cause him to do that?''

"I don't know. Maybe all the grief around here unhinged him.''

"Yes.'' Rose stopped and put a finger to her lips, smiling daringly. "You may know, he was in love with all the previous Missus Richardses. The first of them, Messy Richards, died in the cellar. Something heavy fell on her head—I'm not sure of the details. And then, they told me, Peat tried to shoot himself. I don't know if you noticed the scar by his ear. . . . Next, of course, was the Princess, and she drowned in the pool. . . .''

Tom looked at her closely. "Are you saying Peat had something to do with these . . . accidents?''

"Oh, no!'' Rose denied it quickly, then as quickly added, "Of course, I *was* next on the list. Perhaps it's a good thing Peat was . . . removed. Though I was told . . .'' She never said by whom she'd been told these fascinating things. "Somebody said that Peat was very satisfactory for the first Mrs. Richards—she told *somebody* that he was *fantastic* in the ways of the boudoir. Playing gooses and ganders, as Alex says. I'll never know now, I guess."

"You're lucky."

"Yes. For sure! Messy told *somebody* Peat was so liquid in his ways it was like making love to a dishwasher." Rose laughed uproariously.

What had Alex promised him? That Rose was a second Ludmilla? Tom hadn't seen it yet—not until this moment. The wild laugh was reminiscent, very, and then the way she pulled herself to him, the way she looked like she'd eat him alive. The way . . . the way Tom would have thrown himself on the plate.

But then Alex reappeared. Luckily. Fortunately. It wouldn't do, no, not again.

"Well, Tom, I'm ready," Alex shouted down the gallery.

Yes, he'd want Tom away from her. *Get away from my property!*

"*Rose!*"

"We're coming, Alex." As she walked him dutifully toward Alex, Rose whispered out of the side of her mouth, "And then, of course, there was you, Tom—and Ludmilla."

After all these years, the Polo Lounge at the Beverly Hills Hotel remained Alex's favorite watering hole. He'd spent hours there in the old days with his chums—all the Russians, Toumanoff and Romanov, and Obolensky, a few of the dingy exiled German barons, a Hapsburg prince, a Maltese bridge player or two, and the women. The women!

Alex went into the toilet again while Tom arranged for their booth in the first room, then sat down to wait. He ordered a double martini, very dry, on the rocks with two big olives. Why not? He deserved it.

Well, what if it came to that He and Martha would have to move far from California, to some faraway island group, say the Seychelles, where no one had ever heard of the old Californian Addeys or of the wine-making Morellis, known to all.

Which was the very reason it would never happen. It would've meant the end for Martha Gates and Tom Addey. Particularly for Tom Addey. He had no wish to end his life as the aging and pathetic lover of a vibrant young Martha Gates, target for all the young studs' derision.

Or all the more reason it *should* happen, though: his last chance. Martha was more real to him now, with each passing day, then she'd been that afternoon in the hotel when she'd deceived him. As if she had been sitting right beside him, Tom felt every square inch of her, like a hot iron pressed against him; her smell of all good things—morning coffee and sunny linen and foreign hotel rooms, of the fragrance of the stranger, of more than that, of so much more, of the complete woman. She had kissed him like a virgin and he would never forget it.

He needn't worry. Clara was not going to let it happen. *She knew!* Yet she said nothing that established for a fact that she knew—or that she was angry, or hurt, or indifferent. In this simple strategy, all her new and vastly increased power was based. Wisely, Clara had even offered him the opportunity to flee. Or, if not to flee, to surrender. If he wished to interpret her move to Morelli Vines as a marital separation, he'd been free to do so . . . or not.

Clara Addey was one clever girl. She was to be admired, and feared.

But, Tom tried to cheer himself up, he would not be overly intimidated.

Gin martinis were still tasting very good, and he ordered another as he waited for his friend Alex Spurzov.

Poor Alex.

Poor Alex? Hardly! What a fabulous new chapter of life Alex had been granted: He had found Ludmilla again! How Tom envied him. But why? He had discovered a second Clara while the first was still with him. Or was she?

Watching as Alex appeared in the doorway and marched spryly across the room, it was also clear to Tom that a man like Alex Spurzov was capable of most anything. He could make of Rose anything he wanted. Another Ludmilla? That would be fine.

A jab of envy, a pang of regret hit Tom in the stomach.

"Hallo, Tom!"

Grinning like a monkey, Alex slapped Tom's shoulder and slid effortlessly into the leather booth. Alex was rebrushed and buffed, not a hair out of place; his blazer was crisp, pants pressed, tie and shirt like new. Some old men grew to be unkempt; not Alex. He was dressed to kill, or at least for seduction.

Laughing, Alex announced, "*And so,* Tom—the bloody banker would not allow a picture inside the vault. And I, *of course,* am not so insane that I would remove the Spurzov Egg from there."

"So that's the story. But Hildy did get to see it? A look is as good as a mile."

That had been the plan. Alex had made Hildy Beckmann witness to the existence of the Spurzov Egg. For Alex's purposes it didn't matter in the least whether she got a picture. It was actually better she hadn't.

"She became so excited, Tom, I can tell you, *passionate.* I could have had her there in the vault if we had been alone. . . ."

"Alex! You've got Rose."

Grimacing happily, Alex shrugged. "We are to rename the egg—it is to be the wandering egg of the Fabergé atelier. Ha, ha! Thanks to the genius of your ex-wife, the ever-lovely Thelma Drysdale."

Not that Tom cared one bit. It was all past, such past history, including Thelma Drysdale. How gloomy his life seemed now. Empty of hope. Was he doomed to fade away, to wither, to die? When the waiter came, Tom ordered another martini, not caring, Alex his usual: a Stoly on ice.

Alex put his hand earnestly on Tom's arm.

"Tom . . . my dear, I have had a look in the vault. You are my trustee, executor, whatever it is these ghouls call it. I hate to think of that day—*merde*! But it will come, I know. How dare it? To a man who enjoys life so much? It is *not fair*—are there not enough *unhappy* people around to fill the death draft?"

"Alex," Tom murmured sorrowfully, "I can't help you."

"Yes, you can! In one special way—I have decided when the monster comes for me, then I want little Rose to have my *Egg.* I have nothing else, only money and such, but nothing of *me.* The Egg should go to her, Tom. Can you draw that up, please? She has plenty of money, or will. . . ." He laughed wildly. "When you finish squeezing Dick Richards's nickel. Before you are through with him, my dear, that buffalo will be *shitting*!"

"I'll do that, Alex."

"What ho, my boy! *Cheer up!* How is it with you?"

"Not great, Alex. A little mixed up right now."

"Come to Paris! Rose and I will be off soon. We will take her children with us—dear things! My family, Tom! My new family! I never had one before!"

Tom wanted to remind him of Ludmilla, then decided it was just as well for Alex to forget about her, live for now, in the present—for Rose.

"To your very best, Tom!" Alex beamed. "Ah, Tom, what a wonderful life? *Wouldn't you say?* If our only problems were about women, we could say we'd lived the life of the gods."

And? That was it really. No *ands*.

"You're right, Alex, we're lucky men."

His brilliant smile made Tom happier. Then, in a few seconds, Alex's lips drooped. He touched them to his Stolichnaya.

"You are aware Peat was the one weak link in the chain of happenstance forged by your son Seth?"

"Seth was going to have a talk with Peat before he left. I wonder if he did," Tom said.

"Well . . ." Alex shrugged scornfully. "It doesn't matter now, does it?" He glanced pensively at Tom. "I must admit I'm pleased Peat is out of the way. Also, I admit I myself considered sending him to his maker, if you understand my meaning?"

Understand his meaning? That was clear enough—and within Alex's eyes there was a brief flash of ferocity.

"He saved you the trouble," Tom said quietly.

"Yes. People who work in the kitchen should be more careful."

Tom agreed uneasily, aware again of that *something* in his expression.

Smiling drolly, Alex made the point again. "People forget, my dear, that during the war I engaged in matters of swift retribution. I was a fighting member of the OSS. People do forget. They see an old man, *forgetting* that he was once young and agile."

Very swiftly, an even more blinding sort of illumination danced across the room. Tom put his hand on his martini glass, hoping it wasn't shaking.

"Alex, I never forgot. It might have slipped to the back of my mind. But I promise you I've never forgotten that."

Alex was greatly amused. Again he leaned across the table. Fortunately they were in the corner; nobody could overhear.

And, to be sure, Alex was alone with his attorney in a situation of ironclad attorney-client privilege.

"It did occur to me, as well, Tom, to put the poor lad out of his misery. Such a pity, in a way, that guilt and remorse caught up with him first."

Tom grinned back. "Or *whatever*, Alex. As we know, it's an established fact now that the *poor lad* didn't kill himself." He paused to let his thinking straighten out. "And I'm inclined to think that Seth and his bunch are looking too far afield. I'd speculate, for instance, that our Peat did that dirty deed. He had every reason to hate Cazimir, if you concede"—he qualified it carefully—"that Peat was also in love with Ludmilla." Alex didn't even blink. "It would've been dead-easy for Peat to do it, to coin a phrase. A morning cup of coffee and *blam!*"

Alex frowned. "But the simplicity of that theory annoyed your son. So easy to put the gun to his head, pull the trigger, then press the weapon in his hand. Classic suicide. Ludmilla," Alex added recklessly, "owned such a gun, a small Beretta, as a matter of fact, just like the one in the *poor lad's* hand."

Tom could play along. He had no choice really. "A hellish coincidence, Alex. Of course, we do know Cazimir was completely shattered by Ludmilla's death: motive for taking his own life."

"Against all probability, yes," Alex nodded. "Inspector Maigret and Miss Marples would both be rolling in their graves, my dear."

"Strange things happen, Alex."

"Well, *yes* . . ." Calculatedly, a bland expression crossed Alex's face. "As my executor, my dear, there are perhaps things you should know."

"On the contrary, my friend, I think I know everything I need to know."

Looking put out, Alex sipped more vodka, compressing his lips at the bite of the alcohol.

"You Americans do not understand sacred revenge. People must do certain things. The poor lad—you might have done the same thing in his shoes, Tom."

"Killed myself? I doubt it."

"Your women, Tom . . ." Alex grinned devilishly. "They never made you yearn to end it all?"

"Honestly, Alex? Never! It's never been as bad at that."

"Or think of murder, most just?"

"Well, sure, I've thought about killing certain people. Not seriously, though."

Reassuringly Alex said, "It's nothing to be especially proud of. But I don't think the good God would have any feeling about it. Indifference, maybe . . ."

Alex was like a brick ruin: too old for renovation, too young to be torn down.

But Tom had the drop on him. He smiled forgivingly. He understood. And he was sure of it.

"The law is the law, Alex. Cazimir had it coming to him for any number of good reasons. But murder is murder, whatever the provocation or motivation—naturally, there are greater or lesser degrees . . ."

"Murder One!"

"Sure . . . or *two*, and *three*."

"I think *this* would have been Murder One, my dear."

"If it *had been* murder, maybe so. Fortunately, we were *all* saved the trouble. Cazimir Ben Gazi committed suicide."

"But, my dear," Alex protested gleefully, "it is said by those who rule us that this was no suicide. *It was assassination!*"

Tom leaned comfortably back and lifted his shiny-cold martini.

"To you, *my dear*," he said, using Alex's own endearment. "Now you're talking about something else entirely. It's really unique, Alex. Cazimir's is one of the few cases I've heard of involving a suicide followed by a murder—in *one* victim! Anyhow, *we* don't have to concern ourselves about it. *Our rulers* established the *poor lad* was not a suicide, moreover that he wasn't murdered in California but somewhere off the coast of Spain."

"The very poor . . . peripatetic . . . lad."

"No doubt about it now, Alex," Tom said efficiently. "Our President himself made the finding—whatever misfortune befell our Cazimir, it befell him in another hemisphere entirely."

"Yes," Alex said, "yes, that seems to be the fact of it, my dear." His eyes glistened despondently. "Cheated again! A man could discover a cure for the common nuisance and never get the credit." He smiled at Tom sweetly. "You are a very nasty boy, you know!"

Tom smiled back. "Sorry, Alex. You couldn't get arrested."

Chapter Forty

Nothing could ever be said to have been conclusively decided . . . or ended. Clara remembered a teacher of hers making such a comment once upon a time—that people never really got to understand each other, or for that matter anything else.

Or, as Tom liked to say, phrasing it in the pompous terms of his legal experience: nothing was ever as it seemed on the surface; nothing that people swore to be the truth, the whole truth, and nothing but the truth was, in fact, entirely the truth.

The best people could hope for was compromise—depending on time, place, and the people involved. And this bald *reality*—one didn't call it a truth—was not as difficult to accept as one might imagine.

In the sun of early May in Sonoma County, Clara was out among the Morelli vines. Alberto had said if there was something she really wanted to do, she should walk down the hill toward the main road and check out the new growth, the staking, the state of the weeds, bugs, and water systems.

Take a walk.

Alberto couldn't believe Clara was really serious about helping out, filling in while her brother Fred was away. A week or two of this, Alberto muttered, and she'd be on her way back to the city.

Clara remembered this part of the vineyard so well; it was the oldest of the acreage given to vines. She walked the dirt path, just wide enough to take tilling and harvesting vehicles,

397

kicking at the rocks and loose sod with her boots, soaking the sun up with her skin, feeling the heart of sunshine in her head. Off there, midway between the dirt road and a slanting fence on the other side, there was a single tree, a kind of cedar tree that over the years had been sculpted into a mushroom shape.

The mushroom, a damn good symbol of fertility. Mushrooms grew in damp and silent places in the forest, under bushes, beneath logs, and in the shadow of old redwoods. Some had magical ingredients, it was said; others were poisonous. In this, then, the extremes of existence—fertility and death.

Using an old rotten-ended stake, Clara brushed aside cobwebs the industrious spiders constructed and reconstructed amid the burgeoning greenery of a new generation of grape vines, picking her way between the long, straight rows toward the mushroom tree.

It was funny. She *had* compromised again. Clara wanted to sit, sink, slump. Forget everything else, forget her resolutions. She was *nothing* and the compromise was, finally, in admitting it. There was nothing artistic about her—forget the music and painting. She was a woman of the soil; the daughter of Alberto, a man of the soil. It ran in the family: soil. She should forget all the rest of it, stop feeling sorry that she hadn't fulfilled herself, as people dreamed of doing in such meaningless ways. She was not destined to leave a big, red mark on the history books. Nobody was going to devote a whole chapter to Clara Morelli.

Clara Morelli?

Forget it.

Clara poked the stick into the soft turf, a thick carpet of mossy grass. She remembered it being cushioned like a feather mattress. She sat down under the magical mushroom tree and wondered vaguely what she should wish for.

The view was all the way down the hill to the public road that cut through the Morelli property. She was captain of the ship, as they said, master of her soul.

And what else *should* there be?

In the far distance, on the ascending hills on the other side of the valley, across folding undulations of land as sensuous as any body, she picked out other barns and sheds and warehouses where presses and boxes and bottles were stored.

What did she wish for? What was there to wish for that she didn't have already?

Feeling foolish, half mad or fully happy, Clara grinned at the distant horizon. *Funny* that everything was reduced to utter simplicity—what else *could* she wish for?

Honesty, that was about all she could think of—the wit, the intelligence to be honest with herself, from now on.

Something touched her shoulder. A fly, whatever; absently, she brushed it away. It came back, then a voice.

"And what have we here, pray tell? Who's this pretty peasant girl?"

"Greetings, stranger," Clara said, not looking up. Tom flopped down beside her. "Where'd you come from?"

"I just drove in. Alberto said you were down here."

He was wearing one of Alberto's floppy hats. Seeing him in it might once have made her smile.

"Are you okay?" Tom asked.

Tom sounded so solicitous, but they were like strangers and Clara couldn't really explain why. He'd been that way for weeks now, as if he'd discovered after all the years, suddenly, that she was not the woman he'd thought he had married.

Tom shifted position, also suspicious of what he'd sat upon. He would never be a nature-boy; he was not a man of the soil.

"How is Martha?"

Was that direct and honest enough to suit you, Tom?

He drew a sharp breath, surprised, annoyed, but thought his answer out before replying, "Okay. I saw her last week . . . I think it was."

"Last week? You *think* it was last week?" Clara teased gently.

"That general time frame." He grunted unwillingly, then swiftly shifted ground. "Seth called. He's getting married, believe it or not. To a journalist in Washington. We're invited, if we want to make the trip."

"Do we?"

"Do you want to go?"

"I don't know," Clara said. "And Rossiter? How's *that* going?"

That didn't make Tom very happy.

"I hate to think about it."

"An improvement over Serena, though, you've got to admit," Clara said. "At least, this is a woman—"

"I suppose," he muttered.

"Poor Rossiter. I hope he'll be happy," Clara said, "finally."

But Rossiter could have been happy any number of ways, poor Rossiter. Suppose . . . suppose she had gone on to Palm Springs that day, and suppose Rossiter had not been detoured by Serena's murder? Would they have met at the hotel? And . . . ?

"Who knows?" she asked out loud.

Tom didn't hear. "We had a letter from Alex." He kept saying *we*, she noticed. "Alex and Rose have a big apartment on the Left Bank and we're invited there too, if we want to go. Would you like to go?"

"To Paris?"

"You used to love Paris, Clara," Tom said uncomfortably, frowning, figeting some more, then bursting out, "Clara, I can't figure out what the hell you're up to." He stopped, then resumed haltingly. "You're so quiet . . . so, I don't know what, reserved, or is it hostile. You knock the wind out of me. I'm not sure I know you anymore."

"Maybe you don't. Maybe you never really did."

"I wonder what the hell you're thinking about all the time."

"You haven't been here enough to find out," she said pointedly.

"Well . . ." He was terrifically defensive. "It doesn't seem like you want anybody around, if I may say so. Alberto notices things too. He's worried."

"He's got no reason to worry."

Stubbornly, he said, "I'd like to know just what the hell is bothering you."

"Nothing. Maybe I'm just happy."

"About what?"

She glanced at him disbelievingly. "You think Clara Morelli couldn't have something to make her happy?"

"I didn't say that."

It didn't matter anyway, she told herself. Something had happened to her. Clara might have said that for some peculiar reason it was difficult for her to remember being married to Tom. It had suddenly become impossible to recall what she'd done all those years. It was something that could not have been explained. She felt reborn: It had happened to her, not in the pop-religious sense, but in somehow having her life given back to her, renewed, like a magazine subscription.

"How's the gallery doing?"

He shrugged. "Sputtering along. Martha's spending some time there. We have a woman coming in. . . . Well, goddamn it, Clara, we may as well just close it up. You haven't been over there in weeks—nor has Biff, for that matter."

"So I understand," Clara said. "And how is Martha?"

Tom stared straight at her. Was there something he wanted to tell her? He behaved as if a truth were struggling to the surface, his expression wry.

"Young. And enthusiastic."

Clara laughed. "Can you keep up with such enthusiasm, Tom?"

His face colored and his jaw stiffened. "I do my best, Clara. That's what I want to talk to you about."

"As we learn, Tom, people sometimes receive what they pray for."

"Answered prayers?" he agreed sardonically. "Capote just said it again."

"True, though. You got your Faustian deal, didn't you?"

"How so?" No, he wouldn't like this.

"Youth, eternal youth, Tom. You never stopped chasing tail, did you?"

He flushed again, more angrily now than irritably.

"How did you put that together? I supposed Biff figured it out. The philosopher of North Beach," Tom said bitterly.

"Not necessarily."

"Rose paid me, you know," he said, trying again to change the subject.

"The five hundred thou?"

"Closer to a million. I, uh . . ." He tried to smile. "The question is how should we spend it, Clara?"

"I'm sure you'll find a way."

He was openly insulted. "I? Me? By myself?"

"You're not alone, Tom."

"No?" He shook his head. He was miserable, or at least putting on a good impression of Mr. Misery. "Well, Clara, I am alone, you know."

"Now, come on, Tom, let's be honest. I know what's going on."

"Clara, I'm not sure but what . . . Clara, whatever you think, well, that's long gone by, you know."

She shrugged. Naturally, this was not true. She was not such a fool. "I don't understand what you mean . . . what you want."

"*Clara!*"

Clara shook her head impatiently. "Look, I'm out of some kind of time warp, Tom. I don't know how to tell you. We've passed, like the ships in the night, you know."

"Bullshit!" Grimly he said, "I thought so. Alberto told me when women start acting like you've been acting the last couple of months, it generally means they're pregnant." He nodded doggedly, trying to hold her with his eyes. "So, naturally, I have to wonder."

He didn't really believe she was pregnant. Clara Addey, a woman of her maturity, pregnant? Out of the question! Laughable!

"Well," she said, "I *am* pregnant."

He was stunned, even though he had suggested it. He seemed to go white; he tried another smile.

"Well! I . . ." Faintly, he chuckled, then his cheeks began to flush, the indicator of macho pride. Of course! He, man, had given her child! "Well! What do you know about that!"

What the hell, Clara told herself, he had to know sooner or later. Might as well fire the other barrel.

"The problem is, I don't think it's yours, Tom. The time element is not quite right, you see."

The flush of incipient pride deepened into shock, then, she supposed, something like horror.

"Well . . . for crissakes, Clara!"

"Tom, I don't bear *you* any ill-will," she said.

"Or I you, I suppose you want me to say!"

"If you wish."

"*Whose then, goddamn it?*"

He never stopped asking questions. Did they want to go to Seth's wedding, to Paris to visit Alex and Rose. Whose baby was it?

A very good question. One she was not prepared to answer. One she possibly could not answer with any degree of accuracy. Clara had been very bad. Too often . . . too true.

"All cut and dried, Tom, isn't it? Black and white. Truth and consequence? There can't be much doubt where we stand, can there?"

"Jesus! What the hell is Alberto going to say?"

Clara shrugged, more carelessly than she should have. "He'll be all right. He's used to me by now. I do nothing but shock the socks off him."

"Clara, I cannot believe this is you, that this is happening."

"Why not?" Clara looked him in the eye. His expression, despite the anger, the growing humiliation he might well be feeling, was still evasive. "I wonder what you came here to tell me, Tom? Is it about Martha? Something about Martha, Tom?"

Christ, she suddenly thought, suppose he'd come to inform her that Martha was pregnant, that Clara was going to become a grandmother as well as a mother again.

"Martha is a very young girl, Clara, that's what I'm here to say."

"So you can't handle it?" Very ironic. Too late.

"My God, Clara, she's a child!"

"Well, what the hell did you think she was, Tom? But she's not a child either. She's a woman, and maybe you are in love with her—"

"Maybe I am," he growled.

"And?"

"I told you she's a child!"

Inevitably she understood. "She's not in love with you, is she?"

"She never was," he said hollowly. "It's called infatuation."

"I see," Clara said, "and it's over and you're left high and dry like a whale on the beach."

He looked pained. "Not exactly a whale, Clara. Please . . ."

"No. More of a porpoise . . . a playful dolphin?"

His lip curled sardonically. "Thanks very much."

"I do feel for you. . . . But there's—"

"Clara," he interrupted, "c'mon—"

"Be a sport?"

"Let's go to Paris. You can have the kid. It's not the end of the world. I don't give a goddamn whose it is—you are a little baggage, though, aren't you?"

"As easy as that, Tom?" Clara shook her head. She was about to go on but a loud, hoarse voice broke in, directed at them from the top of the hill.

"Ahoy down there!"

Tom swore and turned. "Who in the hell is that?"

"It's Biff," she murmured.

"Biff?"

Another bit of truth dawned, very slowly, like a winter sunrise. Why Tom should have been so surprised was surprising in itself. But then, Clara had been surprised too. She had discovered something else about herself. Admittedly, Biff was, yes, the dawning of what everybody would say was a very *unusual* sex object.

"Biff!"

Tom was so astonished that he even smiled a little, albeit weakly.

"Well, you see . . ." Of course, she would begin to make excuses. "Biff has been given a Fulbright and . . . well, for the body of his work—"

"Body of his work!"

"Don't project, Tom," she cautioned. "He's coming down, like a friend, and I don't want you hurting his feelings."

"Clara, what about *my* goddamn feelings?"

Clara laughed and leaned toward poor Tom, kissing him lightly on the cheek.

"You've had all the flattery a grown man could ever want, my sweet, worshipped by a young chick, just what you've always wanted."

"Clara!" His voice was whipped, wrung out, beaten. "I told you—"

"Tom, Tom . . . there'll be others."

"Clara, how could you? Cruelly trading me in for an ugly, cigar-smoking thug, a so-called painter? *Biff*, a man named *Biff*? I am insulted, you know."

Clara merely stared at him, wanting very much to laugh, at him, with him. Poor Tom. Poor, poor Tom. He didn't understand, did he? Biff was making her over; Biff was very good at that.

"Tom, I've rediscovered the first rule of magnetism— opposites attract!"

He glowered, his eyes hot and perverse. Clara felt sorry for him at last. He was wounded but wouldn't ever admit it. Tom wouldn't beg either; he was too proud. Contrarily, maybe she should promise him an affair. Affairs were really Tom's style.

Then it was too late. By now Biff was stumbling down the path, clumsily. No, he was not Nature's own gazelle.

Then Clara couldn't suppress the laugh any longer. It burst out of her, mercifully releasing all the good feeling within her. Never had she laughed so loudly, so heartily, so good-naturedly, so lovingly.

Yes, well, something *had* happened. That was it. At last. Something very good. Finally.

ABOUT THE AUTHOR

Born and raised in New York State, BARNEY LEASON did graduate studies in English at Columbia University under Lionel Trilling and Mark van Doren. From there he went to Munich, where he continued his education at Radio Free Europe. As a writer and political analyst he covered eastern Europe and the USSR until 1961, when he joined Fairchild Publications and worked as a correspondent in western and eastern Europe, and then in London as Fairchild bureau chief. After 20 years in Europe he was transferred to California, where he shortly became West Coast bureau chief for *Look* Magazine during its brief revival in 1978–1979. He began writing popular fiction at that time and published his first novel *Rodeo Drive* in 1981. His other published works include *Scandals, Passions, Grand Illusions,* and *Fortunes.*

Barney Leason is married to Jody Jacobs, former society editor for the *Los Angeles Times* who is now writing novels. They've abandoned the heady atmosphere of Los Angeles for an unspecified paradise in northern California.

BANTAM BOOKS
GRAND SLAM SWEEPSTAKES

Win a new Chevrolet Celebrity . . .

It's easy . . . It's fun . . . Here's how to enter:

OFFICIAL ENTRY FORM

Three Bantam book titles on sale this month are hidden in this word puzzle. Identify the books by circling each of these titles in the puzzle. Titles may appear within the puzzle horizontally, vertically, or diagonally . . .

Bantam's titles for August are:

OMAMORI

FANTASTIC VOYAGE II

RICH AND RECKLESS

In each of the books listed above there is another entry blank and puzzle . . . another chance to win!

Be on the lookout for Bantam's September titles: IT'S ALL IN THE PLAYING, FLASHBACK, SO MANY PROMISES. In each of them, you'll find a new puzzle, entry blank and GRAND SLAM Sweepstakes rules . . . and yet another chance to win another brand-new Chevrolet automobile!

MAIL TO: GRAND SLAM SWEEPSTAKES
                     Post Office Box 18
                     New York, New York 10046

Please Print

NAME _____

ADDRESS _____

CITY _____ STATE _____ ZIP _____

OFFICIAL RULES

NO PURCHASE NECESSARY.

To enter identify this month's Bantam Book titles by placing a circle around each word forming each title. There are three titles shown above to be found in this month's puzzle. Mail your entry to: Grand Slam Sweepstakes, P.O. Box 18, New York, N.Y. 10046.

This is a monthly sweepstakes starting February 1, 1988 and ending January 31, 1989. During this sweepstakes period, one automobile winner will be selected each month from all entries that have correctly solved the puzzle. To participate in a particular month's drawing, your entry must be received by the last day of that month. The Grand Slam prize drawing will be held on February 14, 1989 from all entries received during all twelve months of the sweepstakes.

To obtain a free entry blank/puzzle/rules, send a self-addressed stamped envelope to: Winning Titles, P.O. Box 650, Sayreville, N.J. 08872. Residents of Vermont and Washington need not include return postage.

PRIZES: Each month for twelve months a Chevrolet automobile will be awarded with an approximate retail value of $12,000 each.

The Grand Slam Prize Winner will receive 2 Chevrolet automobiles plus $10,000 cash (ARV $34,000).

Winners will be selected under the supervision of Marden-Kane, Inc., an independent judging organization. By entering this sweepstakes each entrant accepts and agrees to be bound by these rules and the decisions of the judges which shall be final and binding. Winners may be required to sign an affidavit of eligibility and release which must be returned within 14 days of receipt. All prizes will be awarded. No substitution or transfer of prizes permitted. Winners will be notified by mail. Odds of winning depend on the total number of eligible entries received.

Sweepstakes open to residents of the U.S. and Canada except employees of Bantam Books, its affiliates, subsidiaries, advertising agencies and Marden-Kane, Inc. Void in the Province of Quebec and wherever else prohibited or restricted by law. Not responsible for lost or misdirected mail or printing errors. Taxes and licensing fees are the sole responsibility of the winners. All cars are standard equipped. Canadian winners will be required to answer a skill testing question.

For a list of winners, send a self-addressed, stamped envelope to: Bantam Winners, P.O. Box 711, Sayreville, N.J. 08872.

Special Offer
Buy a Bantam Book
for only 50¢.

Now you can have Bantam's catalog filled with hundreds of titles plus take advantage of our unique and exciting bonus book offer. A special offer which gives you the opportunity to purchase a Bantam book for only 50¢. Here's how!

By ordering any five books at the regular price per order, you can also choose any other single book listed (up to a $5.95 value) for just 50¢. Some restrictions do apply, but for further details why not send for Bantam's catalog of titles today!

Just send us your name and address and we will send you a catalog!